THE
SWORD
OF
TRUTH

THE GODLING CHRONICLES

THE SWORD OF TRUTH

BRIAN D. ANDERSON

4 Horsemen
Publications, Inc.

DEDICATION

For my wife, Eleni, and my son, a creative genius, Jonathan.

CONTENTS

PROLOGUE

It was all the Dark Knight could do to keep his teeth from chattering. The chill mountain air was thick with a dense fog that soaked into his skin, making every movement of the wind like torture. The only sounds were the crunch and clatter of his horse's hooves and his own labored breathing.

He could feel that he was drawing near to his destination, yet he could see nothing but dull gray fog and the gnarled and vicious shadows of long-dead trees.

He steeled his wits and warily urged his steed onward. He knew what was to come, and it unnerved him. The prospect of death had never bothered him. He had faced it many times before, but this was something different. After today, everything would change. After today, the whole world would tremble. For the first time in his life, he was uncertain. Decades of struggle and planning were culminating in this one moment, this one action. He should have been excited but, for some reason, was unable to shake his sense of foreboding.

His horse spotted the edge of the precipice just before they both would have plummeted to their deaths. It reared fiercely, nearly throwing him from the saddle onto the hard, jagged stone path. Calming his nervous steed, he dismounted and walked to the cliff's edge. He strained his eyes, attempting to penetrate the fog, but could see nothing. Yet he knew what was out there. Reaching down, he picked up a small stone and tossed it over the cliff's edge, but heard nothing.

The trial begins, he thought. He turned and retrieved his sword and scabbard from his saddle and fastened them to his belt. As he peered into the nothingness, his armor felt heavy and cumbersome. Feats of prowess in battle were far different from what he was about to do. Armor would certainly be a hindrance, but he dare not leave it behind. He backed away from the edge of the cliff and closed his eyes, his heart pounding in his ears. For a long moment, he stood motionless as stone.

Suddenly, the sinews of his thick, powerful legs burst to life, propelling him forward at amazing speed. In a flash, he was at the edge and jumped with a heavy grunt. Time stood still as he flew through the air. For a split second, a flash of fear filled his chest as he felt himself begin to fall, but relief and triumph quickly replaced this as his boots struck solid rock. Somehow, with a huge effort, he managed to keep his footing and stumbled to a halt. As he slowly stepped forward, the fog lessened, and he realized he had jumped atop the first in a series of immense natural rock pillars.

"At last," he muttered.

Each pillar was about eight feet apart and could easily accommodate a dozen mounted men. He could make out twelve pillars, but beyond that, the fog thickened again. Experience told him not to get too excited; nothing was ever as simple as it seemed. He could leap the distance easily enough, even with armor on. However, considering the prize that awaited him, something told him there was more to it than that.

Without warning, the ground began to shake violently. The Dark Knight could feel the rock starting to give way beneath his feet. With no time to think, he leaped to the next pillar, only to feel this also begin to crumble the second his boots landed. From pillar to pillar, he raced for his life. In seconds, he knew he would reach the fog again and be unable to see. As he reached the last column, he planted both feet hard on its edge and pushed with all his strength, propelling his body into the void.

His upper thigh struck hard against a lip of rock, flinging his head and torso forward. The sound of grinding metal tore through the dank air as his armor crashed against rough stone. He scrambled and clawed as he felt himself beginning to slip off the edge. Just as he was about to fall, his hand caught a crack in the rock and he pulled himself up. He lay there for a moment, taking stock of his hurts. Nothing serious. His thighs would be bruised, and the hilt of his sword had jammed into his kidney, but overall, he was fine. He listened as the thunder of collapsing pillars echoed, then disappeared.

He rose to his feet, checked his sword, and surveyed his surroundings. Before him lay a square courtyard of plain black granite. On either side were smooth, sheer walls one hundred feet high, and at the far end, carved into the living rock, a flight of steps leading up.

In the center of the courtyard stood a ten-foot obelisk of unadorned white marble. As the Dark Knight neared the obelisk, he heard a low hum. His eyes narrowed and his muscles tensed as his hands slid to the hilt of his sword. The hum grew louder and deeper the closer he came until his body shook with its intensity. He desperately covered his ears but to no avail. He felt his knees begin to weaken; each step became agony as the loud hum grew to a deep roar. As he stepped directly beside the obelisk, he felt blood trickling from his nose.

Almost there, he thought, taking another step.

The moment he passed the obelisk, the hum stopped. It was then that his legs gave way, and he collapsed, his chest heaving and ears ringing. After several minutes, he lifted his head and looked toward the steps. Slowly, he rose to his feet, wiped the blood from his nose, and began his climb.

In the distance, he could see a bright light that obscured his vision. As he finally reached the top, the light lessened and his eyes began to adjust, revealing an immense stone alcove, fifty feet high and nearly twice as wide. The stone was polished white marble, inlaid with veins of pure gold and precious jewels. Standing tall and proud at its center was a gold statue of an ancient warrior. It was ten feet tall and adorned with fine chain mail. Its grim features told of countless battles as its deeply set eyes stared—penetrating and unwavering—with a sense of keen understanding that gave it the distinct impression of life. Atop its brow sat a crown of opal laurels, each leaf veined with silver inlay. Its arms were outstretched with its palms held aloft, and there the Dark Knight saw it. The sword. Its gleaming steel glowed with an unnatural light that spilled down onto the marble floor like a ghostly mist. Its hilt was plain steel, with neither jewel nor marking to tell of its true worth, and the handle was wrapped in hard, unremarkable black leather.

The Dark Knight felt his pulse quicken as he slowly walked forward. It was his; the Sword of Truth was finally his. Closer and closer, he came to his prize. With each step, he drew nearer to the end of his quest. Then, from the corner of his eye, he saw a tall figure.

He was dressed in a pure white linen robe bound at the waist by a thin, white silk rope. A pair of simple calfskin boots could be seen beneath his robe, and he wore a circlet of silver on his brow. His face was smooth and ageless, with a long, hawk-like nose and pronounced chin. His eyes were deep blue and full of sadness and pity. He held no weapon that the Dark Knight could see.

He turned to face the Man in White and unsheathed his sword. "I thought I'd find you here," he said grimly. "Do you intend to fight me unarmed?"

A sad smile crept over the Man in White's face. "I do not intend to fight you at all," he replied.

The Dark Knight burst into laughter. "Some protector you are. You're a coward, unworthy to bear the sword."

"You're right," he said. "I'm not worthy. But neither are you."

"Really?" the Dark Knight mocked, stepping forward menacingly. "We'll see about that. With that sword, I will be able to break the bonds that have held us back for an eternity. We will finally be free! Can't you see that?"

Regret washed over the face of the Man in White. "Free? You mean free to rule? Free to murder? Free to do evil with impunity?"

"No, you fool!" the Dark Knight shouted. "Free to show the world what we truly are. Free to take my..." His voice calmed. "Our rightful place in this cursed world."

"What we truly are, my old friend, has nothing to do with what is in your heart," he replied.

The Dark Knight scowled. "Whatever is in my heart was driven there by those you serve." Slowly, his face softened. "Please, brother, why not join me? I could use your advice and companionship in the times ahead. Together, we could shape the world into a paradise."

Tears began to well in the Man in White's eyes. "There was a time when I would not have hesitated. However, that time is long past. Now I know who you truly are. The paradise you speak of is no paradise at all; it is hell."

"Hell, you say? What do you know of hell? I have seen hell. I have lived in it. Your masters sent me there, and it's time the favor was returned." The Dark Knight's face darkened.

"You sent yourself there with your betrayal," said the Man in White.

"I betrayed you?" the Dark Knight scoffed. "Fool! Your masters have poisoned your mind. Don't you see that? Don't you understand what I'm trying to do?"

The Man in White's eyes narrowed. "I understand all too well. I understand that you will fail. No matter what happens this day, you will fail."

"We shall see," he said ominously. "It's clear to me now that you cannot be reasoned with as I'd hoped." The Dark Knight tensed. "And your blood will spill this day for your foolishness."

In a flash, the Dark Knight leaped forward, slashing his blade at the Man in White's neck. But the Man in White dodged with an unnatural speed and the stroke passed harmlessly.

Again and again, the Dark Knight pressed forward, his fury and frustration growing with each unsuccessful blow. Minutes passed, and the Dark Knight had gained no ground. He began to feel the weight of fatigue burning in his muscles. The Man in White did not attempt to strike; his lack of weapon and armor made it easy for him to avoid the onslaught, and his many years of training made his every step perfect. Slowly, the Dark Knight began to understand his peril. He could not keep this up indefinitely. Eventually, his strength would be gone, and he would be virtually helpless.

Then, in a desperate gamble, the Dark Knight flung his sword at the left leg of his opponent, causing him to shift right and slightly back. Normally, he would never intentionally disarm himself, but this time, the gamble worked. With all his strength, he leaped forward, reaching into his belt, and pulling out a small dagger. His body slammed into the Man in White as he plunged it into his heart.

The Man in White gasped and threw his arms around his killer as both bodies crashed to the floor. The Dark

Knight wrenched himself from the Man in White's grasp, ripping the dagger free. Blood soaked his robe and spilled onto the marble floor. The Man in White's eyes grew dim as he watched the Dark Knight rise and walk to the statue that held the Sword.

This is the end, the Man in White thought as death overcame him. *...the end of the world. I have failed.*

The Dark Knight reached out and grabbed the hilt of the sword. Lightning flashed as he lifted it from its cradle and held it aloft.

"It's mine!" he screamed. "It's miiiiiiiine!"

CHAPTER 1

Gewey Stedding's wagon rolled up the main avenue of the village of Sharpstone, heavy with its cargo of fall hay. Normally this would be neither exciting nor very important, but recent years had been hard, and the sight of commerce filled the villagers with hope. Fall hay meant food for the livestock, meat for the winter, and trade for the spring.

The streets were empty for this time of year. Usually, merchants and travelers from up and down the Goodbranch River kept them busy, but over the last several years, trade had slowed to a trickle. The few people who did pass through did not linger and brought little coin. News of trouble and hardship came with each boat and wagon, regardless of where they came from. The world was in turmoil, and everyone could feel it.

In better times, Sharpstone would be readying for the Festival of Gerath, god of the earth and mountains. Gewey had eagerly looked forward to the festival each year since he was a boy. It was three days of games, music, and some of the best food in the whole kingdom. It ended with the entire town parading to the market square to crown the King and Queen of the festival. As a child, Gewey had dreamed of being crowned King, but as things were, it didn't look like that would ever happen. Last year, the Village Council cut the festival to one day—this year, with little to celebrate and no money to spare, the festival had been all but forgotten. Only a few elders had hung the traditional pumpkin vines above their door, and no one had decorated the statue of Gerath that stood in the village square.

Despite the hardships, the sight of Gewey's wagon made the people smile. Gewey's honest dealings and helpful nature made him very popular in the village. He was always ready to help those in need and never shied away from hard work, even when he worked for free—which lately, happened very frequently. Though only seventeen years old, he stood six feet two inches tall and had the shoulders of a blacksmith. With raven black hair, flawless skin, and chiseled features, it was little wonder that the young girls of the village swooned as he passed. The older women were already talking about who would be a good match for him. Luckily, he hadn't turned eighteen—the time of his coming of age—and he could avoid certain uncomfortable conversations with the Village Mothers.

Called the 'Village Hens' by the men (though only when they couldn't hear), the Village Mothers handled most of the day-to-day operations in Sharpstone. If there was a fire, they organized the reconstruction. If streets needed repair or the river docks rebuilding, the Village Mothers saw it done. The Village Council—headed by the mayor—controlled the finance and commerce, but without the Mothers, Sharpstone would come to a halt.

Gewey had been his own master since his father had died two years earlier of an illness that had swept through the village during an extremely harsh winter. His mother had passed when he was but three, from injuries she received falling from her horse. The memories he had of her were few, and colored by a child's perception. He knew she was kind and beautiful. A painting of her hung above his fireplace. His father would look at it all night on the anniversary of her death and tell Gewey stories about her life and his love for her.

After his father's death, the village council had approached Gewey about selling his farm and taking an apprenticeship with one of the local tradesmen. Gewey's father had been the largest producer of hay in the area, and they had serious doubts as to whether a fifteen-year-old boy would be able to maintain a farm alone. The idea of losing such a resource was unthinkable, and though Gewey had not yet come of age, his father had left him all of his property. Short of petitioning the King, there was nothing they could do to make Gewey give up the land.

Gewey refused every offer, stating that his father wanted him to keep the farm going, and had told him so before he died. The Council was preparing to make one more effort to change his mind when he showed up at the market square with enough hay to supply the whole village for half the year. He had not only bundled and loaded it himself but also turned a nice profit at market. From then on, Gewey was thought of by all as being the master of his own land; his coming of age was never mentioned again. He was treated as any other landowner and even consulted occasionally by the Council.

Gewey's image of himself was somewhat different. He harvested hay, as he had seen his father do a thousand times before. He bartered the way his father had taught him. He held onto the farm because his father would have wanted him to. Nevertheless, in his heart, he was not yet a man. He was merely a boy, still trying to make his father proud. His size and strength made others think him a man, but at night, when he was all alone, his mind was full of fear and doubt.

The village of Sharpstone was just south of the Sarlian Wastes, in the northernmost part of the Kingdom of Megádos. Just to the north was a crossroads that joined the Pithian Highway, leading south to the western gate of the capital, Helenia, then on to the southern ports and the Far Run Road, which spanned the breadth of the entire continent. The land was flat and fertile, and the weather was moderate and prone to early springs. The inhabitants, though not numerous, were kindly and welcomed strangers, so long as they did not cause trouble.

Though not a great producer of goods, the village thrived on being a stop-off point for commerce. They boasted some of the finest blacksmiths and liveries for a hundred miles and provided a welcome respite for many a weary merchant or pilgrim. The inns were clean and comfortable, and frequented by traveling entertainers who often provided a lively nightlife. Overall, Sharpstone was a decent place. That is until the dark times began.

It had been six years since what the villagers called the Long Freeze. The winter did not break, and the planting season came and went. Many villagers became ill and died. Gewey remembered the sadness in his father's eyes each morning as they had stared out on the frozen fields during the first year. The thought of those long days of fruitless labor still made his belly ache with hunger. For an entire year, the ground stayed frozen. When spring finally came, the land was different. It seemed as if the life had been sucked right out of it. The crop was small, livestock suffered, and each year Gewey watched his father's land shrink and dry up further.

The few villagers up and about at that time of the morning waved to Gewey's wagon as he passed. Mostly, they wished him a good day. Others, however, had earnest business and called for him to set aside time for them. This always made Gewey feel uneasy. He was not interested in business. Despite his ability to turn a profit, he hated bartering and trading.

Before the Long Freeze, the avenue leading to the trading court would have been bustling with activity. However, in recent years, shops opened later and later, and a few had even closed, the owners moving to the capital in hope of finding work. As he approached the market square, he could see that it was almost empty, aside from a few vendors who had only just arrived.

Suddenly, a scream pierced the air, making Gewey jump in his seat.

He halted his wagon and saw Thad Marshall, the local baker, running from the square. He jumped down and grabbed the man as he passed. Thad was normally a calm fellow, but it was clear to Gewey that something had terrified him.

"What happened?" Gewey exclaimed.

It took a moment for Thad to steady himself enough to speak.

"My wife...." Thad said. "I just saw my wife." He was shaking uncontrollably.

The baker's wife had died the previous winter. The whole town had turned out for her funeral.

"Your wife?" asked Gewey, uncertain how to react.

"I know it sounds crazy, but I swear that I just saw her standing in the market. I saw her as clear as I see you now."

"Are you sure it was her?" asked Gewey.

"There's no mistake," he cried. "I was with her for thirty-six years. I'd know her anywhere."

Gewey looked thoughtfully at the man. "Well, Master Marshall, I don't doubt your word. The ways of spirits are strange. Who can understand them?"

"You don't understand," the baker replied. "She looked decayed and rotten. It wasn't her spirit I saw."

"You mean you saw your dead wife's body walking in the market?" exclaimed Gewey, surprised.

"That's exactly what I'm saying," Thad said, tears streaming down his face.

"Did anyone else see her?" he asked.

"No ... m-maybe ... I don't know," he stammered.

Gewey helped the baker into the wagon. "Come," he said. "Let's see if we can find out what's going on."

The baker nodded slowly and slumped down in the seat, tears still pouring down his face. Gewey urged the horse forward in the direction of the market. He didn't think the baker would lie, and he wasn't the unstable type, but a grieving man's mind could sometimes play tricks.

Gewey guided his wagon across the square to the far end, near the entrance to the river dock, and halted. Thad doubled over with his face buried in his hands. Gewey hopped down from the wagon and put his hand gently on the baker's arm.

"Come on, Master Marshall," he said, using his most soothing voice. "Show me where you saw her."

Slowly, Thad crept from the wagon and led Gewey to the corner of the market, where he usually set up his stand.

"She was standing right there," he said, pointing a few feet ahead of them. "At first, I thought I was seeing things, but she looked right at me."

Gewey examined the area but could find nothing out of place.

"Wait here," he said. "I'll ask around and see if anyone else saw anything."

Gewey questioned the few people there, but no one had seen anything other than the baker screaming as he ran out of the market.

"What could have scared old Thad so badly, I wonder?" asked Melton Fathing, a local artisan and town gossip. "I was just about to check on him."

"It was nothing," answered Gewey, quickly walking away. He certainly didn't want to humiliate Thad, and Melton would already have started to talk. Besides, he didn't like Melton.

Gewey told Thad that no one else had seen his wife.

"I'm not making this up!" Thad exclaimed.

"I'm not saying you are," replied Gewey, trying to calm the man down. "Why don't you go home? I'll keep an eye out and let you know if anything unusual happens."

"Maybe you're right," said Thad. "Maybe I just need to rest. It's been so hard this last year, losing my wife and all. Business hasn't been the best, either."

The rest of what Thad said trailed off into incoherent mumbling as he stumbled from the square. Gewey noticed Melton staring intently and forced a smile. *Best to let it be*, he thought to himself.

It took him only an hour to unload his wagon. He had always been good at physical labor. His father bragged that his son could outwork ten men. Though this was true, Gewey always held back when others were around. He didn't want people to think he was odd or different, and if people knew how strong he really was, the talk would start.

The rest of the day was uneventful as he sold his hay, most of which went to the livery. Gewey did as he promised and kept watch for anything unusual, but thankfully saw nothing.

His wagon empty and his purse full, Gewey began the long trip back to his farm. He stopped by Thad Marshall's house to check on him, but there was no answer. *Probably sleeping*, he thought.

As he turned toward his wagon, he noticed a shadowy figure approaching from the avenue. The evening shadows obscured his features, but Gewey knew right away who it was. His long strides and graceful motions gave him away.

"Hello, Lee," called Gewey.

The man said nothing. Lee Starfinder was a strange sort. He was nearly as tall as Gewey, though not as wide in the shoulders. He had distinctly sharp, angular features and deep olive skin. He had moved to Sharpstone more than ten years ago, claiming to be a nobleman and scholar, from north of the Razor Edge Mountains, here to retire and live out his days quietly. Gewey, however, thought he had the look of the sea people from the coast of the Western Abyss. He kept to himself and employed several local artisans, so the villagers made little fuss about the man's oddities and reclusive nature.

Lee walked straight up to Gewey and pressed a letter into his hand.

"Wait until you get home to read it," said Lee. "No questions, boy."

Gewey stared at the man, his mouth gaping. Lee spun around and strode off, leaving Gewey baffled. He stared at the letter. It was old and yellow, but the seal was unbroken.

"Great," muttered Gewey. "A long trip made even longer."

Gewey continued on his way home, trying to think about anything other than what the letter might reveal.

CHAPTER 2

The ride home seemed to take forever. Gewey had put the letter in his pocket, but could hardly resist the urge to open it. He tried to push his horse to move faster, but it did no good; she was a workhorse, not a racehorse. By the time he reached his farm, he could barely sit still. He put the wagon and horse away in record time and almost pulled the front door off its hinges on his way inside. The house was dark and cold. Gewey frowned, realizing that the letter would have to wait until he'd tended to the fire and lit the lanterns. Once these tasks were completed, Gewey finally sat down in his father's chair next to the hearth and retrieved the letter from his pocket. He stared at the seal for a moment, and then carefully opened it.

My son,

If you are reading this, my time on this world has passed. As I write, you are but two years old. Should I die before you are old enough to hear what I need to tell you, I will entrust this letter

TO LORD STARFINDER. I HAVE KNOWN HIM FOR MANY YEARS, AND HE HAS SAID HE PLANS TO MOVE HERE SOON TO RETIRE. WHAT I AM GOING TO TELL YOU WILL NOT BE EASY FOR YOU TO UNDERSTAND, BUT YOU MUST TRY.

I AM NOT YOUR REAL FATHER.

Gewey nearly dropped the letter. He felt like a hammer had struck him between the eyes. He read the line again in disbelief and then continued.

BELIEVE ME WHEN I SAY THAT I COULD NOT LOVE YOU MORE, EVEN IF YOU WERE MY OWN FLESH AND BLOOD. YOU WERE GIVEN TO ME TO CARE FOR WHEN YOU WERE AN INFANT. A MERCHANT WHO HAPPENED BY OUR FARM AS HE TRAVELED SOUTH TO MILLHAVEN SPRINGS HAD FOUND YOU. HE TOLD US HE HAD RUN ACROSS A SMALL CARAVAN THAT HAD BEEN ATTACKED BY A BAND OF MARAUDERS, AND THAT HE HAD FOUND YOU IN THE RUBBLE. HE TOLD US HE COULD NOT CARE FOR YOU AND ASKED THAT WE TAKE YOU IN. YOUR MOTHER AND I HAD NO CHILDREN OF OUR OWN AND DID NOT QUESTION SUCH A BLESSING FROM THE GODS. THE MOMENT I LOOKED AT YOU, I KNEW YOU WERE MY SON. I EVEN MANAGED TO DECEIVE THE VILLAGE ELDERS AS TO YOUR IDENTITY, BUT I SUSPECT THEY WANTED TO BE DECEIVED.

SIX MONTHS HAD PASSED WHEN LORD STARFINDER CAME TO VISIT ME. I KNEW HIM IN MY YOUNGER AND MORE ADVENTUROUS DAYS. HE TOLD ME HE HAD COME TO PURCHASE HORSES, BUT I BELIEVE HE HAD OTHER MOTIVES. WE MAY HAVE FINE HORSES HERE, BUT THE WEEKS OF TRAVEL WOULD HAVE MADE SUCH A JOURNEY UNPROFITABLE, AND, AT THE VERY LEAST, UNCOMFORTABLE. I

TOLD HIM THE TRUTH ABOUT HOW YOU CAME TO US, AND HE DIDN'T LOOK SURPRISED WHEN HE HEARD MY STORY. THE FACT IS, I BELIEVE YOU ARE THE REASON HE CAME IN THE FIRST PLACE, AND I BELIEVE YOU ARE THE REASON HE MOVED HERE. HE STAYED FOR TWO WEEKS, BUYING UP NEARLY EVERY HORSE IN THE VILLAGE—MOST OF WHICH HE TURNED RIGHT AROUND AND SOLD AGAIN—AND EACH NIGHT BEFORE SUNDOWN, HE CAME TO VISIT. HE CLAIMED THAT IT WAS TO ENJOY SIMPLE HOSPITALITY AND TELL OLD TALES, AND AT FIRST, HIS VISITS DIDN'T SEEM ODD. LEE WAS ALWAYS ONE FOR A GOOD STORY AND DECENT WINE, BUT I BEGAN TO SUSPECT DIFFERENT REASONS WHEN HE INSISTED ON HOLDING YOU EVERY NIGHT UNTIL YOU WENT TO SLEEP. HE HAD NEVER REALLY CARED FOR CHILDREN, BUT WHEN HE HELD YOU, HE SMILED AND IGNORED EVERYTHING ELSE UNTIL YOU WERE IN YOUR CRIB.

ON HIS LAST VISIT, AFTER HE HAD ROCKED YOU TO SLEEP AND YOUR MOTHER LEFT THE ROOM TO PUT YOU DOWN, HE TOLD ME THAT YOU WERE SPECIAL AND THAT THE GODS HAD BLESSED YOU WITH A GREAT DESTINY. AT FIRST, I THOUGHT HE WAS PLAYING A JOKE, BUT THE LOOK IN HIS EYES TOLD ME OTHERWISE. WHEN I ASKED HIM HOW HE KNEW THIS, HE WAVED ME OFF AND SAID THAT EVENTUALLY IT WOULD BE REVEALED. THE MAN HAS ALWAYS BEEN SOMEWHAT OF A MYSTERY, BUT I BELIEVE HE'S RIGHT. EVEN AS A BABY, I CAN SEE THAT YOU ARE SPECIAL.

SON, YOU ARE DESTINED FOR GREAT THINGS. GO SEE LORD STARFINDER. HE HAS KNOWLEDGE OF THE WORLD THAT YOU WILL ONE DAY NEED. HE CAN BE A LITTLE STRANGE SOMETIMES, BUT MEN LIKE HIM ALWAYS ARE.

REMEMBER, SON, I LOVE YOU WITH ALL MY HEART, NO MATTER WHAT DESTINY HAS IN STORE. FRANKLY, I HOPE LEE'S WRONG, AND THAT YOU STAY WITH YOUR MOTHER AND ME UNTIL WE'RE OLD AND GRAY. I WOULD LOVE NOTHING MORE THAN TO LOOK AT MY GRANDCHILDREN AS I LOOK AT YOU NOW.

ALL MY LOVE,
FATHER

Gewey sat in silence. He felt as if his whole world had been stripped away. Why had his father never told him? This had been written when he was a baby, so surely there had been time. He felt confused and angry. None of it made sense. Why wait so long? Why the deception in the first place?

Gewey read the letter repeatedly as if the words might change and his life would make sense again. But each time, he found new unanswered questions. Finally, he stood up and ran out into the brisk night air. He felt dizzy and leaned against the porch. After a few minutes, he staggered back inside and went to bed. It would be several hours before sleep took him.

He went over his life in his mind, trying to remember some clue, some insight that might help him to understand, but came up with nothing. As far back as he could recall, his father had never been anything but that—his father. He tried to slow his mind and rid himself of his anger, remembering the love his father had always shown him, and the love Gewey felt for him in return.

Gewey fell asleep with one thought in his head: *Lee Starfinder*, he told himself. *Tomorrow I'll go see Lee Starfinder. Maybe he has answers.*

That night's dreams were filled with horror. Visions of death and destruction swirled around him like a storm. Vast armies slaughtered each other, spilling oceans of blood. The sick and dying screamed out in agony. He tried not to look, but could not turn away. Trying to force himself awake only took him deeper into even more terrifying visions. Just when he thought he could no longer take it, the world exploded into a great ball of flame. Slowly, it burned away until there was nothing but utter darkness, so complete that he could feel it. It wrapped around him, pressing in until he wanted to cry out in despair. It penetrated his mind and soul as if it sought to possess him completely. He fought desperately to get out, but there was nothing to fight against. The darkness yielded and contracted with every move he made. Just when he felt as if he would be overcome, a voice boomed out.

"Child," it said. The sheer volume of the voice nearly split Gewey's head in two. "Why do you resist?"

"Who are you?" asked Gewey. His own voice seemed weak and small.

"Who am I?" the voice shot back, almost mocking. "I am he who knows the answers to your questions. I am he who can give you what you seek."

"I don't understand," said Gewey. "What questions?"

"I can tell you who you are, young one," it replied. "The lies that surround you—the reason for your existence can be made clear. I can show you how to use your power to gain all you desire."

Gewey's mind reeled. He felt the malice and hatred in the voice but was compelled to listen. He knew he shouldn't, but he couldn't help himself.

"You're not real," said Gewey finally. "You're in my mind. I'm dreaming."

"Of course you're dreaming," scoffed the voice. "But I am real. In your heart, you know it to be true. You've always known it. Didn't you feel me watching you, protecting you?"

"Protecting me?" asked Gewey. "Protecting me from what?"

"It was I who brought you to safety so long ago," it said. "It was I who has kept you secret from the world. But it is now time." The voice paused. "Time for you to join me."

Suddenly, another voice burst into his mind. "He lies, Gewey! Don't listen to him!"

Gewey felt as if a spell had been broken. "If you know me, then tell me who I am," he said. "If you wish for me to join you, then send for me."

"Of course," answered the first voice. "Just tell me where you are, and you will be with me."

"Don't you know?" asked Gewey. "Aren't you the one who brought me here?"

There was a long silence. Gewey felt the fury of the darkness press in.

"Tell me where you are, boy." Its tone became threatening. "You cannot hide from me. I will find you."

The darkness pressed harder and harder. Gewey wanted to run, but there was nowhere to go—no ground beneath his feet and no light to run to. His limbs felt heavy as panic set in.

"You cannot run," the voice laughed. "You are mine."

The darkness was crushing down on him. Gewey could no longer move or speak.

"Give in," said the voice. "You fight me for nothing. I can help you. I can give you all that you desire."

Gewey let out a final, desperate scream. The voice laughed, then faded away.

Gewey woke up drenched in sweat, his heart pounding like a drum. He could still feel the weight of the darkness on his chest, and the laughter of the voice echoed in his head. It took him a few minutes to calm down enough to get up and pour himself a cup of old wine. He barely tasted it as he quickly drained the cup. Just as he was about to pour another, he heard a horse galloping up to the house. Fear gripped him. He scanned the room for a weapon. The small knife he used for work was still in his pack in the barn, and his axe was in the shed on the side of the house. He spotted a carving knife on a shelf next to the cupboard and snatched it up. The hoof beats stopped, and at once there was a bang at the door.

"Gewey, open up." It was Lee Starfinder.

Still gripping the knife, Gewey crept to the door and cautiously pulled it open. There stood Lee Starfinder, covered in sweat and still wearing his silk nightclothes. In his right hand, he held a small sword. Gewey backed away from the door.

"Come with me," commanded Lee. "We need to leave."

Gewey stood in silence, unable to move.

"No time to lose your wits, boy," said Lee, pushing past him. He scanned the house. "Nothing that can't be left behind, I suppose."

Gewey snapped out of his stupor. "Leave behind?" he cried. "What in blazes are you talking about?"

Lee looked impatient and on edge, not to mention odd in his nightclothes.

"Do you have a saddle?" asked Lee.

"A saddle?" Gewey repeated. "Why do I need a saddle?"

"Please don't ask stupid questions." Lee caught Gewey by the arm and pulled him toward the door. "If you have a saddle, get it. If not, I guess you'll ride bareback. My horse can't carry us both."

Gewey snatched his arm away from Lee's grasp. He leveled his eyes and straightened his shoulders, his fear replaced by anger. There was no way he was leaving without some sort of explanation. Lee noticed Gewey's posture and grinned slightly.

"That's the attitude we'll need in the days to come," said Lee. He motioned for Gewey to sit. "I hope you can appreciate that every minute we delay puts us both in greater danger. And if you hadn't noticed, I am in a hurry." Lee gestured to his own attire.

Gewey nodded and sat in a nearby chair. Lee closed the door but did not sit. Instead, he walked to the window and stared into the night.

"The dream you had tonight was real," Lee began. "The voice you heard was that of the being that is casting the world into darkness. Now that he knows you exist, he'll stop at nothing to find you."

"Why me?" asked Gewey. "Who am I?"

"Don't interrupt, boy," scolded Lee. "Like I said, he'll do anything to find you, but I won't let that happen."

"You're not making any sense," said Gewey. "How could you know about my dream?"

Lee sighed, turning away from the window. "What does it matter?" he said. "The very fact that I do know—that should be enough to stop your arguing. You must come with me now... before it's too late. Something evil is coming for you, and if you don't hurry, it will find you."

Lee could see the confusion on Gewey's face and softened his tone.

"Gewey, I know what was in the letter, and I know you probably have a million questions. I promise that when we're safely away, I'll answer as many as I can. Your father trusted me, and I would ask that you give me the same trust—at least for now."

"He was not my father, and you know it," said Gewey.

"Yes, he was," said Lee. "He loved you, and that's all you should care about. What difference should it make that you were not of his blood? It wasn't blood that bound him to you. It was love, and trust me when I say that means a lot more."

Gewey felt ashamed. "I'm sorry," he offered meekly. "It's just that I don't understand why he never told me."

Lee walked over and placed his hand on Gewey's shoulder. "I'm sure he had his reasons. And considering what happened tonight, I'm grateful that he didn't."

Gewey looked up at Lee questioningly.

"Please just get ready," said Lee. "When the dawn comes, we'll talk."

Lee gently pulled Gewey to his feet.

"No need to pack," said Lee. "I have clothes and provisions at my estate being readied as we speak. I need you to saddle your horse now."

"I don't have a saddle," said Gewey. "Never needed one. Besides, my horse has never been ridden; she's a bloody workhorse."

Lee pondered the situation, then spun around and headed to the door. "I guess you have time to pack a few things after all," he said as he opened the door and headed in the direction of the barn. "But be quick."

Gewey did as he was told. He got dressed and packed a few clothes, personal items, and the last loaf of bread in the house. Once packed, he looked around, doused the flames in the fireplace, and turned off the lanterns. He had just grabbed his wool jacket when Lee burst through the door.

"Good, you're ready," said Lee. "Let's go. Don't worry. If we need anything else, we can pick it up along the way. I've left word with my staff to take care of the farm while we're gone, so don't worry about that either."

Gewey nodded curtly as they stepped outside. Apparently, Lee had been planning this for quite some time. Lee stowed his sword in the wagon and wrapped it in a blanket. Gewey's horse, not accustomed to being handled by a stranger, stamped nervously. Lee's own horse was now tied to the back of the wagon. It wore no saddle; Gewey suspected that Lee had been in too much of a rush to bother with one.

"I suppose it will look less conspicuous if both of us ride into town on your wagon rather than racing in on horseback.

That is, if they don't notice I'm wearing nightclothes," said Lee. His tone was excited, and his movements were graceful and quick. Gewey marveled at how fast Lee could get things done. "Throw your pack on the wagon and let's go."

Gewey calmly obeyed. He still wasn't satisfied with the reasons Lee had given for such a quick departure, but he did now know that, whatever else was happening, the dream had been real, and that thought made him afraid. Even just thinking about it made the weight of the darkness return.

"Stop thinking about it," Lee scolded as he climbed up beside Gewey.

"What do you mean?" Gewey responded, startled. *Surely Lee can't read my mind*, he thought.

"You know what I mean, boy," said Lee. "If you think about him, he may be able to find you. Until we figure out how he located you in your dreams, we must be cautious."

Gewey didn't reply. Instead, he focused his thoughts on the sound of his breath and the movement of the wagon.

It was three miles to Lee's estate, which was situated just north of the village, next to the river. It took them a little more than an hour to get there. Several roads had been built leading to Lee's home; this was more than the village council deemed necessary, but since Lee had been willing to both pay for the construction himself and use local labor, they'd raised few objections. It did, however, lead to rumors about his eccentricities. Some folks even said that he had built tunnels, but Gewey had always ignored such gossip.

Lee's estate was built across fifty acres—a small property for a man of his apparent wealth. But the land was some of the finest in the area, with most of it dedicated to the keeping of his many horses. The house itself, adorned simply in northern fashion, looked modest from the outside. The single-story dwelling had been built mostly of stained cedar with cherry inlay surrounding each window, and the roof was made from red tile imported from the north. Symbols of the Nine Gods were carved into the stone driveway that led from the main avenue to the front door. Although no blooms could currently be seen, a well-tended garden had once dominated the front yard; at its center stood a statue of Gerath, patron god of Sharpstone. Three horses waited in front of the house. Two of these were saddled, and one was packed full of supplies. The large oak door was already open and Millet, one of Lee's servants, stood just inside. He was holding a small box wrapped in silk cloth.

Lee stopped the wagon and leaped down. He retrieved his sword from the cart and placed it in its scabbard, attaching this to his saddle. He walked up to Millet and took the box, whispering something in the servant's ear as he did so. Millet disappeared into the house.

"Saddle up," Lee said to Gewey. "I won't be a moment."

Lee turned and ran into the house while Gewey grabbed his belongings. He'd barely had a chance to stow his gear and mount his horse when Lee returned, dressed in a soft leather travel outfit and a black wool cloak. He carried a long sword sheathed in a plain brown scabbard. Lee walked up to Gewey's horse and attached this sword to his saddle.

"I'd invite you in, but time is short," said Lee, climbing onto his horse. "You'll have the packhorse in tow for now. If we meet anyone we know along the way, we'll say you're accompanying me as I visit relatives in the north. People will get suspicious after a week or so, but Millet has instructions to keep the deception alive for as long as possible."

"Where are we going?" Gewey asked.

"West," answered Lee, pulling the hood over his head.

Gewey pressed the issue. "West where?"

"Save your questions for now," he replied. "We're too close to home, and I won't risk drawing attention. Believe me, boy, what I have to tell you is worth waiting to hear." Lee checked up and down the avenue, and seeing no one, urged his horse on, heading north.

"I thought we were going west," said Gewey.

"Don't be stupid," replied Lee irritably. "If anyone sees us, they need to see us heading north. There's a river crossing used by smugglers not far from here, but we can't be seen making for it. It's the long way around, but there's no choice. Now be quiet. We have a lot of distance to cover before dawn."

To Gewey's relief, they met no one along the way. The cold night air kept him from dozing off. The moon was new, and there was not a cloud in the sky. Gewey looked up at the stars and searched out the constellations his father had taught him when he was small. Pósix, Goddess of the Dawn, shined brightly in the darkened sky, and Gewey thought about the nights that he and his father had spent stargazing.

"Gewey," Lee said suddenly, shocking him to attention. "Dismount."

Lee and Gewey led their horses into the woods on the west side of the road. The forest in this area was thick and treacherous. Gewey could barely see a thing, but Lee seemed to know exactly where he was. The ground was rough and uneven, and Gewey tried not to curse aloud as he tripped over roots and walked headlong into low-hanging branches.

It was nearly dawn, but the thickness of the trees blocked out the light. The air was still and damp, and the only sound he heard was that of their footsteps and the heavy breathing of the horses.

"We're here," Lee said.

Gewey nearly ran into Lee's horse. At first, he couldn't see where 'here' was, but then he spotted a dim light shining ahead, where the forest opened into a small clearing. As they entered this, Gewey noticed that the soft grass was drenched in morning dew and that it was, at most, half an hour past sunrise. Lee began unloading the pack horse and setting up camp.

"We travel at night and rest in the day for the time being," said Lee. "It'll take a couple of days to get used to, but I don't want to risk being seen for now."

Gewey found his own pack and pulled out the loaf of bread. He offered some to Lee, but he refused.

"At least we won't need a fire," Gewey joked, plopping down on a blanket.

Gewey munched on the bread, watching as Lee finished setting up camp and checking the horses. He'd thought of everything; they had blankets, pots, rope, food, and even a small tent in case of bad weather. Gewey wondered how Lee had prepared in such a short time.

When Lee finished his preparations, he pulled out a small sweet cracker from one of the bags and sat across from Gewey.

"Well..." Lee paused. "I guess it's time to tell you what you want to know."

Gewey leaned forward, determined not to miss a single word.

CHAPTER 3

"I guess the best way to start is by telling you a bit about my life, and how I came to live in Sharpstone," Lee began. "Despite what I have told you, I was not born a northern lord. I was born in a small fishing village on the coast of the Western Abyss. My father was a fisherman and died at sea when I was eight. My mother was a beautiful woman, but full of spite and anger. She resented being a lowly fisherman's wife and hated my father for it. When he died, I think she hated him even more. After his death, she joined the Temple of Saraf, God of the Sea, as a novice. Without a husband and burdened with a child, she was left with no other options.

"The Temple sent us both to the city of Hazrah, north of the Razor Mountains. Though I think my mother would have preferred they hadn't, I was made an acolyte so that I could stay with her.

"For the first three years, we lived in Hazrah. I hardly saw the city beyond the Temple doors. I hated it there and longed to leave. One day, Lord Dauvis Nal'Thain came to the Temple looking for a personal attendant. His last attendant had been killed while defending him from an assassination attempt. The High Priestess was reluctant to provide assistance but could not refuse a lord, especially one as powerful as Lord Dauvis. She told him that he could pick an acolyte, just as long as he agreed to pay all his wages and compensate the temple for the loss. She invited Lord Dauvis to stay the night so he could observe us at work during a banquet in his honor.

"None of the others wanted to be chosen, but I was eager. Temple life was dull and monotonous, with endless days of cleaning and scrubbing, and endless nights of prayer and fasting. At the banquet, I did everything I could to be noticed, but Lord Dauvis barely looked at me. I remember how upset I was that night. I just knew I'd be stuck at the temple forever.

"The next morning, to my great surprise, my mother woke me early and told me to pack my belongings. I had been chosen. I think that was the first time I had ever seen tears in her eyes. She helped me pack without a word, then led me to the office of the High Priestess.

"When I entered, Lord Dauvis was standing alone at the back of the room. He wasn't a very tall man; I was only eleven years old, but already stood nearly as tall as he. What he lacked in height, however, he made up for in girth. Though the man must have weighed three hundred pounds, he moved with surprising agility.

"My mother put her hand on my shoulder, whispered, 'Farewell,' and left the room. It was the last time I was to see her.

"Lord Dauvis looked me up and down and grunted. 'I expected more,' he said. I wasn't sure if he was talking to me or to himself, so I kept quiet.

"'What's your name, boy?' he asked.

"'Lee Starfinder,' I replied. I did my best not to sound afraid.

"Lord Dauvis explained what my duties would be. Mostly, they consisted of running messages, doing chores, and seeing that his meals were ready on time. All of that was fine by me. Anything was better than rotting away at the Temple, and from the sound of it, the work for Lord Dauvis would be a lot easier as well.

"The High Priestess was waiting for us at the entrance. She bowed to Lord Dauvis and asked that he send regular reports of me. He nodded and thanked her for her hospitality. She gestured toward me and said, 'Do not dishonor this temple, boy, or I will know about it.' I remember smiling with excitement as I walked out of the temple doors for the last time.

"Life with Lord Dauvis was harder than I had thought it would be. He was unmarried and had no children, so I spent every waking hour attending his needs. For five years I ran his errands, arranged his schedule, and saw to his meals. I don't think I stopped moving for more than a minute, but to tell you the truth, I loved it. I was living life outside of the Temple. Hazrah was a bustling metropolis that breathed a life of its own, and my duties frequently had me traveling to nearby towns and villages. I learned more about the world in one month under the service of Lord Dauvis than I had in my entire life. As I got older, he gave me more responsibilities. Eventually, I acted as his proxy during minor business deals and spoke in his stead at meetings with local politicians.

"I think I would have been happy to live out my life in service to Lord Dauvis, but the gods had other plans. When I was sixteen, the two of us were traveling to Pendleton—a village two days' ride to the west—to mediate a labor dispute. Suddenly, our coach was attacked. Apparently, the mayor was afraid that he would be caught pocketing gold intended for village construction. His plan was to make it look as if bandits had robbed and killed us, stealing all the accounting records and making any investigation impossible.

"When they attacked, I tried my best to protect Lord Dauvis, but I had never been taught to fight and was quickly overcome. I was knocked to the ground and bleeding from a knife wound to my arm. A large man jumped onto my chest and was about to slit my throat. I braced myself, knowing I was about to die, when suddenly the man's head separated from his shoulders and rolled to the ground beside me. I looked up and saw Lord Dauvis swinging his sword and fighting like a madman. He took on five bandits single-handedly; one after the other fell to his sword, but in the end, it wasn't enough. In desperation, one of the bandits flung a long knife at Lord Dauvis that pierced him through the belly. Ultimately, the attackers were all dead and Lord Dauvis lay dying. I remember how scared I was as I watched him pull out the knife. Blood soaked his waistcoat and spilled to the ground, but he bore the pain in silence.

"I helped him into the coach and hurried back to the manor. By the time the physician arrived, Lord Dauvis was near death. It took three servants to force me out of the room, and even then, I didn't wander more than a few feet from his chamber door. Hours seemed like days, and when the physician finally emerged, he told me that Lord Dauvis was asking for me.

"He looked so pale and weak, lying there in his bed. No one was in the room but the two of us. He beckoned me to come closer and smiled.

"'Lee,' he said, 'I don't have much time, so listen carefully.' He reached up and took my hand. 'It was no accident that you are in my service. A week before you came here, I was told by the Oracle of Manisalia that I was to take you into my home and protect you. She said you were important, and that one day you would help save the world. I wasn't sure if I believed her, but I wasn't about to take the chance. Now, I think that I do believe.'

"He called out for the housekeeper, who brought him a scroll sealed with the crest of his family.

"'I'm leaving you everything,' he said. I was stunned. 'My wealth and title will be passed to you. I've already made all the arrangements, so there will be no one who can dispute your claim.'

"I couldn't believe what I was hearing. 'Why?' I cried. 'Why would you do this?'

"'Because of what else the Oracle told me,' he answered, still smiling.

"'What else did she tell you, my lord?' I asked. I could feel his grip loosen. He was slipping away.

"He pressed the scroll into my hands and said, 'Promise me you will take care of my house and servants. You're a Nal'Thain now.'

"Tears were streaming down my face. 'I promise,' I wept.

"Lord Dauvis closed his eyes and whispered his last words: 'Go see the Oracle.'"

Lee paused and wiped his eyes.

"In the weeks that followed, I set about the business of learning to be a lord. I was now looked upon as Lee Nal'Thain, the son of Dauvis Nal'Thain.

"I sent for my mother at the temple but learned that she had left the order shortly after I went to serve Lord Dauvis and had left no clue as to her whereabouts. I spent a small fortune trying to find her but eventually gave up the search.

"It was almost a year before I went to see the Oracle. I was afraid of what she would tell me, so I kept putting it off. Millet was the one who finally convinced me to go. You've met him at my estate. He's been with me a long time.

"It was a seven-day journey to Manisalia. The town was quiet; it had a few shops, an inn, and a livery, but little else. I had pictured a city filled with pilgrims and thought I'd be able to see the Temple towering from a mile away. But I didn't. I actually had to ask for directions.

"The Temple of the Oracle turned out to be a small closed pavilion set upon a massive marble floor. The floor had been built on a foundation where you would expect a temple to be; according to legend, it was located on the very spot where the gods first breathed life into humankind. A short flight of alabaster steps covering the small distance from the ground to the 'temple floor' was the only other man-made structure. Later, I learned that three temples had originally been built there. All had collapsed one after the other, only days after they had been built, leaving only the foundation and the floor intact. Taking it as a sign from the gods and fearing for the safety of the Oracle, it was decided not to attempt building a fourth.

"I had planned on a long stay. I figured I would be one of many waiting to see her, but as soon as I walked up, a young girl dressed in white linen robes approached me.

"'It's about time you got here, Lord Starfinder,' she said, using my given name. She took my hand. 'Come, she's waiting.'

"Needless to say, I was surprised. But I let her lead me up the stairs—past men and women who looked as if they'd been waiting for a long time—and straight into the pavilion. I looked around for a moment. A large green carpet covered the entire floor, and pillows lay scattered everywhere. A few uncomfortable-looking chairs lined the walls, and a number of dim lanterns hung from ropes strung across the pavilion's support beams. Whatever I expected, this wasn't it, and for a moment, I thought someone was playing a joke on me. The pavilion's sole occupant was sitting on the floor, legs crossed, holding a rag and playing tug-o-war with a puppy. She was wearing green cotton trousers and a brown tunic. Her feet were bare, and she wore no jewelry; nothing about her indicated that she was indeed the famous Oracle of Manisalia. She ignored me at first, clearly enjoying herself, and I was just about to walk out when she finally spoke.

"'Do you like dogs?' she asked me. 'Personally, I think they're better than people. More loyal. Certainly smarter.'

"I just stood there, staring like an idiot. Here before me was the great Oracle of Manisalia. People spoke of her wisdom all over the world. Kings and lords bowed to her will.

In fact, she was the very reason I was now a lord instead of wasting away back at the Temple of Saraf. The woman had the ear of the entire known world, and here she was, barefoot on the floor, playing with a mongrel puppy. It wasn't exactly inspiring."

Gewey grinned, trying to imagine the scene.

"She looked at me and smiled. Her skin was flawless, as if age could not touch her; but if the stories about her were true, then she must have been very old. Her jet-black hair was tied back in a loose braid, showing no hint of gray. Her eyes were sky blue and twinkled in the dim light. When she met my gaze, I felt small and insignificant—as though she had turned me into a child.

"'I take it I'm not what you expected,' she said. 'Would you feel better if I have my assistant come in and chant in an ancient language? She knows one. She's a very bright young girl.' Clearly, the Oracle was having fun with me. 'I guess you want to know what I told poor Dauvis about you.'

"I sat in front of her on one of the pillows and told her my story. She listened patiently, but I had the feeling that she knew what I was going to say before I said it. Still, it felt good to tell someone. When I finished, she stood up and got a bowl of figs from the corner and we sat in silence and ate. When we finished eating, she reached over and put her hand on my cheek.

"'So young, yet so strong,' she said, her voice soft and melodic. 'You've been through a lot, but there is much more to come. First, it's time you knew who you are, and why I told Dauvis to care for you.'

"I remember how nervous I was, but I thought I was ready to hear it.

"'You are the son of Saraf, God of the Sea,' she told me.

"I was speechless. I couldn't believe what she was saying. I refused to. I wanted to leave, but the Oracle leaned forward and grabbed my wrist. Her strength was surprising.

"'I know it's hard to understand,' she said, 'but it's true. Saraf seduced your mother eighteen years ago. How it happened and why he did it, I don't know. Perhaps one day, if you see your mother again, she can tell you. But that part of the story hasn't been revealed to me.'

"She released me and picked up the puppy that had been lying quietly beside her. 'One day you will be given a great treasure, and you will have to leave your whole life behind to protect this treasure. If you refuse, or if you fail, darkness will consume the world. You have been chosen because of who and what you are. Your courage and wisdom will be put to the test, but if you face the challenge, you can save us all. What the treasure is, I do not know, but once you touch it for the first time, you will have no doubts. You will know what to do. The only question will be if you're willing to do it. The cost will be great, and once paid, your life will never be the same. Until then, you must train your mind and body. As the son of Saraf, you can achieve things far beyond the abilities of normal men. You have power you've never dreamed of, and the time is coming when you'll need it.'

"She lowered her eyes and stroked the sleeping puppy. I expected her to say something else, but she just sat there silently.

"'Is that it?' I asked, but she just continued petting that bloody puppy. Finally, I got up and left the pavilion, not sure what to believe. None of it made sense to me.

"For the next few years, I tried to forget about what she told me and lived the life of a Hazrahinian lord. But the more I tried to forget, the more miserable I became. I renewed the search for my mother, but once again came up empty-handed. I thought that if I found her, she could tell me it was all lies and I could feel normal again. Eventually, I decided it was time to begin training for what was to come, even though I had no idea what exactly that was.

"It turned out that the Oracle was right. As I trained, I discovered that I was stronger and faster than other men. It took me mere weeks to learn new sword techniques that took other people years to master. My eyesight was sharper and my hearing keener. The more I trained, the more I came to believe the Oracle; but it wasn't until I first saw you that I knew for a fact she had told me the truth."

Lee stood up and stretched his legs. He walked over to where he had tied his horse and stroked its mane.

"My father said you first saw me when I was a baby," said Gewey. "He said you came down to buy horses, though he really didn't believe that. He also said he thought I was the reason you moved to Sharpstone."

Lee laughed softly. "Harman always was a bright one," he said. "And he was right. Looking back, I wish I had confided in him more. But at the time, it seemed safer to keep him in the dark." He walked back to the blanket and kneeled down. "The truth is, it was I who had Millet bring you to your father. I knew I couldn't keep you safe. A lord showing up out of nowhere with a child... It would draw too much attention. Millet disguised himself as a merchant and told your father he had found you in the wreckage of a raided caravan. I knew your father's heart and was sure he'd take you in."

"If all this is true, then how did you end up with me in the first place?" asked Gewey. "How did my father come into this? And why has it all been such a secret?"

"I was just getting to that," he replied. "Be patient and I'll tell you."

Gewey sighed and motioned for Lee to continue.

"I trained for years, preparing myself," said Lee. "But for what, I still didn't know. By the time I was twenty-eight, I had learned everything the local masters had to teach, so I ventured out in search of anyone who could train me. It was on one of those trips that I met your father.

"He had left Sharpstone in search of his fortune. He was courting your mother at the time. Your grandfather had left him little in the way of a living, so he left home hoping to find work as a man at arms. With what he saved, he hoped to buy a farm and earn the right to marry your mother. I think she would have married him regardless, but Harman was a proud man, and he couldn't imagine taking a wife without the means to support her.

"When I first encountered your father, I was making my way around the eastern end of the Razor Edge Mountains, on my way back to Hazrah. I had just finished studying under a sword master in Vallhavin, and had stopped for the night in a small village. What I didn't know was that this particular village was home to a band of raiders and cutthroats that had been wreaking havoc in every town and village for a hundred miles. I was sitting in the common room of the inn, sharing a bottle of wine with Millet. He always came with me on these trips—he's convinced that I can't take care of myself—and to tell the truth, there were times I would have gone mad but for his company. Earlier I had heard talk of a sword-master and battle strategist somewhere in the northwest near the steppes; I was trying to decide whether to cancel my trip home and seek him out when I noticed two men huddled in the corner, staring at me.

"At once, I knew their intentions. One of the abilities I had discovered was that I could sense when someone means harm. Sometimes, I can almost hear their thoughts. I immediately told Millet to go to our room and wait for me there.

"I didn't have to wait long. As soon as Millet headed for the room, one of the men got up and followed him. I wasn't wearing my sword, and, for all his accomplishments, Millet is no warrior. I stood up and pretended not to notice that the second man was still watching me as I walked toward the bar. As fast as I could, I grabbed a mug off a table and flung it at the man in the corner. It hit him squarely in the throat and he fell over, gasping. I ran upstairs and was just in time to see the first man drawing a knife as he knocked at my door. I charged in, trying to get to him before Millet could answer, but the man saw me coming and ran down the hall to the back steps. Foolishly, I chased after him.

"By the time I caught up to him, he'd made it out of the back entrance and was heading across the street to a nearby house. I was just reaching out to grab for him when I felt a pain shoot through my left shoulder. It took a second for me to realize that I'd been struck by an arrow. Three more men—one carrying a bow—jumped out from around the side of the house. I was unarmed, wounded, and outnumbered, and all I could think was that the bloody Oracle had been wrong after all.

"I thought I was about to die right there in the street. But suddenly, out of nowhere, your father stepped in front of me, swinging his sword wildly. I think it was the sheer ferocity of his attack that saved us, being that his skills with a blade were crude at best. Later, he told me his father had served the King as a soldier and had taught him basic sword fighting when he was a boy, but he had never learned much beyond that. The men turned and ran, and your father, being a much wiser man than I, did not chase after them. Instead, he helped me back to the inn where he and Millet tended my wounds. The innkeeper warned us about the raiders, saying that they would definitely return and that we should leave as soon as possible. Millet fussed and complained about me traveling wounded, but there was no choice. Your father came with us, and I hired him as a bodyguard. I introduced myself to him as Lee Starfinder—not Nal'Thain. In those days, I never traveled under the name of my crest.

"I decided not to return to Hazrah, and headed west to seek out the sword master. As it turned out, the attack did me some good. The wound took only two weeks to heal. I kept this from your father, of course, but it was more proof of my heritage.

"I eventually found the sword master and studied under him for a year. When my studies were done, your father told me he wanted to go home. He had saved enough money to buy a small farm and take his bride. He feared that if he waited any longer, she might marry another. I'm sure your father told you, but she was quite beautiful; even so, I don't think she would have married anyone else even if he'd stayed away for ten years. She truly loved him. I was sorry to see him go, but I knew from the look in his eyes that he was determined. I didn't see him again for many years.

"I eventually returned home for good, or so I thought. I continued training myself, as there were no more masters left to teach me. Life went on as normal, and I found myself becoming forgetful of what the oracle had told me.

"It was the night of a massive blizzard when Millet woke me and told me a messenger from the Oracle was waiting in my study to see me. I went downstairs, and to my surprise, found the young girl who had once led me to the pavilion all those years ago. Though she was no longer a young girl, I recognized her right away. She looked frightened and was shivering from the cold. In her arms, she held a baby wrapped in linen.

"'It's time,' she said.

"'What do you mean?' I asked, knowing perfectly well what she meant.

"She didn't say another word. She just walked up, placed you in my arms, and ran out, disappearing into the storm."

Gewey's jaw tightened. "Let me get this straight," he said. "I was dumped off during a storm in the middle of the night, and you decided I was the treasure, just like that. You then left me with my father and moved hundreds of miles to Sharpstone to watch over me. And now, for whatever bizarre reason, some evil being is on our trail. Have I missed anything?"

"Don't make light of this," Lee scolded. "I have sacrificed much, and you will listen to what I have to say."

"Fine," said Gewey, raising no objection.

Lee continued. "Like I said, when the girl handed you to me, I had no idea what was happening. I looked down at you sleeping in my arms and remembered what the Oracle had said: when the time came, I would know what to do. Well, I didn't, at least not until I pulled back the blanket you were wrapped in and touched your face with my finger. It was then that I understood why you are so important. The second I touched your skin, I knew what you really are." Lee paused and leaned in. "You are a god, Gewey. In fact, you are the only child ever born from the union of two gods."

Gewey burst into laughter. "You're crazy!" he exclaimed, jumping to his feet. "And to think I was starting to believe you. I actually left my farm trusting that you might know something."

Lee frowned. "There is one way to show you," he said. He walked over to Gewey and reached out his hand.

"What's this?" asked Gewey, clearly amused.

"Take my hand," said Lee.

Gewey hesitated.

"Just do it," said Lee. "If this doesn't make you believe me, you can go home and forget everything I've said."

Gewey shrugged. "Fine," he said, taking Lee's hand.

It was as if a bolt of lightning had struck him. Time stood still, and Gewey felt as if the whole universe had opened up. He could see straight into Lee's mind, and in that moment, he knew everything Lee had told him was true. He let go of Lee's hand, shaking from the experience.

"The first time is the worst," Lee said. "After a while, you'll learn to control it. It's how those of us carrying the blood of a god can recognize one another. There are others like me—half man, half god. I've met a few of them. But you're different. You're full-blooded. One of a kind."

Gewey still couldn't speak. The idea was more than he could handle. His head began to spin faster and faster with the enormity of it all. After a few seconds, he fell to the ground, unconscious.

He awoke with Lee kneeling over him, smiling broadly. "Boy, if you're going to be any kind of god, we can't have you passing out like this." He began laughing.

Gewey managed to sit up, still feeling lightheaded and more than a bit embarrassed.

"How can this be?" asked Gewey. "I haven't got the power of a god. I bleed, I sleep, and I eat. What kind of god does all that?"

"One who's bound to the earth," answered Lee. "I don't have all the answers, but I have learned much. I've searched books all across the land looking for answers to the very questions you ask. Some I've found, but others are still a mystery. Like me, you're stronger and faster than normal men; and like me, you can see and hear far better. But I'm only a half-god. Some things I can teach you, but discovering your true power is something you're going to have to do on your own."

Gewey got to his feet. "Let's say I believe you," he said. "Why are we running? The voice in my dream... If I'm a god, why should I fear it?"

Lee's eyes narrowed. "What do you know about the Dark Knight of Angrääl?" he asked in an ominous tone.

Gewey shrugged and said, "Rumors mostly. I've heard he's a thousand years old, and that he slays children in the night. To be honest, I've always ignored such tales. I figured they were just stories meant to frighten children."

"As far as being a thousand years old, I doubt it," said Lee. "As far as killing children, I daresay he would without hesitation. Whatever you've heard, just remember this: he is real. He's the reason we've been brought together."

Lee looked at the sky. It was two hours past sunrise. "We need to rest. I'll tell you more once we set out this evening. In the meantime, sleep close to me. I should be able to stop the Dark Knight from entering your dreams."

With that, Lee lay on his blanket and closed his eyes. Gewey's head was buzzing with questions, but he tried to follow Lee's example. He began to feel fatigue seeping into his bones, and—god or no god—he needed rest like anyone else. He was about to ask Lee one final question but heard him breathing deeply and steadily. Gewey couldn't imagine how he could fall asleep so quickly, especially with all this excitement.

It took him more than two hours before sleep came, and thankfully, the dream didn't return.

CHAPTER 4

Gewey awoke an hour before sunset. Lee was nearly finished breaking camp. Gewey packed his own gear and ate the rest of the bread he had brought. When they were ready to leave, Lee mounted his horse and motioned for Gewey to do the same.

"There's a hunting trail a mile west of here that will lead us to the crossing," Lee said. "We should get there just after dark."

"I thought you were going to tell me about the Dark Knight," said Gewey.

"We can talk along the way," Lee replied. "I don't want to be caught sitting in the open too long. It could be dangerous."

Gewey nodded and mounted his horse. The forest had thinned, enabling them once again to ride, and it wasn't long before they found the trail.

"You said you'd heard of the Dark Knight of Angrääl," Lee began. "That's good. It's because of him we're doing this. He's the reason darkness has spread throughout the land. You're old enough to remember the Long Freeze."

"I remember," answered Gewey. "I almost starved."

"It was a sign of the Dark Knight's power growing," Lee continued. "I don't know much about him, unfortunately, but I do know that he's stolen the Sword of Truth. With it, he's locked the door to heaven, and as he masters the use of his power, his corrupting influence changes the world."

"The Sword of Truth?" said Gewey. "I've never heard of it."

"I'm not surprised," Lee replied. "Knowledge of the sword has been a closely guarded secret for thousands of years. Only a few people—members of certain temples, and perhaps a handful of scholars—know of its existence. I only stumbled upon it by accident when studying from a collection of rare books that Lord Dauvis had left me. Apparently, the sword was forged at the time of creation. It was meant to be a key to the door between heaven and earth. Why the gods would make such a thing, I don't know. But whoever possesses it acquires great and terrible power—a power not meant for mortal men."

"How did he get it?" asked Gewey. "You would think a thing like that would be protected."

"How he got the sword isn't so important as what he plans to do with it. I believe he's locked the door to heaven so that he can find a way to rule as a god. With the door locked, the gods are powerless to stop him. If he succeeds, all of creation will be his to control."

"None of this answers how I got here," Gewey noted. "If I'm a god, why am I not locked away with the others?"

"Quite right," Lee acknowledged. "It's a question I've spent many years trying to answer. As near as I can tell, you were brought to the earth and given human form before the door to heaven was sealed. Maybe the gods saw this coming, maybe not. Regardless of how it happened, the fact is that you are here, and you're the only one who can defeat the Dark Knight and reopen the door."

"I still don't understand," said Gewey. "If I'm a god, then why do I seem so human?"

"Again, I'm not certain. But I think that when you were trapped on Earth, it changed you, making you mortal. The gods can take human form. Perhaps you were locked in this form when the door to heaven closed. You still have your powers, but it seems you're also mortal."

"My powers?" Gewey said, sounding doubtful. "I know I'm pretty strong, but other than that, I'm just like everyone else."

"There's where you're wrong," Lee retorted. "You have abilities that you have yet to discover. Some I know of, and can teach you; others, I can only guess at. Many things you will only discover yourself through trial and error. You are the only one of your kind, so no one really knows the full potential of your abilities. The good news is that the Dark Knight doesn't know either."

"What is he?" asked Gewey. "Is he a god?"

"No," answered Lee. "He's a man, or at least he was. All I know is that he was part of an order charged with protecting the door to heaven. He betrayed them and took the Sword. The order was destroyed, and its temples abandoned."

"How did he find me in my dreams?" asked Gewey. "And why now? Why not last year, or the year before?"

"You had just discovered that you weren't who you thought you were," said Lee. "Reading your father's letter must have awakened something inside you that the Dark Knight could detect. I was lucky to have sensed him before he tricked you into revealing your exact location."

"So that was you!" Gewey exclaimed. "You were the other voice."

Lee nodded. "Yes, that was me. I've felt his presence once before and I was lucky to escape. He knows who I am, but I have managed to conceal my whereabouts. I knew that if he found you, he would move against you. The second his mind touched yours, he knew both what you are, and the threat that you pose. Unfortunately for us, he also knows that you don't yet understand your powers, and he'll try to kill you before you can discover them. That's why we must hide for the time being, at least until you're ready to face him. His power grows stronger each day. Poor Thad Marshall's wife is all the proof I need of that."

"You saw her?" Gewey asked.

"Yes," Lee answered. "It was I who ... disposed of her. Not a pleasant task, I might add. Melton Fathing would have discovered me if he hadn't been busy gossiping about Thad's outburst. I was lucky to have seen her in time. I can't imagine how the people of Sharpstone would react to the living dead."

"So, she was alive?" asked Gewey. "How can that be?"

Lee shook his head. "I don't know if alive is how I'd describe her. It was as if her spirit had been forced back into her body. I don't think she knew where she was, or why. What the Dark Knight has done to cause this is a mystery, but there's no doubt that it was him."

Gewey rubbed his temples in disbelief. "What did you do with her?"

Lee shot Gewey a look that said not to ask that question again.

"Say I buy all this," said Gewey. "What do we do now? Where do we go?"

"For now, our destination must be a secret," Lee responded. "Even from you. I can protect your mind when you sleep, but if we're separated, and he finds you while you dream, he could force you to give yourself away. I was only barely able to intervene the last time. But the closer we are to each other, the more I can help. In the meantime, I'll start training you to shield your mind."

It was fully dark by now, and the stars were shining brightly in the heavens as they neared the river. Two lights from the ferry could be seen in the distance. Gewey knew about the crossing, but he'd never used it before, and the thought of being on the water at night unnerved him.

"Wait here," said Lee. "I'll secure the ferry for us."

Half an hour passed and Gewey began to get nervous. Finally, Lee returned with a scowl on his face.

"Let's go," Lee growled. "He's agreed to take us across. And of course, he's charging double to do it at night. The oarsmen want an extra copper each."

"Can't say I blame them," said Gewey.

Lee shot Gewey an angry look. "Just be quiet and let me do all the talking," he said. "Last thing I need is you saying something stupid and giving us away."

Gewey wanted to respond but held his tongue. He followed Lee to the waiting ferry, which was nothing more than a large wooden raft. The ferryman was making ready to cast off, grumbling and cursing about being wakened from his bed and muttering something about 'good-for-nothing foreigners'.

"Well, come on, you two," said the ferryman. "The sooner we get across, the sooner I can get back to bed. Why you can't wait 'til mornin', I don't know."

Gewey boarded as Lee secured the horses and helped the ferryman untie the raft. The crossing made Gewey nauseous, and he was relieved when they reached the opposite bank.

After they disembarked and settled their fee, Lee led them south along the western bank of the river for the next few hours until they came to Far Run Road.

"We'll take the road for a while," Lee explained. "When it gets close to dawn, we'll find a spot to camp. The village of Terriston is about two nights' ride, so we can travel the road until then."

"Great," Gewey said, clearly relieved. "By then, I'll be looking forward to a soft bed."

Lee laughed. "We won't be visiting; we'll be going around it. We're still too close to home to risk being seen."

Gewey's heart sank. He hated sleeping outdoors, and he realized that the days of comfortable beds and hot meals were gone—at least for a while.

"You're going to have to toughen up, boy," Lee scolded. "Believe me, a few nights sleeping under the stars is nothing compared to what is in store for us."

"Yeah," Gewey replied, smirking. "But we sleep under the sun, don't we?"

"Don't get smart with me," said Lee. "The last thing I need is for you to start acting your age."

Gewey suddenly filled with rage. He hated being reminded of just how young he really was. It wasn't his fault he looked like a grown man. He never wanted to be robbed of a childhood. He never wanted to be forced to live the life of someone ten years older. And he certainly never asked to be the savior of the world or to be hunted down by an evil, sword-stealing knight.

Lee could seemingly feel Gewey's mood change, even in the dark. "Calm yourself. You need to learn to control your anger."

Gewey took a deep breath and let his anger subside. The rest of the night, they traveled in silence, leaving the road before sunrise to make camp. Lee unpacked some bread and dried meat and gave some to Gewey, who ate it gratefully; they had only stopped a few times that night, and they hadn't eaten at all until now. Belly full, Gewey lay on his blanket and enjoyed the remainder of the cool night.

"Tell me about my father," Gewey said, finally.

Lee was lying a few feet away. "I'm not sure what to tell you. I didn't know him that well. He was brave and honorable, that's for sure. After I moved to Sharpstone, I tried to keep my distance. I didn't want to interfere with him raising you."

"You traveled together for a year," Gewey pointed out. "You must have gotten to know him a bit in that time."

Lee rolled over and faced Gewey. "He was my bodyguard, and our interactions were based on that relationship. Besides, I was studying swordsmanship and battle strategy for most of that time. It left little room for bonding."

"You sent me to be raised by him," challenged Gewey. "And you're telling me that you didn't know him? I don't believe you." Gewey rolled over, sulking.

Lee sighed. "I had good reasons to send you to Harman. He saved my life without even knowing me, and in the year he was with me, I never heard a dishonest word pass his lips."

Gewey closed his eyes and tried to picture his father's face. "That can't be the only reason."

"No, it wasn't," Lee admitted. "One of the things you'll discover is that if you try hard enough, you can look into people's hearts and see them for who they really are. I looked into Harman's heart and knew the man he was. Of all the people I've known, his heart was the most pure. When you were first brought to me, I knew there was only one man I could trust to protect you."

This made Gewey smile. He suddenly felt whole again as he let the love for his father rush over him. Gradually, sleep began to take over.

The next evening passed uneventfully. Gewey's heart felt light as Lee told him stories of his travels to pass the time. He asked Lee to retell the story of how he met his father, and Lee was happy to oblige, this time adding a few extra details about Harman's heroism.

"We need to train you to close your mind," said Lee, after they had made camp. "This won't be easy, but you'll have to trust me." Lee motioned for Gewey to sit across from him.

Lee reached over and grabbed Gewey's hands. Gewey felt the same shock of recognition the moment his hand touched Lee's, but this time it was more intense. He felt the presence of Lee's mind pressing in on his.

"Keep me out," Lee instructed.

"How?" asked Gewey. Beads of sweat were forming on his forehead.

"Picture your mind as a gate that you have to keep closed," he replied. "Keep me out."

Gewey tried, but Lee's will was too strong. Slowly, Lee forced his way into Gewey's mind until he had complete control.

"Stop!" Gewey screamed.

Lee released his hold. "You'll have to do better than that, boy. That's just a taste of what's to come."

Gewey collapsed on his back, breathing heavily, his head pounding.

Lee helped him to his feet. "Steady," he said. "It's a shock when someone seizes your mind, but you must learn to keep me out."

"I can't," Gewey gasped. "You're too strong."

Lee suddenly slapped Gewey's face. "Never say 'I can't' to me again. You can, and you will. Dig deep. Find the strength. You're a god, so act like one."

Gewey's ears were ringing. "What was that for?" he yelled. Rage filled his chest.

"That was for weakness," Lee replied as he sat back down. "Come, try again."

Gewey fought the urge to strike back. He sat down and readied himself for another assault. It was midday before Lee allowed him to sleep. By then, Gewey was nearly blind from exhaustion and was asleep almost before he rested his head.

They repeated the lesson the next night, but this time Gewey was able to keep Lee out a bit longer. Lee, however, showed no sign of being pleased at Gewey's progress. He shouted and cursed each time Gewey failed. A few times, they nearly came to blows, but Gewey managed to check his anger and frustration.

The third night, they made their way around the village of Terriston, being careful to avoid encountering anyone along the way. Being inconspicuous, Gewey discovered, meant a day without Lee's harsh training; their lessons could get quite loud at times, and they couldn't risk attracting attention.

It was well into the fourth night before they were back on the road again. Gewey wasn't looking forward to camp and the subsequent lesson, but he had become determined to beat Lee. The previous night had been uneventful, but Lee still seemed on edge. He and Gewey had hardly spoken, and when they did, their interactions were short and unpleasant.

When they made camp, Lee unpacked only their blankets and a bit of bread and dried meat. That night's lesson was the harshest yet. Gewey felt as if his mind would break, but in one instance, he almost managed to keep Lee out. He lay down to sleep when it was over, but noticed Lee sitting upright, staring into the brush.

"What's wrong?" asked Gewey. "You seem upset."

"I'm not sure," Lee replied. "I think we're being followed."

"Followed?" said Gewey, startled. "By who?"

Lee shook his head. "I don't know, but I think we'll stay off the road for a few days."

Gewey nodded. The idea of being followed disturbed him; that Lee seemed worried disturbed him even more. Sleep came slowly, and he did not rest well. The next evening, they packed up and headed deeper into the woods.

The Forest of Simon Bal was one of the largest in the world, spanning hundreds of miles in every direction. There were no trails, and it didn't take long for Gewey to miss the comfort of the road. Lee changed direction so often that Gewey no longer knew where he was.

It was an hour before sunrise when Gewey heard it. It was the sound of a horse walking over uneven terrain. Lee drew his sword and motioned for Gewey to do the same. They waited for a time, trying not to make a sound. After a few minutes, the sound of the hoofbeats faded.

"Who was that?" whispered Gewey.

"I don't know," said Lee. "But one thing's for sure: whoever it was, it's no accident they are traveling the same way that we are. I left a trail so confusing that only an experienced woodsman could follow it. We'll stop here for now. Hopefully, it will seem like our trail has disappeared and our pursuer will be thrown off."

Finding a nearby hill to wait out the coming day, they didn't bother to unpack the horses. Both of them kept their swords close.

CHAPTER 5

They slept very little the next day and hardly spoke a word to each other. Lee waited until it was fully dark before they continued. They zigzagged through the forest for hours, stopping from time to time to listen for sounds of pursuit. Much to Gewey's relief, there were none. After a time, the flat ground transitioned into steep wooded hillsides, which made changing direction increasingly difficult.

"You do know where we are, don't you?" Gewey asked, breaking the silence.

Lee scowled. "Would you rather guide us?" he replied irritably.

Gewey shook his head and kept quiet.

It was about two hours before sunrise when Lee brought them to a sudden halt and leaped from the saddle, drawing his sword. He motioned for Gewey to stay still and disappeared into the night. Gewey's heart was pounding, and he drew his own sword, peering into the darkness. Ten minutes later, Lee reappeared.

"What's going on?" asked Gewey.

"There's an encampment just ahead," Lee whispered. "Looks like bandits."

"Bandits?" said Gewey. "What are they doing?"

Lee mounted his horse and urged them forward. "Not noticing us, apparently. It looks as if they've found some sport, so I doubt they'll see us pass."

"What kind of sport?" Gewey inquired.

"They've captured an elf," Lee responded. "How that band of morons managed it, I don't know, but I imagine they'll be busy with her for a while."

Gewey halted. "It's a woman? What will they do to her?"

Lee turned. "It's not a woman; it's an elf. And you don't want to know what they're going to do."

"You don't mean to let them kill her, do you?" Gewey asked, appalled.

Lee reined in his horse. "That's exactly what I mean to do, boy. We don't have time for heroics, and even if we did, she's a bloody elf."

Gewey got down from his horse. "I don't care what she is," he said determinedly. "I'm going to save her. You can help me, or you can sit here and do nothing. I don't care either way." Gewey began to creep off into the darkness to look for the bandits' camp.

"Fool," Lee grumbled. He dismounted and caught up to Gewey.

"You're not ready for this, boy." Lee grabbed his shoulder and pulled Gewey behind him. "Just stay in the brush and let me take care of it."

Gewey followed behind Lee as quietly as he could. They had only walked a few yards when they heard the yells and curses of the bandit camp. The glow of the bandits' fire became brighter as they approached. Gewey could smell the stench of unwashed bodies mingling with scorched, burned meat. When they got close enough, Gewey could make out six bandits, each with a long knife at his side. A few bedrolls were cast carelessly about, and a single bandit guarded six horses tied off several yards from the fire. The rest were gathered around what appeared to be a young woman. She was on her knees, gagged and bound, with her wrists tied behind her back. A man who seemed to be their leader was squatting in front of her, while the rest passed a large jug of wine around, laughing hideously.

"Well, well, well, me lovely," the bandit leader chuckled. "Look what we 'ave 'ere, lads. Thought you could sneak up on ol' Durst, did ya?"

The elf glared defiantly at the bandit leader.

"Oy!!! Ain't she a tough one?" a heavyset bandit joked. "I think she's sweet on ya, cap'n."

"Well, lads," said the leader, flashing an evil grin. "I am quite the ladies' man, after all."

This brought gales of harsh laughter from the rest of the band. The leader stood up and grabbed the jug, draining it dry.

"Stay here," whispered Lee, and silently moved around the camp to where the horses were being kept. With the lone guard's attention focused on the elf, he neither noticed Lee's approach, nor his knife until it had plunged into the back of his neck. Before the first guard hit the ground, Lee had already drawn his sword and was rushing in on the rest of the group. Gewey had never seen anyone move so fast. He killed two more bandits before the others even noticed he was there. The leader managed to unsheathe his long knife and lunge clumsily at Lee. Lee easily dodged the blow and sent the man tumbling to the ground. The two remaining bandits tried to flee, but Lee quickly caught them and ran both of them through.

The bandit leader got to his feet. "I'll not go alone!" he screamed, bolting toward the elf with his knife in hand.

Realizing Lee was too far away to do anything, Gewey sprang to his feet and rushed headlong toward the bandit leader. He threw himself at the bandit just before he was able to plunge his knife into the elf's chest. The two of them went crashing to the ground with the bandit landing on top, pinning Gewey. The boy feared for his life as the bandit began hacking at him maniacally. He instinctively lifted his arms to defend himself and felt pain shoot through his body as the knife found flesh. He could see blood splatter as one final blow struck home, deep in his chest. It was then that Lee reached them, thrusting his sword through the bandit leader's back. Lee moved to Gewey's side as the man gasped and fell to the ground.

"Fool," he cursed as he tore open Gewey's shirt. Blood poured from the gaping wounds covering his arms and chest. "I told you to stay put."

"I'm sorry, Lee," he said weakly. "I guess I'm not much of a hero."

Lee smiled. "Nonsense. Your father would have been very proud of you."

Lee tore Gewey's shirt into strips and pressed one of them to the wound in his chest; the rest he wrapped around the cuts on his arms. "I'll be back. I have a salve that will stop the bleeding."

Lee dashed off, leaving Gewey lying on the ground and wondering if this was the end for him. He turned his head and noticed the elf woman, still bound, staring at him.

"Don't worry, Miss," said Gewey. "I'll have Lee untie you when he gets back."

The elf woman gave no reaction. Gewey had never seen an elf before, and he'd heard very little about them. She looked almost human. She was thin—though clearly not frail—and her skin was dark bronze. Her long auburn hair fell loosely about her shoulders, and despite the bruises on her face, Gewey could tell that she was quite beautiful. He guessed she was about as tall as most human women; in fact, her narrow piercing eyes and her distinctly elfish ears were the only features that suggested she was anything else.

It was only a few minutes before Lee returned and began tending to Gewey's wounds.

"Stop," said Gewey. "Untie her first."

Lee shook his head, but he could see that Gewey was determined.

"Very well," he sighed, walking over to the elf woman and cutting her bonds.

She got up and stared at Lee for a moment. Lee tensed, ready to draw his weapon. She backed away slowly until she reached the edge of the bandit camp, then turned and ran into the woods.

"You're welcome," Lee called after her.

Lee finished dressing Gewey's wounds and pulled him close to the still-burning fire.

"What now?" asked Gewey. His wounds were beginning to throb.

Lee was staring at the fire. "Now we have to risk going into town," he said. "If you were human, I'd say we'll sit here until you die. But thankfully, as a God, you'll heal—one of the advantages, I suppose."

Gewey tried to laugh, but the pain in his chest stopped him. "Couldn't we just wait here until I heal?"

Lee shook his head. "No. We need medicine and clean bandages. You may heal on your own, but without proper treatment, it could take months instead of weeks. Besides, our provisions won't be enough to last that long. Eventually, we'll run out of food and have to go into town, anyway."

Gewey felt guilty. If only he had known how to fight, they wouldn't be in this mess. "Once I'm better, I want you to teach me the sword."

"Believe me," Lee replied, "you'll learn to fight. I'll see to that."

"I never want this to happen to me again," Gewey declared. "I want to be able to fight my own battles. I want to be more like you."

Lee cocked his head and smiled. "You'll be far better than I. Actually, I was impressed with how well you did this time."

Gewey looked shocked. "What are you talking about? I was nearly killed."

"Maybe, but you managed to fight an armed bandit alone and with no training. And let's not forget, you saved the life of that elf."

Gewey shrugged. "Why did she run off? We meant her no harm."

"Elves are a strange lot," Lee replied. "Not much is known about them. They tend to keep to themselves. I know they don't like humans."

"Why don't they like humans?" asked Gewey, trying to keep his mind off the pain.

"Five hundred years ago, man and elf lived in peace," Lee began. "They more or less stayed out of each other's way. That is until King Luthon IV of Maltona desecrated their most sacred temple. He was a greedy, selfish ruler. He'd made war on his neighbors for so long that he bankrupted his nation. The Temple of the Four Winds—the seat of elfish spiritual power—rested on the border of his kingdom and was rumored to hold vast treasures. For hundreds of years, humans had left the Temple in the elves' control, but Luthon decided to break tradition and claim it for himself. This, of course, sent the elves into a frenzy.

"At first, the war was contained in Maltona, but as the elves closed in, Luthon convinced neighboring kingdoms that the elves wouldn't stop once Maltona fell. Thus, the Great War between elf and man began. For twenty years it spread and raged, leaving the landscape in ruin. Eventually, both sides came to an uneasy truce and agreed to keep to their own lands, never to have dealings with one another again."

"So man started it?" Gewey asked. "No wonder they hate us."

"Yes, but that wasn't the end of it," Lee continued. "The war split the Elven nations apart. Many didn't want the truce, and they began raiding human villages. They slaughtered entire families, burning everything in sight. The other Elven tribes, fearing a second war with man, turned on their own kin. For ten more years, there was civil war, leaving the elves a scattered, broken people. After that, they receded into the shadows. Few have seen them since, and fewer still know much about them."

Gewey pictured the elf woman in his mind—how proud and defiant she seemed, and how beautiful. He couldn't imagine such a war.

"I've spoken too much," said Lee. "You should rest. There's a village ten miles from here, and I need to scout it before we go. You'll have to wait here until I return."

Gewey was already drifting off. "I'll be fine," he said sleepily. "But before you go, tell me one more thing. Why were you willing to leave her to die?"

"You have to understand, Gewey," Lee replied. "The story I told you is from long ago, and there aren't many who still know the tale. Men choose to forget the war, convincing themselves that the elves' hatred of them is uncalled for, returning hate with more hate. Dealings with elves are dangerous at best. Their loathing runs deep, and their cunning is formidable. They live about five times longer than an average man, so there are elves still walking the earth who can remember what the war did to their people. They've become poisoned by their own memory, and in turn, they poison the minds of their children. They're not the people they once were. Believe me when I tell you, releasing that elf has put us in more danger than we were in already. I'm still not sure she won't come back and try to kill us."

"But we saved her," said Gewey. "Why would she want to kill us?"

"You're human to her eyes," Lee answered grimly. "And that's reason enough. Now, you need to sleep."

Gewey obeyed and let himself drift off. The face of the elf woman haunted his dreams.

The next morning, Gewey awoke to find that Lee had already left, but not before he'd taken the time to leave wafers and dried meat at Gewey's bedside, along with his sword. His wounds still throbbed, but Gewey managed to sit up and eat. After he finished, he got to his feet and walked around for a bit. His legs felt weak at first, but the more he walked, the stronger he felt. After a while, he became bored and decided to try to take a nap.

As Gewey lay there, he listened to the sounds of the forest. At first, he heard only what anyone would hear, but as his mind stilled, he was able to take in more and more. It was subtle to begin with—the sound of a robin making its nest, then the rustling of a grass snake slithering through the brush. Gradually, his awareness grew and grew until he felt as if he could hear the very growing of the trees. Though everything around him lived and breathed, it did not feel chaotic. Instead, it was like a chorus of life in perfect harmony. He lay there for hours, listening to the music of the forest, until he heard the sound of footsteps approaching in the distance.

He got up and grabbed his sword, wincing in pain. A few minutes later, Lee arrived, frowning.

"Why are you on your feet?" he scolded.

Gewey told him what he had experienced.

"That's very good," said Lee. "But you need to rest for a bit longer. I don't want you to reopen your wounds." Lee instructed Gewey to take off his shirt so that he could check his bandages. As he removed the dressings, Lee stared in disbelief.

"And I thought I healed fast!" he said in amazement. "Your wounds have closed already. It will still take some time for you to heal completely, but I think we'll be able to move on sooner than I thought."

Gewey was pleased. "I do feel much better. In fact, I think I'm ready to leave now."

"Not so fast," Lee advised. "I've secured a room at an inn, and we're not expected there until nightfall tomorrow. We'll risk one more day here and move on in the afternoon. It's ten miles to the village of Gath, so you'll need to gather your strength."

"If you say so," Gewey sighed. "What do we do in the meantime?"

Lee grinned. "I suggest you lay back down and listen to the forest. It's good practice."

Gewey grumbled with discontent. He hated being idle; years of farm work had driven the laziness right out of him. At first, he kept insisting that he was well enough to travel, but Lee wouldn't budge.

Finally, after much argument, Gewey gave in and spent the rest of the day listening to the forest as he had been told to do.

It felt like he had lain there forever before it was time to leave. Gewey spent most of the night, and the next morning, staring at the trees. Lee had given him an herbal tea to help him sleep, but it only made him light-headed and dizzy. Lee insisted that Gewey continue to rest while he packed. When he was done, he checked Gewey's bandages once more and tossed him a fine linen shirt and expensive riding trousers.

"What's this?" asked Gewey.

"Just get dressed," Lee instructed.

Gewey dressed and mounted his horse. Pain shot through his body as he climbed up, but he was able to hide it from Lee.

"I would have helped you," said Lee.

"No need," Gewey insisted. "I can manage."

The sun was just setting when they reached the road outside Gath. The village was much larger than Sharpstone, and the streets were busier than Gewey was used to seeing this late in the evening. Vendors were still pulling their carts about, looking for prime locations along the main avenue, and lights shone in every shop window.

The sound of a blacksmith's hammer rang through the air, and the smell of the nearby stables made Gewey's heart long for home. The street they traveled twisted and turned until he had trouble remembering which way they had come; Gewey thought he would certainly be lost if they had to make a quick getaway, but Lee seemed to know exactly where he was going.

"There, up ahead," Lee directed, pointing to a sign that read The Fated Bandit. "I've instructed the innkeeper to have our meals brought to our room. I've told him that I'm a horse merchant traveling with my son. Don't speak unless you must; your accent gives you away."

Gewey frowned. "What do you mean?"

"I mean, you sound like a farmer from Sharpstone. Your father may have educated you somewhat, but you don't sound like the son of a wealthy merchant."

Gewey's face soured. "There's nothing wrong with the way I sound," he said, offended.

"Look, boy," Lee said. "You'll stay in the room and not come out. We need to keep you out of sight until you're well enough to travel, so stick to the plan for now. The first person that hears your voice will immediately see through our story, so if you must speak, keep it short."

They tied their horses to the hitching post and Lee went inside. Gewey stayed with the horses to watch their belongings. It wasn't long before a young boy came from around the back of the building and began unpacking the horses. Gewey wanted to help, but he stopped himself; a spoiled merchant's son wouldn't offer to lend a hand. Lee walked outside and gave the lad a copper coin.

"See that our horses are well taken care of," Lee ordered. He then turned to Gewey. "Let's go. Our meal is waiting."

The inn was as clean as the inns in Sharpstone, though a bit larger. The common room was filled with travelers of all sorts—merchants, pilgrims, and even a pair of lords from the south. To the delight of the gathered crowd, a flutist had taken up residence in the corner, playing a jaunty, well-known festival dance. Serving maids were running about as the innkeeper barked orders to a thin, blond-haired youth. Gewey breathed in the air and smiled. This was a welcome change from the woods and trails.

Lee led him up the stairs and down a hall to their room. It was small, but accommodating. Two beds lined opposite walls, and a brass washbasin, already filled with hot water, sat in the corner. On a small table were two plates piled high with roast mutton and spring peas. A loaf of hot bread steamed in the center, and a cup of honeyed wine sat beside each plate. Gewey's mouth watered at the prospect of his first hot meal in days.

A few minutes later, there was a knock at the door. It was the young blond lad from the common room. He had brought up their belongings, and he informed them that the other boy had seen to their horses. Lee thanked him and passed out yet another copper piece.

"Throwing quite a bit of money around," Gewey observed. "Don't you think that will draw attention?"

"It would be noticed more if I didn't," Lee replied. "Like I said, we're supposed to be wealthy horse merchants. That type likes to show off." Lee paused. "And don't try to lecture me, boy. Of the two of us, I'm the one who has been more than twenty miles from Sharpstone."

"I didn't mean anything by it," said Gewey. "I just..."

"You need to understand the danger we are in," Lee interrupted. "Right now, we're exposed. Until you're healed, you must not question even the smallest thing I say."

Gewey nodded and then stripped off his clothes to wash up. To his embarrassment, Lee insisted on helping him and changing his bandages. After they were both washed, they sat down to eat. The food was still hot, and Gewey moaned with satisfaction as he took the first bite.

Gewey felt recharged after a wash and a hot meal, and he asked Lee if they could go down to the common room and listen to the music. Lee angrily repeated his earlier warning about the danger they were in. "Besides," he said, "you still need to heal."

"I don't see how a few minutes of sitting in a corner and enjoying myself could put us in danger," Gewey protested. "Anyway, I feel much stronger now. I promise I won't say a word to anyone!"

Lee looked as if he was ready to strangle the boy. "There will be no further discussion," he said through his teeth. "In the morning, I have to pretend to be interested in horse trading, and I expect you to stay in this room at all times. Understand?"

Gewey didn't answer, instead easing himself down onto the bed and staring at the ceiling. Lee unpacked a few things, set his sword next to his bed, and went to sleep. Gewey stayed awake for a while, thinking about home.

The next morning, he woke to find Lee already dressed and breakfast waiting on the table.

"I checked your wounds while you slept," Lee said. "It looks as if you'll be ready to travel in just a few days. You're healing twice as fast as I'd hoped."

"Great," yawned Gewey. "I don't want to be stuck in this place any longer than I have to."

"In any case, I'll be back by dark," Lee said, clearly not looking forward to playing the role of a merchant. Lee's discomfort made Gewey feel a little better.

"What should I do?" asked Gewey.

"Stay here and bloody heal," Lee growled as he walked out the door.

The day passed slowly as Gewey tried to occupy himself. At first, he tried listening to the sounds of the town, but unlike the harmony of the forest, the sounds of Gath were confused and chaotic. He wasn't able to stand it for more than a few seconds.

When sunset came and Lee hadn't returned, Gewey began to worry. After another hour passed, supper and hot water were brought to the room, but he was too anxious to eat. Just as Gewey had finally decided to go looking for Lee, he burst through the door, breathing heavily.

"What happened?" asked Gewey. "Where have you been?"

"It seems our presence has been noticed," Lee answered. "I spotted someone following me through the streets, but I think I lost him."

"Could you tell who it was?"

"No. Whoever it was moved so fast that I almost didn't notice him until it was too late. It took more than an hour before I was sure I wouldn't lead him back here."

"What do we do?" asked Gewey.

"I've already sent for the horses," said Lee. "I hate to have you travel before you're healed, but I don't see any other choice."

Gewey looked at Lee reassuringly. "I'll be fine. There's barely any pain at all."

"Still, I don't want you doing too much too soon," said Lee, sitting down at the table. "We have some time before the horses are ready, so we might as well eat before we go."

They ate and packed, finishing just as the blond youth from the inn came to inform them that their horses were ready and waiting. They gathered their things and left. While Lee loaded the packhorse, Gewey couldn't help but feel exposed and vulnerable. He kept expecting something to happen, but the night was quiet. They mounted their horses and slowly made their way west, out of town.

As they passed the last building within the town limits, Gewey could swear he saw a shadow moving behind him before ducking out of sight.

CHAPTER 6

"Aren't we leaving the road?" Gewey asked after they had ridden a while.

"No," said Lee. "We're still being followed, and I plan to catch whoever it is."

Gewey smiled. "Good, I hate running."

Lee threw the hood of his cloak over his head. "Maybe so, but if I tell you to run, you do it."

Gewey's smile vanished. "I'm not running if it means leaving you behind," he said with determination.

"You'll do as I say," Lee shot back. "If danger comes, I can handle it much better if I don't have to watch you."

"I don't need watching," Gewey protested.

"For now, you do," said Lee. "Until I've had time to train you, you're a liability in a fight. But don't worry; your time will come soon enough."

Gewey didn't like being thought of as a liability, but he could hardly argue; the last time he fought, he'd been nearly killed.

They rode on until they found a decent spot to camp. Lee lit a fire and told Gewey to get some sleep.

"Aren't we a bit out in the open?" asked Gewey.

Lee was changing into a black shirt and a set of black leather trousers. "Like I said, I intend to find out who's following us. You try to get some rest. I'll be nearby." Lee disappeared into the darkness.

Sleeping in the day for so long had made it hard for Gewey to do so at night, so he stared at the small fire while listening to the crackle of the dry branches. Morning came, and he still hadn't slept. His wounds felt much better, though. In fact, when he reached under the dressings, he could feel that they were almost completely healed. He wondered if there would be a scar. The wounds on his arms had already turned light pink, and the one to his chest had closed and was well on its way to being no more than a minor irritation.

Lee appeared out of the nearby brush, looking stern and focused. He unpacked their breakfast and checked Gewey's bandages.

"Amazing," said Lee. "You seem to heal more quickly by the minute. I can't wait to see how powerful you'll become."

"Did you see anyone last night?" asked Gewey.

"Yes, but whoever it was moved off before I could catch him," Lee said. He spat angrily. "From now on, we stay on our guard. This one is fast and knows how to move without being seen."

"Shouldn't we get off the road?" Gewey asked. "Maybe we can lose him."

Lee shook his head. "We won't be able to lose him there; he's too good, too fast. And though they don't look like they'll be a problem for much longer, your injuries will still slow us down. No, we need to catch him—and kill him."

These final words sent a chill down Gewey's spine. When he had watched Lee kill the bandits, it was fast and furious; he hadn't had the time to consider what was about to happen. This time, they were planning to capture and kill someone. Somehow it felt different—calculated, vicious.

"How do you plan to catch him?" Gewey asked.

"I don't know," Lee admitted, squatting down to pick at the grass. "It's four days until we reach the next town. I have until then to figure it out. That is ... unless he attacks us first."

The next two nights were the same. Lee set up camp, then scoured the area, hoping to get lucky in finding their pursuer. But he met with no success. Gewey could see the frustration on Lee's face. He hadn't slept, and the fatigue began to show in his eyes. Gewey urged him to rest for at least a few hours, but Lee ignored his advice.

On the third night, they set up camp and had just begun to eat their meal when Gewey saw Lee's neck stiffen and his hand move slowly to the knife in his belt.

"What is it?" Gewey whispered. Lee shook his head almost imperceptibly. Just as his hand reached the handle of his knife, they heard a rustle in the bushes just beyond the light of their fire. Lee and Gewey both jumped to their feet and drew their weapons.

"Peace," said a female voice. "I mean you no ill will."

From out of the darkness came the elf woman they had saved from the bandits. She moved with such grace and precision that her footsteps seemed to glide over the ground. Gewey stared in awe. She was wearing a shirt and trousers made of fine cloth, which appeared to change color and hue as she passed through the firelight.

Her hair was now done in a series of tight braids, tied together by a thin leather strap. Over her shoulder, she carried a short bow and a quiver of arrows. In her hand, she held a long knife.

"So it's you who's been following us," growled Lee.

"Yes," she answered. "And with very little difficulty, I must say." Her mouth turned to a sinister grin. "Your clumsy efforts to catch me have kept me quite entertained."

"Those bandits didn't seem to have much trouble catching you," Lee shot back.

The elf woman's jaw tightened. "There were twenty of them before they met me. The six you encountered were all that was left."

"What do you want?" Lee asked. "Why are you following us?"

"What I want is none of your affair," she answered. "I follow you because it pleases me to do so."

"You play a dangerous game, elf," said Lee. "You're lucky I didn't kill you the moment you stepped out of the shadows."

The elf woman laughed. "Bold words, half-man."

Lee's back stiffened. "What did you call me?" he asked, his tone low and threatening.

"I know what you are," she said. "I knew the moment I saw you. Only a half-man can move as you do."

"If you know that, then you also know it won't be easy to kill me," said Lee.

"Maybe it will, maybe it won't," she said. "I've dealt with your kind before. But it's not you that I'm interested in— it's your young friend." Her eyes set upon Gewey. "You're no half-man, yet here you stand when, by all accounts, you should be dead."

"And that's none of your affair," Lee said before Gewey could answer. "Again, I ask you, what do you want?"

The elf woman sheathed her blade. "For now, I want you to come with me. There's something I need to show you." She turned and began to walk away.

Gewey started to follow, but Lee grabbed his collar and pulled him back.

"You think I'm a fool?" Lee snapped. "You must ... if you imagine I'll follow you blindly into the night."

The elf paused. "You may have strength, half-man, but I believe the instincts of your young companion are better. But if you need assurance..." She turned to face them and got down on one knee. "I swear by the angels of the night and the guardian who watches the souls of my kin that I mean you no harm." With that, she rose.

"I'm going with her," said Gewey. "I don't think she wants to hurt us."

Lee grumbled and nodded. "Very well," he said, putting away his weapon. "I know nothing about the oaths of an elf or what your people now hold sacred, but you're right about one thing. I do trust his instincts. But know that if you betray us, it will be the last thing you do."

"As you say," the elf laughed, then led them north into the nearby woods.

Lee walked directly behind the elf, his hand never leaving the hilt of his sword. Gewey followed, trying to keep himself from gawking at the silhouetted figure of the Elven woman moving through the forest. He thought back on the tale Lee had told him about the war and shook his head, wondering.

How could man make war on such beautiful people?

They walked for several minutes until they came to a steep hill. The Elven woman stopped and turned.

"Before we go on, I must ask you a favor," she said.

"What favor?" asked Lee.

"I wasn't speaking to you, half-man," she said.

Lee glared at the elf. "You will speak to..."

"What is it I can do for you?" Gewey asked, cutting Lee off.

Lee was furious.

The elf looked straight into Gewey's eyes. "If what I have to show you is of value, I want you to allow me to accompany you."

"Out of the question," Lee asserted. "You have no business with us. If you feel in our debt for saving you, I release you from your obligation."

"It is not for you to release me from anything," she replied. "You know nothing of my motives, and I will tell you nothing except that I will not harm you. I will follow you with or without your permission. All I ask is that you let me do so openly."

"It would be an honor to have you join us," Gewey said before Lee could stop him. "But I must warn you, our road is dangerous."

"I have already guessed that," she said. "And I thank you. Now come and see what the night has caught."

She led them up the hill to where a small patch of thin pines grew.

Lying face down was a man—bound, gagged, and unconscious. A horse was tied to a tree, and the man's belongings had been tossed on the ground next to him.

"He's been following you," she said. "I overheard him asking someone on the road about two men traveling west, one young, and one older. He described you perfectly. I thought you might want to question him before I slit his throat."

Lee walked to the unconscious man and rolled him over. To his great surprise, it was Millet.

"Millet!" Lee shouted. "What have you done to him?"

"You know him?" asked the elf.

"He's my servant and my friend," said Lee as he drew his knife and cut Millet's bonds.

"Forgive me," she said. "I didn't know."

Lee examined him. He had a few bruises but otherwise looked unharmed. "Why is he unconscious?" asked Lee, cradling Millet in his arms.

"I forced him to drink jawas tea," she answered. "He'll be awake soon. In the meantime, I suggest you gather your things and bring them here. This is a much better location. I'll watch over your servant until you return."

Lee reluctantly agreed, leaving Gewey to keep watch on the hill. He didn't want Millet to wake up only to see an armed elf at his side.

Millet was still unconscious when Lee returned. They built a small fire and Lee unpacked medicine to heal Millet's bruises.

The elf woman sat far from the fire, her eyes closed. Gewey couldn't keep his eyes off her. Finally, he shyly walked over and sat next to her.

"What's your name?" he asked.

She slowly opened her eyes and looked at Gewey. "I am called Kaylia." Her voice was soft and feminine, yet strong.

"I'm Gewey," he said awkwardly. He looked over at Lee, who was tending to Millet. "He's not so bad. If it wasn't for him, I'd be dead right now."

"Perhaps," she said.

"Why do you want to come with us?" asked Gewey.

Kaylia closed her eyes again. "I have my reasons."

Gewey stared at her in silence for a while.

"Why do you stare?" Kaylia asked. Her tone wasn't judgmental or accusing, but it made Gewey blush all the same.

"I don't know," said Gewey. "I don't seem to be able to help myself. I'm sorry."

Kaylia smiled. "Most humans turn their eyes from my kind. Strange that you do not."

"I'm just curious about you," he said. "I never thought I'd meet an elf."

"Did you want to?" she asked.

"I never gave it much thought," he replied. "But now that you're here, I'm glad that I've had the chance."

Kaylia looked at him peculiarly. "You don't fear me. Why?"

"Should I?" asked Gewey. "You said you didn't want to hurt us."

"I could be lying," she replied.

Gewey shook his head. "Why would you? I'm not an expert in battle, but I think that if you'd wanted to hurt us, you could have picked us off with your bow."

"True," Kaylia agreed. "It's just that I find it odd you're so willing to take me as a companion. You're clearly not like other humans."

"You might be surprised ... if you get to know a few," he replied.

"Perhaps," said Kaylia. "I have a feeling I'll know soon enough."

Millet began to stir by the fire. Lee was still cradling his head in his lap.

"My ... my lord?" Millet asked weakly.

"Yes, my old friend," said Lee, smiling down at him. "You're safe."

"An elf," he said. "She attacked me on the road. How did you find me?"

"Don't worry about it," said Lee. "Rest for now. I'll explain later."

"Of course," said Millet, lowering his eyes. "I'm sorry. I couldn't let you go alone."

"He is not alone," said Kaylia.

Millet looked over and saw the elf woman. "You!" he screamed, trying to get up. "my lord, she's the one. She's the one who attacked me."

Lee held him. "I know," he said soothingly. "Don't worry, she won't do it again. Go back to sleep and I'll explain everything in the morning."

"If it's all the same to you, my lord," he said, "I've slept quite enough." He sat up and tried to stand, but his legs were still sore from his bindings, and his head still swam from being drugged.

"Easy, Millet," Lee advised. "Take your time."

"Perhaps I'll just sit for a while," Millet said. "At least until that blasted tea wears off. Strong stuff, that is."

Millet was wearing a dark leather woodsman's outfit. His round features and pale skin gave the impression that he was city-born and ill-suited for life in the country, but the stories Lee had told of him painted a different picture. He may have seemed soft, but Gewey guessed that the man had a strength that wasn't readily apparent. Lee had described him as crafty, resourceful, and—most of all—loyal. Gewey could tell that Lee was pleased to see him.

"If you don't mind, I would like to know what I've missed," said Millet, still glaring at Kaylia.

Lee recounted the events of the past days, leaving out any mention of Gewey's heritage. Gewey figured this to be for Kaylia's benefit. When he finished, Millet shook his head and sighed. "That explains how I lost you in the forest," he said. "You must have been less than a stone's throw away when I passed you."

"That was you?" Gewey asked.

"Indeed," Millet answered. "I was on your trail the day after you left. Don't worry, Master Gewey, your farm is being well tended. I left instructions for the staff to say that the two of you will be away for many weeks and that Lord Starfinder had made arrangements to tend your farm."

"I'm sure everything is in order, Millet," Lee said. "But you shouldn't have come. This isn't like our other journeys, old friend. I don't know if we'll ever return."

"I know," said Millet. "And if you think for one second that I'll be left behind to rot, then you're not nearly as bright as I thought. Besides, I'm tired of village life. It's high time I had another adventure. One more before the end. Wouldn't you say, my lord?"

Lee slapped Millet on the shoulder. "Yes, I would."

Lee and Millet spent the rest of the night talking quietly by the fire, while Gewey and Kaylia sat in silence until dawn. After they packed the gear, Lee gathered everyone around.

"The village of Harvesting Shallows is one more day's ride," said Lee. "Kaylia will have to wait for us on the other side of the town. The last thing we need is to be seen traveling with an elf."

Kaylia nodded in agreement.

"When we get there," he continued, "we'll trade our steeds in for a wagon and horses better suited to the job. From then on, we'll act as pilgrims. I already have the proper clothing for us, so that won't be an issue. Anyone looking for me and Gewey won't be looking for four pilgrims, and that should make it easier to hide Kaylia's identity."

"Wise plan," Kaylia said. "I'll scout ahead for now. You won't see me again until you leave Harvesting Shallows." With that, she took off through the woods and disappeared.

"Elves are strange folk," said Millet. "I'm not sure it's a good idea to let her travel with us, my lord."

"I doubt we could have stopped her," said Lee. "Besides, Gewey's the one who agreed to let her come along."

Millet glared disapprovingly at Gewey.

The day was uneventful. They passed a few people on the road, but no one took any special notice of the three travelers. When they arrived in Harvesting Shallows, it was an hour after sunset. Lee and Gewey got a room at an inn while Millet stabled the horses. Once in the privacy of their room, Lee checked Gewey's wounds.

"Your arms are completely healed," said Lee with satisfaction. "And at this rate, your chest will be healed in a few more days."

Gewey had almost forgotten his injuries. The wound on his chest itched from time to time, but other than that, he felt fine.

When Millet arrived, they unpacked their things and headed down to the common room to eat. Gewey was thrilled to be allowed out of his room.

"I don't want you talking to anyone," warned Lee. "We're still trying to go unnoticed."

Gewey nodded his head enthusiastically. "Don't worry, Lee. For the rest of the night, I'm a mute."

Lee gave Gewey a sideways look. "Just keep your conversation confined to the three of us."

Millet couldn't help but smile. "He reminds me of you," he whispered into Lee's ear.

Lee chuckled softly.

The common room wasn't as nice as the one in Gath, but there was a lovely young woman in the corner singing folk tunes, most of which Gewey knew. The crowd was also a bit more common than at the last inn, but that was fine by him. He didn't like pretending to be rich and stuck up. In his mind, he was still just a simple farmer, though he hadn't realized until that moment just how proud of this he was.

"Where do we go from here?" asked Gewey over a bowl of hot beef stew.

"We'll keep to the west road for now," said Lee. "The additional company has forced me to rethink the plan, but it looks like it's going to turn out for the best. We'll move more slowly, but we'll draw a lot less attention."

Millet nodded in agreement. "Sir, if I may? Sooner or later our lady friend will get curious about the true nature of our trip. How do you plan to deal with certain … revelations?"

"What do you mean?" asked Gewey.

"What I mean is, although she may know the true nature of Lord Starfinder, yours is something quite different. From what I understand about her kind, it may become a problem."

"I don't follow," said Gewey. "Why should my 'nature' be a problem for her?" Until then, Gewey hadn't been sure how much Millet knew about him, but clearly, Lee had confided everything.

"What Millet means," said Lee, "is that your kind is not exactly held in high regard by hers. When she finds out, there's no telling how she'll react. It's one of the reasons I didn't want her with us."

Gewey looked confused. "It would help if I knew what you are talking about."

"When I told you about the war, I left out an important detail," said Lee. "Man was losing until the gods intervened. They gave mankind the means to turn the tide; needless to say, this left a bad taste in the mouths of the elves where your kind is concerned."

"I see your point," Gewey said thoughtfully. "How do we handle it?"

"With great care, I would think," said Millet. "She may be dangerous, but given her current choice of traveling companions, she may not take it as poorly as we fear. Frankly, I'm surprised she let me live."

Lee contemplated the situation. "For now, we need to keep things to ourselves," he said, finally. "Short of killing her, there's no way to be rid of her company. Besides, she may be of use in the days to come."

"We're not killing her," Gewey snapped. "I gave my word."

"Calm down, boy," said Lee. "I have no intention of killing her, and if I did, I doubt it would be easy. She said she killed at least fourteen bandits before she was captured, and I believe her. I tried to catch her myself for two straight nights and couldn't, and I'm not someone you can easily avoid. No ... I think killing her is out of the question. Still, we need to be careful until we find out what she really wants."

"Isn't it obvious?" Gewey asked. "We saved her life, and she feels she owes us."

"I don't think it's as simple as that," Lee replied. "Traveling openly with our kind is risky enough, considering the way humans feel about elves. However, should her people discover it, I don't think they would be happy—and that's putting it mildly. If she simply wanted to return the favor, she could follow us unseen and wait for an opportunity. No... I don't think it's a matter of a simple debt."

"We could just ask her," Gewey suggested. Lee and Millet both laughed.

"Yes, young master," said Millet. "That may be the solution, but I doubt she would be very forthcoming."

"Millet's right," said Lee. "She won't tell you until she's ready. But do ask if you feel the need. You never know, she might surprise us."

The conversation steered toward more pleasant topics as the warm stew filled their bellies and lifted their spirits. When they were finished, they retired to the room. There were only two beds provided, so Millet insisted on sleeping on the floor. Gewey protested, but Millet wouldn't listen.

"I may look soft, Master Gewey," said Millet. "But let me assure you that I am not. Besides, you are still injured, and Lord Starfinder is far less able to deal with hardship than I."

Lee smiled, rubbing his eyes. "Don't try to argue with him, Gewey; the man will stay up all night badgering you if you try." Lee stretched his arms and yawned. "If he says he's sleeping on the floor, that's what he'll do, and there's nothing on earth that can stop him. Believe me, I've tried to change his mind before, and you saw how well that went."

Millet looked displeased. "If you're referring to me following you and Master Gewey, need I remind you that I had told you even before you left that I had no intention of letting you go off and getting yourself killed. I daresay that you are quite incapable of managing without me."

"I wouldn't presume to dispute you," said Lee. Millet smiled. "Very wise, my Lord." Gewey decided it was best to let Millet have his way and went to sleep. The morning came, and for once Gewey had risen before Lee.

However, Millet was nowhere to be seen.

"Wake up," said Gewey, shaking Lee.

"What is it, boy?" he asked groggily.

"Millet's gone."

The door opened. "I'm not gone," Millet said, carrying a platter with three bowls of porridge and three cups of fresh milk. "While the two of you have lazed around wasting the day, I procured us a wagon and two fine horses to pull it. And I've restocked our provisions and had them delivered to the inn."

Lee rolled out of bed and took the milk and porridge. "You see, Gewey? The man's a freak of nature. Who else could get all that done before breakfast?"

"Indeed," said Millet, and offered Gewey his breakfast, which the boy accepted gratefully. While eating, Gewey noticed that their gear had been packed, and three sets of pilgrim's robes had been laid out for them. He could see why Lee held Millet in such high esteem. The sun was barely up, and he had already done a day's worth of work.

Millet was the first to finish his breakfast and put on his robes.

"I'll remove the gear to the wagon," he said. "Do hurry. We don't want to keep our elf friend waiting."

"Wow," said Gewey as he watched Millet walk out the door with their gear over his back.

"You got that right," said Lee. "He may look like a soft city dweller to you, but that man is as tough as a spring bull."

Gewey nodded in agreement. "I can't believe you wanted to leave him behind."

"I fear for his safety," Lee said, looking pained. "I don't know what I would do if something were to happen to him."

Gewey got up and put his hand on Lee's shoulder. "We'll protect him."

"Until you're ready, I'll be doing the protecting," said Lee.

Gewey frowned. "I just meant..."

"I know what you meant," Lee interjected. "And don't think I don't appreciate it. But now I have two people to watch out for—not to mention an elf."

"Don't worry," said Gewey. "I'll be ready when the time comes."

"I know you will," Lee said, rising to his feet. "And speaking of being ready, it's time we got going."

They put on their robes and left the inn. Millet was waiting out front with the wagon, an impatient look on his face. The wagon was covered and had two benches, one running along either side of the interior. Gewey examined the new animals Millet had bought. They were of good stock—strong and solid, fit for the long journey ahead. Gewey climbed into the back of the wagon with the supplies as Lee sat up front next to Millet, who insisted on doing the driving.

When they reached the outskirts of the village, they saw someone in pilgrim's robes standing alongside the road.

"I see all went well." It was Kaylia. She hopped into the back of the wagon across from Gewey without waiting for Millet to stop.

"I don't remember you taking robes with you," said Gewey. Kaylia gave a mischievous smile. "You should pay more attention, young one."

"We're headed to the city of Kaltinor," said Lee. "At our pace, it should take us at least six days to get there. Remember, should anyone ask, we're pilgrims from the Eastern Temple of Ayliazarah on our way west to worship at the Temple of the Far Sky."

Gewey had heard of these places from the stories his father had told him when he was a child. Ayliazarah, the Goddess of Fertility and Love, was worshiped in almost every city and village. Even the towns too small to have a temple usually had a shrine or two in her honor. The Temple of the Far Sky was on the coast of the Western Abyss, atop the Cliffs of Heaven, where all of the nine gods were worshipped. It was by far the oldest temple in existence, and thousands of pilgrims journeyed there each year. As Gewey saw the disgust on Kaylia face, he remembered what Lee had told him about the way elves felt about the gods.

"Tell me about yourself," Gewey said to Kaylia.

"You know all that you need to know about me for now," she said brusquely.

"Fine, then tell me about the elves," he pressed.

Kaylia looked at him darkly, her fierce eyes burning from underneath her hood. "You do not need to know anything about my people, other than to stay away from them."

"If elves hate humans so much, why do you want to travel with us?"

"Save your questions," said Kaylia. "I'm sure your friends told you that you would get no answers from me." She pulled her robes close. "You should listen to them."

For the rest of the day, Lee and Millet discussed possible routes west while Kaylia listened quietly, occasionally offering advice. Gewey dozed on and off, though he was still determined to question Kaylia again. He desperately wanted to learn more about the elves; they seemed magical, yet treacherous—like beautiful predators. Every movement Kaylia made flowed like water, and her voice was like soft music. Gewey caught himself staring at her over and over again, though she didn't seem to notice—if she did, she ignored it. That night, they set up camp just off the road. Kaylia disappeared as soon as they settled in.

"Where do you think she went?" asked Gewey.

"I don't know," said Lee. "But I'm sure she'll be back by morning."

"Do elves sleep?" he asked.

"I would think so," said Lee. "But how often, I couldn't say. Most of what I know about elves is from the few books I've read on the subject, and most of these were about the elves of old. Very little is written about what they are like now. Best not to worry about it. Get some rest."

Lee removed Gewey's bandages and examined the wound on his chest. It had almost completely healed, so Lee decided a bandage was no longer necessary. The pink lines on his arms that told where his cuts had been had vanished completely.

The morning came, and just as Lee had said, Kaylia returned. They climbed onto the wagon and slowly moved on.

CHAPTER 7

The day was hot, and sitting in the back of the wagon in full robes was miserable. Kaylia, however, seemed unaffected.

"How old are you?" Gewey asked Kaylia, renewing his efforts to get information. "I hear your people live a long time."

"I'm older than you," she said without looking up.

Gewey was undeterred. "I'm just trying to get to know you."

"There's no need," said Kaylia. "You already know everything you need to know."

"But that's practically nothing," Gewey insisted. "If we're going to travel together, don't you think we should know more about each other?"

"I do not," she replied. "At least not now."

Gewey kept pressing, determined to learn more about her. "Do you have a last name, or are you just Kaylia?"

Kaylia reached into her robe, pulled out a flask, and drank deeply.

"What's that?" asked Gewey.

Kaylia handed him the flask. He noticed a sweet smell as he lifted it to his mouth. Despite the heat, the liquid was cool, and it tasted like honeyed water.

"Thank you," said Gewey, handing her back the flask.

Suddenly, he felt woozy and his vision blurred. The last thing Gewey saw as he dropped to the bottom of the wagon was Kaylia's grinning face.

Lee turned and saw Gewey sprawled next to the supplies. "What happened?"

"The boy wanted to know more about elves," said Kaylia. "So I introduced him to jawas tea."

Lee laughed aloud. "A lesson he won't soon forget, I imagine.

"Wouldn't you agree, Millet?"

Millet was not amused; his own experience with jawas tea still lingered in his memory. "I don't think it's a good idea to drug the boy," he said sourly. "If we are attacked, it won't do to have to carry him."

"You're right, of course," Lee acknowledged. He turned to Kaylia. "In the future, please let the boy remain conscious."

Kaylia shrugged. "If you say so."

When Gewey awoke, the wagon had stopped. Millet was preparing the noon meal, while Kaylia and Lee were checking the horses.

"What happened?" Gewey asked. His vision was still fuzzy, and his head swam.

"Our elf friend happened," said Millet. "She drugged you with jawas tea."

Gewey rubbed his eyes. "Why did she do that?"

"I expect she wanted you to stop asking questions," Millet replied. "In the future, I suggest that you refrain from accepting food or drink from a stranger, especially if that stranger is an elf."

"I think you might be right," said Gewey as he slowly climbed out of the wagon. *At least I learned one thing,* he thought. *Jawas tea doesn't affect elves.*

Gewey ate his food as far away from Kaylia as he could, and when they were done, he insisted on trading trade places with Lee in the wagon.

Once they were underway, Gewey turned to Millet. "You've been with Lee for a long time, right?"

Millet nodded. "A very long time."

"What was he like when he was young?" asked Gewey.

"Rash," Millet answered. "Very rash."

Gewey paused, considering what he should ask about next. "Have you been to Kaltinor before?"

"Yes, but not for many years," Millet replied. "I'm sure you'll find it exciting. Compared to Sharpstone, it's a very large city."

Gewey tried to picture what it would be like. Gath was the largest town he'd seen so far. He'd heard stories about some of the great cities—their tall buildings reaching to the heavens, their wide brick streets large enough to accommodate twenty wagons at once. He wondered if Kaltinor would be like that.

"What's the biggest city you've seen?" asked Gewey.

Millet thought it over for a moment. "That would have to be Baltria," he said finally. "Though it wasn't the most impressive city I've visited."

For the next few hours, Millet entertained Gewey with tales of the wonderful places he had seen. He didn't mind the flood of questions and answered each one with courtesy and patience.

"Stop the wagon," Kaylia said suddenly. "Now!"

Millet stopped the wagon and Kaylia jumped out to scan the woods. After a few minutes, she got back in the wagon and told Millet to continue on.

"What did you see?" Lee asked, his hand on his sword.

"Hopefully nothing that need concern us," Kaylia answered.

"I'm concerned, and I'm responsible for the lives of my friends," Lee said. "So you need to tell me what you saw."

"There's a small group of elves traveling south of the road. If they ignore us, we'll be fine. If not..." Kaylia trailed off, her eyes meeting Lee's with a mutual understanding.

Lee closed his eyes and listened to the sounds of the woods. In the distance, he heard four elves matching their pace.

"They follow us," Lee said warily. "Don't say anything to Millet or Gewey yet."

Kaylia nodded. "Agreed. If all goes well, it won't be necessary. They may not know I'm here."

"And if they do?" Lee asked.

"Then I will have to speak to them," Kaylia replied, clearly troubled by the prospect.

The day passed slowly for Lee and Kaylia. Millet and Gewey realized something was wrong, but after a while, they decided to ignore it. Millet continued to regale the boy with tales of his travels.

When night fell, they made camp. Gewey helped Millet build the fire and prepare the meal. Lee sat on a blanket, sharpening and oiling his sword, his eyes fixed on the surrounding forest. Kaylia was leaning against the wagon, her head bowed in thought.

Lee sheathed his sword and walked over to Kaylia.

"They're still here," he said.

"I know," Kaylia responded. "I must speak to them. Wait here until I return."

Lee sat next to the fire while Millet and Gewey ate, eyes closed, listening into the night.

"What are you doing?" asked Gewey.

"I'm listening," Lee growled. "So be quiet."

Gewey noticed Kaylia's absence. "Where's...?"

Lee's eyes popped open, glaring at Gewey. Gewey tried to listen as he had done in Gath, but he couldn't concentrate. Frustrated, he threw down his bowl and stormed over to his bedroll.

Suddenly, Kaylia reappeared and sat next to the fire.

"Where did you go?" asked Gewey.

Kaylia pushed back her hood; her face was stone and her eyes narrow slits. "I was speaking to my kin."

Gewey leaped to his feet. "What?"

"Don't worry," she said. "We're in no danger."

Lee grunted and tossed a twig into the fire.

"That's good news," said Millet. "But it would have been nice to know that elves were nearby."

"There was no need to tell you," said Lee. "At least, not at the time."

"How long have you known they were out there?" Gewey seethed.

"What difference does it make?" he answered. "You couldn't have done anything about it other than worry. If they'd attacked, we'd all be dead, anyway."

This did little to calm Gewey. "I don't care!" he yelled. "If my life's in danger, I have a right to know!"

Kaylia fixed her gaze on Gewey. "Shut your mouth," she said.

Her voice was steel. "What right do you have to question anything? Those around you are willing to sacrifice themselves to protect you. Isn't that enough?" With that, she turned and headed off into the night.

Gewey started to follow her, but Lee stopped him.

"Leave her," Lee advised.

Gewey pushed past him and chased after her, anyway.

"Rash," said Millet. "Very rash. But I must say, he is handling his situation remarkably well, all things considered."

Lee sat down. "How am I going to keep him alive long enough to get him ready? It's been less than a month, and already he's nearly been killed."

"Yes," Millet replied. "But he wasn't killed, was he? The boy will learn, just as you did."

"I almost failed," Lee said. "When I attacked the bandit camp, I chased two of them down. That's when Gewey got hurt. When I left him alone."

Millet nodded. "That sounds familiar; you never could stand to let anyone escape."

"It's all too familiar," Lee agreed. "It almost got Gewey killed. If I had just let them go, the boy would have never been injured. I keep making the same mistakes over and over again."

Millet smiled softly and placed his hand on Lee's shoulder.

"You've always expected too much of yourself, Lee Starfinder. Your job is one of a protector, but you are also a teacher. The boy survived and learned from the experience. If you think he can learn without danger, you're wrong. Even I know that. You can't protect him from everything, and you shouldn't try." Millet stood up and walked over to his blanket. "I believe in you, and I believe in the boy," he said as he lay down. "You should too."

Lee remained by the fire, mulling Millet's words over in his head.

Meanwhile, Gewey wandered aimlessly, hoping to find Kaylia.

"Kaylia," he called out in a whisper. He repeated it several times, but there was no reply. He was about to give up and start back to the camp when he realized that he was hopelessly lost. After meandering for a bit longer, he decided there was nothing to do but sit and wait for daylight.

Gewey heard a voice from behind him. "You're very foolish. You know elves wander these woods, yet you venture off alone in the dark."

Startled, Gewey quickly got to his feet. Turning around, he was able to make out Kaylia's features in the darkness. "I was looking for you," he said. "And besides, you told us they wouldn't attack."

"You continue to take my word on its merit," said Kaylia. "The word of an elf. How strange." The Elven woman sat on the ground and crossed her legs. "Sit."

Gewey sat across from Kaylia. After looking him up and down for a moment, she began to speak. "You're not like other humans, are you? And I don't just mean your attitude toward my kind. There's something else different about you. Something that your friends are afraid I'll discover."

"Yes, there is," Gewey replied nervously. "And believe me, I would like nothing more than to tell you."

"So why don't you?"

"I can't," Gewey insisted. "I don't think you'd like what you'd find out."

"I'll make you a deal," Kaylia proposed. "We'll sit here and talk for a while, and I'll tell you about my people; after that, you can decide the wisdom of sharing your secret. That is what you want, isn't it? To know more about elves and our ways?"

"I would love to know more about your people," Gewey agreed. "And you."

"Then we have an agreement," she said, pulling back her hood.

"You asked how old I am: I am one hundred and three years old. That is young for my kind. In fact, not much older than you by our standards. We can live for well over five hundred years. My father, who fought in the Great War, died eighty years ago. I've wandered ever since."

"Why are you wandering?" asked Gewey.

"I search for my destiny," Kaylia answered. "I was given a task when my father died, and I seek to complete it."

Gewey was intrigued. "What's the task?"

"My father was great among my people and had the power of foresight. As he lay dying, he told me that it was my task to find redemption for my people and that I should never stop searching for it. He said that one day the Elven people would be healed by my hand. Since then, I have sought the meaning of his words."

"You've wandered for eighty years?"

"I have," she replied. "I hope to one day fulfill my destiny and help my people become great—as they were before the Great War."

"Lee told me your kind hate humans," said Gewey. "But the war has been over for five hundred years. Certainly, enough time has passed to move on."

"You wouldn't understand. The Great War changed us. You would have to know what we once were to comprehend how devastating it has been for us."

"Then we should start there," Gewey said enthusiastically. "Tell me about your people."

"A tall order," Kaylia responded. "And a tale longer than time will allow. But I will tell you enough to satisfy your curiosity."

Kaylia got to her feet to look at the night sky. The stars twinkled like fireflies over a lake, and the half-moon lit her face, making her features soft and radiant.

"The story of my people begins with the creation," she began.

"Unlike you humans, we believe that the world was created by a single god. In the very beginning, there were only elves and the earth. Our ancestors were charged as caretakers for all living things, and for thousands of years, we lived in harmony with nature. God blessed us with dominion over all things, and the wisdom to keep the world in balance. But as time passed, we became arrogant and forgetful of our duties. As a result, the One God sent the many gods, and with them ... man.

"We prayed and lamented in hope that God would take pity on us and forgive us our sins. But God heard our prayers and knew them to be prideful. The many gods were now the keepers of the world, and man was favored above us. God could see the anger behind our prayers and removed his blessings. We lost the ability to speak with the Father of All Things, and my people fell into despair. But then he took pity on us and sent the spirits and angels down to carry our prayers to him. They watch over us and guard the souls of our kin until the day God returns to pass His judgment. On that day we will see the Father, and we will both answer for our sins and be rewarded for our good deeds.

"You are the first human in over five hundred years to hear these words," Kaylia continued. "There are many stories about the time before the gods came, and I promise I will tell them all if you wish to hear them—but for now, you know enough to understand the faith of my people."

"Thank you," said Gewey. "I would love to hear as much as you can tell me."

Kaylia smiled warmly. "If all humans were as open as you, I doubt the Great War would have ever happened."

"Do you hate humans?" Gewey asked.

"No," Kaylia answered. "But I pity them."

"Why?"

"They put their hopes in gods that are selfish and cruel," she explained. "The gods have enslaved man and made them their dogs. They gave them the gift of victory over the elves and allowed them to become powerful, but then denied them the wisdom to use that power. Such beings are not worthy of worship. The gods saved the humans from annihilation that would have been caused by their own arrogance; then, instead of reigning in their destruction, they set them loose to burn the world—and destroy my people."

"You're talking about the Great War," Gewey interjected. "Lee told me a little about that. He said that the gods intervened so that man could win."

"They did more than you could know," she said. "Long ago, my people were vast in number and bound together by strong nations. The gods cast fear and doubt into our hearts.

Our armies splintered, and we turned on each other. Kin fought kin, and man took advantage of our weakness and destroyed us."

Gewey looked perplexed. "But Lee told me that the elves fought each other after they made peace with man."

"The half-man only knows what human lies have told," Kaylia said. "Mankind was beaten. There were no more battles to be fought. His armies were smashed, and his cities in ruins. My people had but to march across the land and slaughter the few that remained, and man would have been gone forever. But instead, we took pity on the humans and left them in peace. It was then that the gods cursed us. We knew hatred for our own kind for the first time, and it consumed us. We prayed to the spirits for help, but the gods imprisoned them, holding them until we had lost all hope. The humans did not show us the pity we had shown them. Man waited until we had all but destroyed ourselves, then swept down on us like a plague. The few who escaped found refuge in the forests and mountains where humans seldom went. Since then, we have struggled to rebuild and free ourselves of the curse the gods put on us."

"I'm sorry," Gewey said. "I had no idea how much your people have suffered."

"Don't be," Kaylia responded. "My people will rise again. The suffering of my kin will make us wise—worthy to face the Father."

She sat back down. "Now you know about us. I have shared secrets known to no other human. Will you not share your secret with me?"

Gewey felt ashamed. It was his very own kind—the gods—who'd destroyed her people. How could he tell her what he was?

"Now that I've heard your story, I'm even more afraid to tell you," he said.

"If what I've told you isn't enough, then know this," said Kaylia, her eyes on fire. "I travel with you, humans. This I told my kin, and I bargained to save your lives. One day I will face judgment and probable death. In the eyes of my people, there is nothing worse I could do than have human companions. It is forbidden."

Gewey gasped. "They're going to kill you? When?"

"When my journey with you ends, I will return home to answer for my crime," she replied. "That is how I prevented my kin from attacking. Knowing this, what could you possibly tell me that would alter the path I have chosen?"

Gewey made up his mind. "I'll tell you, but please understand that I only found out myself a short time ago." He took a deep breath and steeled his nerves. "You said that there is nothing worse than having a human as a companion. But there is. I'm worse."

Kaylia looked confused. "You're dancing around the issue," she said. "Just be direct and let me be the judge."

"The boy is a god," said Lee from the darkness. He walked up slowly and stood beside Gewey. "I had a feeling you'd do something stupid, boy, so I came to find you."

Kaylia laughed loudly. "You don't say," she teased, seemingly not surprised by Lee's sudden appearance. "A god! A living, breathing god, here in my presence. You're right. That would be worse than traveling with a human."

"This is no joke, elf," Lee warned. "The tale you told makes me even more certain that you should not know what the boy is. But now you do anyway. The only question is, what happens next?" Lee drifted in front of Gewey and slid his hand to the hilt of his sword.

Kaylia's face shifted from amusement to rage as she realized Lee was serious. "You speak the truth!" Her hand touched her sword, but she did not grab it. "I must ponder this. Go back to camp. If you see me in the morning, I expect you to tell me all that you know."

"And what if we don't see you?" Gewey asked. "I can't help what I am, and I didn't ask for it. I would never do anything to harm you ... or your people."

Kaylia said nothing.

"Come," Lee said, lifting Gewey to his feet. "Leave her be." Lee guided them back to the camp where Millet sat by the fire waiting.

"How did it go?" asked Millet.

"Not as bad as it could have," Lee answered. "We'll know by morning."

"Things will work out," said Millet. "Don't worry."

"Lee..." Gewey started, but Lee immediately cut him off.

"Go to sleep," he advised. "We'll talk tomorrow."

Gewey lay down but was unable to stay asleep for more than a few minutes at a time. He kept hearing Kaylia's story in his head, and seeing the rage on her face when she found out what he really was.

How could the gods do this to her people? he wondered. I've got to find a way to make it right.

Gewey was awake to see the dawn. Lee and Millet were still asleep. He hoped to see Kaylia, but she had not returned. He hated himself for telling her. He hated himself for what his kind had done.

Most of all, he hated the gods for creating this mess in the first place.

"I'll hear your tale, young one." It was Kaylia. She was standing by the wagon, her eyes fixed on Gewey.

Gewey got up and began to walk toward her.

"Stay where you are. I said I would hear your tale, not suffer your company." She paused. "At least, not yet."

Gewey looked at the others, still sleeping soundly. If Kaylia decided to attack, there would be nothing to stop her.

Kaylia sensed his fear and said, "I have no intention of harming you. I gave you my word, and I'll keep it. But know this. If my people find out about your existence, they will hunt you down until the end of creation. Whether or not I will tell them depends on you."

Gewey nodded slowly and began telling his story, leaving out no detail. He told her about how he'd grown up, about his father, how he'd found out about his true nature, and, of course, about the Dark Knight. When he finished, Kaylia looked at him thoughtfully and walked over.

"I find no guilt in you. I will help you complete your task. I swear to this."

"Thank you," said Gewey, his relief clearly showing. "But why? Won't your people kill you if they find out?"

Kaylia smiled. "They're going to kill me anyway," she said. "And I can only die once. Besides, from what you have told me, it is unlikely I will live to face their judgment."

Gewey bowed his head and sighed with relief. He heard Millet stir.

Millet rose and turned toward Gewey, stretching the stiffness from his joints. "Up with the dawn, I see." He noticed Kaylia standing there and smiled. "I see that you've decided to join us. Wonderful—absolutely wonderful."

Lee was the last to rouse. He pretended not to notice Kaylia's return, but Gewey suspected he had been awake to hear their whole conversation. After eating, they packed up and continued on their way to Kaltinor.

CHAPTER 8

Gewey returned to his seat in the back of the wagon with Kaylia. He kept the conversation light, telling her about his youth and life in Sharpstone.

To his surprise, she seemed to take great interest in his past, asking questions about the way he lived and the people he knew. Gewey had never thought of village life as anything other than dull and common, but Kaylia seemed to enjoy hearing about it.

"It must have been difficult to leave such a wonderful life behind," said Kaylia.

"Actually, I've just learned to appreciate what I've lost," Gewey admitted. "Still, I don't see how my life would impress you."

Kaylia leaned back and explained, "A simple existence is what elves long for, though it doesn't surprise me that humans find such a life common and unfulfilling. But then, you aren't human, are you? Perhaps there is hope that you can learn to appreciate simple things."

"The simple things will have to wait," interjected Lee from up front. "He needs to learn to tap into his power. From now on, midday meal will be preceded by lessons, as will supper. Your training has been delayed for far too long, and we've got a lot of catching up to do now that you're more or less healed."

"I would be happy to assist," Kaylia offered. "I may not be a half-man, but I am not without skills."

"Your help will be welcome," said Lee. "And you," he said, turning to Gewey, "will do as I and Kaylia instruct. Do you understand?" Gewey nodded happily, beaming with anticipation.

"You may not be so excited when you find out what's in store," chuckled Lee.

Kaylia giggled almost girlishly, but with a sinister grin on her face.

"Elf training is hard, young one. Believe me when I tell you that if you were human, you would never survive it."

"That settles it then," Lee said. "We start today." Gewey could hardly contain himself. Finally, he would learn to fight. He had grown tired of feeling as if he were weak and helpless. If danger came, he needed to be able to fight, and he was determined to prove himself. Whatever the future held, he would be ready.

When they stopped for a midday meal, Lee told Gewey to follow him into the woods. He was already out of the wagon when he remembered his sword and started back for it.

"You have your sword ready when I'm ready, or not at all," yelled Lee, marching on into the woods.

Gewey obeyed and followed Lee, unarmed.

They soon found a clearing and Lee came to a halt. "Attack me," he said.

Gewey stared but did nothing.

In a flash, Lee stepped forward. Moving his leg behind Gewey's, and bringing his arm hard across the boy's chest, he sent him crashing to the ground. "I said attack me," he yelled again. "Or I swear you'll wish you were never born!"

Gewey jumped up angrily and ran straight at Lee. With uncanny speed, Lee stepped aside, grabbed Gewey's shoulder, and jerked the boy's head and torso backward. Gewey's feet flew into the air, and he landed in the grass with a soft thud.

Lee looked down at Gewey, shaking his head. "Pathetic," he growled. "You will not touch a sword until you throw me to the ground at least once." He took several strides and then turned to face his young pupil. "Again."

Although still dazed, Gewey got to his feet. Again and again, he came at Lee—again and again he was sent sprawling. This went on for the better part of an hour until Lee motioned for Gewey to halt.

"I hope you show Kaylia more than you've shown me," Lee muttered.

When they returned to the wagon, Millet and Kaylia had already eaten and were waiting nearby. Millet had two plates of dried meat and a large piece of flatbread set aside for them.

"We'll eat as we travel," said Lee, taking the food from Millet.

Millet nodded curtly, handed Gewey his food, and climbed into the wagon. Gewey could feel the soreness sinking in from the dozens of falls he had taken at the hands of Lee, but he didn't complain. He got in the wagon and went over in his mind each time Lee had thrown him, trying to work out his mistakes.

Kaylia smiled slightly and said, "That's good. Think about what you did wrong. See it in your mind—each motion, every shift on your feet. Remember the feeling in your muscles. Feel the sensation when you lost your balance. What brought you to that point? When did you lose control? Most importantly, how could you have prevented it?"

Gewey looked at Kaylia. His face was stone with concentration. "I can see it now," he said. "Why can't I see it while it's happening?"

"You will in time," Kaylia replied, then handed him a flask.

"Drink this."

"What's in it?" he asked, eying the flask suspiciously.

"Jawas tea," she answered.

"Are you crazy?" Gewey asked sharply, handing it back.

Kaylia refused to accept it, shaking her head. "Jawas tea has a strong effect on humans, but as you are not exactly human, you should be able to withstand its negative effects. If you can, you will find that it has amazing qualities."

"But it put me out cold the last time," Gewey protested.

"And you must prevent that," she replied. "This time, I want you to feel it inside you and stop it from taking control. You are not to fail, understand?"

"I'll try," said Gewey, warily opening the flask.

"No," Kaylia said sternly. "I said you are not to fail."

Gewey nodded and put the flask to his lips. As the cold liquid poured down his throat he could feel the effects setting in immediately. But this time, he was ready for it. He fought to keep his eyes open and retain feeling in his limbs, but after only a few seconds, he knew he was losing the battle.

"Don't think about the way you feel," whispered Kaylia— or at least, it sounded like a whisper to him as his head swam. "Think about your body as a whole. Command it. You are in control. You will not allow the tea to win."

For a moment, Gewey felt his strength returning, but it was short-lived. Eventually, the jawas tea took over, and he slumped down in his seat, unconscious.

Kaylia reached over and slid his body into the corner.

When he woke, it was already dark, and the wagon had stopped. Gewey crawled out and knelt down groggily. Millet, Kaylia, and Lee were already eating.

"I guess we'll get a late start," said Kaylia, setting down her bowl.

She had removed her pilgrim's robes and donned her shirt and trousers. She pulled out a small knife and threw it with a flick of her wrist. The knife stuck in the ground less than an inch from Gewey's foot. "You'll need that," she said.

Kaylia led Gewey into the forest. The moon was out, providing the only source of light. Gewey's heartbeat quickened the further they walked. He began to wonder when the training would start, and then suddenly he noticed—he was alone.

"Kaylia," he called nervously, but there was no answer.

Gewey strained his eyes, hoping to catch sight of some movement or shadow. But the night played tricks. He began to see things in the shadows that weren't there; shapes he thought might be Kaylia turned out to be nothing more than a bush or a stump.

"The night can be a weapon, young one," Kaylia's voice whispered from the darkness, seemingly from everywhere. "It plants fear in the heart of your enemies. It is a cloak and a dagger. It can serve you well until you are ready to strike."

In the blink of an eye, Kaylia was behind him, her knife at his throat. "You're dead," she said, then lowered the knife. "You must learn to see through the curtain of darkness and use your foe's ignorance against him."

"I don't understand," said Gewey.

"Of course you don't. We elves spend our lives moving in the shadows. Not even your half-man friend can match me in the dark. An elf can put an arrow through the eye of a buck from two hundred paces in total darkness. Take out your knife. It's time you learned to defend yourself."

"I've never fought with a knife," said Gewey.

"I guessed," Kaylia replied sarcastically. Then, in the blink of an eye, she was on him, her blade slashing through the air like lightning.

Gewey felt the cold blade across the back of his hand. He dropped his weapon, clutching his hand and cursing loudly.

"You are uninjured," Kaylia said. Gewey looked at his hand. There was no blood.

"My blade is dull," she explained. "For now. Were you an elf, you would not be so fortunate."

"I don't want special treatment," he complained. "I can take it."

"Just like you were able to take the jawas tea," she scoffed. "No, I think you need to learn more before your real training begins."

Gewey sulked as he bent down to pick up his knife, but he didn't say a word.

For the rest of the lesson, Kaylia instructed Gewey on the basics of knife fighting. Gewey felt as if it was a bit too basic, but he did as he was told.

"You move like a drunken ox," she observed when they were finished.

"It's my first time," said Gewey. "Besides, all I did was thrust and slash at nothing for close to an hour."

"And when you do so with purpose, we'll move on," she answered. "I hope you show more enthusiasm when the half-man trains you." Gewey felt angry and embarrassed.

"Can you find your way back to camp?" asked Kaylia.

"Yes," Gewey lied.

"Good," she said, vanishing into the woods.

It took Gewey more than an hour to find his way back to camp.

Lee and Kaylia were talking quietly near the wagon, and Millet was sitting by the fire, poking it with a stick. Gewey walked over and sat across from Millet, his face twisted in anger.

"What's wrong, young master?" asked Millet. "You look upset."

"I don't think I'm cut out for this," said Gewey. "I thought I'd do so much better, but so far, I've failed at everything."

Millet chucked.

"What's so funny?" barked Gewey.

"Nothing lad," said Millet. "I just remember Lord Starfinder speaking similar words a long time ago."

"You're just saying that to make me feel better," said Gewey. He tossed a twig into the fire.

"I'm doing no such thing. I'm telling you the truth. When Lord Starfinder came home after his first day of training, he was quite literally in tears. In fact, he didn't go back for a week; I had to convince him."

The thought of Lee pouting and crying made Gewey smile.

"Don't take too much pleasure from that," scolded Millet. "He wasn't hardened by years of farm work, and he is only half of what you are ... if you catch my meaning. Yet look at him now: hard, strong, and skilled beyond anything you could imagine."

Gewey glanced over at Lee and thought about the fight with the bandits. He had never seen anyone move so fast. *He must really be holding back with me*, he thought.

"You've been with Lee for a long time, yet I notice you still call him 'my lord'," Gewey observed.

"Of course I do," said Millet, surprised. "He is my friend, yes; but he's also my lord and master. My family has served the house Nal'Thain for generations, and I would not dishonor them by treating the master of the house with over-familiarity. We are friends, and my love for him goes far beyond that of servant and lord, but I can never let that distract me from my duty."

Gewey looked puzzled. "But he's not really a Nal'Thain. He told me he started as Dauvis Nal'Thain's servant."

"He told you correctly," said Millet. "I remember when he arrived. I was very jealous that he had been picked to serve the master of the house and I had not. But after a time we became friends, and when he rose to be the master, I became his personal assistant."

"What did you call him before he was made a lord?" asked Gewey.

"By his name, of course," Millet answered. "But enough about that." Millet got to his feet and went over to his blanket. "You need to eat and rest."

"Thank you, Millet," Gewey said gratefully. "Thank you for the talk. I feel better."

"I'm happy to hear it," said Millet as he lay down.

Gewey went to sleep that night feeling determined. He would not fail, and he would not give up.

For the next few days, Gewey trained harder and harder. On three occasions he nearly threw Lee to the ground, once he managed to find Kaylia in the shadows, and he even learned to stay awake after drinking jawas tea—though just barely. Neither Lee nor Kaylia openly showed that they were pleased, but Gewey could tell they were, and it filled him with pride.

As they neared Kaltinor, Gewey noticed the landscape changing. The forest became thinner, and the road was criss-crossed with little streams spanned with wooden bridges, some in desperate need of repair. They passed farms more frequently, but many looked abandoned, their fields untended and grown over with weeds. The air was becoming colder each day, and the sun rarely peeked out from the overcast sky.

"What's happened here?" Gewey asked Lee, the day before they were to arrive in Kaltinor.

"The Dark Knight," answered Lee. "As his power grows, you'll see more of this. Even more reason for us to hurry. He'll bring a hard winter ... and bring it early."

"I wish I knew where we're going," said Gewey.

"If I could tell you, I would," Lee assured him. "But there is still a danger that the Dark Knight could enter your mind, and we've had to stop your mental training in favor of more practical things. If we did both, you'd collapse from exhaustion, and we need you strong."

"This may not be a problem," interjected Kaylia. "One of the benefits of jawas tea is that it strengthens an elf's mental abilities.

Even the strongest mind could not enter uninvited. Though Gewey is not an elf, there is a chance it may give him the same advantage."

Lee raised an eyebrow. "Really? I had no idea jawas had that power."

Kaylia smirked. "There's much I know that you don't, half-man," she said.

"Perhaps," said Lee. "Still, I will test if it's effective."

That night after had Gewey finished his training with Kaylia, Lee beckoned him over. They repeated the exercise Lee had taught him, except this time Lee told Gewey not to try and keep the gate of his mind closed. Much to his amazement, Lee found himself completely unable to enter Gewey's mind; the jawas tea seemed to work exactly as Kaylia had claimed it would.

"How long is it effective for?" Lee asked Kaylia, who was standing nearby.

"One dose will last for at least two days," Kaylia answered. "But more importantly, it builds in your system. Among my people, there are those who can journey inside the mind of another. We use jawas to strengthen that ability."

"But from what I've just seen, it would block minds—not make it easier to enter them," said Lee.

Kaylia's mouth twisted in disgust. "If your intention is to invade a mind, you're right, jawas prevents this from happening. But we do not enter uninvited, as you might. With jawas, we can touch the thoughts of another with greater ease, and at greater distance."

"That could prove quite useful," said Lee, stroking his chin. "How much do you have?"

"Enough to last many weeks," she answered. "At least six, I should think."

"Is it hard to find?"

"Not in this area," Kaylia replied. "I shall gather more for the journey while I wait for you to leave the city."

"You'll be coming with us into Kaltinor," Lee said flatly. "It's very important we gather information before we continue further west. The Dark Knight's power grows, and we need to know what lies ahead. This may take a few days, and I might need you with me."

Kaylia looked concerned. "And what if I'm discovered? That could prove to be a problem."

"You won't be discovered," said Lee. "I have friends in Kaltinor that can hide you if need be, but I don't think it will come to that. We'll be staying in the Temple of Ayliazarah, so you can stay silent and hooded the entire time—like a good little pilgrim."

It was obvious that Lee was trying to get under Kaylia's skin. The two were constantly throwing thinly veiled insults at one another. This time, Lee had the advantage. Kaylia couldn't conceal the fact that the idea of staying in a temple built for one of the gods made her uncomfortable.

"I will bow and stay silent," she seethed, "but if you think I will pretend to worship..."

Lee doubled over with laughter, further fueling Kaylia's anger.

"Calm yourself, elf," he said, grinning widely. "Pilgrims do not usually pray until they reach their destination."

This did little to calm Kaylia down. With her teeth clenched and back straight, she turned and strode off into the night. When she returned, she moved her blanket far away from the others.

The next day, Gewey noticed more travelers along the road.

Kaylia took special care to remain unseen, despite the fact that her hood completely covered her features. As they rode on past midday, the sheer volume of traffic told Gewey that the city was near.

The farms they passed were no longer abandoned, though the fields were empty from the harvest. Along the way, they were stopped by a man driving a wagon loaded with bricks and masonry tools. Thinking them pilgrims from the east, he asked for news. Lee told him that times were dark and getting darker; the man replied that it was the same here and continued on his unhappy way. This darkened Lee's mood, and he hardly spoke for hours.

"I guess our ruse will be put to the test," Millet said as the sun began to go down.

Gewey leaned forward and spotted an encampment ahead. "Who are they?"

"That, my boy, is a group of real monks," Lee answered. "I can see ten of them from here."

"Do we have to stop?" Gewey asked, nervously.

"If we don't, they'll wonder why," Lee responded. "Besides, if we can't fool them, there's no way we'll fool the temple."

Lee pulled off the road to the edge of the encampment. A tall, hooded monk walked up to the wagon next to Millet.

"Welcome brothers ... and sister," he added, noticing Kaylia's hooded figure in the back. Even through the robes, it was impossible to hide her feminine shape. "I'm Brother Salvo. Please take your ease with us. We have plenty to share."

"Thank you, Brother," said Millet, taking the lead. "We will be pleased and grateful to share your fire. I'm Brother Milton, this is Brother Leston," he said, pointing at Lee. "And in the wagon are Brother Gewton and Sister Kaymaya."

Millet stepped from the wagon and stood in front of the man.

After exchanging a few words, Millet told the rest to climb down and see to the horses and gear. Lee jumped down while Kaylia and Gewey climbed from the back. Gewey was confused by the sudden role reversal, but Lee acted as if following Millet's orders was second nature.

The encampment was a beehive of activity as the monks and pilgrims prepared supper. No one spoke to them at first, which pleased Gewey. Kaylia was doing everything she could not to get too close to anyone, but eventually, Lee leaned over and whispered in her ear. Gewey saw her nod, then walk over and offer assistance to several monks who were preparing bedding for the group.

"This is not a time to avoid contact," Lee whispered to Gewey as he passed. "That would be noticed."

Gewey wondered how Kaylia would avoid giving herself away, but no one gave her a second look. Luckily, she was not the only female pilgrim in camp, and Gewey observed that the other women hardly ever removed their hoods or spoke. It seemed as though their ruse was intact, at least for now. By nightfall, several other groups had arrived at Brother Salvo's encampment; by the time dinner was served, their number reached about thirty. Millet and the others gathered near the wagon to eat and talk privately.

"A dangerous game," Kaylia grumbled under her breath.

"But necessary," Lee insisted.

"I agree," said Millet. "This is a good chance to test our deception."

Kaylia clearly didn't think so. "You had me working openly with these—these monks. If one of these oafs had bumped into me and discovered my identity, what then?"

"I'm counting on your elf dexterity to prevent that," Lee replied. "If you had not behaved as a pilgrim should, it could have put us in danger. And please, don't call them oafs. Men and women like these here do nothing but good works. Their lives are dedicated to it."

Just then, Gewey saw the figure of Brother Salvo approaching.

"Brother Milton," called the tall monk.

Millet stood and bowed low. "I thank you for sharing your meal," he said. "As do my companions." Gewey, Lee, and Kaylia bowed their heads in turn.

"We're happy to have you among us," said Brother Salvo. "Pilgrims on the road have become more and more rare these days. It's good to see those willing to make the journey of faith. May I sit with you?"

"Of course," said Millet, offering his blanket. Millet sat next to Kaylia so that he could face Brother Salvo directly.

"Where do you come from?" Salvo asked.

"We are from the Temple of Ayliazarah in the eastern kingdom of Palinsali," answered Millet. "We're on our way to the Temple of the Far Sky."

"Ahhh," said Salvo. "Servants of sacred love. We haven't seen many in these parts for some time. You have a long journey ahead. The Temple of the Far Sky is many weeks from here."

"All the more reason to thank you for your hospitality," Millet said graciously.

Brother Salvo pushed back his hood. He was older than he sounded, yet he was still quite handsome. The years showed in his eyes, but his blond hair and squared features suggested the type of maturity that Gewey had heard the women of Sharpstone speak of with admiration and desire. His skin had a golden hue that could only have been the result of years of hard work in the sun.

"You won't find much generosity beyond this point," Brother Salvo lamented. "The world is being consumed by darkness. All the news we get here is filled with sadness."

"Are you part of a temple?" asked Millet.

"No," said Salvo. "I follow Saraf, but for the past few years, I have maintained this encampment. We serve as a refuge for pilgrims and travelers, though lately there have only been a few. This is the largest group we've had in months."

"I see," Millet said thoughtfully. "But why do the pilgrims not take refuge in the city temples? It's less than a day's ride from here."

Brother Salvo smiled feebly. "I see that things aren't as bad in the east. Here, the temples are turning everyone away—and it's the same in the western kingdoms. The High Priestess of the Temple of Ayliazarah in Kaltinor has actually turned out her own novices and acolytes."

Millet looked mortified. "How could she? She has no right."

"I agree," said Salvo, "but there's little that can be done."

"What has caused this?" Kaylia asked suddenly.

Gewey felt Lee stiffen next to him.

"I don't know, Sister," Salvo replied. "But I've heard stories—terrible stories."

"What kind of stories?" asked Millet before Kaylia could speak again.

"It is said that Angrääl is alive again and that the dead are rising from their graves," whispered Salvo. "Stories are spreading everywhere of an evil power, bringing darkness across the land."

"Angrääl?" said Gewey.

"Please, don't speak that name too loudly," Salvo warned, looking around to see if they had been heard. "You may be too young to know the story, but a thousand years ago, Angrääl was a kingdom far to the north, well beyond the White Wilderness. Legend says that the Demon King Rätsterfel rose up to challenge the gods. The war raged for a hundred years. Eventually, he was destroyed in a battle with heaven itself—but not before he had laid waste to half the world. Some say he has returned to take his revenge."

"Do you believe that?" asked Gewey.

Brother Salvo lowered his eyes. "I'm not sure what I believe anymore," he said. "But I do know that I've never seen such hardship in the world. There is something sinister behind it. I can feel it. Whether or not it's the return of the Demon King is impossible to say, but there is a pestilence spreading, and it's growing stronger. If it wasn't for the help I get from passing pilgrims and the few nobles still dedicated to the gods, I wouldn't be able to do what little I manage." He sighed heavily and shook his head.

Millet reached over and put his hand on Brother Salvo's shoulder. "Have faith, Brother. Things will get better. What you do here is important; there's nothing little about kindness."

Brother Salvo looked up and smiled. "Thank you, Brother. It's hard not to despair sometimes. Your words comfort me." He rose to his feet. "Now, I must attend to my other duties. Please stay as long as you wish."

"Thank you, Brother Salvo," said Millet. "But we'll be leaving at sunrise."

"Then I hope you'll stop here on your return journey," he said and walked back into the heart of the encampment.

"Surprising," said Kaylia.

"Surprising, how?" Gewey asked.

"Such kindness in a human is to be admired," she said. "My people would be very interested to see it."

"It appears you have as much to learn about us as we do about you," said Millet.

"So it seems," she replied.

"I'm worried," said Lee. "I had intended for us to stay a few days at the temple in Kaltinor, but if what Brother Salvo says is true, we may have to make other plans."

"That would be fine by me," said Kaylia. "I never thought it to be a wise plan."

"It's a good thing you're not in charge then," Lee said, glancing at Kaylia. "We need information, and the temple is the best place to get it. Without it, we travel blind."

"So, what do you suggest—as the leader?" Kaylia asked sarcastically.

Lee smiled devilishly. "I could say we've killed an elf, and that we need somewhere to dispose of her body. They'd let us stay in the High Priestess' apartment if we did that!"

Kaylia glared at Lee from underneath her hood. "You could try," she hissed.

"Enough of this," said Gewey. "Let's just get there. Maybe they'll simply let us stay."

"The first intelligent thing I've heard all night," Millet declared. "I, for one, am going to sleep. If you two wish to insult one another, be my guest. But please do it quietly."

There was silence among the group. Though tension remained between Lee and Kaylia, they eventually decided Millet was right and lay down to sleep.

CHAPTER 9

In the morning, they said their goodbyes to Brother Salvo. Millet gave him two gold coins that Lee had provided and promised to stop there again when they returned home. As they pulled away, Gewey wondered if they would be able to keep that promise. The more he learned, the more it seemed unlikely he would ever see his home again. Kaylia was deep in thought, her robes pulled tight around her.

"Are you all right?" asked Gewey.

"I'm fine," answered Kaylia. "I was just thinking about the people at the encampment. They weren't what I expected."

"What did you expect?" Gewey asked.

"I don't know," Kaylia admitted. "I suppose I expected them to be more brutish. I didn't expect to see the kindness they show to one another."

"Millet's right," said Gewey. "You have a lot to learn about humans."

Kaylia was silent.

"The story Brother Salvo told about the Demon King," said Gewey. "Have you heard it before?"

"Yes," said Kaylia "Though it's told differently among my people. In our tales, he's a hero."

"How could someone called the Demon King be a hero?" asked Gewey.

Kaylia laughed and said, "We don't call him the Demon King, we simply call him King Rätsterfel. In our stories, he stood up to the tyranny of the gods and tried to free the world."

"I wonder which story is true?" Gewey said pensively.

"Perhaps neither," Kaylia replied. "It was long ago, and storytelling among my people is not what it was. Much of our history was lost with the fall of our nations."

"That must be hard," said Gewey. "My people depend on their stories as a way to connect them to our ancestors. If we didn't have them, we'd be lost."

"You keep referring to the humans as 'your' people," she said.

"Yet they are not. Being raised as a human does not make you human. If they found out what you are, do you think they would bow down and worship you, or would they run in fear and disgust? Though I admit the monks surprised me with their kindness and selflessness, I wonder how kind they would have been if they discovered what I am? What if they knew they had shared a meal with an elf? Do you think they would just ignore it and smile?"

"And what about your people?" interjected Lee, who had been listening from the front of the wagon. "They want to murder you just for traveling with humans. Are they any better?"

"You're right, half-man," Kaylia acknowledged. "The old hatreds run deep on both sides. I cannot claim differently. Perhaps on this journey, we can find a way to change that."

"Wouldn't that be something," Millet added. "Now that would be an adventure I would be proud to be part of."

"I think you speak for us all, old friend," said Lee.

For the rest of the morning, conversation between Kaylia and Lee was more civil than usual. They even exchanged a few stories while Gewey listened with a pleased grin.

It was just before noon when they reached the gates of Kaltinor. They had expected the gates to be open during the day, but instead, they were shut tight and protected by four members of the city guard. Millet pulled up and halted the wagon.

"What's your business?" the guard captain inquired. As the captain spoke with Millet, the other three guards moved to the back of the wagon and looked inside. Gewey and Kaylia bowed their heads and stayed quiet.

"We're just pilgrims passing through," said Millet.

"Pilgrims, you say?" said the captain. "I'm sure you saw the monks camped back the way you came, and I'm sure they told you the temples will not receive you. We have no room here for a bunch of poor pilgrims. Best you move on."

"They did tell us," Millet affirmed. "All the same, we are just passing through." He reached down and handed something to the guard captain.

The captain looked at it for a moment, then quickly put it in his pocket. "Your stay here can be no longer than three days. Any longer and you'll be arrested. Understand?"

Millet nodded. "Completely."

The captain ordered his men to open the gates. Millet glanced over at Lee and sighed with relief. There was a loud screech of metal on metal as the gates slowly swung open. Millet urged the horses forward and passed through.

"We've managed to bribe our way through the gates with little problem," said Lee. "Let's see if our luck holds at the temple." He glanced back at Gewey. "If you want, you can walk beside the wagon. I know you've never seen a city before, and you won't see much of it from back there." Gewey smiled with excitement and leaped from the wagon.

The streets of Kaltinor were thirty feet wide and paved with smooth stones. Most of the buildings along the main avenue were two stories tall; the bottom levels held shops of all kinds, while the upper floors held residences where Gewey could see people eating and talking on small balconies. In just a few minutes, he had counted at least five taverns and three inns—a far cry from what he'd grown up with in Sharpstone. People of all kinds surrounded him; commoners, lords, monks, and merchants all moved about at a pace that astounded him. In the distance, towering above it all, stood a large manor of deep gray stone. At four stories high, it was by far the largest building Gewey had ever seen.

"What do you think, young master?" Millet asked. Gewey could barely hear him over the noise of the city.

"It's amazing," he said breathlessly. "I can't imagine what it would be like to live here."

"Like living in a hornets' nest," muttered Kaylia, who had jumped down beside Gewey. "It's unnatural."

"I agree," said Millet. "Over the years, I've come to appreciate living in the country."

Lee laughed. "So I guess all that about hating the smell of horses and pigs, not to mention the constant complaining about not having proper shops and clothing, was nothing but hogwash."

"Not hogwash, my lord," answered Millet. "I guess I've just changed more than I realized."

"We've both changed," said Lee, thoughtfully.

They wound their way west through the city's temple district and approached the Temple of Ayliazarah. The temple was made from red granite and bore elaborate carvings of the goddess along the outer wall. At the front, a stone staircase led up to an arched entranceway with two large oak doors. Statues of Ayliazarah, each one holding a harp in one hand and the Moon in the other, stood on either side of the door.

Millet stopped the wagon, and they climbed down.

"Remember," Millet advised. "Speak only when spoken to and say nothing of what Brother Salvo told us."

When they got to the door, Millet pounded it several times with his fist. It opened a few moments later, and there stood an old woman dressed in fine white linen robes embroidered with intricate interlacing gold patterns. Her head was covered in a thin gold silk scarf, and she carried a long white ash walking stick.

"What's your business here?" the old woman asked.

"We're pilgrims on our way to the Temple of the Far Sky," replied Millet. "We thought we might stay the night and see the temple while we're here."

"You thought wrong," said the woman. "We have no room for vagabonds. Be gone." She started to close the door, but Millet's hand shot out and stopped her.

"We are not vagabonds," Millet said sternly. "As I said, we are pilgrims, and we demand entrance to the temple."

"You demand?" the woman scoffed. "You will leave now, or I will call the city guards."

"Who is it?" asked a woman's voice from within the temple. "What do they want?"

"It's no one, Your Holiness," the old woman replied, turning her head inside the door. "Riff-raff, nothing more."

"Let them in," said the voice. "Let me see this 'riff-raff,' if you please."

The old woman glowered at Millet as she slowly opened the door.

Once inside, they saw a floor made from polished black marble that spanned an enormous room lined with gold columns. The walls were covered with tapestries and frescoes depicting the nine gods, and several immense glass chandeliers hung from the twenty-foot ceiling. In the center of the room stood a ten-foot statue of Ayliazarah, a perfect replica of those outside the door, except for the fact that this one was made of solid gold. At the far end were two spiral staircases leading to the upper level.

Just inside the door stood a woman dressed in white satin robes. She was holding a large, leather-bound book. She was younger than the woman who answered the door by at least twenty years, although her face looked careworn. Her light brown hair fell down over her shoulders in tight curls ornamented with tiny white flowers. She smiled brightly at Millet and the others as they entered.

"I don't know, Maybell," said the woman. "They look a bit scruffy, but I wouldn't say they're riff-raff." Her voice was cheerful and kind.

"Thank you for allowing us entrance, Your Holiness," Millet said, bowing low.

The others bowed as well but said nothing. Millet introduced them, using the same names he had given to Brother Salvo.

"I'm Sister Salmitaya, High Priestess here in Kaltinor," she said. "To what do I owe the pleasure of your visit?"

"We are but simple pilgrims on our way to the Temple of the Far Sky," Millet replied. "We seek lodging and a short respite from our travels."

"I tried to make them leave, Your Holiness," said Maybell. "But they wouldn't listen."

"Nonsense," laughed Salmitaya. "Times may be hard, but if these people managed to gain entry to the city, then who am I to turn them away? How did you get past the gate, by the way?"

"I'm ashamed to say, Your Holiness," said Millet. "We bribed our way in."

Salmitaya raised her eyebrows. "Is that so? It's interesting that mere pilgrims would have money enough for bribes."

"We have saved for many years to come on this pilgrimage," answered Millet. "This temple is among those we planned to visit along the way."

"I wish I had known," she said. "I could have saved you the cost of a bribe."

"Some pilgrims send word and money ahead," said Millet, understanding her meaning. "But I think that takes away from the lesson one is supposed to learn along the way. We have not, however, come empty-handed. We intend to make all proper contributions before we depart."

Salmitaya laughed. "Please, Brother Milton. You don't need to bother. It's my pleasure to offer the hospitality of this temple. You may stay as long as you wish."

"Thank you, Your Holiness," said Millet, bowing low.

"Thank you, Brother," she replied, bowing in return. "Sometimes it's easy to forget that this is a place of worship and contemplation. In these dark times, we have been all but driven to beg in the streets."

"It pains me to hear that," said Millet. "Is there anything we can do to help?"

"Sadly, there isn't," Salmitaya replied. "Our troubles go deeper than you can guess." Her eyes became sorrowful. "But this is not a conversation we should have here and now." She shook off her sadness and her smile returned. "Maybell will see to your needs. I hope you will join me for supper later."

"We would be honored," said Millet. "All but Sister Kaymaya, that is. She has taken the vow of the Sacred Word."

"Then I will see to it that she is accommodated," said Salmitaya. "Now, if you will excuse me, I have things to attend to." She bowed her head.

Millet and the others bowed low and watched as the High Priestess hummed softly while she walked across the floor to the stairs.

"Do you wish for me to have someone see to your things?" asked Maybell, still glaring suspiciously.

"To the horses and wagon, yes," answered Millet. "But we'll see to our own things."

"As you wish," she said. "I'll wait here." The four of them returned to the wagon and gathered their personal gear, leaving the provisions in the wagon. When they walked back inside, Maybell was tapping her foot impatiently, her arms crossed.

"If you please," she said sourly. "Follow me." She led them to the far left corner of the enormous room, where a large tapestry hung. As they approached, they saw that it covered an archway leading to the rear chambers. Maybell pulled back the tapestry and motioned for the group to enter. She then led them through a series of narrow hallways with evenly spaced doors and floors made from polished wood. The walls were made of rough brick and bore no decoration.

"As you can see," said Maybell, "despite the beauty of the rest of the temple, we live a simple life."

"I haven't noticed any other novices or priestesses," Millet observed. "Are they all praying?"

"There are only a few of us," answered Maybell. "The rest have left."

"Why?" Millet asked. "In times like these, you would think this place would be filled with the faithful."

"It is," she said, shooting an angry glance back at Millet. "The faithful are what we have here."

Millet decided not to pursue the matter further.

"Here we are," said Maybell, opening one of the doors. "You three will stay here, and you," she said to Kaylia, "can follow me. We keep a private chamber ready for those who have taken the vow of the Sacred Word."

Maybell led Kaylia down the hall to a door with a six-inch circle carved in the center. Inside the circle were carved three smaller, interwoven rings.

"This is where you will stay," Maybell said as she opened the door. "Your vows will be respected while you remain within these walls, and I will have your meals and wash water brought to you." Kaylia nodded and entered the room.

"I'll tell your friends how to find you," Maybell said as she left the room, closing the door behind her.

The room was drab. The plain brick walls were unadorned, and a worn rug covered part of the floor. A bed and a small table were the only furnishings. Kaylia sat cross-legged on the rug and waited.

The room the others shared was just as bare. Bunk beds lined opposite walls, and a table and bench sat at the rear. They had just begun to unpack when there was a knock at the door. Millet opened it to find Maybell, still bearing a sour expression.

"A basin and hot water will be brought for you," she said curtly. "Afterward, you are to make yourself ready for supper with Her Holiness. If you do not have clean robes, they will be provided."

"Thank you," said Millet. "Clean robes would be appreciated."

"If you wish to see your companion, she is down the hall in the room bearing the symbol of the Sacred Word," said Maybell. "Now, if you'll excuse me, I have more important things to attend to." She turned away and marched down the hall.

"I don't think she likes us very much," said Millet, closing the door.

"You can say that again," Gewey agreed. "I didn't think we were going to make it past the front door. Lucky for us, the High Priestess was there."

Lee looked worried. "Yes. Very lucky."

"I know that look, my lord," said Millet. "What are you thinking?"

"I'm not sure," Lee replied. "Something's not right here."

"I agree," said Millet. "The temple shouldn't be this empty, regardless of how bad the times have become."

Lee nodded. "It's not just that. It's a feeling I got when you were talking to the High Priestess. Something doesn't fit. From what Brother Salvo told us, I expected a less hospitable welcome."

"Quite right, my lord," said Millet. "If there is something amiss, I'll wager we'll find out about it soon enough. In the meantime, I'd better check on Kaylia and explain the vow of the Sacred Word."

Lee smiled with amusement. "She's going to love it. Don't you think?"

"That's not nice, my lord," scolded Millet. "Besides, it's the only way I could think of to keep her isolated."

"You did well, my friend," said Lee. "Now go explain everything to Kaylia."

"What is the vow of the Sacred Word?" asked Gewey once Millet had left.

"The vow of the Sacred Word, my young friend, is what only the most faithful swear before their pilgrimage," Lee explained. "They don't speak unless spoken to. Their eyes must be lowered in submission, and they must keep their heads covered at all times. They eat alone, sleep alone, and must meditate for three hours a day. They maintain chastity and humility throughout their pilgrimage and for one year after. Should they fail, they are required to present themselves to the High Priestess of their temple for penance. This usually means locking themselves in a small room for the remainder of their lives. Most go insane."

"That sounds tough," said Gewey. "Why do they do it?"

"To prove their faith," he replied. "Why else?"

A few minutes later, Millet returned.

"How did she react?" asked Lee.

"Well enough, my lord, but I should have told her before we arrived. She did agree that it was the best way to stay unnoticed, but she wasn't happy about the three hours of meditation each day. Especially when I told her that it must be done in full view of the world rather than in the privacy of her room."

Lee grinned mischievously. "She'll be fine," he said. "Showing a bit of humility is good for the soul."

"Indeed, my lord," said Millet. "Perhaps we could all do with some."

"I've been meaning to ask," said Gewey. "Why is it Millet pretends to be our leader in public?"

Lee threw his head back, laughing loudly. "Because I am quite possibly the worst actor in the world," he said. "Millet is much better at playing a role than I am, so we decided long ago that in cases like this, it's best to let him take the lead."

"You had no trouble pretending to be a lord from the north who wanted to live out his days in the country," Gewey noted.

"First of all," Lee replied, "I am a lord from the north, even though I wasn't born one. Secondly, I was raised in a small village and understood quite well how to behave. Third, I intended to be as inconspicuous as possible when I moved there, and you've seen how well that worked out. I was a topic of conversation more often than the weather."

"You did have a habit of causing tongues to wag," said Gewey, smiling.

"My point exactly," said Lee. "When it comes to blending in, Millet is the better man."

Just then, a young lady in brown novice robes brought them water and clean robes.

"I'm Celandine," she said. "Her Holiness asked me to tell you that supper will be ready in one hour. I will return then to escort you to her."

"Can I ask you a question?" said Millet.

"Certainly," she replied.

"How many people are at the temple? Counting you, I've only seen three."

"Then you've seen us all," Celandine stated.

Millet looked shocked. "Where did the others go?"

"That is a question best asked of Her Holiness," she answered.

"Now, if you'll excuse me."

"Only three people in the whole temple," Gewey said, once Celandine had left. "How is that possible?"

"Definitely a question I'll be asking 'Her Holiness'," said Millet.

The three washed and dressed, and an hour later, Celandine came to escort them to dinner. They were led back out into the main part of the temple and up the spiral stairs. The upper-level halls were well decorated with art and sculptures, and the floor was covered with fine, hand-woven carpets. They walked to the end of a wide hall, where they stopped at a large polished oak door with gold inlay.

"You will be dining in Her Holiness' private apartment," said Celandine as she knocked gently on the door. After a moment, Maybell opened the door from within and gestured for them to enter.

The first room of the apartment was lavish beyond anything Gewey had ever seen. The walls were covered in beautiful tapestries, and gold lanterns hung from the ceiling. Glass cases displaying gold figurines lined the doorway leading to the next room, and a small marble statue of Ayliazarah stood in each corner. In the center of the room was a large rectangular table covered by a white silk tablecloth.

A large cushioned chair was at the head of the table, and two smaller chairs were placed on either side.

"Please sit," Maybell instructed. "Her Holiness will be here shortly."

They took their seats as Celandine left the room. A moment later, a young boy entered carrying a platter filled with cups of wine. He placed a cup in front of each of them, and one in front of both empty chairs.

Millet noticed Maybell had moved off into the corner and was surveying the group. "Will you be joining us?" he asked.

"She will," said High Priestess Salmitaya, as she entered from the next room.

The High Priestess took her cup and raised it high. "Let us drink to Ayliazarah, Goddess of Love and Fertility. May she cast down her blessing and lift the shadow that has descended on our poor city."

Everyone lifted their cups and drank deeply. The wine was sweet and of excellent vintage.

"Tell me, Your Holiness," said Millet. "Is it true there are only three of you?"

Salmitaya sighed heavily. "I fear it is so. This temple once housed over one hundred of the faithful, but those days are long gone."

"How could such a thing happen?" asked Millet.

"We were a victim of our own arrogance and shortsightedness," she explained. "My predecessors involved themselves in political maneuvering and were constantly at odds with the governors and local lords. They became more interested in their own ambitions than in the welfare of the temple. In time, they created some very powerful enemies.

"By the time I became High Priestess, there was open hostility between the temple and the government. I tried to repair relations, but sadly, my skills as a politician leave much to be desired."

"Couldn't the other temples help?" Millet asked. "Surely they wouldn't want to see a temple fail."

Salmitaya smiled sadly. "The other temples were as bad—if not worse—than this one. The whole city became a battleground of government versus religion. As you can see, religion lost."

"How could they hope to shut down a temple?" said Millet. "Didn't the people of the city protest?"

"Why would they?" said Salmitaya. "Governor Mattlin passed laws denying the temples the ability to do good works within the city. Instead, they fed and clothed the people while we were forced to watch and could do nothing. And when we protested, we were threatened. Without good works to show, faith in the Temple quickly diminished."

"Why not go to the King?" asked Millet. "Surely he could help."

"King Grayling III is nothing more than a puppet," she replied. "He does the bidding of our enemies."

"That still doesn't explain why there are only three of you," Lee interjected.

"Good," she said, laughing gently. "I was afraid the rest of you lacked the ability to speak."

"Forgive me, your Holiness," Lee said in his best rural accent.

"Me and my young friend are not accustomed to such distinguished company. I hope I didn't offend you."

"Not at all," she said. "In fact, I insist that you feel free to speak your mind. To address what you said, we are all that is left after a long campaign by the governor to shut us down. Most of our novices, monks, and priestesses were from here in Kaltinor. The magistrate began to persecute anyone related to a member of any temple within the city walls. Those that didn't leave out of fear for their loved ones were threatened with imprisonment. The few we had that came here from abroad eventually left to join other temples and missions. Only my remaining influence with the Council of Nobles has prevented our complete demise."

"What about temples in other cities?" asked Gewey. "Couldn't they help?"

"I wish they could, child," she said, her eyes fixed on Gewey. "But the world has become a dark place. They simply can't spare any of what little resources they have. No—I'm afraid we're on our own."

"There's an encampment not far to the east," said Millet. "A man named Brother Salvo runs it. He is good and kind. Perhaps he could help?"

The High Priestess suddenly burst with laughter. "I know Brother Salvo," she said. "It is I, along with what's left of the other temples, that bribes the governor into helping him maintain his camp. He thinks we do nothing and accuses us of turning people out. What he doesn't understand is that at this point, even if we were left alone, we are nearly bankrupt. The King has taxed our coffers dry at the bidding of the lords. You saw for yourself what it takes for a pilgrim to enter the city. I could help a few get in, but we don't have the means to feed or house them for more than a few weeks."

Gewey was staring at the riches in the room around him.

"I can see your mind, young one," she said. "You stare at the treasures in this room and only see how much food and shelter it could provide."

"I wasn't..." Gewey stammered.

"It's all right," said Salmitaya. "I take no offense, and you're not wrong. What we have in the way of gold and other valuables could purchase much if we would actually be allowed to reap the profits. But keeping these things is the only way I can ensure that one day I might restore this place to its former glory. You see ... if I sold off or traded our treasures, the tax levied on us would close our doors forever. Together, they are considered relics and can't be taxed—at least, not yet. As things stand, I can barely feed the three of us. The boy who served you earlier puts himself in great danger when he comes here. His mother loved this place, and when she became ill, the sisters and brothers cared for her until she passed. I've tried to stop him from coming, but he is very persistent."

"This is all so unfair," cried Gewey. "I don't understand how someone could do this to a temple."

"In a way, we brought it upon ourselves," she explained. "If we had stayed faithful to our purpose and left politics alone, we might be having a much different conversation."

Just then, Celandine entered the room, followed by the young boy. They carried trays filled with food and placed them on the table. The boy ran off and returned with plates and silverware that he quickly put in front of the party.

"Wonderful," said the High Priestess, "Enough of this sad talk. Let us enjoy the meal Sister Celandine has prepared."

"Won't she be joining us?" asked Millet.

"What a good idea!" Salmitaya replied. "You heard him, sister. Join us." Celandine nodded her head and retrieved a chair from the next room.

"Don't bother serving us, Sister," said Salmitaya. "We'll serve ourselves." She turned back toward her guests and continued.

"Forgive the lack of formality. Celandine is our only cook these days, and it's usually just three of us. She doubles as server on the rare occasions we have guests."

"We are used to serving ourselves, Holiness," said Millet. "Besides, we're pilgrims—not lords."

They passed the trays around until everyone's plate was full. The food was good. Though not extravagant, it was better than anything Gewey had tasted in a long time. The conversation was light and cheerful. The High Priestess asked about their travels, and Millet mixed in truth with lies as he told their story. She seemed very interested in Gewey's farm upbringing. They had told her that he was raised on a farm and had come to the temple after his father died.

"What do you think of the city, Brother Gewton?" asked Salmitaya. "I bet it's much different than what you're used to."

"Yes, it is, Your Holiness," answered Gewey.

"I have a meeting with the governor tomorrow," said Salmitaya. "It's pointless, but unfortunately I must attend. I was thinking you might come with me. Would you like that?"

"We would love to come, Holiness," Millet answered quickly.

"I'm sorry, Brother Milton," she said. "I could explain away one lonely young pilgrim, but a group may cause problems. I'm sure you won't mind if the boy accompanies me. The governor wants me there at the crack of dawn, and he takes pleasure in making me wait. I could use the company, and Brother Gewton would get the chance to see the manor. It's a beautiful house, actually."

"Of course," said Millet. "I'm sure Brother Gewton will be happy to accompany you, Your Holiness."

Lee tried to hide the concern on his face. Gewey, on the other hand, looked excited. The chance to see inside the governor's manor was something he would have hated to pass up.

"It's settled, then," she declared. "I will wake you in the morning and bring you with me. Expect to be away for most of the day. There's no telling how long I'll be made to wait."

When they finished dinner, Maybell and Celandine cleared the table.

Salmitaya stood up. "While I would love to stay up and talk, I must now excuse myself. It's rare that I have the pleasure of stimulating conversation, but the morning comes early and brings with it a trying day. If you will agree to linger for a few days, I would love to speak with you more. We don't get much news from the world here."

"We had indeed hoped to stay for a bit," said Millet. "Thank you again for your hospitality, Holiness. Now, I think I could use some sleep myself."

Salmitaya bowed. "Until tomorrow, then."

They all bowed in turn and watched as the High Priestess and Maybell walked from the room. Celandine led them back to their chambers and bid them goodnight.

"I don't like it," Lee said, once Celandine had gone. "Something's wrong. I don't like that she's taking such a strong interest in the boy."

"It may be just as she says," said Millet.

There was a knock at the door. It was Kaylia. She sat on one of the beds and they told her about the events of the evening.

"I agree with the half-man," said Kaylia. "Something is wrong here. Her story is too perfect. It fits too well ... if you believe her over Brother Salvo."

"It's not only that," said Lee. "If Salmitaya is to be believed, then Brother Salvo may just be unaware of the true circumstances. He didn't strike me as a liar. But from the moment she invited us in, I got the feeling that she knew we were coming."

"I think you're all being ridiculous," said Gewey. "If she wanted to hide something, why would she let us stay here in the first place? Why risk us finding out? You say her story fits too well. Would you rather that it didn't fit?"

"I would rather not feel as though we were walking straight into a trap," said Lee.

Kaylia nodded. "We should leave now ... before the trap is sprung."

"No," said Lee. "At least, not yet. If there is something going on here, we need to know whether or not it involves us. Hopefully, things are as Salmitaya says, and I'm just being paranoid. But if she does have motives that could hinder us, we need to know."

"And what about the boy?" Kaylia asked. "You don't really intend to let him go off with that woman, do you?"

"I don't see that we have a choice," Millet answered. "If he refuses, it could raise suspicion. If we're wrong, and the High Priestess is telling the truth, then we will have insulted her and ruined any chance we might have of gathering information during our stay."

"I'm going," Gewey said hotly. "I can make this decision for myself."

"Indeed, you can," Millet said. "But you need to trust in our experience."

"Listen to him," Kaylia advised Gewey. "We are trying to out-maneuver a possible predator in her home territory. You need to watch and listen. One day it will be you making these decisions, and when the time comes, you will need to know how."

"I'm not a child," Gewey protested. "You act like I don't know anything."

"You don't," snapped Lee. "You are a child, regardless of how old you may look—and you're too important for me to let you discover that fact on your own. Until you're ready, you'll do as you're told."

Gewey crossed his arms and glared furiously at Lee.

"I need you to pay attention tomorrow," Lee instructed. "If Salmitaya is up to something, we need to know what."

Kaylia handed Gewey a flask of jawas tea. "Drink this," she said. "Now that it no longer knocks you out, you can use it to relax and help you sleep."

Gewey took the flask and drank. Immediately, the tension left his body, and he felt his troubles begin to lift away.

Kaylia returned to her room and Lee, Gewey, and Millet went to bed. Gewey, aided by the jawas tea, went right to sleep, but Lee and Millet stayed awake talking for a while longer.

"If I might be so bold, my lord," said Millet, "you should remember that the boy has been on his own, without a father, for more than two years. He may be still little more than a child, but he's been treated as a man for quite some time."

"What do you suggest?" asked Lee. "The boy must learn, and I don't know how else to teach him."

"I think that perhaps you should trust the boy's instincts from time to time," Millet responded. "The fact of the matter is that you intended to let him go with the High Priestess all along. I think all he wants is to be consulted."

"Funny that you should talk about trusting his instincts," Lee remarked. "When I first met Kaylia, I told her that it was the one thing I did trust. Still, he is inexperienced. Instincts are no substitute for good judgment. I hope mine is good enough."

"You do show wisdom, my lord," yawned Millet. "Occasionally. But you should learn to accept that some things are beyond your control."

Lee chuckled. "Anyway, we'd better get some rest. Goodnight, Millet," said Lee.

"Pleasant dreams, my lord," he replied.

CHAPTER 10

Gewey woke up early and donned his robes. Millet and Lee were still sleeping. Not wanting to wake them, Gewey went to look around the temple. He wandered the narrow corridors for a while until he found his way back to the main hall. The dawn light shone dimly through small windows set high on the surrounding walls. The gold statue of Ayliazarah glowed eerily. As Gewey approached it, he felt a cold chill that made the hair on his arms stand up.

"I was just about to wake you," said Salmitaya, appearing from the direction of the staircase. "We'll leave in just a bit. Would you like breakfast before we go?"

"No, thank you," Gewey replied.

"You should eat," she insisted. "Please join me." She motioned for Gewey to follow and led him back to the same chamber in which they had eaten the night before. Waiting at the table were a bowl of porridge and a glass of apple juice.

"Good to see another morning person," Salmitaya said with a smile. "Poor Celandine and Maybell simply hate an early rise." She pointed to the food. "Please, Brother. I hope you don't mind porridge? Last night's fare was more lavish than we usually have. I'm afraid this is a bit more like what we're accustomed to lately."

Gewey nodded. "This is perfect, Holiness. I love porridge and juice."

"Before these dark times plagued this place, I had good friends here," she said. "In private, they called me Taya. I would have you do the same. Maybell refuses and Celandine, well ... to get that girl to speak more than a few words would be a miracle."

Gewey blushed. "I would be honored. What are we going to do today, Holi—Taya?" he asked after swallowing a large mouthful of porridge.

"The same thing I always do when I see Governor Mattlin," she answered. "I'll ask for the littlest thing, and he'll act like I just told him that the city is on fire." She suddenly looked dismayed. "How's your porridge, Brother Gewton?"

"Delicious," Gewey replied. But even as he said this, he began to feel dizzy. He tried to stand up, only to stumble into the wall.

Salmitaya made no move to help him. She smiled a sinister smile. "Is something the matter, my child?"

"You..." was all Gewey could manage to say before he collapsed in a heap on the floor.

Salmitaya got up and stood over Gewey. "Such an attractive boy," she said, as two city guards entered the room. "Bind him and take him to my carriage." The guards nodded and dragged Gewey away.

"Such a pretty, pretty boy," she said and laughed softly.

When Gewey finally awoke, it was to utter darkness. He feared he had been blinded until he realized he'd simply been blindfolded.

He couldn't initially remember what had happened to him, but then it suddenly came rushing back—Salmitaya! She must have drugged him. But why? His body was seated upright, and when he tried to move, he found that both his hands and feet were shackled. He tested them, but they were too strong for him to break. As his head cleared, he could sense that he was in a wagon or carriage, moving steadily along.

Gewey's thoughts were interrupted by the sound of Salmitaya's voice. "I see that the young prince has awakened. Wonderful! I was getting lonely."

"What's going on here?" Gewey asked angrily. "Why did you drug me?"

"Why, why, why. With youth, it's always why," she mocked. "It's actually the how that's more interesting to me. One bite of that porridge should have been enough to put you to sleep for twelve hours. But you, my pretty young friend, ate nearly the entire bowl—yet here you are, awake after only six hours. Do you know what that makes you?"

"What?" growled Gewey.

"A mystery," she replied. "One that I intend to solve before I deliver you."

"Deliver me to who?"

"All in good time," said Salmitaya.

Six hours, Gewey thought. She has a six-hour head start. But that's nothing for Lee. Then it hit him: They won't expect me back until after nightfall. By then, who knows where we'll be?

"I get the shackles, but why the blindfold?" asked Gewey. "What are you afraid of me seeing?"

"Afraid? I wouldn't go so far as to say afraid. But given how much moonbane root it took to knock you out, you clearly warrant a little extra caution."

"This won't work, you know," Gewey said. "Eventually, my friends will find me."

Salmitaya snickered. "Your friends are dead. Lee Starfinder, Millet Gristall, and that wretched elf are all dead. They died the moment you were taken."

Hearing the names of his friends and her knowledge of Kaylia's true identity sent fear into his heart. Still, he was defiant. "You lie!" he shouted.

"Of course, I'm not lying," Salmitaya replied. "How do you think I know your true identities, Gewey?"

"How do you know who we are?" he asked, trying not to let the fear show in his voice.

"You keep asking the wrong questions," she said. "The inexperience of youth is so delicious."

Gewey recoiled as he felt her hand on his chest.

"Do I make you nervous?" she asked, laughing lightly as she withdrew her hand.

"You make me sick," he said, his skin crawling. "You're evil."

"What does a farm boy know about evil?" she asked. "I've seen real evil, child. The elf you were traveling with—you know, the one the guards killed this morning." Her tone was amused yet filled with hatred. "She was evil."

"Kaylia is not evil, you witch!" Gewey raged. "She is good and kind, and a thousand times better than you'll ever be!"

Gewey's ears rang as he felt the impact of Salmitaya's hand across his face.

"Never compare me to an elf again," she warned. "Or this trip will become very unpleasant."

Gewey felt a touch of satisfaction at having made her lose control.

"How long will this trip take?" he asked.

"Finally," said Salmitaya, her voice now calmer. "It appears I've knocked some sense into you. That is an excellent question. One your mentors would be proud that you asked. Gather information slowly, boy. Don't ask the big questions like 'Why are you doing this?' or 'Where are we going?' right away. If you want to try and escape, it's the little details that will help. Unfortunately for you, I already know this, so you won't be getting any details from me."

"It's not like I can go anywhere," Gewey said, shaking his shackles. "Why not tell me?"

"I'll tell you what," she replied arrogantly. "You get to ask one question, and one question only."

Gewey thought hard, but he couldn't come up with anything he thought would help him. "Who are you taking me to?" he asked finally.

Salmitaya shook her head. "Disappointing. You ask a question you already know the answer to."

"Tell me," Gewey demanded.

"I would hate to deny him the pleasure of proper introductions," said Salmitaya. "So instead, I'll answer your question with a question: who do you run from?"

Gewey could barely contain his terror as the realization washed over him. *He found me*, he thought.

Salmitaya instantly picked up on his fear. "That's right, boy. And he's very excited to meet you. The only thing I'm wondering is why the Great One would be so interested in a simple farm boy. The answer is obvious: you're not just a simple farm boy, are you? What is it, I wonder?" She stroked Gewey's cheek. "You are pretty. And you certainly have a strong constitution. But there's more, isn't there?"

Gewey smirked. "You ask the wrong questions," he said. "You should take your own advice."

Salmitaya laughed aloud. "And just what is the right question, child? Enlighten me."

Gewey's tone became dangerous. "How long will it take for you to die once I get loose from these chains?"

"Such fire," said Salmitaya. "I wonder if you will be so brave when you face him. Somehow, I doubt it."

"Why do you serve him?" Gewey asked. "You're a High Priestess of Ayliazarah; how can you betray your faith?"

"You speak from ignorance," she answered. "Long ago, I followed the teachings without question, but my faith was misplaced, as you will soon learn. For years, I watched as the world became a cesspool, riddled with corruption and plagued by despair. Did the gods intervene? Did they make their presence known? Of course they didn't, because the truth about the gods is that they care nothing for us."

"And your master does?" he scoffed.

"My master will set the human race free," she said. "He will release us from servitude and pointless worship. At last, humans will be free to become what they were meant to be: the true masters of this world. When that happens, I will be there to bathe in the glory of my master's victory. And somehow, you're connected to that end."

"I have nothing to do with it," Gewey bluffed. "I'm just a farmer."

"I hope you're better at farming than you are at lying," said Salmitaya.

"I could take a lesson from you," Gewey said, his voice dripping with contempt. "You're the High Priestess of deception."

Salmitaya chuckled. "Perhaps," she allowed. "The secret is to mix truth and lies together, like your friend Millet did."

Hearing Millet's name infuriated Gewey, but he managed to keep the anger inside. "What's the real reason the temple failed?" he asked.

"It's just as I said," she replied. "The only difference being that I was the one behind the persecution and threats. The governor was very happy to help, especially when he discovered how rich I would make him. Luckily, the king is a weakling and easily bought—much more easily than the governor, in fact."

"I still don't get why the other temples didn't stop you," said Gewey. *Keep her talking,* he thought. *Maybe she'll give something away.*

"That's the best part," she said. "They are the ones that helped. A few couldn't be corrupted and had to be dealt with, but for the most part, they were all too happy to sell out."

"I don't believe you," said Gewey.

"Really?" she mocked. "How do you think I knew to be at the door when you and your friends arrived? How do you think I knew you were coming?"

"You didn't," said Gewey, after thinking about it for a moment. "We had to bribe our way into the city. If you knew we were coming, you would have sent word to let us in."

"Dear boy," she said. "Had I cleared the path for you, your suspicions would have been raised. No, you had to believe it was your cunning that got you through the gates. Of course, the guards informed me that you were here, and I had left them instructions to find a way to let you pass if your friends were too stupid to bribe the captain. But make no mistake—I've known every move you've made for quite a while."

"You know what I think? I think you just got lucky," Gewey said.

"No argument there," she said. "I knew what to look for, but it wasn't until you talked to my friend Brother Salvo that I knew you were here."

Gewey couldn't believe what he was hearing. "Brother Salvo works for you?"

"Not exactly," said Salmitaya. "But there are those among him who are my eyes and ears outside of the city. I told them what to watch out for, and it was reported to me as soon as you were spotted. I must admit, it was more than fortunate that you pretended to be pilgrims of Ayliazarah—a deception that brought you right to my doorstep—though I could have arranged a meeting, regardless."

"I still don't understand how you know our names," said Gewey.

"Your names were given to me over a week ago, foolish boy," she replied. "Your name is known by all of His agents. There was never any chance you would escape."

"How did you know about Kaylia?" Gewey asked. "She's only been with us a short while."

"You don't really think I would provide rooms that would give you privacy, do you?" she said, then paused for a long moment. "Smart boy. Keep me talking. But nothing I've said will do you any good."

Gewey suddenly began laughing.

"I'm glad you find this amusing," she said, her voice showing irritation. "Perhaps I'll make you grovel a bit before the Great Master takes you."

"You don't understand," Gewey said. "It's not what you said."

"What then?" she asked.

"Two things," said Gewey. "One: I'd bet you didn't see the bodies of my friends before you left."

"And what's the other thing?" For the first time, Salmitaya sounded uncertain.

"The second thing," he said, "is that you actually thought that your plan to kill them would succeed. You have no idea what you've done. You're in a lot more danger than I am."

Gewey's head flew back as she struck him.

"Guard!" shouted Salmitaya.

"Yes, Holiness," a low, rough voice replied.

"Keep an eye on him," she said. "I'll ride up front for a while. If he speaks or tries to escape, make him regret it."

"As you wish, Holiness," the man replied.

The carriage stopped, and Gewey could hear the door opening and closing.

"You heard her, boy," said the guard. "Not a sound out of you."

Gewey remained silent. He hoped what he said was true. He had to believe that his friends still lived and were coming for him. He shifted in his seat and smiled slightly.

They're coming, he thought.

CHAPTER 11

Millet woke to find that Gewey had already left. He could see by the dim light of the oil lantern that Lee was still sound asleep. *Best to let him rest a bit more*, he thought. He got up as quietly as he could and began to straighten up the room.

"Don't bother being quiet," said Lee. "I'm awake."

"Good," Millet said, smiling. "Then you won't mind getting out of bed so I can make it."

Lee smiled sleepily. "Did you see Gewey leave?"

"No, my lord," Millet replied. "He was already gone when I awoke."

"I hope he doesn't do anything stupid," Lee muttered. "I don't trust that woman."

"Don't worry. I'm sure the lad can handle himself," said Millet.

Barely were the words out of his mouth when a series of loud thumps sounded from immediately outside the door. These were followed by a muffled scream. Lee jumped out of bed and grabbed the knife he had hidden under his pillow. Millet rushed to his pack, searching for a weapon, but before he could find one, Lee threw open the door and ran out. Lying in the hall were four city guards, all dead, blood pouring from their multiple wounds. Kaylia stood over them, still dressed in her underclothes, her long knife at the ready.

"How you've stayed alive this long I can't imagine," she said. "I heard them coming from all the way down the hall."

"Thank the gods for that," Millet said from behind Lee. "my lord, we need to find Gewey."

Lee was still staring at the bodies and the half-naked elf standing over them. *How did I miss this?* he thought. *I should have heard them.*

"Pay attention, half-man," Kaylia said sternly. "Get your things together. I'll be right back."

Kaylia ran down the hall to her room.

Millet grabbed Lee by the arms. "Are you all right, my lord?"

"I'm fine," answered Lee. "Gather our things. Don't bother with the robes."

A few minutes later Kaylia reappeared with her pack, still holding her knife. Instead of her pilgrim's robe, she wore a brown, waist-length hooded riding cloak over the same shirt and trousers she'd been wearing the day they'd met. "This should disguise me as well as the robes did," she explained in response to Lee's questioning look.

"I take it we're no longer pilgrims," said Millet.

"It seems like the pilgrim disguise didn't work," Lee admitted.

Once they'd gathered their gear, Lee led them down the hall to the entrance leading into the main temple. He peered out from behind the tapestry that covered the doorway and saw Maybell kneeling in front of the statue of Ayliazarah.

"Quickly," Lee whispered.

Lee burst from behind the tapestry, sword in hand, and ran toward the praying woman. She looked up at him, eyes wide in shock, as he grabbed her roughly and pinned her to the floor.

"What's the meaning of this?" she screamed, struggling in vain against Lee's iron grip.

"Why don't you ask the guards that you sent to kill us?" Lee asked harshly.

"I—I don't know what you're talking about!" Maybell stammered. "What guards?"

"Listen to me very carefully," Lee said in a low, dangerous whisper. "You will answer my questions, or I'll let my friend here deal with you." He looked at Kaylia, who pulled back her hood.

"An elf!" Maybell cried out, terrified. "Ayliazarah protect me."

"The gods can't protect you from me, woman," said Kaylia with a malevolent grin.

"What do you want?" Maybell pleaded.

"Nothing you can't provide," said Lee. "First, you will tell us where to find our wagon and horses. Then you will help us leave the city. Finally, you will tell us where our young friend is."

"He's with Her Holiness," she said. "You already know that."

"Let me question her," Kaylia offered, stroking her blade.

Horror and fear took hold of the old woman. She started to weep uncontrollably. "Please, I'm begging you," she said between her sobs. "I spent the night at the Temple of Islisema. Her Holiness sent me there last night after dinner. I just got back. I know nothing."

"Millet," said Lee. "Go upstairs and look around. See if that witch left any clues."

Millet nodded and immediately ran up the stairs.

Lee looked directly into Maybell's eyes. "I'll ask you again," he said. "Do you know what Salmitaya did to our friend?"

Maybell looked straight back at Lee. "I swear by the gods I do not! I don't know what's happening here!"

Lee sighed. "She tells the truth. She knows nothing."

"How can you be sure?" asked Kaylia.

"I can tell," Lee replied. "She doesn't possess the skill to deceive me. Remember what I am; it takes a trained mind to hide the truth from me."

"Perhaps she is trained," said Kaylia.

"No," said Lee. "If she were, I would know that too."

Lee allowed the shaking, still terrified woman to get up. They waited in grim silence until Millet returned. He came running down the stairs.

"I found something," he said, handing a letter to Lee.

Lee took the letter and read it aloud.

"Salmitaya,"

"You are to watch for three travelers. They will be disguised as pilgrims and will be using false names. Their real names are Lee Starfinder, Millet Gristall, and Gewey Stedding. Two are older, the other young. It is possible that they have picked up another companion along the way. The young one called Gewey is to be brought to me unharmed. The others are to be killed. Do not underestimate them, Salmitaya. And do not fail as you have in the past, or you shall find reward swiftly turns to punishment."

It was signed simply "Y."

"He knows who we are," said Lee, clutching the letter angrily.

"Somehow he knows our names, and now he has the boy."

Kaylia's eyes shone with fierce determination. "There's only one thing to do: find him and get him back. But first, we must leave the city."

"That shouldn't be hard," said Millet. "They're trying to keep people out, not in. But unless you want to delay long enough to buy proper horses for riding, then we either leave behind our gear and run after them, or try to catch them riding in a wagon."

"I suggest we do both," said Kaylia. "Millet, you can take the wagon while Lee and I run ahead and catch them. They think us dead, so it's unlikely they'll be in much of a hurry. Once we're outside of the city, all we need to do is find out if anyone has seen a carriage with an armed escort."

"What makes you think that's how they'll travel?" asked Millet.

"The boy is strong, and won't go willingly," Kaylia reasoned. "They'll need a wagon or carriage to carry him, and I can't picture a high priestess in a wagon. The letter said to be cautious, so it's likely she'll bring an escort. Being that she ordered the attack on us earlier, she clearly has access to the city guard."

"That's a lie!" spat Maybell. "Her Holiness would never order the spilling of blood within her own temple."

"Then explain the letter," said Lee. "Does a High Priestess go about the business of murder? Does she abduct people? Once we're gone, I suggest you look closely at what's been happening here." Maybell glared at Lee, hatred burning in her eyes.

"Did you see her receive this letter?" Millet asked Maybell.

"No," the woman answered. "Why?"

"I wonder how she received word so quickly..." Millet began, stroking his chin. Suddenly, his eyes lit up. "Sister Maybell, does Salmitaya keep a messenger flock?"

"Of course she does," Maybell replied, trying her best to keep her composure. "All temples do."

"That explains part of it, at least," said Lee. "Still, we have no idea how the sender of this letter got our names in the first place, or how he knew our cover story."

"What's a messenger flock?" Kaylia interrupted.

"Fauna birds," answered Millet. "Generally, there are cages on the roof to house them. Each bird flies between two homes. Tie a letter to their leg and release them, and they can carry a message in a single day that would normally take a week."

Kaylia nodded slowly. "Caged birds," she said, grimacing in disgust.

"Let's stay focused," Lee said. "Millet, you and Kaylia stay here while the good sister and I go get our things."

"I'll not help you if you intend to hurt Her Holiness," Maybell said defiantly. "No matter what that elf may do to me."

"I'll make you a deal then," said Lee. "If no harm has come to our friend, then no harm will come to Salmitaya. If she's the woman you think she is, you should have nothing to worry about. But I daresay that if you are smart and do a bit of investigating, you may end up wishing we had not made this bargain."

"Do I have your word?" Maybell asked.

"You do," Lee replied.

"Then come with me," she said. "The sooner you have your things, the sooner I'm rid of you."

Maybell then pulled herself from Lee's grasp and marched toward the door with a speed surprising for someone of her age. She didn't even bother with her walking stick, and it took a concerted effort for Lee to catch up.

"The half-man risks much letting the old woman live," said Kaylia.

Millet frowned. "If he says she knows nothing, then she knows nothing. Lord Starfinder will not kill the innocent."

"There are no innocents," Kaylia said darkly. "She could give us away."

"I've thought of that," said Millet. "You still have some of that jawas tea, don't you?"

Kaylia pulled back her cloak, revealing a flask tied to her belt.

"Good," said Millet. "We'll give her enough to put her out for at least twelve hours."

"She still knows too much about us," Kaylia insisted.

"That may be," Millet replied. "But the fact is, we are not killing her. Do you understand?"

Kaylia looked hard into Millet's eyes and said, "You have a good heart, Millet Gristall. But that will not save us from danger, nor will it change the fact that I am not bound by your master's promises. I agreed to come with you, not take his orders."

Millet stared hard at the elf, and the two waited in silence until Lee returned with Maybell at his side.

"Everything is ready," said Lee. "Let's get moving. One of the stable boys saw a carriage with an escort of city guards heading to the west gate."

"I thought a bit of jawas tea might be in order," said Millet, gesturing to Maybell.

"That won't be necessary," said Lee. "Sister Maybell will be coming with us."

Kaylia shook her head with a scowl. "You get more foolish by the minute, half-man."

"Don't worry," Lee assured her. "We had a chance to talk on our way to get the horses and wagon. She has agreed not to give us away, and she will see to it that we pass through the gate unhindered. In return, she wants to be the one to escort the High Priestess back to the temple when we catch them."

"Not to be contrary, my lord," Millet began, "but won't taking her with us slow us down?"

Lee smiled devilishly. "Us, no," he said. "You, on the other hand..."

"That's not funny," Millet said sternly.

"It's not meant to be," said Lee. "Maybell will ride with you on the wagon, while Kaylia and I run ahead to catch up with Gewey and Salmitaya. Once we have them, we'll bring them back, and Maybell will escort the priestess back to the temple."

"I must agree with Millet," said Kaylia. "We should drug her and leave her."

"Maybe," said Lee. "But that's not what we're going to do. You, my elf friend, can either help me free Gewey, or you can go your own way."

"Very well," she said begrudgingly. "We'll do as you say ... for now."

"My lord," Millet interrupted, "before we leave, we should find out where the other sister is."

"She didn't stay at the temple last night either," answered Maybell. "But where she went, I don't know."

"Clever," said Millet. "No witnesses."

"I wish we were as clever," Kaylia said, glaring at Maybell.

"However, being that we are not, we should leave before the guards are missed."

"Agreed," said Lee. "The west gate is not far. We need to get there quickly."

They left the temple and got into the waiting wagon. Maybell rode in the front with Millet, while Lee and Kaylia rode in the back. When they reached the west gate, they were stopped by the city guards. Lee tensed and gripped his sword. But Maybell was true to her word.

"I'm from the temple of Ayliazarah on business for High Priestess Salmitaya," she told the guard. "These people are my escorts." The guard nodded and opened the gate.

Lee turned to Kaylia and smirked. "I told you," he said.

"A stupid gamble either way," said Kaylia, unimpressed. "The woman can still betray us."

"True," Lee acknowledged, "but she can also give us valuable information. It's clear that the Dark Knight knows who we are, and what we're doing. She may be able to help us figure out how this happened."

"If she's truly innocent, why would she have any information we need?" Kaylia asked.

"I assure you, she wasn't lying about her innocence," Lee replied. "But she may still know things—things she may not think important, but that are valuable to us, nonetheless."

They rode for an hour before they thought it was safe enough to ask strangers if they had seen anything. It did not take long to find someone with good information.

"Aye," said a man walking on the side of the road carrying a woodcutter's axe. "I saw a carriage. Right grand sight it was. Must have been ten men guardin' it. Have to be awful rich to afford ten guards."

"Where were they going?" Millet inquired.

"Don't rightly know where they were headed for," said the man. "But they were on their way west when I seen 'em."

Millet thanked the man and tossed him a copper coin.

"That has to be them," Lee said as he jumped out of the wagon.

He turned toward Millet. "You and Maybell stay on this road. There's a crossroads a mile from here. When you reach it, head south until you get to the village of Fair Harvest. Get a room at the inn and wait for us there."

Millet nodded and watched as Lee and Kaylia ran headlong down the road, quickly disappearing from sight. Maybell crossed her arms over her chest and frowned. "We will not be staying in the same room," she stated flatly.

Millet groaned and urged the horses onward, wishing he were back in Sharpstone.

CHAPTER 12

Gewey sat in dark silence for hours as the carriage plodded along. When the temperature dropped, he figured it was getting close to nightfall. If they stopped, it might give him a chance to get his bearings. Maybe he'd even get a chance to escape. He was sure Lee would come for him. From Gewey's perspective, a bunch like this wouldn't stand a chance against a man like Lee Starfinder.

His thoughts were interrupted as he felt the carriage stop and heard the door open.

"Bring him," he heard Salmitaya order from outside the door.

A guard grabbed Gewey by the front of his robe and pulled him roughly from the carriage. He felt himself falling before landing hard on the ground.

"Careful," Salmitaya warned. "We don't want him damaged. At least, not yet."

The guard hoisted Gewey to his feet, gruffly instructing him to stay put. Gewey did as he was told and waited, listening to the sounds of the people around him. He could make out ten different voices, most likely guards. It sounded as if they were setting up camp, but Gewey couldn't be sure. After half an hour, he was led away from the carriage and through the entrance of a nearby tent. The guard stopped and forced him to the ground. He lay there for a moment and then struggled to his knees. He could hear a guard breathing heavily nearby.

"Leave us," Salmitaya ordered.

Gewey felt cold hands on his face as Salmitaya removed his blindfold. He blinked at the bright lamplight filling the tent. When his eyes adjusted, he saw Salmitaya standing in front of him. She was no longer wearing her robes; instead, she wore a blue silk dress tied at the waist by a thin silver belt. Her braided hair fell neatly down her back, and her ears and neck were adorned with diamonds and gold.

"The clothes suit you," said Gewey sarcastically. "It's better than the costume you were wearing when I met you."

Salmitaya smiled warmly, seemingly unaffected by Gewey's jabs. "We were both in disguise, I think," she said. "Are you hungry?"

"No," he replied. "I've lost my appetite."

"Don't be silly," she chided. "How on earth do you expect to escape if you don't keep up your strength?"

"You don't need to worry about my strength," Gewey said confidently. "I'll be free long before I starve."

"Perhaps," said Salmitaya. "Perhaps you'll be free this very night." She walked across the tent and sat in a waiting chair.

"What do you want?" asked Gewey.

Salmitaya laughed playfully. "What makes you think I want something?" she asked, trying to sound innocent.

"I may be young, but I'm not stupid," said Gewey. "You never get something for nothing."

"So true," she said. "And as it turns out, you do have something I want. Give it to me, and I might just forget I ever found you."

"I have nothing to give you," said Gewey. "And even if I did, what makes you think I'd let you have it?"

"You'll give it to me because it's in your best interests to do so," she replied. "And it's such a little thing at that."

"Get to the point," he snapped.

"As you wish," she said. "What I want is information. Why are you so important to the Great Master? Why do I have to risk exposure, traveling to the ends of the bloody earth, just to deliver one farm boy?"

"Like I said," Gewey responded, "I have nothing to give you. I don't know the things you want to know."

"I think you do," she said sweetly. "And one way or another, you will tell me."

At that moment, a guard came in carrying a bowl of stew and a cup of water. He placed the cup and bowl in front of Gewey and then stood at the tent's entrance.

"One more thing," she said, turning to leave. "You will eat, or the guards will beat you until you do so. Your choice."

Gewey looked at the food. He thought it was most likely drugged, but he took it and ate, nonetheless. Immediately, he felt the drugs take hold much more strongly than the first time. Salmitaya had apparently learned her lesson well. He concentrated on keeping his wits about him in the same way he did with the jawas tea. He felt weak, but he was able to remain conscious. Deciding he might be to able take advantage of this, he fell over and pretended to be in a drug-induced sleep.

A short time later, he heard Salmitaya enter the tent and felt her hand brush back his hair.

"What's your secret?" she wondered aloud.

Gewey cracked open his eyes and watched Salmitaya as she left the tent. A guard stood just inside the entrance, watching him intently. He scanned the area as well as he could from his position, but the tent was bare and contained nothing he could use to his advantage. He could do little under the guard's watchful gaze, so he decided to bide his time. If he was going to escape, he would first have to do something about the guard; how he would manage this while in shackles, he had no idea.

A couple of hours later, an opportunity presented itself. The guard briefly stepped out and returned with a small stool. The man promptly sat down, and it wasn't long before Gewey heard him snoring.

Gewey tested his movements, but the rattle of the chains caused the guard to stir.

He was just about to try again when a hooded woman in novice robes walked into the tent. She looked at the sleeping guard and drew something from her sleeve. In a flash, her hand shot out and struck the guard's neck. The man woke suddenly, clutching at the point of impact, then abruptly fell from the stool.

"We don't have much time," the woman said as she ran over to Gewey.

He instantly recognized the voice of Celandine, the novice from the temple in Kaltinor. "What are you doing here?"

"Saving your life," she answered as she knelt down and began unshackling him. "Luckily, the governor didn't send his best men along; I thought it would take longer to find a way to get you out."

"Why are you helping me?" Gewey asked.

"Do you really think this the time for questions?" Celandine replied curtly. "We have a clear path to the woods behind the camp."

She ran back over to the guard and took his knife and sword. "I hope you know how to use this," she said, tossing the sword to Gewey.

Celandine used the knife to cut a hole in the back of the tent and then motioned for Gewey to follow as she stepped into the night.

It was dark, but Gewey could make out the tree line twenty yards away. The camp was quiet, aside from the sound of sleeping men. Celandine led Gewey rapidly across the field, and they vanished into the trees.

They ran for about fifteen minutes before they stopped.

"Wait," said Celandine. She took off her robe, revealing a plain shirt tucked into light tan pants. Her honey blond hair was wrapped tightly in a black scarf, and even in the dark Gewey could tell that she was beautiful. He wondered how he'd failed to notice this at the temple.

"I left some supplies under that bush," she said, pointing to a nearby huckleberry bush and tossing her robe at Gewey. "Get the packs and put this inside."

Gewey obeyed. Just as she said, there were two journey packs hidden under the bush. He picked them up and stuffed the robe inside as Celandine fastened the knife she had stolen to her belt.

"I'd guess we have about an hour before they discover you're gone," she said. "We need to move."

They ran west until they reached a small stream and then turned south. They followed the stream for an hour, crossing it several times in order to throw off pursuit. Gewey was impressed by her endurance.

"Are you able to continue?" Celandine asked as they ran.

"Yes," said Gewey. "I can go on for quite a while."

"Good. We don't stop till dawn."

True to her word, they ran south until the morning light shone through the trees. They stopped at the foot of a small hill and sat on the forest floor.

"You see well at night," Gewey said, catching his breath. "You didn't fall once."

Celandine smiled faintly. "That comes from my mother's side."

They sat in awkward silence for a few minutes.

"You need to tell me what's going on here," said Gewey, when he could take the silence no longer.

"What's going on is that Salmitaya is not the only one on a mission to deliver you," she replied.

Gewey jumped to his feet. "What are you saying?"

"Calm yourself," she said. "I have the same goals as your companions."

"How would you know about our goals?" Gewey asked. "Who are you?"

"I'm one of the good guys," she said. "I'm here to help you."

"I've heard that before," he noted. "Do you have proof?"

"You mean, other than the fact that I stopped you from being taken to Angrääl in chains?" she said sarcastically. "No, not really."

Gewey was taken aback. "You know where they were taking me? How?"

"Unlike dear, trusting Maybell, I've been suspicious of Salmitaya for a while," she answered. "Over time, I made a habit of secretly reading all the letters she received. It didn't take long to figure out who the 'High Priestess' really serves."

"But who do you serve?" asked Gewey. "You don't seem like a novice."

"Actually, I am a novice—just not the kind you would have heard about," she replied. "My order isn't widely known, but it's very old. We once protected Heaven itself, and we still battle the darkness to this day. I came to Kaltinor two years ago to investigate the failure of temples throughout the city."

"When you found out about the temples, why didn't you do something?" Gewey asked accusingly. "It doesn't look like you've done anything to help."

"We've done more than you could know," she shot back. "But there are more important things than rescuing a few temples."

"Like what? What could be more important than that?"

"Like finding you and making sure you're delivered safely," she replied.

"Why should I be important?" he asked suspiciously.

"I don't know," said Celandine. "But ... if the Dark One wants you captured, then it's obvious that you are."

"I'm not going anywhere unless you tell me where we're going, and who exactly it is that wants me," Gewey said stubbornly. "So you can save us both some time and just tell me."

"West," she said. "We're going west. Beyond that, I really don't know. There's a temple where you'll be safe, but I don't know exactly where it is."

Gewey laughed. "So we just head west and hope we find this so-called temple? Sounds like a great plan."

Celandine's eyes narrowed. "I said that I don't know where it is—not that I couldn't find it. The location is kept a secret that only a few of us know. I know where to make contact, and from there we'll be taken to the temple."

"What about my friends?" Gewey asked. "How will they know where to find me?"

"If they still live, they're on their own," she said bluntly. "We can't risk going back to find them. If you're captured again, your enemies won't be so careless twice."

"I'm not abandoning my friends," Gewey protested. "They are alive, and they wouldn't leave me behind."

"I think they probably are alive," she agreed. "I doubt the buffoons Salmitaya sent to kill them succeeded. But I'm no warrior, and neither are you. If we go after them, we will be caught, and then your friends will have risked their lives for nothing. Salmitaya is arrogant, but not stupid. If she gets her hands on you again, it will take an army to free you."

"How did you know about Salmitaya's plans in the first place?" Gewey asked. "How did you know to follow her?"

"She sent me away after dinner to spend the night at another temple," she answered. "A habit of hers when she wants to do things unseen. She tells us that one of the other temples wants to ensure a blessing by having a follower of Ayliazarah under their roof. Maybell believed her, but that woman would believe anything. I, on the other hand, packed what I needed and hid outside the temple until morning. I saw the guards arrive, then later drag you out and put you into the carriage. I knew they had left some men behind to deal with your friends, but unfortunately, I had neither the time nor the means to help them. Instead, I followed Salmitaya, hoping for a chance to free you."

Gewey was unsure. "Assuming I believe you, what should we do now?"

"We head west to Althetas," she replied. "We need to find a way to get there unnoticed, and unfortunately I don't have much in the way of supplies or money, so we'll have to improvise."

"Do you know where we are now?" he asked.

"We're north of the Spirit Hills," answered Celandine. "We have enough food to pass through, and there's a town on the southwestern slopes where we should be able to re-supply. From there, we can hopefully find a way further west."

"I still don't feel right about leaving my friends," Gewey said.

"We'll try to send word to them when we can," she replied. "But we have to keep moving. I doubt the guards will be able to keep up with us, but Salmitaya won't give up easily. She'll send trackers."

Celandine got to her feet and held out her hand. Gewey thought for a moment, then pursed his lips.

"I'll go with you," he said, taking her hand. "But don't think that means I've given up on finding my friends. As soon as we're safe, you must promise to find them."

"You have my word," she said, pulling Gewey to his feet.

"Then let's go," he said.

They crossed the stream and headed south toward the hills.

Gewey still wanted to turn back and find Lee, but he knew Celandine was probably right. And if even she wasn't, there was no other choice.

To turn back now would deliver him straight into the clutches of Salmitaya.

CHAPTER 13

Lee and Kaylia ran west along the road at a pace no normal human could match. Lee worried about being noticed, but he knew they had to risk it if they wanted to catch up with Salmitaya. Each time they came to a crossroads, they were forced to stop and make sure their quarry hadn't turned. Fortunately, a carriage with a ten-guard escort left an easy trail to follow.

As the hours passed, Lee worried that Kaylia's strength would give out. He could run a full day without tiring, but he had no experience with the stamina of elves, and he couldn't afford to leave her behind. With a good plan of attack, he was sure he could kill ten city guards, but it would only take one to get to Gewey and cut his throat.

He needed the elf to ensure that didn't happen.

"Do you need to stop?" Lee asked at one of the crossroads.

"Elves are stronger than you know," she replied. "We do not tire easily."

Lee nodded and took off west. Just as the sun was going down, Kaylia grabbed Lee's arm, stopping him.

"They're one mile ahead," said Kaylia. "I can smell them."

They waited until it was fully dark before approaching the camp. Two tents had been erected in a small clearing twenty yards off the road. A carriage pulled by a team of six horses had been pulled just to the side. As they'd been told, ten guards were busy about the camp, building fires and cooking meals. They couldn't see Gewey anywhere.

"Looks like they've been here for more than an hour," Lee noted. "Gewey's probably in one of the tents."

"But which one?" Kaylia asked. "We shouldn't move until we know."

"Agreed," he said. "I'll keep watch from here. You go around through the woods and check from there. Be back here in an hour."

Kaylia nodded and took off through the brush.

Lee watched as Salmitaya wandered through the camp, her head held high as she shouted orders to her men. She walked in and out of both tents but gave no indication as to where Gewey was being held.

An hour later, Kaylia returned.

"These guards should be easy to deal with," she said. "They have no idea how to secure a camp; the entire perimeter is left unwatched. They'll be bunched together near the fires in two groups. Once we know where Gewey is, we can take them out."

Lee nodded, watching as a guard carried a bowl and cup into one of the tents. A little while later, Salmitaya emerged from that tent and went into the other.

"He's in there," said Lee, pointing to the tent Salmitaya had just exited. "I count nine men by the fires, so that leaves only one guarding Gewey."

"We should wait until they're sleeping before we strike," Kaylia proposed. "If one of them raises the alarm, the guard in the tent could kill the boy before we can get to him."

Lee nodded in agreement. They settled in, never taking their eyes off the camp. Lee watched as the guard inside the tent was relieved, careful to take note of the length of time it took for him to return to the fire. It was then they saw a woman in novice robes enter where Gewey was being held.

"How did she get here?" Lee asked anxiously. "Did you see her before?"

Kaylia shook her head. "I think we have a new player in this game. We'll need to move soon."

Lee went over the plan with Kaylia. She was to enter the tent holding Gewey and deal with the guard there, while Lee would take care of the guards by the fire nearest to the tent. If the alarm were raised, Lee would then fall back and join Kaylia and finish off the remaining guards as they approached. If there were no alarm, then Kaylia would wait with Gewey while Lee took out the rest of the guards on his own.

"The important thing is that once we have Gewey, we don't lose sight of him," said Lee. "They may be clumsy fools, but it only takes one to cause us to fail."

"A good plan," she said. "But you should be the one to free the boy. I can kill the other guards more quietly than you."

"Probably," Lee replied. "And it's why you'll be the first in the tent. Slaughtering city guards in their sleep may not be honorable, but it should be easy. If the tent guard is awake, I need him down fast."

"I think you don't like the idea of an elf killing humans in their sleep," she said.

"And I think you like the idea far too much," Lee retorted.

It was then they saw a guard rise from his bedroll and walk toward the tent holding a flask. Lee and Kaylia lay silent. A second later, the man bolted out again, yelling at the top of his lungs. The camp instantly erupted into a beehive of activity. Salmitaya came out of her tent and sprinted to where they were holding Gewey.

"We should pull back before they see us," Kaylia suggested.

"I can hide in shadows too," said Lee, sounding insulted. "If they come near, we'll move—but not until then."

Salmitaya left the tent, while two guards carried a third man next to the fire and threw him roughly to the ground. The remaining guards gathered around the High Priestess to receive their orders. They then headed for the nearby forest in small groups, leaving only the two guards with Salmitaya.

"It would seem our young friend has escaped," Kaylia observed. "And unless I'm wrong, the novice had something to do with it."

"We'll wait a few minutes, then go down and see for ourselves," said Lee. "I'll take the near guard; you take the one walking toward Salmitaya."

The elf smiled ominously and sprung to her feet, rushing toward the camp. Lee chased after her, but it was too late. Kaylia had killed the first guard and had the second on the ground before he could get close. Lee turned toward Salmitaya, hoping to reach the woman before Kaylia did. He made it just in time.

"Enough," said Lee, standing in front of the terrified woman. "I gave my word she would not be harmed."

"I gave no such word," Kaylia replied, holding her bloody knife.

"If you harm her, I'll kill you," warned Lee. "Please don't make me do that."

Kaylia walked over to the shaking woman. "She deserves to die, Lee. You know it."

"Yes, she does," he agreed. "Nonetheless, I ask you to preserve my honor and let her live."

Kaylia studied Lee for a long moment. "I would not want to dishonor you. And I would not want to kill you, either." She locked eyes with Salmitaya, cleaning her knife on the High Priestess' dress. "But should we meet again, woman, my blade will send you to the Father."

Salmitaya collapsed to the ground, weeping.

"Check the tents," Lee said. "See what you can find out." Kaylia took one more look at Salmitaya and obeyed.

Lee turned to the High Priestess. "Calm yourself," he snapped.

"That demon wants to kill me!" Salmitaya cried.

"True," Lee acknowledged. "And I may yet let her if you've harmed my friend. Where is he?"

"I don't know," she answered. "He's escaped."

"I guessed as much. I wonder how Angrääl will reward your failure."

"I don't know what you're talking about," she lied. "I serve the temple."

Lee reached down and helped Salmitaya to her feet. "My dear," he said calmly, "it's that kind of lie that will earn you some private time with my elf friend. I promised that you would not be harmed, but as you've seen, stopping Kaylia could prove to be quite difficult. And I've heard Elven interrogation methods can be rather ... unpleasant."

"You wouldn't," she cried.

Lee's tone turned dangerous. "You kidnapped my friend and tried to have me murdered," he fumed. "It is all I can do not to kill you myself."

Kaylia returned holding a set of iron shackles. "Someone freed him and took him into the forest," she said, throwing the shackles at Salmitaya's feet. "I examined the guard. He was poisoned with a stylus needle."

Lee raised an eyebrow. "Elf poison? Why would an elf want to save Gewey?"

"If it was the same girl we saw entering the tent, she was no elf," Kaylia noted. "But clearly she's familiar with elf tactics."

"In that case, I hope she turns out to be on our side," Lee said, his concern showing in his voice. "Do you think you can track them?"

"Perhaps," she said. "The guards in the woods will slow me down, but I should be able to tell which direction they ran. That is unless this girl hides like an elf as well."

"I'll gather three of their horses and meet you two miles east of here," said Lee. "Find out what you can." Kaylia started off toward the woods.

"Kaylia," called Lee.

She paused and turned her head slightly.

"Try not to kill all the guards," he said.

Kaylia smiled and disappeared into the night.

"She'll kill every one of them," Salmitaya said, her words dripping with contempt. "Elves only understand blood."

"And yet, you live," Lee pointed out. He saddled three horses, then chased off the others so that the guards could not follow. He mounted one horse and signaled for Salmitaya to mount another.

"If you try to escape," he warned, "I swear, I'll hog tie you and carry you over my saddle."

Salmitaya glared angrily.

They rode east for two miles before hiding in the woods next to the road. "Now that I have you alone," said Lee, "you'll answer a few more questions for me."

Salmitaya lowered her eyes, looking defeated.

"How long have you served the Dark Knight?" he asked.

"The Dark Knight?" she scoffed. "I serve the power of Angräal that seeks to release us from slavery. The Dark Knight is merely an instrument."

"You'll find that I'm not easily distracted," said Lee. "How long?"

"Eight years," she replied.

"How many others are there?" he asked.

Salmitaya laughed. "How should I know? We are not told the identity of others. No knowledge—no betrayal."

Lee pressed the matter further. "Of course. But surely you've run into others from time to time."

"I have," she admitted. "But never the same person twice, and not for more than for a few moments. If you want me to give you names, I can't. Torture me all you want, I don't know."

"Is there a way you recognize others like you?" asked Lee. "A signal, or some sort of clothing?"

"The only way I can tell is if a person bears the seal of the Great Lord himself," she explained. "It's a hand holding broken scales. I've seen it many times, but we all have orders to destroy it right away once received. That's the only way I know." She turned away and faced the darkness of the forest. "Ask me nothing more. I have no knowledge of plans or strategy. I know nothing that can help you."

"Perhaps," Lee said. "But you still have to convince one more person."

"The bloody elf? She would cut my throat before listening to me."

"It's not the elf you need to convince," Lee chuckled. "Your fate rests in the hands of Sister Maybell."

Salmitaya's eyes widened. "You brought her with you? Where is she?"

"She's safe," he answered. "Waiting for us to return this very moment, in fact."

"She's a fool," spat Salmitaya. "A blind old fool."

"I spared your life because of a promise I made to that blind old fool," Lee warned. "You had better pray she holds me to it."

Lee could sense her sudden fear.

Kaylia showed up with a look of concern and confusion on her face. Lee walked with her out of earshot of Salmitaya.

"Whoever this woman is, she's clever and moves with great speed," Kaylia whispered. "It would take me two days to catch them if I persisted, so I doubt the guards have any chance at all."

"That would be good news if we knew who she was," Lee said.

"Could you tell where they're going?"

"I think they're heading into the Spirit Hills," she replied. "Any other direction would take them back to the road. I doubt they'll risk exposure until they're well away from here."

"There's a village on the southwest slopes that they'll likely stop at for supplies," said Lee. "Even at a dead run, it would take them three days to make their way through such rough terrain. On horseback, we can reach the village ahead of them if we take the road and go around. Unless they sprout wings and learn to fly, we should be able to head them off."

"What of the woman?" Kaylia asked. "You don't intend to leave her here, do you?"

"We'll ride to Fair Harvest first," Lee responded. "I promised to deliver her to Sister Maybell. A delay, I know, but we should still be able to beat Gewey and this mystery woman by a full day."

"Very well," said Kaylia. "I don't like delays, but I would like to see this reunion." A sinister smile crept over her face.

Lee threw his head back in laughter. "No doubt Maybell will be quite put out." He paused, struck by a sudden thought. "By the way, did you leave any of the guards alive?"

"Yes," answered Kaylia. "But I doubt they'll venture into the forest after dark again."

Lee smiled. "We're off, then."

The three mounted their horses and headed east until they reached a crossroads, where they turned south toward Fair Harvest.

It took them until mid-morning to arrive, and by that time, their horses were spent. Lee knew he would have to purchase replacements if they expected to catch Gewey.

Fair Harvest was little more than a large camp supported by a few local farmers and traders. The town had only one road, with a few small shops and dwellings scattered on either side; the inn at the southwest corner of the village was by far the largest building. Seeing the state of things, Lee grew concerned that he wouldn't be able to find decent horses. They approached the inn, tied their mounts to the hitching post, and led Salmitaya inside.

The interior of the inn was even less impressive than the exterior. Three tables and a small bar were the grand sum of the common room.

Two locals sat in the corner drinking ale while the barmaid leaned against the wall, playing with her hair.

The innkeeper, who had been rummaging around behind the bar, rose to his feet as they approached. "Can I help you?" he asked, staring at the hooded figure of Kaylia.

"We have two friends staying here," said Lee. "Could you tell someone to get them for me?"

"Indeed, sir," said the innkeeper. "They're here all right. You'll be taking them along with you, I trust?"

"Why do you ask?" Lee said warily. "Has there been trouble?"

"Not so much trouble," he replied, "but I swear that woman could drive a nitfly mad. I mean, look around. Does this look like a palace to you?" The man gestured to the meager décor. "You'd think she was the Queen herself by the way she makes demands."

Lee smiled. "Could you go get them, please?" he asked, tossing the man a copper.

"Yes, sir," said the innkeeper. "Right away." He disappeared up the stairs.

Seconds later, Millet came running downstairs and pulled Lee into a tight embrace. "Thank the gods you're here; that woman is driving me mad." Releasing his grip on Lee, Millet noticed Salmitaya.

"I see you have her, but what about the boy?"

"Let's go upstairs where we can talk," said Lee. "Where's Maybell?"

"In her room," said Millet sourly, leading them upstairs. "She refuses to come out until she gets a proper bath. The wash basin isn't to her liking."

"Well, she can get one back in Kaltinor if she wants," Lee quipped, slapping Millet on the shoulder.

"Indeed," Millet huffed.

"We'll take care of this one first," Lee instructed, holding Salmitaya by the arm. "Show us to Maybell's room."

Millet knocked on the old woman's door.

"Unless you're here with a proper bathtub and hot water, go away!" Maybell called from behind the door.

"Open up," Lee said sternly.

They heard the woman scuffling around, and then the door swung open.

"We have someone here to see you," Lee said, pushing Salmitaya inside.

Maybell immediately noticed the blood on Salmitaya's dress. "You said she wouldn't be harmed!"

"And she hasn't been," said Lee. "That's not her blood."

Maybell looked in horror at the bloodstained dress. "Then whose blood is it?"

"Before I get to that," said Lee, looking at Salmitaya. "I think Her Holiness has a few things she'd like to tell you. The deal is that she lives so long as she tells the truth."

Salmitaya glared at Lee. "Very well," she said, then turned toward Maybell. "What I am going to tell you is the complete truth. Once you've heard it, you are to decide my fate. On the head of Ayliazarah and the essence of my soul, I swear that my words are not false."

Salmitaya proceeded to tell Maybell how she had conspired with the governor to close the temples. She told her about the murders and deceptions she had been a part of. Maybell listened carefully, but her face betrayed no emotion—not even when Salmitaya confessed to serving Angrääl and kidnapping Gewey for the Dark Knight.

When she was finished, Maybell stood up tall and straight. She looked directly into Salmitaya's eyes.

"I cast you out," said Maybell, her voice quiet and calm. "The eyes of the temple will no longer see you. Your name will be stricken from the Book of the Eternal Light and shall not be spoken again. I give you your life, only so that you may see the day when you and your master suffer as you have made others suffer." She paused, still locking eyes with Salmitaya. "Now, leave from my sight before I forget myself and kill you where you stand."

"Put her in your room, Millet," said Lee. He then looked over to Kaylia. "Give her some jawas tea and leave her there. She can make her way back to Kaltinor, or wherever else she wants to go, when she wakes up."

As soon as the door closed, Maybell sat on the bed and wept.

"Millet will see that you get safely back to Kaltinor," Lee said, placing his hand gently on Maybell's shoulder. "If, of course, that's where you want to go."

Maybell wiped her tears and said, "I can't go back. No matter what I said, that woman has power enough to keep herself safely locked away in the temple. She could crush an old woman like me."

"Then where do you want to go?" Lee asked. Maybell opened her mouth to reply, but Kaylia and Millet returned before she could give her answer.

"Kaylia and I need to leave as soon as we're able," Lee explained. "Millet, you'll take the wagon south to the Old Road of Santismal, then continue west. Whoever freed Gewey is likely to pass through Vine Run on the southwest slope of the Spirit Hills. Kaylia and I will try to cut them off while you follow behind."

"You never told me what happened to Gewey," said Millet. "Where is he?"

Lee related the events of the past day and explained their plan.

"I will see to the horses now," said Millet. "You should eat and rest for a bit."

"One more thing," Lee said, turning toward Maybell. "Sister, if you wish, you can accompany Millet until you either reach another temple or figure out where it is you want to go."

Millet froze. "But my lord…" he began.

"Thank you," Maybell interrupted. "That is very kind. I'm sure Millet and I will become fast friends."

Millet looked pained as he turned and left. Kaylia said nothing, but Lee could tell she was not happy.

"If you'll excuse us, Sister," Lee said, motioning for Kaylia to join him in the hall.

"She will slow us down," Kaylia asserted. "You should leave her."

"You're right," Lee acknowledged. "But I won't. She's a lady of worth and honor, and I will not abandon such a person."

"Answer me this, half-man," she countered. "When you came upon me in the forest, was it you who decided to come to my aid?"

Lee had no answer.

"I see," she said.

"The fact is, I was wrong and Gewey was right," Lee said, finally. "Given the same choice again, I would help you."

"You misunderstand," she replied. "Helping me was foolish. You were right to want to leave me. And know this: given the same choice today, I would leave you."

Lee chuckled.

"Something amuses you?" asked Kaylia.

"It's just … that is the first thing I've heard you say that I don't believe," said Lee. "Come, let's eat."

CHAPTER 14

It was well into the afternoon when Gewey and Celandine reached the foot of the Spirit Hills. Though they had stopped running, Gewey was beginning to feel the fatigue in his legs as they walked onward.

"I don't think we're being followed," said Celandine. "All the same, we should be well into the hills before we stop."

"Where are you from?" Gewey asked, trying to make conversation.

"Baltria," she answered. "But I haven't been there since I was a child."

"Do you remember what it was like?"

"Vaguely. Mostly just flashes of memory. I do remember the smell of the salt air coming in off the bay. My father would take me to see the ships, and that smell always told me when we were close. What about you? Where are you from?"

"Nowhere you would have heard of," said Gewey, not wanting to give away too much about himself.

"Don't worry," she said, sensing his trepidation. "While I'd love to know why you're deemed to be so important, I'm not going to force it out of you."

"What do you know about me?" Gewey inquired.

"I was given your description and name, and was told that if I found you, I should keep you safe until you could be delivered to the temple."

Gewey looked puzzled. "Why would your temple care about me?"

"We have spies among the Dark Knight's followers, and when we learned that he was after you, we knew we had to get to you first," Celandine answered. "Other than that, I don't know much."

"What's your temple like?" Gewey asked.

"It's a place of training and worship," she explained. "Only a few of us are permitted to go there, and I must admit I'm curious why a farm boy is worth this journey."

"Me too," Gewey said.

Celandine laughed. Her laugh sounded like a song to Gewey, and it made him have thoughts that caused him to blush.

"How old are you?" she asked.

"Why?" Gewey replied. "How old do I look?"

"Your size says a grown man in his twenties," she remarked. "But your eyes tell a different story."

"I'm seventeen," he announced. "But I've been my own man for two years."

Celandine smiled sweetly and looked closely at him. "You are very young, but I have no doubt that you are your own man. I meant no offense."

"It's just that Lee and the others treat me like a child," he admitted. "Back home, I have my own land and run a farm by myself. Here, I feel like I'm growing up all over again."

"But when it comes to the world, you are," Celandine replied.

"Your friends only want to protect you, as do I."

"I don't need protecting," Gewey said bitterly. "I can take care of myself."

"I could tell," she teased. "Salmitaya must have been terrified."

"I would have escaped sooner or later!" Gewey protested. "I didn't need rescuing."

"Be that as it may," she said sternly, "I did rescue you, and I would think you would show a little appreciation."

Gewey felt ashamed. "I'm sorry. I do appreciate your help, Celandine. I really do. I just get sick of feeling so bloody helpless."

"I understand," she said sympathetically. "I know what it's like to feel helpless, but trust me, once you get to the temple, you'll never have to feel that way again."

"I hope you're right," Gewey replied earnestly.

"One more thing," said Celandine. "My friends call me Dina—or at least, they did when I had friends."

Gewey smiled. "Dina, then."

By the time the sun went down, they were well into the interior of the Spirit Hills. They built a small fire at the base of one of the hills and split a loaf of flatbread Dina had brought.

After they ate, Gewey lay down on the grass to rest, using his journey pack as a pillow. The stars were obscured by the constant overcast clouds, and he felt the chill of the damp night air creep into his clothing.

Lee's words about the coming of a hard winter echoed in his head, and suddenly his mind went to thoughts of the villagers in Sharpstone. They had seen too many hard winters—too many deaths.

Somehow, he would find a way to make things right.

Dina was huddled close to the fire, already asleep. Gewey watched the firelight as it danced across her face. He wanted to go to her and feel the softness of her cheek against his hand. She stirred for a moment, and Gewey felt himself blush with embarrassment. He rolled over and tried to sleep, but he couldn't take his mind off her.

Finally, he got up and walked off into the night, careful not to wake her. He closed his eyes and breathed the cold air into his lungs.

Remembering Kaylia's lessons, he focused his mind on the darkness that surrounded him. The trees in this part of the hills were thick and numerous, so Gewey decided to practice moving through the shadows.

It wasn't long before he had forgotten Dina and lost himself in his training. The darkness opened itself up to him, showing him where to hide, how to move, and where to strike.

"You move like an elf," said a voice from behind him. Gewey spun around and saw a thin, old man dressed in animal skins and holding a gnarled tree branch as a walking stick. His long gray hair was tangled and unkempt, and his wiry beard fell down his chest. Gewey, realizing that he had left his sword back at the fire, took a quick step backward.

"Who are you?" he stammered.

"The spirits tell me that you are something special," the old man answered. "I wanted to see for myself."

"Spirits?" Gewey asked. "What spirits?"

"They tell me you need my help," he continued as if Gewey hadn't spoken. "Yes, they do. They tell me things. Things you should know. Things you shouldn't. They're very clever."

"Tell me who you are," Gewey demanded. "What do you want?"

"He asks what we want. He does. What could we want? Nothing, that's what. We have all we need. But you want something, don't you? You want something very badly. Don't worry. No, don't you worry. You'll have it. Yes, indeed, you will. I'll give it."

"What will you give me?" Gewey asked, confused.

"No, not yet," said the old man. "Not now, but soon. Very soon."

The old man turned and walked away, disappearing behind a nearby tree. Gewey chased after him, but he was nowhere to be found. He searched for over an hour, but to no avail. It was as if the old man had vanished like a puff of smoke.

When he went back to the camp, he woke Dina and told her what had happened.

"Did he say anything else?" she asked.

"Nothing," he answered.

Dina thought for a while. "I don't know," she said finally. "The Spirit Hills are said to be an odd place—haunted even— but I've never heard of anything like this."

"What should we do?" Gewey wondered.

"What can we do?" she replied. "I say we get some rest and see what happens. It doesn't sound like whoever it was is finished with you, but I don't see how we can do anything about that."

The next day, Gewey and Dina hardly spoke a word. The Spirit Hills seemed to be living up to their name; Gewey held tight to his sword, ready to strike at every snap of a twig, while Dina continually looked back and forth over her shoulder as if expecting to see ghosts emerge from every shadow. As they moved deeper into the hills, Gewey could feel the air becoming thicker. By mid-afternoon, he was struggling to breathe.

"We're being watched," Dina whispered.

"From where?" Gewey asked.

"Everywhere," she replied. "I can feel their eyes on us."

Suddenly, a voice came from behind them. "Eyes, you say?" Gewey's heart nearly leaped out of his chest. It was the old man. He was sitting on the ground under a tree they had just passed.

"Not eyes," said the old man. His voice was mirthful, and he was still wearing his animal skins. His walking stick lay across his lap. "No, not eyes. But they see you. Of course, they do."

"Who sees us?" asked Gewey. "Who's out there?"

The old man laughed heartily. "A child of heaven you are," said the old man to Gewey. "You walk the Spirit Hills. They see you. They love you. They want you to stay. But you mustn't. No, no. They'll keep you for themselves. But I'll keep them away. Yes, I'll threaten to leave them, I will. Leave them alone. No more old man Felsafell to talk to."

"Is that your name?" Gewey asked. "Felsafell?"

"Yes, my name," he answered. "I'm at your service. I'll tell you what you seek to know. But first, you come. We sit and talk. So long since I've heard other voices. Welcome they are, to tired ears and blurry eyes."

Felsafell grabbed his walking stick and hopped to his feet. He walked past Gewey and Dina, beckoning them to follow. They looked at each other, confused.

"You mustn't fear," Felsafell assured them. "I mean no harm. The spirits will obey. They'll leave you be. Come along now, quickly. An old man must eat and rest."

Reluctantly, Gewey and Dina followed. Felsafell led them through the hills and valleys for over an hour until Gewey knew he was hopelessly lost. Finally, as they rounded one of the larger hills, they saw Felsafell's house.

It looked as if it were built entirely of small twigs and grass. There were two windows covered by cloth curtains, but there was no glass.

Smoke rose from a chimney atop the steep thatched roof, and the air was filled with the scent of bread and meat. A small porch stretched from the front of the house, with three wicker chairs lined up beneath one of the windows.

"We're here, my friends," said Felsafell. "Come in. Take food and rest. The spirits are quiet now. They are indeed."

Felsafell opened the door and showed them in. The interior was simple, much like Gewey's own home. The walls were lined with tools and animal skins. In the fireplace was a spit where a wild pig slowly roasted. On the table were two large jugs and a loaf of fresh bread. Two beds sat in the corner of the room. A bedroll lay on the ground next to the fireplace.

"Sit and eat," Felsafell instructed. "Time for talk when our bellies are full. Sit and rest."

Gewey and Dina sat at the table while Felsafell ran to the corner and brought back three cups. He filled the cups with cider, then went to the roasting pig and began cutting off large slices and putting them on a platter.

"A simple meal of meat and bread," said Felsafell as he brought the platter to the table and sat down. "No fancy things, you know. But I have all that is needed."

"Thank you," said Gewey graciously. "Roast pig and bread is most welcome."

Felsafell smiled broadly, showing a mouthful of crooked teeth.

"Too kind," he said. "I'll try hard to speak as men do. So long with the ghosts and spirits. No voice, but old Felsafell's to keep me company."

"How long have you been here?" asked Dina, tearing off a piece of bread.

"Questions later, dear friends," Felsafell replied. "Questions after food and rest. An old man can travel far, but not forever. No, he can't."

After they ate, Felsafell poured a cup of cherry wine from the second jug and passed it around. For a while he closed his eyes, humming softly and holding the cup in both hands. Gewey noticed the light through the window beginning to dim as evening drew near.

"Time for rest," said Felsafell. "You take the beds. Old Felsafell sleeps by the fire. But don't you worry. We will speak before the dawn."

Dina and Gewey lay down in the beds, which were remarkably soft and comfortable. Felsafell lay down on the bedroll in front of the fire and was fast asleep in seconds.

"What do you think?" Gewey whispered. "Is he crazy?"

"Maybe," Dina answered. "But I don't think he's dangerous. Still, we should be wary."

Gewey nodded in agreement. He tried to stay awake, but it wasn't long before a full stomach and a soft bed got the better of him.

"Rested enough, my friend," said Felsafell, shaking Gewey softly. "Time for questions. Time for answers."

Felsafell walked across the room and opened the front door. "On the porch, we'll talk. All your answers are out here."

Gewey heard Felsafell walk across the porch and sit in one of the chairs. He took a deep breath and got out of bed. Dina was still sleeping soundly. He approached the open door and peered outside. Felsafell was seated, smoking a pipe and gazing into the night.

"Time for answers, child of heaven," he said.

CHAPTER 15

Gewey pulled out a chair across from Felsafell and sat down. The old man had a quirky smile. The pipe filled the night air with a sweet odor that reminded Gewey of his father, who had himself smoked a pipe on occasion. "It's answers you seek," Felsafell began. "Yet you don't know all the questions."

"Why did you call me 'child of heaven'?" asked Gewey. "What do you know about me?"

"I know many things. The spirits are clever. They share with old Felsafell the things they know. Yes, they do indeed. They say the earthbound son of two shepherds comes to visit. They say he needs to know things. Things known by none."

"What do I need to know?" Gewey asked impatiently.

"Your strength," Felsafell replied. "You do not know it. From the earth, it comes, and there you'll find it. Your father left it there."

"My father? Do you know who he is?"

Felsafell nodded. "A farmer, of course. Just like you. He left his land in your care. Search the earth and find your strength."

"I don't understand," Gewey said. "Where exactly should I search?"

"Old Felsafell is not the source," he answered. "The spirits are a tricky lot. What they say may not be what they mean. But more there is to tell before the dawn greets us. Though dawn is not what it used to be."

"Tell me, then," Gewey urged him.

Felsafell smiled. "Of course, the young are always full of haste. But hurry you must, for the darkness comes. It closes the eyes and deafens the ears. The spirits fear it will be their end. They see as their doom approaches."

"You're talking about the Dark Knight. What do you know about him?"

"The Cold One in his castle," Felsafell continued. "He wants you. And he will have you. By his power, you will fall. But fall you must, to open your eyes."

"You mean I'm beaten?" Gewey cried out. "I lose?"

"Beaten, yes," Felsafell affirmed.

Gewey's face dropped in despair. "What's the point of all this if I can't win? Why even tell me?"

"Now you know," said Felsafell. "You know what you didn't. Will you stop? I think you will not. But more to tell before the dawn greets us. Would you hear it?"

Gewey sighed and looked up at the old man. "Yes, I'll hear it."

"Your friends are true," he declared. "But be warned. One will leave this world. The one who is bravest will give all. This friend will save you with courage and love."

"Who will die?" Gewey demanded. "Tell me."

"I know not. If the spirits know, they refuse to say."

"But they must," Gewey said in anguish. "You have to make them."

"I cannot," he replied. "Love me, they do indeed. I stay with them and talk to them when others flee. But I am not master here."

"Is there anything I can do?" begged Gewey.

"There's always something to be done," he answered. "But change what is to be? I cannot say. The spirits are clever, but they only see. They do not push and pull the world as men and elves. But more there is to tell before dawn greets us. It comes soon, and as it comes, you must go."

"Tell me then," Gewey said, "do my friends still live?"

"Good news I have for you. Indeed, they live, but be warned: the child of two worlds and the child of one. Their future is uncertain. By your words, you will see one live or die. You must see this approach before time runs out."

"I don't understand," Gewey implored.

"You will when the time is right. Some secrets are not for me to tell. But soon enough, you'll see your friends. They wait for you."

"Where are they?"

"They're not far," he said. "You need not search. They will find you. Take comfort. There is one more thing to tell that you must hear. The dawn is saying hello, and your time with old Felsafell is at an end."

Gewey leaned forward. "What is it?"

"Before the time when good and evil take up arms, you must decide. To seek the friendship of your mother's child, or leave to fate that child's future."

"My mother?" Gewey exclaimed. "My mother didn't have any other children. First, you tell me a friend will die saving me, and then you ramble on about my mother. You know what I think? I think you're just a crazy old man."

Gewey got up and stormed off the porch. He stopped after a few yards and gazed toward the forest. The dawn light was beginning to filter through the trees, revealing a light mist that covered the surrounding hills.

"Old, for sure," Felsafell called out, laughing. "Crazy, yes. But that changes nothing. No, it does not. You know what I say is no lie. Deny it as you wish; it matters not to me.

My time nears its end and old bones will rest at last. But come inside and take repast. You must go before the dawn turns to day."

Gewey stifled his anger and followed Felsafell inside. Dina was just waking. Gewey thought she looked beautiful as she sat up and stretched her arms.

"Good morning," she said. "You slept well, I hope?"

"Yes," Gewey replied. "But we need to get moving soon. I think I've had enough of this place."

Dina looked concerned. "Did something happen?"

"Nothing important," Gewey answered. "But I want to get out of these hills by tomorrow."

Felsafell had already laid out two bowls of porridge and cups of water. "Eat first," he insisted. "But eat fast. You must go if you would see your friends."

Gewey and Dina ate breakfast and gathered their packs. As they left the cottage, Felsafell handed each of them a loaf of bread and a few slices of roast pork wrapped in cloth. They thanked him, though Gewey was still clearly upset by their conversation.

"Head west from here," Felsafell instructed. "The path you find will lead you safely away. Farewell."

Gewey nodded but said nothing more before setting off in the direction Felsafell had told them. Dina followed close behind, humming sweetly.

"What's that song?" asked Gewey. "It sounds familiar."

"I doubt you know it," she said. "My mother sang it to me when I was very young."

"Where is she now?"

"She died when I was a small girl," she said sadly. "I don't remember much about her."

"I'm sorry," Gewey replied. "My mother died when I was young, too."

"No sad talk this morning," she said, smiling brightly. "Did the old man talk to you?"

"Yes," Gewey said, shaking his head. "Turns out he was just a crazy old man."

"Really? I'm not so sure. There's something about him."

"Did he speak to you?" Gewey asked.

Dina nodded. "He woke me up in the middle of the night while you were still sleeping. He knew things—things nobody else knows."

"What did he say?"

"Nothing I want to tell right now," she answered. "Some of his words were troubling, and I would prefer to have a pleasant morning."

"I agree," Gewey said. He tried to put it out of his mind, but he couldn't stop thinking about what Felsafell had told him. He would fall to the power of the Dark Knight. Even worse, one of his friends would die. He swore he wouldn't let that happen.

They found the trail Felsafell had told them about and headed south. The rest of the day was uneventful. Gewey kept their conversation light, saying nothing of his talk with the old man. The trail seemed to defy the rugged terrain, staying level and smooth, and by the evening they had managed to cover many miles. They decided not to camp and instead continued on; they were both still remarkably full of energy. Gewey attributed it to sleeping in a soft bed and eating a hearty breakfast, but Dina told him she thought it was the spirits urging them on.

"I think they're trying to help us," she remarked. "It's almost like they're giving me strength."

"I don't know," said Gewey. "But I do feel rested."

"At your age, you should always feel rested," she teased.

"How old are you?" Gewey snapped. "You can't be much older than I am."

"You'd be surprised," she laughed. "I'm older than I look."

"That's not an answer."

"No, it's not," she said with a wry smile. "But you never ask a lady her age."

The night air was near freezing, but Gewey and Dina didn't seem to notice. They walked cheerfully down the trail, talking and laughing.

Daybreak came and went. Still, neither of them felt any hint of fatigue. They were nearing the southern end of the Spirit Hills, and Dina guessed that the road leading west to the hillside village of Vine Run was less than half a day away.

"Once we reach the road, it's a straight shot to the village," Dina explained. "If we hurry, we should get there by midday tomorrow."

This lifted Gewey's spirits. He hoped Lee would be waiting in the village so he could talk to him about what Felsafell had said.

By noon, they had reached the road and headed west. The path was cut straight through the hills and spanned as wide as thirty feet in some places. As they traveled, Gewey saw immense stone carvings of ancient kings lining the road. Some of these stood more than twenty feet high. They sat down to eat in the shadow of one of these massive carvings.

"Do you know who put them here?" Gewey asked.

"This is the Old Road of Santismal," Dina stated. "Long ago, this was the heart of a great kingdom, and this road cut right through the middle of it. It's said that the Kingdom of Santismal was the richest and most powerful the world had ever seen."

"What happened to it?" he asked, gazing at the weathered statue.

"Some say war, others say famine." Dina shrugged. "No one really knows. All that's left are a few scattered ruins and this road. Some parts are still paved in stone, but most of it has been washed away by time."

Gewey marveled at the thought of a massive paved road and the work it must have taken to build it, not to mention the effort it would take to transport the statues.

"They must have been a great people," said Gewey. "Have you seen the ruins?"

"Some," Dina replied. "Even in ruins, the buildings stand taller than any today."

"I hope I get to see them one day," he said.

"I'm sure you will," she affirmed.

When sunset came, their energy finally ran out, and they made camp. They finished off the meat and bread Felsafell had given them and lay down on the soft grass. Two straight days of walking, with only very short stops, made sleep come quickly.

Gewey awoke to a bitter cold. The fire had died, and he could see that Dina was shivering in her sleep. He reached over and shook her awake. Dina rubbed her eyes and stretched.

"A bit chilly this morning," she yawned.

"Winter's coming early this year," Gewey remarked.

"It's only a few hours until we reach Vine Run," said Dina. "There's an inn there where we can rest for a bit."

The thought of a warm fire and blankets energized Gewey. He got some flatbread from his pack and split it with Dina. Shivering, the two ate next to the remains of their fire.

As they approached the village, Gewey could immediately tell why it was called Vine Run. The surrounding hills had been cleared and turned into massive vineyards that stretched on for hundreds of yards in all directions. It had clearly been beautiful once, but now the vines were bare and withered. The ground was a dull gray, matching the cloudy sky.

The village itself also showed signs of decay. The multicolored brick houses were cracked and in dire need of repair. Several of the wooden structures had burned to the ground, and the streets were practically abandoned. Only a few people walked about, and they all stared at Gewey and Dina as they passed.

When they reached the inn, Gewey was thankful to be away from such a depressing sight. Happily, the inn's common room turned out to be a complete contrast to the rest of the desolate town. It was packed with at least thirty people, and a fire roared in the hearth, filling the room with warmth and cheer. A flute could be heard from the far corner, and the crowd was singing merrily along. Gewey and Dina pushed their way to the counter, where a short, round woman with a pleasant smile stood swaying to the music.

"Greetings to you, sir," she said. "Just arrived?"

"Yes, we have," said Dina, before Gewey could speak. "We need a room and a hot meal."

"That's grand!" the woman exclaimed, clapping her hands together. "Always plenty of room here. As for the meal, you just missed the midday supper, but I can get you some bread and maybe a bit of lamb if those scoundrels in the back haven't eaten it all."

She reached to a shelf behind her and grabbed a large jug and two cups. "Maybe this will make it up to you," she said. "The finest wine for a thousand miles. We make it right here, or at least, we did in the past. Vines aren't what they used to be, you know. They'll come back though, you just wait and see. In the meantime, we have plenty of spirits to go around."

"Thank you," said Gewey, taking the wine. "I'm looking for some friends who might have come through here."

"If it's friends you're after, you'll make plenty tonight," said the bar matron. "Young Bartol Greenward turns eighteen today—half the town will be in and out of here. But don't you worry—if it's quiet you want, you won't hear a peep from the back. Our walls are thick. But I hope you join us for a while. It looks to be a grand party."

"What about strangers?" Gewey asked. "Have any come through here in the past couple of days?"

The woman crinkled her nose in thought. "Can't really tell," she said. "Been out sick until this morning. Dreadful sick. Feeling better now, though. Ready for the celebration." An old man pushed his way behind the counter and whispered something into her ear.

"Yes, I am, you old goat," she said crossly. "I was just about to show them to their room, wasn't I?" she asked, turning toward Gewey and Dina.

"Yes, you were," Gewey said, clearly amused by her reaction.

The bar matron turned back to the old man. "You see? Now go back to your wine and leave me be."

The woman led Gewey and Dina through a door in the corner of the common room. Gewey scanned the crowd, trying to catch sight of Lee, Millet, or Kaylia, but he didn't see any of them.

"I forgot to ask," said the woman. "How many rooms will you be needing?" Gewey froze and could feel himself blushing.

"I ... uh..." he stammered.

"Forgive my husband," Dina said. "He sometimes forgets we're no longer bound by our parents. One room will be fine."

"That's quite all right," said the woman. "My old goat of a husband forgets we're even married at all." She unlocked the door and handed Dina the key. "You keep this, my love. Men can't be trusted with anything. Now I must get back. The old goat will bring you some water for the basin. I'll see your meal is brought in as well, if you want."

"Yes, thank you," said Dina.

"Grand," said the woman. "I'm Minnie if you need anything. And my husband's name... Well, you can just call him old goat. He answers to that more than anything else." With that, Minnie scurried off down the hall.

The room was simple but comfortable. The washbasin in the corner was large enough to stand in, and the small table and chairs were well-made. But the thing that Gewey noticed most of all was the single bed.

"Husband?" he asked.

Dina smiled. "I suppose I could have said brother. But I was taken off guard, and we can't afford two rooms."

"You weren't the only one taken off guard."

"Don't worry," she said playfully. "Being my husband won't be so bad."

Gewey couldn't meet her eyes for fear his embarrassment would show.

A little while later, Minnie's husband brought their wash water. "I'll bring your meal in half an hour," he said sourly before skulking out of the room.

"It'll feel good to be clean," said Dina. "I have fresh clothes for you in my pack." She stood there staring at Gewey with eyebrows raised.

"What?" exclaimed Gewey.

"Turn around, if you don't mind," Dina instructed. "Unless you intend to watch me bathe."

Gewey blushed for what felt like the hundredth time and turned to face the door. He felt his heart race as he heard Dina bathing behind him. By the time she was finished and dressed, he could hardly breathe.

"Your turn," she said, drying her hair with a towel that had been placed on the bed. Gewey didn't move.

"Come now," she teased. "I'll look away." Gewey's hands shook as he disrobed and began to wash.

"Very nice," Dina said suggestively.

Gewey spun around, nearly knocking over the basin, but Dina was still facing the door.

"That's not funny," he fumed.

"I'm sorry," Dina laughed. "I'll be good. I promise."

Gewey washed and dressed as fast as he could.

There was a knock at the door, and Minnie's husband brought them their meal. It was far more than the bar matron had said there might be; clearly, she'd gotten to the leftover lamb before anyone else.

As they ate, Gewey tried not to think about his earlier embarrassment, but he was still unable to look Dina in the eye.

"I think I'll save the wine for the journey," Dina said, holding up the jug Minnie had given them.

"Good idea."

"I suppose we should see if your friends are anywhere about," she said, finishing her last bite of lamb. Gewey nodded in agreement.

The common room was still bustling with partygoers. Several tables had been pushed aside and a dance contest had broken out in the center of the floor. It reminded Gewey of birthdays back home.

He scanned the room, hoping to catch a glimpse of his companions, but he couldn't see much through the crowd. He forced his way to the far wall and stood on a chair. Without warning, he was lifted off his feet and thrown over a broad shoulder. Before he could do anything, he was being spun around. He struggled to free himself, but his assailant lifted him up and sat him down hard in a chair. It was Lee. Gewey saw Dina approaching from behind him with her knife drawn.

"Dina, stop!" Gewey cried. "I've found them."

Dina put her knife back in her belt and covered it with her shirt.

"I see your taste in travel companions has improved," said Lee, smiling widely.

"How did you find me?" Gewey asked.

"Luck, combined with a bit of skill," Lee answered, laughing and slapping Gewey on the back. He turned to

Dina. "So you're the one who helped my young friend. Celandine, right?"

"Please, call me Dina," she said. "And you're Lee Starfinder. Where are your companions?"

"I see you and your husband decided to join us," said Minnie as she passed by with a tray of wine. "And found a friend, I see!" She disappeared into the crowd.

"Husband?" Lee exclaimed, bursting into laughter. "You've been busy."

"It's not funny," Gewey objected. "Anyway, where's Kaylia and Millet?"

"Kaylia's in her room," Lee replied. "And Millet should be here by tomorrow. But I don't think we should talk here."

Lee led them to the room where Kaylia was staying. She smiled brightly when Gewey entered, but the smile vanished when Dina followed behind. She regarded the other woman with open suspicion.

"I see we have yet another traveler," Kaylia noted. "I take it she's the one we saw at Salmitaya's camp?"

"You saw us escape?" Gewey asked, surprised.

"I think we need to slow down," said Lee. He proceeded to tell Gewey and Dina the events of the past few days.

"I would have given anything to hear Sister Maybell cast out that witch," Dina said once Lee had finished. "She was right not to return to Kaltinor, though. Salmitaya would have killed her."

"Since we arrived, we've just been waiting," Lee continued. "Kaylia hasn't enjoyed it too much. I don't think she's ever stayed at an inn—too many humans for her taste."

Kaylia looked at Dina. "You don't seem surprised to discover that I'm an elf," she said coolly. "I assume Gewey told you. It makes me wonder what else he's told you."

"There have been many surprises in the last few days," Dina replied. "One more doesn't shock me."

"I told her nothing," Gewey asserted. "Give me a little credit."

"From the look of things, you have a story to tell as well," Lee said.

"Yes," Kaylia agreed, still eying Dina warily. "So it seems, and I would love to hear it."

Dina told her story up until the rescue of Gewey, at which point Gewey took over. Lee and Kaylia listened intently to every detail. When Gewey got to the part about Felsafell, Lee and Kaylia both sat up straight, paying even closer attention. Gewey left out the details of what the old man had told him while sitting together on the porch, preferring to save that for a more private conversation with Lee. When he was finished, Lee got up, laughing.

"My boy," he said. "You have had some adventure. Worthy of one of my tales."

Kaylia wasn't amused. Her eyes turned back to Dina. "I take it you intend to accompany us?"

"I intend to do what I set out to do," Dina responded. "Nothing has changed. I will deliver Gewey to the temple as I was instructed."

Abruptly, Lee's tone became serious. "You may go where you wish," he said. "But I have no intention of delivering Gewey into the hands of anyone unless I have a very good reason to do so. And so far, you've been rather vague as to who sent you."

Dina lowered her head and took a deep breath. "I was sent by the High Lady of Valshara. I am a novice in the Order of Amon Dähl."

Lee's eyes widened. "That's quite a claim. Do you intend to back it up?"

Dina reached inside her shirt and pulled out a thin silver chain with a small white medallion hanging on its end. Engraved on the medallion was a man in a hooded robe, holding a dagger in one hand and a ring of laurels in the other.

"That could be a fake," Lee said.

"The image could be faked," Dina acknowledged, "but not the metal."

Lee reached out and took the medallion in his hand. It was hot to the touch and burned his fingers, causing him to quickly withdraw in pain.

Dina smiled and held the medallion firmly in her hand. "Each of us is bonded to the Order by this symbol. No one can touch it unless they have received the blessing of Amon Dähl."

Lee stared in wonder. "I thought your order was destroyed."

"We haven't survived for two thousand years because we're fools," Dina boasted. "The Beast of Angrääl tried to destroy us and many died, but we were able to escape with the Order intact."

"How many are left?" Lee asked.

"Not many," she answered sadly. "But we have never been dependent on numbers. When we get to Althetas, I'll contact the Order and they'll take us to the temple. Once we get there, Gewey should be safe."

"Althetas is four weeks on horseback," said Kaylia. "Twice that, as we travel now. We should leave immediately and send Millet and Maybell somewhere safe."

"I'm not abandoning them!" Lee shouted, his temper flaring.

"They're known to our enemies, and I'll not leave their safety to chance."

Dina looked displeased. "You don't understand," she said. "Gewey must go with me, and me alone. I cannot bring anyone else."

"My friends go with me or I don't go at all," Gewey stated with resolve. "That means all of them, and I don't care if it takes us a year to get there."

"Very well," Dina said after a long moment. "You don't leave me with much choice."

"It's settled then," Gewey declared. "We leave as soon as Millet and Maybell arrive." He touched Lee on the shoulder and whispered, "I need to speak to you in private."

Lee nodded his head in agreement. "The boy and I must talk alone," he said to the others. "Dina, I think your husband may feel more comfortable staying in my room tonight."

Kaylia raised an eyebrow at Gewey, a slight smile on her face. "You told people you are married?"

"It was Dina's idea," Gewey muttered, feeling every bit as uncomfortable as he sounded.

Dina wore an amused grin. "It seemed like the thing to do at the time."

"Well then," Kaylia said. "We wouldn't want people wondering why a husband and wife who came together didn't stay together."

"Good point," Lee added, barely able to contain his amusement. "I'm sorry, Gewey. The life of a married man can be tough."

"This is not funny," Gewey growled.

"It's not meant to be," Lee replied. "Kaylia's right, though. If you said you're married, you have to keep up the ruse, at least until we've left here. Don't worry, I have an extra blanket in my pack—assuming you'll be sleeping on the floor, that is."

Dina sauntered over to Gewey and slipped her arm around him.

"Yes, he will," she teased.

Gewey turned bright red and pulled away from Dina. "That's enough," he protested, trying not to stutter. "Lee, I need to speak to you now." He grabbed Lee's arm and pulled him from the room.

Lee took Gewey to his room and locked the door.

"That was not funny," Gewey hissed.

"It's just one night," Lee chuckled. "You've survived being kidnapped by agents of the Dark Knight; I'm sure you can survive one night alone in a room with a beautiful woman."

"You mean to make me go through with this?" Gewey asked incredulously.

"Amusing or not, Kaylia makes a good point. We don't want to raise unwanted questions. Better for you to leave with people thinking that a young couple was just passing through. But that's not what you wanted to talk to me about, is it?"

"No, it isn't," Gewey said. He proceeded to tell Lee about the details of their encounter with Felsafell and what the old man had told him on the porch.

"He is a strange one," Lee remarked.

"You've met him?"

"Many years ago," Lee answered. "I had heard of a crazy old hermit who lived in the Spirit Hills. It was said that he could speak to the spirits and that they told him the future, so I sought him out. I must have wandered those hills for five days before I found him. Well, to be honest, he actually found me."

"What did he tell you?"

"To get out of his hills and never come back," Lee remembered. "Of course, he didn't say it like that, but the message was the same. I approached him, but he vanished before I could get close. I tried to find him, but I ended up lost for days. He did leave behind some roast pork and bread for me, though."

Gewey laughed. "He gave us the same. But what do you make of his words to me?"

"I don't know," Lee admitted, frowning. "I need to think on it for a while." He then slapped Gewey on the back, forcing a smile. "You shouldn't worry about it for now. There's a few hours before bed, so why don't we join the others in the common room for a little entertainment?"

Gewey's eyes brightened. "That sounds like a wonderful idea."

"You should invite your wife to join us," Lee quipped. "I'm sure she wouldn't want her dear husband unattended."

Gewey scowled. "I'll see if Kaylia will come too."

"Good luck," said Lee. "I don't think merry-making with a room full of humans is her cup of tea."

As Lee predicted, Kaylia refused to join them, but Dina was more than happy to keep an eye on Gewey. They listened to the music and even joined in the dancing. Dina pulled Gewey onto the floor during one of the more energetic tunes. Unfortunately for him, knowing how to dance was not one of the skills that came along with being a god. It was all he could do to keep from stepping on Dina's feet, and he nearly fell over twice.

"One of your lessons is going to have to be how to dance with a woman," Lee announced, doubling over with laughter.

Gewey was not amused. "I'm a farmer. When would I need to dance?" he said defensively.

"Your father was a farmer," said Lee, "and he could dance very well. Let me show you."

Lee walked over to Dina, who was laughing and talking with

Minnie. He extended his hand and Dina accepted, smiling as she bowed her head.

Gewey felt a tinge of jealousy as he watched Lee spin Dina around the room. When the song ended, Lee could see it in his eyes.

Lee put his hand on Gewey's shoulder. "That's why you should learn to dance, my boy."

"I don't know what you mean," Gewey lied.

"Of course not," he laughed.

They continued to make merry until the party started to wind down. Minnie was busy cleaning up, while her husband was helping those who had drunk too much wine to the door.

When they went upstairs, Lee gave Gewey a blanket and went to his own room. Gewey nervously followed Dina into their room and placed the blanket on the floor.

"Don't worry," Dina said reassuringly. "It's no different to when we were in the Spirit Hills. Just get some sleep."

Gewey gave her a tight smile and stretched out onto the floor. He knew she was right, but it felt like something had changed since then—at least in his mind. He wondered if it was the same for her, but he couldn't build up the courage to ask. He closed his eyes and drifted off to sleep, wanting to sneak a look at her, but not daring to take the chance.

CHAPTER 16

It was two hours past midday when the covered wagon carrying Millet and Maybell pulled up in front of the inn. Millet was hunched over, looking very unhappy. Maybell was complaining about Millet's driving, claiming that he was not fit to drive a plow horse, let alone a wagon or carriage. Even so, Millet helped her down from the wagon and opened the tavern door for her when they arrived at the Vine Run Inn.

When they entered, Lee and Dina were talking casually at a table in the common room, while Gewey sat in the corner receiving marital advice from Minnie. Lee saw them come in and motioned for Millet to join them. Gewey excused himself and hurried over to Millet, embracing him.

"It is good to see you too," said Millet. "I see you're unharmed."

Gewey beamed at the sight of the man. "I'm glad you're here," he said. "So much has happened." He led Millet over to the table, where Lee and Dina waited. Maybell followed close behind.

"How was your journey?" asked Lee.

Millet scowled. "Interesting, my lord," he said delicately. "And long."

"That's an understatement," Maybell huffed. Her eyes widened when she saw Dina. "Sister Celandine! I'm surprised to see you. You must be this mystery woman they spoke of."

"Good to see you, Sister Maybell," Dina said, bowing her head. "I am indeed the 'mystery woman'."

"I knew there was more to you than meets the eye," Maybell remarked, "but I certainly didn't expect this. Explain yourself."

"I don't think..." Millet began.

"Of course you don't," Maybell cut in. "I will hear the story. There is no one here to spy on us."

Indeed, the inn was empty with the exception of Minnie, who was well out of earshot and busy adding up the profits from the previous evening's party. Lee nodded in agreement and began recounting the events of their travels. When his story was finished, Maybell began to chuckle softly.

"What's so funny?" Lee asked.

"I thought my adventures were over," she explained. "To think that an old woman like me gets to see the temple of Valshara. Is it true that the Knights of Amon Dähl are trained there?"

"It is," Dina answered. "But this temple is not the original one. That was destroyed fifteen years ago by the Dark Knight. To my understanding, the current Temple of Valshara was once a monastery where members of the order went to retire. Only the elders knew its location, so we were able to keep it hidden. Even now, its location is only known to a few."

"Even so," Maybell said, "I'm excited to see it."

"I really didn't expect you to come that far with us," said Lee.

"We'll be passing by several temples where you would be much safer."

"Nonsense," she replied. "My years in this world are nearly done. I would rather them spent making a difference. You may think me just a worthless old woman, but I am not without skills."

"And what might those be?" Millet asked sourly.

Maybell shot Millet an angry glance. "For one, I know the laws and customs of every city and town from here to the abyss. For another, I have connections with temples everywhere and can gather information we will need."

"Still, it's a long journey," Lee warned, "and conditions will be harsh."

"I'm tougher than I look," she countered. "I may have been locked away in a temple for many years, but I'm no stranger to hardship."

Suddenly, her expression became desperate. "Please. Let me go with you. I need to go with you. I thought I would spend the rest of my days watching the decay of the temples. Now I have a chance to be useful again."

Lee looked at Gewey and shrugged his shoulders. "I leave it up to you."

Gewey thought for a moment. "I would be very happy if you accompanied us," he declared.

Millet sighed loudly.

"You just mind your manners," Maybell said to Millet. "Or I'll teach you why novices fear my name in every temple from here to the northwestern steppes."

Lee laughed loudly. "Millet, my old friend, I think you may have finally met your match."

"Indeed," Millet grumbled.

"So, where to now?" Gewey asked.

"With such a large group, we might try to find a caravan headed west," Lee suggested. "Delhammer is four days from here. It's large enough for us to go unnoticed, and we might be able to hitch onto a caravan from there."

Dina thought for a moment. "While we're there, we should see what information might be found at the temples. Maybell, you can help there."

"Won't Salmitaya be expecting that? She might have sent word ahead," Gewey noted.

"She has more pressing issues," Maybell replied. "She may have been a High Priestess, but I have been in the Order since before she was born—certainly long enough to have my voice heard. If she were going to move against me, she would have done it in Kaltinor. Now that I'm out of her reach, she wouldn't dare show her face in another temple."

"Still, we should be cautious," Lee advised. "Even if she can't hinder us through the temples, she may have sent word to other agents of Angrääl."

"I'll be discreet," Maybell assured him. "But that is something that can be discussed later. For now, I would like to clean up."

Dina took Maybell to her room so that she could wash and change. This time, she did not complain about the lack of a proper bathtub.

Lee told Kaylia to gather her things and had Gewey check the wagon.

It was nearly dark before they were all ready to go. Minnie scolded them for leaving at such a late hour and insisted that they eat before departing. She even packed each of them a meal for the road. Lee gave the woman five silvers, enough for them to have stayed for an entire week. Minnie thanked him and, despite Lee's objections, gave him a case of their best wine.

"You seem like a man who can appreciate it," she said as her husband loaded it into the wagon. "Most of the folks who pass through here wouldn't know good wine from well water."

Lee bowed graciously and climbed onto the back of the wagon.

Millet and Maybell took the front; should they run into any curious strangers, they would say that Millet was her younger brother and that they were headed west to resettle. Lee jokingly suggested that Gewey and Dina maintain the guise of a married couple, but Gewey fiercely refused.

They continued down the Old Road of Santismal through the night, stopping a few hours before dawn to make camp. Kaylia told Gewey it was time they continued with their lessons and took him into an area of tree-covered hills. By the end of the lesson, he was able to find Kaylia in the shadows, and he even managed to avoid being found for more than five minutes. The lessons with the knife advanced to include more complicated tactics and maneuvers, which Gewey took to right away.

"You've improved," Kaylia noted. "Soon you'll be ready to start actual Elven training."

Gewey's heart swelled with pride. "I practiced in the Spirit Hills."

"Those hills are dangerous," she warned. "As is the hermit who lives there."

"He didn't seem dangerous. A bit crazy maybe, but not dangerous."

"He speaks to the spirits that live there," she said. "And not all spirits are harmless. We elves have ventured there many times to speak to Felsafell and gain his knowledge, but we knew our peril."

"What peril?"

"It is said Felsafell feels all that the spirits feel," she answered. "Their joy, their fear, their anger, but mostly their loneliness. They yearn for the souls of man and elf to join them. Should you have stayed too long, they might have trapped you there forever."

"Is that what happened to Felsafell?"

"No one really knows who or what he is. He's very old though—some say older than the elves. Some say he's really a spirit in human form. No one knows for sure, but what is known is that seeking his wisdom means risking being lost in the hills forever."

Gewey shuddered at the thought that he had spent the night in the old man's house, and eaten at his table.

"I wonder why he let me go," Gewey said, almost inaudibly.

"I've never heard of anyone who has seen where he lives, save you. Whatever he had to tell you must have been important. But beware of his words. They aren't always what they seem."

Gewey nodded, thinking about what he had been told of his own death, and the death of a friend, hoping he had merely misinterpreted Felsafell's words. "Believe me," he said. "I hope I find more meanings than those I have at present."

Kaylia took Gewey's hands and looked into his eyes. "I know you value the council of the half-man," she said sincerely. "You trust his judgment. But he is not all-knowing and cannot give you all the answers. I would help you if you let me. If you trust me with what you were told, I will help you decipher its meaning."

Gewey thought for a moment. "Yes, I would welcome it," he said. "But not tonight. I'm too tired."

Kaylia placed her hand on his cheek. "Of course," she said softly. "When you're ready, I will help if I can."

Gewey felt more at ease when they returned to camp. For some reason, the thought of being able to confide in Kaylia made him feel as though a huge weight had been lifted from his shoulders. He noticed her watching him with a look of compassion as he lay down to sleep.

They only slept for a few hours before packing up camp and starting out again. Gewey was concerned that Maybell hadn't rested enough, but she seemed full of energy and eager to get going.

The noon lesson with Lee was Gewey's best showing thus far. He found himself using the moves he'd learned from Kaylia to slip through Lee's grasp. On his third attempt, he sent Lee to the ground.

"Excellent!" Lee shouted enthusiastically. "Tomorrow we start teaching you the sword. I see that your lessons with the elf have done you good."

"Thank you," said Gewey. "Her lessons have been helpful."

"I envy that you get to train with an elf. I've always wanted to learn their ways of combat and stealth."

"I'm sure Kaylia would teach you, if you asked," Gewey asserted. "It might be good if you spent some time with her."

"I may do just that," Lee acknowledged. "When we have time." He looked thoughtfully at Gewey. "If you want to ask her about what Felsafell told you, you can."

Gewey looked up at Lee, shocked. "Did she tell you about our conversation?"

"No," Lee said, smiling. "But I noticed that she recognized his name when you told us about him, and I thought she might offer you her counsel. I would warn you to be careful, though. It's obvious she's taken a keen interest in you. The only question is, what direction will that interest take?"

"What do you mean?"

"Nothing," Lee answered, waving his hand dismissively. "Just be careful. She doesn't appear to be the type that gives her affections lightly."

"You don't mean..." Gewey stammered. "You don't think she..."

Lee burst out in laughter. "No," he said. "But that would be a dilemma, considering the way you look at Dina."

Gewey blushed. "I don't know what you're talking about," he said, unable to look Lee in the eye.

Lee spotted a fallen tree and sat down. "Sit," he said. "We should talk."

Gewey sat next to Lee with his eyes fixed firmly on the ground.

"If things had been different, your father would be where I am now," Lee explained. "But unfortunately, it's left to me."

Gewey was mortified. "If you're about to have that talk with me, my father did have it ... when I was ten."

Lee shook his head, smiling. "Not that talk. You're a young man now—a handsome one at that—and your body has far outpaced your maturity." Gewey looked offended, but Lee raised his hand. "I don't mean to say you're immature. The entire village depended on you after you inherited the farm from your father, and you didn't let them down even once. But dealing with women is much more difficult than running a farm. Your feelings for Dina are obvious. I'm sure she knows it, too."

Gewey's eyes shot wide.

"Don't be embarrassed," Lee said, putting his hand on Gewey's shoulder. "I don't think she takes it for anything more than boyish infatuation. But when you're young, you never feel love just a little. It's bigger and more powerful than any enemy you'll face. You must understand something, Gewey. You are a god bound to earth as a human, and you have a great task ahead of you. I would never tell you not to explore your feelings, but I would warn you of the dangers. If Dina doesn't feel the same as you, the pain might be unbearable, and it could end up even worse if the feelings are mutual. All I ask is that you don't push the issue. If things happen, so be it, but please take it slowly and speak to me when you don't know what to do. Love for you will be a touchy thing. As a god, you can't know where it will lead." Lee chuckled to himself. "Even as a man, it's like walking through the forest deaf and blind."

"Have you ever loved?" Gewey asked.

Lee's eyes suddenly became distant. "I told you that the Oracle said I would have to sacrifice everything," he said. "I once had a wife and son."

"What happened to them?"

"I left them behind," Lee confessed. "My road would have put them in too much danger. I couldn't have that."

"Where are they now?"

"Safe in Hazrah," Lee answered. "But it's not something I enjoy talking about."

"I'm sorry, I didn't mean to..."

"It's fine," Lee assured him. "I made my choice. But I want you to promise to talk to me as things... progress."

"I promise."

Suddenly, Lee looked as if he had been struck by lightning.

"What is it?" Gewey asked impatiently.

"Bound to earth," Lee mused. "You're bound to earth."

"You're not making sense."

"Felsafell said your strength was in the earth!" Lee said excitedly. "I think I understand what he meant. You see, my father is Saraf, God of the Seas, so when I'm near the water I can listen to its heartbeat and gain strength. I have to sit and meditate to draw on this power, but maybe you can draw from it directly, as you fight."

"How would I do that?" Gewey asked, puzzled.

"First you must learn to hear the earth. The sword can wait. Kaylia's teaching you the knife. That will have to do for now. Tomorrow, we will try to tap into your true power."

That night, Kaylia seemed different during training. Gewey was able to find her in the shadow three out of four times, and he was able to avoid her for over twenty minutes. Finally, she told him the lesson was over and started back to camp.

"Wait," Gewey said.

Kaylia stopped but didn't turn around. "What is it?"

"You said you would help me to understand what Felsafell told me. I'm ready to tell you."

"Perhaps you shouldn't," Kaylia advised.

"I don't understand. Why not?"

"My judgment is compromised," she replied. "I'm sorry."

"Tell me what's wrong," Gewey pleaded. "Maybe I can help?"

Kaylia laughed softly. "It's not something you would understand."

"Is it because I'm so young?"

"Age is not something elves look at to determine ability," she explained. "I'm old by human standards but not much more than a child to my own people. The reason you wouldn't understand is that you're not an elf."

"I could try. I might surprise you."

"I think you might," Kaylia agreed. "But I need to work this out on my own. Don't worry, I'll be all right."

That night, Kaylia slept far from the others. Gewey stopped wondering what was troubling her. His thoughts wandered to what Lee had told him about Elven feelings, but that only raised questions in his mind that made him laugh at himself. If Kaylia were human, he would take her words to mean something else; but she was right; he didn't understand elves.

The next day, Kaylia sat in silence with her hood pulled far over her face as they rode in the wagon. Dina laughed merrily as Lee spun tales of his past adventures. Gewey loved Lee's stories -especially the ones that included Gewey's father—and he never tired of hearing them.

He tried to tell a few of his own, but every time Dina looked at him, his tongue felt heavy and useless, and eventually, he stopped trying.

"Kaylia," Dina said, trying to make conversation. "Surely you have some adventures you could share to pass the time."

Kaylia didn't look up. "I have no desire to pass the time," she said flatly.

Dina cleared her throat. "Okay, then. How's your training going, Gewey?"

"You'd have to ask my teachers."

"He needs to work harder," Lee chimed in. "But I think he shows promise."

"You should feel fortunate," said Dina. "Not many people get to train with a man like Lee, let alone an elven warrior."

"I'm no warrior," Kaylia snapped. "There are no Elven warriors. You humans know nothing."

"I'm sorry," Dina said sincerely, reaching over to touch Kaylia's knee. "I didn't mean to offend you."

Kaylia's hand immediately shot out, grabbing Dina by the wrist. Her eyes fixed stonily on Dina's. "Abomination," she hissed. She reached down and drew her knife. Dina screamed and tried to climb over Lee to get away, but Kaylia was too fast. Before anyone could move, she had caught Dina and pulled her to the floor of the wagon, knife pressed to her throat.

"Abomination!" she repeated, louder than the first time.

Gewey was stunned. "Afisul Si Damon!" he shouted in desperation. The words spilled out of his mouth before he had even the slightest idea of what he was saying.

Kaylia stopped abruptly, her eyes wide. She stared at Gewey, utter amazement on her face. "How?" she cried. "How do you know these words?"

Without waiting for an answer, Kaylia leaped from the wagon and ran. Gewey tried to go after her, but she was out of sight before he could make it more than a few feet.

Millet and Maybell sat shocked, trying to piece together what had just happened. Lee reached down and helped Dina to her feet.

"What was that about?" he demanded. "Why did she attack you?"

Dina was shaking terribly. She tried to calm herself. "I was careless," she said, "and Kaylia realized what I am."

"And what is that?" Lee inquired.

"My father was a blacksmith from Baltria," she told him quietly. "But my mother was an elf. That's why she called me an abomination."

The wagon fell silent. Everyone stared at Dina with a combination of wonder and confusion.

"How can that be?" Lee asked. "Such a thing is impossible."

"No, not impossible. But as far as I know, I'm the first. And what I am puts me in danger from both worlds. I thought my human blood would mask my identity from Kaylia, but when her hand touched mine, she could sense the Elven blood in me."

"But you look human," Gewey remarked.

"Yes, I do," she acknowledged. "But do you remember when you asked me how old I am?"

Gewey nodded.

"I'm thirty-eight years old," she revealed. "But my Elven blood makes me look like I'm barely out of my teens."

"How did it happen?" Millet interjected. "With the hatred that exists between the races, it's hard to imagine."

"How does anything happen?" she replied. "My father came across my mother injured in the forest when he was out hunting. He told me that he knew he loved her from the moment he first saw her. She had been attacked by soldiers who'd heard of a large group of elves in the forest near to the city. But as it turned out, my mother was the only one. She had left her people on what my father described to me as a 'soul quest'. She was attacked while she was meditating, so she didn't hear them coming until they were already upon her. They left her for dead, and if my father hadn't found her and cared for her, she certainly would have died.

"Once she had healed, she discovered that my father had moved her to a small village thirty miles north so he could care for her without raising suspicions. He'd sold everything he possessed to have enough money to keep her alive and away from other humans. Soon, she realized that she loved him as well."

"How were they able to stay together?" Millet asked. "Eventually, they would have been discovered."

"They were," Dina said sadly. "My father did everything he could to keep her safe; at one point he moved to an even more secluded area so that they wouldn't be found."

"But they were found," said Lee. "Weren't they?"

"Yes," said Dina. "But it was the elves that found them. I was only three when it happened. I remember my father embracing my mother and begging her to come with us, but she knew that was impossible. The elves didn't know about me. They only knew that my mother loved a human. She knew they would kill me if they found out there was a child, so she sent my father and me away. I never saw her again."

"I don't understand why they would want you dead," said Gewey. "You're innocent in all this."

"Elves see themselves as separate from humanity in every way you can imagine," Dina explained. "The idea of a half-elf, half-human child shatters that belief. Frankly, it would be just as bad for me if humans found out. Thankfully, they have no way of knowing unless they discover my age or I tell them directly, as I've just told you."

"What now, my lord?" Millet asked.

"I'll tell you what now," Maybell cut in. "Someone needs to talk some sense into that elf. I don't care what you are, Celandine. You're a part of what's going on here, and a good person to boot. If Kaylia can't see that, then to blazes with her."

Dina smiled appreciatively. "Thank you," she said. "But I don't see what could help."

"You said something," Lee said to Gewey. "Something that made her stop. What was it?"

"I don't know," Gewey answered. "It just came out. I have no idea where it came from."

"You should go look for her then," Lee suggested. "Perhaps she'll listen to you."

Gewey nodded and got out of the wagon. He hoped finding her in the daytime would be easier than it was at night. As it turned out, he didn't have to look very hard at all. He found her a few hundred yards off the road, kneeling next to a tiny stream. Her eyes were closed and her knife was buried in the ground beside her.

"Kaylia," Gewey said softly. "Are you all right?"

Kaylia didn't move.

"Kaylia," he repeated.

Still, she didn't move.

Gewey sat on the grass behind her, not knowing what to do next. Twenty minutes passed before Kaylia spoke.

"Where did you learn those words?" she whispered.

"I don't know," he replied. "They just came out. What do they mean?"

"It's a declaration. Literally translated, it means my spirit flies to yours."

Gewey was taken aback. "I wasn't trying to declare anything," he said quickly. "I just wanted to stop you from killing Dina."

"What you said to me is rare and sacred," she said, continuing as though she hadn't heard him. "It's something that few elves have spoken since the Great War."

"What do you mean by a declaration? Please, tell me what's going on."

Kaylia turned to Gewey and opened her eyes. "Do you love me?" she asked.

"I..." Gewey didn't know what to say.

"If not, then you should never have spoken those words."

"I don't understand," said Gewey. "I really don't."

"Then understand this," she said. "The language you spoke is known only to the elves. It is the language of our ancestors, and even among my people, only a few know it entirely. What you said can only be spoken to someone that you love ... and for only one reason."

"What reason?" he asked nervously.

"It means that you wish to be joined with me."

"Joined?" Gewey exclaimed. "You mean..."

"Yes," she said. "That is exactly what I mean."

"You can't think I was asking you that, do you?"

"What then?" she snapped. "Why did you say it?"

"I don't know," he replied hastily. "I didn't know what it meant. It just came out."

"But it came from somewhere," she insisted. "And it cannot be ignored."

"I take it back then. Just pretend I didn't say it."

Anger flashed across Kaylia's face. "Because you are not an elf, I will pretend you did not make that offer. Once you say the words of joining, they cannot be unsaid."

"What do we do now?" he asked.

"I either accept you as my mate ... or refuse."

Gewey laughed with relief. "That's easy then. Just refuse."

"If I do, then I must leave you, never to be in your sight again. I am not prepared to do that just yet."

"You mean we either get married or you have to leave? That's ridiculous."

"I'm sorry you think so," Kaylia lamented. "But to my people, it is very serious. However, I have one year to consider it. If at the end of that time I decide you are not a worthy mate, then I shall refuse."

"And what happens in the meantime?" he asked, afraid to hear the answer.

"In the meantime, nothing. But be warned; elves are protective of their suitors. Careful you don't let your eyes stray too far."

Gewey immediately thought of Dina. "What do you intend to do about Celandine?" he asked anxiously.

Kaylia thought for a long moment. "It appears I can do nothing," she said finally. "Your words have bound me. If you wish her unharmed, I will accept it."

"Thank you," Gewey said, relieved.

Kaylia smiled. "Send her to me. She and I should talk. Don't worry, I won't harm her."

Gewey nodded and returned to the wagon.

"What happened?" asked Lee. "Did you find her?"

"She wants to speak to Dina alone," Gewey said.

Dina looked worried.

"She swears she won't attack you again," he assured her.

Reluctantly, Dina went to join Kaylia.

"What happened?" Lee asked. "What did she say to you?"

"I don't want to talk about it," Gewey replied. "Not yet, at least."

An hour later, Kaylia and Dina came walking back to the wagon.

"Kaylia has agreed to teach me about my Elven heritage," Dina said as they climbed in.

Kaylia nodded in affirmation.

"And that's it?" Millet pressed. "No more attempts to kill her?"

"That depends," Kaylia said.

"On what?" Lee asked.

Kaylia did not respond. She simply smiled a knowing smile as the wagon continued down the road.

CHAPTER 17

Gewey spent the day trying to avoid conversation with the others. Kaylia was sitting next to Dina, whispering in her ear. When Lee asked what they were talking about, Kaylia told him to mind his own business. Gewey was not looking forward to the midday lesson. He knew Lee would press him about what had happened with Kaylia. The fact was, he wasn't quite sure himself. When the time came, Gewey followed Lee to a quiet spot off the road.

"Sit," Lee instructed.

Gewey sat down on the grass and crossed his legs.

"Close your eyes and listen to the sound of the earth," Lee continued. "Not the way you hear the forest. Stretch out with your thoughts and feel its rhythm, its heartbeat. Let it flow into you and give you strength."

Gewey did as he was told. At first, he felt nothing. Then, like a sound heard from a great distance, it was there, pulsing steadily. The more he listened, the nearer it came, until it beat in his mind like a great drum. Beads of sweat formed on his forehead as the beat grew louder.

"You must let it in," Lee urged him. "Let it pass into you."

But Gewey couldn't. The beat pounded against him until he thought it would tear him to ribbons. He let out a scream and collapsed.

When he came to, Lee was standing over him with a concerned look on his face. He put a water skin to Gewey's mouth and poured. Gewey tried to drink, but he began to cough and splutter as the water stung his swollen throat.

"Easy, Gewey," Lee soothed him. "You'll be fine."

"What happened?" asked Gewey, carefully trying to sit up. Lee put his hand on Gewey's back and steadied him. "You're much more powerful than I thought. I had you do too much, too soon. From now on, we take it slow."

"No," Gewey insisted. "We try again. Taking it slow won't defeat the Dark Knight."

"Neither will getting yourself killed," Lee countered. "The amount of power you unleashed could have destroyed you. Look around."

Gewey surveyed the area and saw that large sections of the ground had been completely torn apart.

"You see," Lee said. "You must learn to control this power, otherwise, there's no telling how much damage you could do to yourself and those around you."

Gewey nodded slowly. "I see what you mean."

"That's enough for today," said Lee, lifting Gewey to his feet.

"Now, if you wouldn't mind, what in blazes happened between you and that elf?"

"Lee, I really don't think..."

"Listen to me, and listen to me well," said Lee, cutting him off. "If it doesn't affect what we have to do, then fine, keep it to yourself. But you need to remember that I have more than just you to worry about. If there's anything that could possibly jeopardize any of us, I need to know about it."

Gewey sat back down on the grass and thought for a moment.

"I'm not sure if it will affect us. At least, not all of us. And maybe not for a while."

Lee sat next to him. "You can trust me, Gewey. Whatever it is, I'll understand."

Gewey looked at Lee, then told him what had happened with Kaylia. When Gewey finished, Lee sat there with his mouth open for a minute, not knowing what to say.

"Now do you see why I didn't want to talk about it?" Gewey asked, troubled.

"I do indeed," Lee finally managed to say. "Do you intend to marry her?"

"Don't be ridiculous. I'm not even of age, and besides, she's an elf."

"Yes," said Lee. "And you're a god. And it doesn't appear that she cares if you're of age or not. As I understand it, she is barely of age herself in the way elves measure years." He shook his head. "I told you to be careful."

"How was I supposed to know?" Gewey cried. "The words just came out. I didn't know what they meant."

"That was interesting," Lee said pensively. "There must be some reason for this."

"That's what she said, too," Gewey noted.

"I really don't know what to tell you," Lee said, laughing. "You certainly do get yourself into some tight spots. I suggest you try not to let your eyes wander to Dina too often. Heaven knows what kind of trouble that could cause."

Gewey wanted to deny it, but he knew his attraction to Dina often caused his eyes to wander. "I'll try," he said.

"Two beautiful women," Lee remarked. "I suppose there are worse things to happen to a young man. Then again ... perhaps not."

Lee hopped to his feet and pulled Gewey up. "Maybe your mother was Ayliazarah, Goddess of Love," he quipped, slapping Gewey on the back.

Gewey was not amused.

They headed back to the wagon and continued on their way. Kaylia had her hood pulled back, allowing Gewey to look at her closely. There was no doubt that she was beautiful, but he had never imagined a romantic relationship could be possible with an elf. But then, of course, he wasn't really a human. His head began to swim, so he decided to try to take a nap. *At least if I'm asleep, I'll escape for a bit*, he thought.

He woke just as they were about to stop and make camp. Millet and Maybell were arguing about where the best spot would be. Lee, Kaylia, and Dina were all looking at him, trying not to laugh.

"What?" Gewey asked, trying to shake off the cobwebs in his head.

"The things you say," said Dina. "Enough to make a lady blush."

"What do mean?" Gewey asked. "What did I say?"

"More interesting," said Kaylia, "is who were you talking to in your dreams?"

"I don't know," he said, flustered. "I was bloody dreaming. Can't I dream in peace?"

"Don't let them tease you," laughed Lee. "They're just having a bit of fun."

Gewey rubbed his eyes. "Enough then," he said irritably. "I'm not in the mood." He was nervous about the lesson with Kaylia. He wasn't sure how to talk to her anymore. He didn't know a thing about elves, and the thought of saying the wrong thing unnerved him. When the time came, however, Kaylia acted as if nothing had happened.

"Lee has told me you will not be learning the sword for a while," she said. "So we need to step up your knife training. It's not as brutish, but every bit as deadly."

"Do elves ever use a sword?" Gewey asked.

"Sometimes," she answered. "But it's not something we prefer. The sword can be necessary in a full-on battle, but in the type of fighting we're likely to encounter, I think you'll find it very advantageous to have skill with a knife."

Gewey was grateful that the conversation didn't stray from the lesson to more uncomfortable subjects. Kaylia pushed him hard throughout, showing him ways to keep an opponent blind and off-balance. He found it was very much like the way he had learned to hide in shadows.

When Kaylia attacked, she was never directly in front of an opponent, nor did she press an advantage.

"The sword is a direct assault," she shouted to him in between strikes. "Powerful, but slow and deliberate. The knife, on the other hand..."

She paused, deftly tossing her weapon from hand to hand. "The knife is an ambush!" Suddenly she was on him, striking quickly and mercilessly from nearly every conceivable angle. For an hour, he tried to imitate her movements. He watched her body twist into seemingly impossible positions that he simply could not match.

"You must learn to be more flexible," she said. "You must see as your opponent sees, move where he cannot reach, then strike where he cannot defend. It is no different from our other exercises, only that you are hiding in plain sight."

"I think I understand," he said. "I'll do better next time."

"You did well this time," she replied.

Gewey raised an eyebrow. "A compliment?"

"The nature of our relationship requires that I be completely honest with you," she explained. "As a teacher, I do not give praise easily, even when warranted. But as a suitor, you will receive my honesty in all things. I suggest you do not abuse that privilege."

Gewey almost winced at the word 'suitor.' "Thank you," he managed. "I won't."

When they returned to camp, Lee was sitting next to the fire talking with the others. A box wrapped in cloth was at his feet—the same one Gewey remembered Millet handing to him the night they had left Sharpstone.

"What's in the box?" Gewey asked as they approached.

"I was hoping Kaylia might help me with that," answered Lee.

Kaylia and Gewey sat by the fire as Lee unwrapped the box. It was made from dark, polished wood and had strange lettering carved on the lid.

"Do you recognize the language?" Lee asked Kaylia.

"Yes," she said. "It's the ancient language of my ancestors."

"Can you read it?" he asked.

"I can try," she said. "But I'm sorry to say I know very little. Only a few Elven scholars know it well enough to read it fluently."

Lee handed her the box. She looked at it intently for several minutes.

"The first line isn't difficult," she said. "It simply reads, 'Unto the creator I sing'. That's a common phrase used in many of our ceremonies. The second line is a bit more difficult. I think it says, 'The time will come to receive your gifts', but I may be wrong. The third line ... and again, I'm not sure ... seems to say, 'This book I keep until the end of time.'"

"That's it?" Lee asked, sounding disappointed. "Nothing more?"

"Like I said, I may be wrong," Kaylia told him. "But I believe I'm close."

"What is it, exactly?" asked Gewey.

"I don't know," Lee admitted. "I've never been able to open it."

"What do you mean?" Gewey asked. "Just take a bloody axe and break it."

Lee laughed. "I actually tried that once in a moment of frustration. But as you can see, it didn't even make a scratch. I tried for years to discover what it is, but I haven't found anything written describing such an object."

"I know what it is," Maybell interjected.

"You do?" Kaylia and Lee asked simultaneously.

"Indeed, I do," said Maybell with a nod. "And you were close on the translation, elf."

"I had no idea you could read ancient elfish," Kaylia said, amused.

"I can't," she answered. "But I know that phrase well enough. And if I'm right, I know what's inside that box."

"Well, tell us then," Lee said impatiently.

Maybell gave Lee a withering look, then continued. "It should say: 'Unto the creator I sing, His gift to me I humbly receive. The end of days I fear not, for his book shall guide me.'"

"What does it mean?" asked Lee.

"It refers to a prophecy I first heard about when I was studying as a novice in the Great Library of Halmanteris," she explained.

"Do you know the whole thing?" Lee asked.

"No," she answered. "But I know someone who might. She's a Sister living in the Temple of Ayliazarah in Gristol. I've known her for many years. She is without a doubt the most learned Sister in the Order. It's on our way to Althetas. Perhaps we should stop on the way?"

"We might," said Lee. "Can you tell me anything about what's inside the box?"

"I can only guess," she said. "I think it might contain the Book of Souls. It is said that it was written at the time of creation and contains all the secrets of the gods."

Kaylia's eyes grew wide. "It couldn't be."

"Why not?" Lee asked. "What do you know about it?"

"The Book of Souls was kept by the elves until the time of the Great War," she explained. "It was thought to have been lost forever. If that is the book, then it rightfully belongs to the elves."

"If that is the book, then it rightly belongs to everyone," Maybell corrected her. "But you're right; it was said that the elves guarded it for centuries. But let's not jump to conclusions. We don't even yet know if it is actually the book that's in there."

"Good point," Millet agreed. "And being that we don't know how to open it, this discussion is pointless."

"Where did you get it?" asked Maybell.

"It was among Lord Dauvis's possessions," Lee replied. "I've always thought it was something important, but I could never figure what. Where he acquired it, I don't know."

"Lord Dauvis?" Maybell asked. "Of Hazrah? Then you must be Lee Nal'Thain. I've heard of you. You inherited his property and title when he died."

Lee nodded. "I keep that name secret. I imagine news of my inheritance is well known throughout the temples, but I would ask that you keep this to yourself."

"The death of Lord Dauvis was spoken of at the time," Maybell acknowledged. "As was his successor. A lord of such wealth and influence is always of interest to us. But now I have a more important question: Why do a Lord of Hazrah and an elf take so much care to keep the true identity of a farm boy a secret? Not to mention the training you give to him. Dina here doesn't seem to know much, but perhaps you could tell me."

"These are things you're better off not knowing," said Lee.

"You think I might betray you?" she responded, sounding offended. "I know enough to do that already if I so choose. Face the facts: I will either work it out on my own eventually, or I'll learn the truth when we get to Valshara."

"She's right," Gewey said. "Besides, I don't want people risking their lives without knowing why."

"Boy," Lee snapped. "You need to listen to me and keep your mouth shut."

Gewey looked at Kaylia. "What do you think?"

Kaylia took a deep breath. "I would keep this secret for as long as possible," she said. "But you're right; people should know why they risk their lives. And I think sister Maybell would figure it out on her own, eventually." Kaylia then looked at Dina. "But there are two people here who know nothing. Would they both keep your secret?"

"If you would share it," Dina affirmed, "I will keep it, even from my own order. Though I suspect what you have to say is the very reason I'm taking you to them in the first place."

"If you need an oath from me," Maybell said, "the best one I can give is my word. I will not betray you, and I will keep your secret with me until death."

Gewey looked around the fire. All eyes were on him. "Lee, if I reveal myself, then I reveal you as well."

"That doesn't matter much," said Lee. "I'm not the important one. Besides, the world has seen many of my kind, so it would be no great shock to see another." He stared into the fire. "Do as you will."

Gewey took a breath, then told them the story from beginning to end. When he was finished, Maybell and Dina were staring at him in amazement.

"Is this true?" Maybell whispered. "You are a god walking the earth?"

"I am," said Gewey. "But trust me, I don't feel like one. Until Lee proved it to me, I had no idea. It still doesn't seem real sometimes."

"Do you remember being in heaven?" asked Dina.

"I don't know that I was ever in heaven," he replied. "For all I know, I was born in this world. I have no memory beyond my childhood."

The camp was quiet for a long time. Dina and Maybell just sat there, staring at Gewey.

"Well now," said Maybell, breaking the silence. "This is exciting. I would say this calls for some of that wine we have in the wagon."

She went over, retrieved one of the bottles, and passed it around.

"Do you know who your real mother and father are?" Dina asked, swallowing a mouthful of wine.

"No," said Gewey. "Like I said, I didn't even know I was a god until just recently. Whoever they are, they left me no clues."

"I think it's important that we find out what's inside that box," Maybell said to Lee. "If it is the Book of Souls, then it could hold the key to why the boy is here."

"I agree," said Kaylia. "But the book is said to be written in ancient elfish. Even if we open it, we have no way to read it."

Lee looked thoughtfully at the box. "I do think we should open it and see what it contains, but it's more important to get Gewey to a safe place where he can train. We can stop and see this woman in Gristol, but we can't stay for long. If she can't help, the book will have to wait."

"I disagree," Kaylia contended. "If that is the Book of Souls, then it's the key to far more than Gewey's power—it's the key to victory. If we can open it and understand it, this will give us the knowledge we need to defeat the Dark Knight. Gewey may not even need to be put in danger at all."

"What are you saying?" Lee asked.

"I'm saying that Gewey may not have to fight," she answered. "The book may show us another way."

"This is all well and good," said Lee. "But like you said, who can read it?"

"The elves can," Gewey said suddenly, his eyes turning to Kaylia. "You're thinking about taking it to your people, aren't you?"

Kaylia smiled sweetly at Gewey and nodded. "That's right."

"You can't," Gewey protested. "You've already said that they'll kill you."

"I'll face their judgment eventually," she replied. "If it means victory without bloodshed, I'll gladly take the risk."

"I'm sorry," Lee cut in. "But I'm not sending it to the elves. At least, not yet. First, we'll try Gristol and see if the box can be opened. It may not be the Book of Souls at all. For all we know, it could be a recipe for lamb stew. No, it stays with me for now."

Gewey smiled with satisfaction, but Kaylia did not look pleased.

"Kaylia," said Dina. "I would like to hear more about the elves before I sleep."

"Of course," she replied, and led her away, out of earshot. When the wine was gone, they began settling into their blankets. For a while, Gewey lay watching Kaylia as she shared her Elven heritage with Dina. Then, just as he felt himself beginning to drift off, they returned to the fire and lay down. He could feel the eyes of both women on him, so he rolled over onto his side to face away from them.

"You haven't been taking your jawas tea," Kaylia said quietly.

Gewey had not heard her approach and nearly rolled off his blanket in surprise. He took the flask from her hands and swallowed a large mouthful. He felt the familiar sensation of relaxation flowing through his limbs.

"Can I ask a favor of you?"

"Of course," answered Gewey.

"Would you allow me to touch your mind? The jawas should make it easy ... if you allow it."

"Why?" Gewey asked, concerned.

"I want to see who you really are," she said. "And you will see me. If you refuse, I will understand."

"I ... I'm not sure. How would you do it?"

"It's not difficult," Kaylia assured him. "When you are falling asleep, you will feel my mind touching yours. When you do, just let me in."

"What will happen?" he asked, nervous and unsure.

"That depends," she replied gently. "Perhaps nothing. Perhaps everything. There's really no way to know."

Gewey thought for a moment. "I guess it would be all right."

Kaylia nodded and returned to her blanket. Gewey allowed the jawas to take over and began to drift off.

It was then that he felt Kaylia's presence, like a gentle knock on the door to his mind. Instead of trying to keep it shut, as Lee had taught him, he allowed it to open. He felt a warm breeze enter and wrap itself around him. It was as if kindness itself had become tangible.

"I'm here." It was Kaylia, but her voice sounded distant. "Can you see me?"

"Where are you?" asked Gewey. All he could see was a deep blue mist swirling everywhere. "I can't see you."

"Don't look with your eyes," she advised. Her voice was like a thousand tiny bells. "Just imagine what you want to see and then make it so."

Gewey imagined the mist lifting. It cleared slowly, revealing a lush forest. He could smell the earth and trees around him. Standing next to a tall pine was Kaylia, dressed in a flowing white dress. Her auburn hair fell loosely down her back, and her skin glistened like the night sky.

"Can you see me now?" she asked, smiling.

He was completely awed by her stunning beauty. "Yes," he answered. "You look ... different."

Kaylia's laughter sounded almost childlike. "Here, we look as we are. I see you tall and straight, dressed in gold robes."

Gewey tried to look at himself, but he appeared out of focus.

"Why can't I see myself?"

Kaylia walked lightly across the forest floor until she was less than a foot in front of him.

"It takes time to learn to see yourself. But that's not why we're here. Come with me." She took his hand. "Let me show you things you never dreamed of."

"Where are we going?" he asked as he let himself be led away.

"Inside your mind," she answered. "And inside mine. It's doubtful you'll remember what you've seen when you wake—at least, not until you've been properly trained. But the impressions will last."

Gewey felt a tinge of disappointment. "Will you tell me about it tomorrow?"

"No, not unless I feel you need to know. But don't worry, I swear I won't force you to reveal anything you don't want to."

The last thing Gewey remembered was a sensation of flying, with Kaylia's hand locked firmly in his. When he woke the next morning, Kaylia was still sleeping nearby.

There was a sweet smile on her face.

CHAPTER 18

Gewey was at first afraid that his experience with Kaylia would make things even more awkward than they already were, but he soon found the opposite to be true. For some reason, conversation with her the next day was much easier. He even told her some stories about his life back in Sharpstone. Dina was quiet, but her eyes kept wandering to Gewey. He pretended not to notice, but it was hard to ignore her.

He hoped Kaylia was unaware of Dina's gaze, but he held little hope that anything would escape the elf's attention. By the time they reached Delhammer, Gewey was quite ready for a change of scenery.

The city wasn't as big as Kaltinor, but at least the gates, though guarded, were open. Millet stopped and asked one of the guards about the quality and location of the inns. The man was more than happy to help once he had been given a copper.

The streets were busy, but much cleaner than those in Kaltinor. It seemed that commerce had not been affected by hard times, and the people were cheerful and smiled as they passed by.

The inn they found was decent. The common room was filled with patrons enjoying the antics of a juggler and magician, something Gewey had never seen before. Lee paid for the rooms while Millet stabled the horses. Gewey shared a room with Lee, while Dina and Kaylia shared another. Millet and Maybell each got a room of their own, though both of them protested, arguing that they were perfectly willing to share, and even sleep on the floor if necessary.

Once they were settled, Maybell left in search of the temple district, insisting that Dina accompany her. Millet and Lee went looking for a caravan headed west. Gewey persuaded Kaylia to join him in the common room and watch the acrobat, who, as it turned out, also played the lute and sang. Kaylia was uneasy at first, but she soon realized that no one was paying her any attention. As she grew more comfortable, she even laughed at some of the more silly songs.

Lee and Millet were the first to return. They joined them at the table. "I see your aversion to being seen in public has lessened," Millet said cheerfully.

"I didn't want Gewey to be left unprotected," she answered unenthusiastically. "And luckily, these people don't seem so interested in the comings and goings of others. A hooded woman doesn't seem so out of place here."

"I think you'll find that to be more and more the case, the further west we go," Millet replied.

"Did you find a caravan?" asked Gewey, still watching the entertainment with glee.

"We did," Lee confirmed. "It doesn't depart for two days. Still, I think it's the best way to travel unnoticed."

"I think I could use a break anyway," Gewey noted. "This seems like a fun place."

"We can't be reckless," Lee said sternly. "And we can't afford to expose ourselves too much."

"If the entertainment here is as good at night as it is at midday, then I think I'll be happy not leaving the inn," said Gewey.

The acrobat was juggling six apples, taking a bite from each one as it passed, before making them disappear.

Seeing Gewey in such high spirits, Millet couldn't help but smile affectionately. "I think the lad does need a bit of fun in his life right now, my lord. Who knows when he'll get another chance, given what the future may hold?"

Lee sighed. "You're right, of course. I forget sometimes that he's only seventeen."

"He's sitting right here," Gewey said, waving his hand in front of Lee's face. "And I just want to enjoy myself while we wait. Don't you?"

"Good point," said Lee, slamming his hands on the table. "I think we could all do with a bit of fun. Wait here."

Lee got up and went to the bar. Gewey saw the barman nod enthusiastically as Lee whispered into his ear.

"What did you do?" asked Gewey when Lee returned.

"You'll see tonight," Lee said with a sly grin.

Kaylia shook her head, unimpressed. "I think I'll be staying in my room tonight."

"Not a chance," Lee said, pulling out a red scarf from his pocket.

"This, my dear, is traditional attire in this region, and it should cover up your more ... obvious attributes. Besides, Gewey needs looking after, and it seems like you've volunteered for the job."

"Mind your tongue," Kaylia fumed.

"I didn't think you could blush," Lee teased, paying no mind to Kaylia's anger. "I guess I was wrong."

Just then, Maybell and Dina returned.

"How are things at the temples?" asked Lee.

"Better than I expected," Maybell replied. "I spoke to the High Priestesses at the temples of Gerath and Ayliazarah.

They've been suspicious of Salmitaya for some time. Apparently, the witch wasn't as careful as she thought."

"So why didn't they move against her?" Lee inquired.

"It's not as easy as you think to oust a High Priestess," she answered. "Even a corrupt one. Besides, Salmitaya was well protected within Kaltinor—and still is, from what I've learned. We have no soldiers to simply march in and remove her. But I am pleased to say that if she is caught outside the city walls, she will spend the rest of her life in a temple prison."

"What else did you find out?" Lee asked.

"Not much," she admitted. "At least, nothing useful."

Lee looked concerned. "I had hoped we could get an idea of what we might run into as we travel further west."

"Communication between the temples has become spotty at best," added Dina. "I spoke to a few of the Sisters, and from what they told me, suspicion between the temples has become a plague. They hear the rumors about the growing strength in the north, and even claim there are agents of Angrääl living openly in some cities, gathering followers."

Lee scratched his chin. "I want you to go to the other temples tomorrow and see if you can find out anything else. For now, we should all keep our eyes and ears open." Everyone nodded in agreement.

"But now, my friends, Millet and I have an errand to run and must leave you," Lee said. "Be washed by sundown, Gewey; I have a surprise for you."

Gewey looked confused as he watched Millet and Lee leave the inn. "A surprise? What could he possibly be up to?" he wondered aloud.

"With that one, who knows?" Maybell replied. "But if you don't mind, I haven't seen an acrobat in years."

They all watched until the acrobat had finished, then retired to their rooms to wash and get ready for supper. The smell from the kitchen promised roast lamb and fresh bread. Gewey's mouth watered at the thought.

Lee entered the room just as Gewey had finished bathing. He was carrying a bundle tied with twine. "Here," Lee said, tossing him the bundle.

Gewey opened it. Inside were a set of new clothes and a pair of fine leather boots. The long tunic was gold silk with silver embroidery, and the pants were of the same design. A polished black leather belt completed the outfit. Gewey stared, not knowing what to say.

"Well?" Lee asked happily. "Are you going to try them on or not?"

"I don't get it. Why did you give me this?"

"To wear at your coming-of-age celebration," he said matter-of-factly.

"My what?" Gewey cried. "I'm only seventeen."

"True," Lee replied, smiling. "But the way I see it, the age of a god should be counted differently. Besides, who knows if you'll have the chance to celebrate a real coming-of-age party?"

"True," Gewey acknowledged, holding up the clothes in front of him. "We might be dead by then."

Lee laughed heartily. "Not what I had in mind, but a good point," he admitted. "Now get dressed. I'm going to Millet's room to get ready. I'll send him for you when it's time."

An hour later, Millet showed up at Gewey's door dressed in fine blue linens, looking very much a city dweller. His face beamed with delight when he saw Gewey in his new finery.

"Now that's proper dress," Millet remarked. "You look very much the young lord."

Gewey felt awkward. He had never worn anything fancier than festival robes before. He couldn't stop pulling and tugging at the long tunic, and the heeled boots made him feel as if he would tip forward at any moment.

"You'll get used to it," Millet laughed. "One day, I suspect you may dress like this all the time."

That idea didn't please Gewey. He felt far more comfortable in his own clothes—the clothes of a farmer. He smiled anyway and tried to stop fidgeting.

When Gewey entered the common room, everyone smiled cheerfully and clapped their hands with approval at the sight of him. He saw that the others were dressed in fine attire as well. Lee was decked out in a bright red suit with gold buttons. Dina and Maybell both wore emerald green dresses with matching scarves wrapped tightly around their heads. Their hair, adorned with tiny white flowers, fell loosely from underneath the scarves. Dina's eyes were painted, giving them an elfish quality that made Kaylia appear less obvious. Kaylia wore a similar dress, but hers was light blue and tied at the waist with a deep blue sash.

Minstrels were just arriving and tuning their instruments in the corner. The dozen or so patrons looked on, whispering, with smiles still on their faces.

"Now that's more like it," said Lee, as he threw his arm around Gewey's shoulder and led him to the table. "First we feast, then we celebrate." He jumped up on a chair and addressed the entire room. "You are all welcome to join us. Let everyone celebrate and be merry." This was met with enthusiastic cheers and applause.

By the time the meal was served, the minstrels were already playing. The crowd in the common room swelled as word of the celebration got out. Before long, more than fifty people were gathered in the hall, all laughing and feasting.

"Not bad for a last-minute arrangement," Lee said as he surveyed the room. "Even if I do say so myself."

"It's wonderful," Gewey agreed. "Thank you."

"Not exactly discreet, my lord," Millet pointed out.

"You're right about that," Lee replied. "But sometimes the right thing isn't necessarily the smart thing."

Millet smiled. "Quite right, my lord." Lee smiled at Gewey and hopped up on his chair.

"Ladies and gentlemen," he shouted above the crowd. He had to repeat this several times before everyone settled down and paid attention. "Tonight we celebrate the coming of age of a young man who I have come to know and love. Through adversity and hardship, he has shown himself to be a man of honor and respect, and is most deserving of our admiration."

Voices yelling "Here, here!" and the beating of mugs on tables sounded throughout the room.

"In the years I've known him, I have never seen him falter or turn a blind eye to someone in need. I consider it a privilege to be here with him today, and to be part of this celebration." Lee looked down at Gewey, his eyes showing a touch of sadness. "I only wish his father were here today to see him. He would have been so proud of the man I see before me. I look at you, and I see him. His bravery and loyalty live on."

Gewey felt a lump in his throat and choked back his tears.

"So, without further ado," Lee continued, "I present to you, Gewey Stedding!"

The crowd erupted in cheers and yells. The stomping of feet and slamming of mugs shook the room. Gewey stood and bowed low.

"Thank you," he said, once the crowd had calmed down. "I'm not much for making speeches, but I do want to say this to my friends: I love you all. I am honored to have you with me, and I hope that we have more reasons to celebrate in the days ahead."

He bowed again, then turned to embrace Lee. The room erupted once more.

"Thank you for this," Gewey said, tightening their embrace.

Soon, the wine was flowing. The room became alive with music and dance. Gewey danced with Dina, careful not to step on her feet this time. It was during the second song that he felt a tap on his shoulder—it was Kaylia. Dina smiled and politely stepped aside.

To his great surprise, he found dancing with Kaylia was easy and natural; he was able to anticipate her every movement. They spun gracefully around the room like a top. Gewey found himself laughing out loud and full of joy.

Lee cut in for the third song, but by then Gewey was feeling dizzy and was ready to sit, anyway. He sat at the table and watched as Lee picked Kaylia up by the waist and spun her around. The elf threw her head back with laughter.

Dina sat down beside Gewey. "You look every bit the man," she said. "How do you feel?"

"Happy," he answered. "Very happy."

"Kaylia's very beautiful," she said, looking at the elf. "Don't you think?"

Gewey felt himself blush. "Yes, she is," he said shyly, trying not to meet her eyes. "But so are you," he added.

Dina placed her hand lightly over his. "Careful," she said, giggling playfully. "You wouldn't want two women competing for your favor, would you?"

Gewey tried to think of something to say but was only able to manage a nervous grin. Dina squeezed his hand quickly, then asked Millet to dance. Millet was more than happy to oblige; Maybell had been bending his ear for most of the evening about etiquette and customs in the western cities.

The night wore on, but the party gave no indication of dying down. Gewey was sitting across from Kaylia when suddenly he saw her back stiffen and eyes narrow.

"What is it?" he whispered.

"An elf," she said.

"Here?" Gewey asked, startled. "Where?"

Kaylia nodded subtly toward the door. Gewey scanned the room and saw a tall, hooded figure standing alone in the corner.

"We need to tell Lee," Gewey urged her.

"Not yet," she said. "I doubt he's here to fight. He wouldn't risk it among so many humans." With that, Kaylia got up and started to the back.

"Where are you going?" Gewey asked anxiously.

"To talk," she replied.

"Then I'm coming with you," he said and moved to her side before she could protest.

Kaylia paused a moment, then proceeded to her room. It was only a few minutes before there was a soft knock at the door. Kaylia opened it, and the tall hooded figure stepped quickly inside. He looked at Gewey for a long moment before turning to lock the door.

"You wish for this human to be present?" the elf asked.

"He wishes it," Kaylia replied gravely. "And I do not object."

"Very well," he said, pushing back his hood. His skin was much darker than Kaylia's, but his sharp features and Elven ears clearly stated his kinship to her. Gewey thought it must be wonderful to live among such people.

"I'm Linis, of the western tribes," he announced. "I've come to warn you and give aid."

Kaylia was taken aback. "Warn me? How would you even know me? It's been many years since the western tribe have had dealings this far from their home."

"You've been away from your people for a long time, Kaylia," he replied. Kaylia was shocked to hear him use her name. "Much has changed."

"Speak your intent," Kaylia demanded. "Or leave."

Linis sat down on the edge of the bed. "You are known to many of our kin. Word of your pending judgment has traveled fast and far."

"What of it?" Kaylia asked defiantly. "How is this your concern?"

"You will not live to be judged," he answered. "The elders have sent word that you are to be killed, and even now you are being hunted."

"I gather from your words that you are not among the hunters," she observed.

"No," Linis replied. "I am not here to kill you, and I do not wish you judged at all."

"But I have broken the law," she countered. "And do not wish to avoid judgment."

"Old laws for an old world," Linis scoffed. "The elders are holding on to a life that no longer exists. The time for the old hatred is over. If we are to survive, we must learn to live with the humans. We cannot hide from the rest of the world forever. Eventually, it will find us."

"You speak of a second split!" Kaylia cried, outraged. "I will not be a part of it."

"The choice is no longer yours," he said. "The elders break with tradition by ordering your death without trial. They fear the words you may speak, and seek to silence you before you become a threat to their power. You are already a part of this, like it or not."

"How did this happen?" she asked solemnly. Her face was pained with the thought of her people turning on each other once again.

"It started five years ago," Linis began. "My tribe was approached by a man claiming to be from a stronghold in the north. He told us there were armies preparing to march on the kingdoms of the west. He offered to return our lands for us to rule, so long as we agreed to become their allies.

"We contacted the other tribes, only to find that they had been given similar offers. Many wanted to take the offer in hopes of achieving our former glory, but others knew it for what it was—a lie. My tribe sent scouts north to gather information. When they returned, they said that the land of Angrääl was alive again, and was indeed gathering strength.

"Our elders remembered the old stories and rejoiced, believing that Rätsterfel had returned once again to battle the gods. But some of us refused to believe this. Some of us had actually gone out to see the world while the elders locked themselves away, letting their hatred of humankind stew and fester.

"We tried to reason with them, but they threatened us with death or banishment, forbidding us to speak of it. It was then we made contact with the humans."

Kaylia sat up straight. "You did what?"

Linis laughed. "Is it really so surprising?" he asked, motioning toward Gewey. "You travel with humans yourself. Have you not found that they are not the demons we've made them out to be?"

"Do the other tribes know?" Kaylia asked.

"Some," he replied. "Most choose to do nothing as the world passes them by. But we will not be so foolish. Darkness is consuming the land, and if we do nothing to stop it, we shall be consumed along with it."

"How do you move around?" she asked. "If you're known to associate with humans, aren't you hunted? I imagine you would at least be called forth for judgment."

Linis held his head high and proud. "I will not face the judgment of fools," he said determinedly. "As for being hunted, most choose to leave us alone for the time being. Those that have come after us have been turned back. We are more numerous than you can imagine. We even have a few locations in human cities where we can gather and walk about the city openly."

Kaylia's mouth gaped. "How did you accomplish this?" she asked skeptically.

"It took time, but we opened relations with a few of the lords. After a while, we gained their trust. Many humans still view us as killers and assassins, but that attitude is slowly beginning to change. It's a thing never seen in a hundred lifetimes."

"I'd like to see that," Gewey said sincerely. "I think it would be wonderful for elf and human to live side by side."

Linis nodded in approval. "You choose your companions wisely, I see. But we're a long way from peaceful co-existence. For now, it's our task to break down old ideas and replace them with new ones. Perhaps human and elf will one day live together, but we still have much work to do."

"You said you were here to warn us," Gewey reminded him.

"Yes, my young friend." Linis turned back to Kaylia. "A small group of elves is waiting just outside the city with the intention of killing you and any that travel with you. I'm here to make sure that doesn't happen."

"How?" asked Kaylia. "I travel with others that would make escape impossible. Unless you can grow wings and fly us away from here, they will catch us."

"Don't underestimate what a determined Seeker can do," Linis advised.

"What's a Seeker?" Gewey asked.

"In human terms, it would be woodsman or tracker," he answered. "It takes two hundred years to attain the rank of Seeker, and in the whole of the world we have no equal in the art of evasion."

Gewey stared in wonder. He had thought Kaylia could never be surpassed in skill when it came to avoiding being seen, but she was only one hundred and three years old. Linis had trained for two hundred years. It was difficult for him to grasp the concept.

Kaylia saw the look on his face and smiled. "You see, Gewey, there is still much to learn. For both of us."

Linis laughed. "You will find me to be a willing teacher. And from the way you move, it seems as though Kaylia has already given you some instruction. She has done well. You are fortunate to have such a graceful teacher."

Upon hearing Linis speak well of Kaylia, a pang of jealousy suddenly struck Gewey's chest.

"Five of my kin are waiting just outside the city walls," Linis continued. "Tomorrow night we will escort you west, where you can be safe for a time. You should inform your companions of our intent and tell them to bring only what they can carry. I will return at dusk tomorrow. Be ready." He rose from the bed and put his hands on Kaylia's shoulders. "All will be well, Kaylia. I know I have given you much to think about, but you must trust me. There is no other way for you and your friends to escape." With that, he left.

Gewey was still boiling with jealousy as Kaylia sat on the bed and looked up at him. "That's quite enough," she scolded.

"I don't know what you mean," Gewey lied. Somehow, though, he knew she could feel what he was feeling.

"You have no cause to be jealous," she explained. "If he approached me with interest, he would have immediately sensed there is a suitor; unless he was prepared to challenge you, he would not interfere."

"I'm not jealous," he replied stubbornly.

"Of course you are," she said. "It's perfectly natural. It's a consequence of touching the mind of someone you've spoken the declaration to. I told you those ancient words have meaning. But they also have power."

"If you knew this would happen, why did you want to touch my mind to begin with?" he cried, suddenly feeling violated.

"I felt it was necessary to know you more ... intimately," she answered. "I suppose I should have warned you there might be some emotional repercussions." Kaylia had the look of a mischievous child. "Now, I think it's time to rejoin the party. We can inform the others later." She took hold of Gewey's hand.

"No!" he yelled, jerking his hand away. "You told me you wouldn't hold back, but it's all you do."

Kaylia lowered her eyes. "You're right, of course. I should have warned you." She held out her hand. "I will try to be more considerate."

Gewey paused, allowing his anger to subside. "Thank you," he finally said.

He took her hand, and they returned to the common room, where the others were still enjoying the celebration. Lee was dancing with Maybell, who was laughing like a young girl as he swept her across the dance floor, while Millet and Dina toasted each other's health for what was probably the tenth time. The rest of the room buzzed with merry-making as the minstrels played on and on, each song livelier than the last.

When things finally died down around midnight, Kaylia had everyone join her in her room. She told them in detail about her conversation with Linis, and the ambush that awaited them when they left Delhammer.

"Do you trust him?" Lee asked.

"I probably would have been able to tell if he was lying," Kaylia answered. "If he says there are elves waiting to kill us outside the city walls, then I think we should take it very seriously. Linis says he can help us avoid detection, and we should accept his help."

"I agree," Gewey added. "I think he was telling the truth."

Lee looked intently at Kaylia. "Fine," he said reluctantly. "We'll trust your judgment."

"Thank you," Kaylia replied.

"I was talking to Gewey," he said, rising to his feet. "Now, we should all get some rest. I have a feeling that we're going to need it."

Dina cleared her throat and tilted her head toward Maybell. "Excuse me," she said. "But aren't you forgetting something?"

"Ahh," Lee said, suddenly realizing what she meant. He turned to the old woman. "Maybell, from the sound of it, we'll be walking for quite some time. You may want to take refuge here."

"Young man," she said indignantly. "I can walk you into the ground. Don't let the age on my face make you think

I'm feeble. I will not be left behind. I said I'm going to the temple of Valshara, and I mean to do just that."

"Very well," Lee conceded with a certain amount of admiration. "We'll be leaving early tomorrow. Millet and I will divide the gear and sell what we won't need in the morning."

"I fear that means the wine as well," Millet lamented. "Such a pity."

They said goodnight and retired to their rooms.

Gewey was so excited at the thought of meeting more elves, it took two large swallows of jawas to calm his mind enough to be able to sleep.

CHAPTER 19

When Gewey awoke the next morning, his things had been packed for him. Lee had already left, so he made his way down to the common room, following the smell of porridge and biscuits. Maybell was sitting at a table, sipping on a cup of apple juice.

"Good morning," Gewey said, taking the seat across from her.

Maybell smiled warmly. "Well, if it isn't the young man. Come to keep an old woman company?"

"Absolutely," he said. "Have you eaten?"

"Not yet," she replied. "I was waiting for the others to roll out of bed. But now that you're here, I say to blazes with them."

Gewey chuckled. "I agree."

The two of them ate while Maybell told him stories about the different temples she had seen. Gewey marveled at her ability to remember every detail.

"Now that I have you to myself," she said. "I must ask: What do you intend to do about the two women who now compete for your affections?"

Gewey was stunned. "I don't..." he stammered.

"I may be old," she said, cutting him off, "but I'm not blind. Both Kaylia and Celandine seem to be quite taken with you—not that I blame them. But that does present you with a difficult situation."

"I don't think Dina sees me that way," Gewey countered.

"Perhaps not," Maybell laughed. "But she has at least shown interest, and I don't think Kaylia is very happy about it."

"I haven't noticed anything," Gewey said. In truth, it seemed to him that Kaylia and Dina were getting along quite well.

"Of course you haven't," she chided. "You're a man. I just want you to be careful. The last thing you need is to have a broken heart on your conscience."

"What can I do?" he asked sincerely.

"Either choose one or choose neither," Maybell replied. "I do not envy you. Both Kaylia and Celandine are remarkable and beautiful young women. It's an impossible choice. But it's one I fear you'll eventually have to make."

Gewey's head reeled at the idea. He wished he had stayed in bed.

"Good morning," Dina said, as she and Kaylia entered the common room and sat down at the table. Kaylia was once again wearing her hooded cloak. Gewey was unable to look either of them in the eye.

"Have you been teasing the young man, Sister?" Dina asked playfully.

"Not at all," Maybell replied. "We were just talking about the choices a man who has come of age is faced with."

"Is that so?" Kaylia asked. "I hope he listened."

"I think he did," Maybell said, reaching across the table and patting Gewey's hand.

Lee and Millet returned a few hours later, each carrying a large sack filled with supplies. Lee spent the better part of an hour separating the goods into individual packs small enough for everyone to carry. Maybell insisted on carrying her own provisions but eventually relented when Gewey pleaded with her.

By dusk, they had made all their preparations and waited in the common room. Eventually, Kaylia stood up and motioned for the others to do the same.

"Linis approaches," Kaylia noted. "Everyone, gather your things."

Lee raised an eyebrow. "How can you tell?" he asked skeptically.

"We elves can sense when others are near," she revealed. "But we can discuss this later; right now, we must leave this place."

Outside, they saw the elf, cloaked and hooded, waiting by the corner of the inn. Kaylia made the introductions, and Linis bowed to each in turn.

"Once we arrive at the gate, you must follow me very carefully," Linis instructed. "My kinsmen are waiting for us about one mile south of the city. Those waiting to ambush you are three miles west."

"If elves can tell when others are near, won't they sense you moving?" Gewey asked.

"We have ways of masking our presence," he answered. "If we are discovered, two of us will stay with you while the others try to distract them. Now we must hurry. I have paid the gate guard to be absent for the next twenty minutes, but after that, we may be questioned."

Linis led them at a quick pace through the city streets. Gewey kept looking back to check on Maybell, but to his surprise, she seemed to have no trouble keeping up.

Just as Linis had assured them, the west gate was unguarded when they passed through.

"Follow me along the wall," Linis whispered. "In three hundred yards, there's a path leading southwest. My people wait for us at its end."

The path was barely visible in the fading daylight. The group tried to keep pace with Linis, but in minutes, he was out of sight.

At first, Gewey was nervous, but then Linis reappeared along with five other elves. They were all cloaked and hooded in the same dark brown. Two had bows across their backs, and each carried a long knife at their side. They stood in silence as the group approached.

"These are my kinsmen," Linis told them. "All worthy Seekers."

Gewey and the others bowed and introduced themselves. All except Kaylia.

The elves said nothing for a moment, and then one of them stepped forward. He was a bit taller than Linis, and broader in the shoulders. He pushed back his hood, revealing close-cropped black hair and the same defining sharp features Gewey had come to admire.

"I am Haltris," he said. "My brethren are Sitrisa, Maltora, Santisos, and Prustos. We are honored to be of service." He turned to Kaylia. "It is a special privilege to meet someone so distinguished among our kin." They all bowed low.

Linis's eyes lit up as he regarded Maybell. "You bring wisdom, I see. How wonderful! If we survive the night, I hope you will favor me with stories of your times and travels."

"An elf of exceedingly good taste and intelligence, I see," Maybell laughed. "I would be happy to share what I know with you. Though by your standards, I think I'm quite young."

"Wisdom cannot be measured in years," said Linis. "Nor can value. I look forward to speaking with you."

"What's your plan to avoid the other elves?" Lee asked, stepping forward. "From what I've seen of your people, it's not going to be easy."

"No, it won't be," Linis acknowledged. "Prustos and Maltora will try to lead them away so we can slip by unnoticed. Our people are not easily fooled, but your pursuers are not Seekers as we are."

Prustos and Maltora nodded sharply at Linis, then disappeared into the forest.

"Don't worry," Linis assured them. "They have never failed. Even among Seekers, they are renowned for their skills. Now come, we have far to go before the dawn."

Linis and Santisos led the way, while Sitrisa guarded the rear. Lee dropped back and joined Sitrisa.

After a few hours, Linis called for a halt. "We rest," he said.

"I hope it's not on my account," said Maybell. "I'm not tired just yet."

"I would think you strong as any here," Linis laughed. "And wise enough to know when you need to stop."

"Then why do we rest now?" Lee asked.

"Because we're being chased," Linis replied. "A pursuer will assume you will run as fast and as hard as you can. A smart predator will bide its time and wait until you're spent, then strike. If you remain strong, you can turn the predator into prey."

"I see the wisdom," Lee said, nodding respectfully. "I wish I had known long ago that elves such as you existed. I could have learned much."

Linis smiled humbly. "Years ago, I would have killed you the second I saw you. I'm ashamed to say that my current attitude toward humans is a fairly recent development."

"What changed your mind?" Lee asked.

Linis sat on the forest floor and motioned for Lee to join him.

"Many years ago, I was sent to find one of our kin. She had left her people on a Soul Quest. When she hadn't returned after several years, her father asked me to find her. It took me three years, but I succeeded, only to find that she had taken a human man as a mate. I reported what I had found to her father, and he ordered her execution."

Lee's eyes shot over to Dina, who was several yards away, tending to the meal. "Was there a child?"

"Strange you should ask," Linis remarked. "In fact, there was a child. But its mother knew that I'd seen her, and she sent her mate and the child away to a human city. When I returned, she pleaded with me to spare her husband and child. She explained how the human had saved her and sacrificed everything to care for her. My heart was moved by her story."

"What did you do?"

"I told her to run. She could never allow herself to be seen by another elf, and she could never let it be known that a child came from her union with a human."

"You let her live?" Lee asked, shocked.

"I did," he replied solemnly. "What became of her, I don't know. After that, my perceptions began to change. If one of our kind could find love with a human, what did that say about our beliefs?"

Lee sat in silent thought for a moment. "What would you do if you found that child today?" he asked, finally.

"I would welcome her," Linis replied. "She may very well be the future of all the people of the world."

"You swear that she would not be harmed?" Lee pressed him.

"Of course," said Linis. "But why do you ask?"

Lee's eyes went to Dina. "That child is with you now."

Linis followed Lee's gaze. "She must not know," he said. "At least, not now."

"Why?" Lee replied indignantly. "She has the right to know."

"And I will tell her," Linis assured him. "I assume she thinks that her mother is dead, and if she learns what I have told you, she may try to seek her out. If she is the offspring of a human and an elf, then she may very well be the catalyst that unites our two races. But if she exposes herself too soon, she will not live long enough to fulfill that destiny."

"I think you should leave that decision to her," Lee suggested. "She is not rash or foolhardy. If you speak to her and explain things, I know she'll do the right thing."

"I'll consider your words," he said thoughtfully. "Until then, I would ask you to keep silent about this."

Lee nodded. "I'll keep it to myself for the time being."

Just then, Santisos walked over to where the two of them were sitting. "We should move on," he advised. "I don't think we are pursued as yet."

Linis got to his feet and gathered the group together. They walked for another two hours, then rested again for a short time.

Lee watched to see if Linis approached Dina, but to his disappointment, the elf didn't speak to her.

Dawn was just breaking when Prustos and Maltora returned. Their faces were expressionless. Linis spoke privately with them for a few moments, then rejoined the group.

"Our pursuers have been led away," Linis announced. An audible sigh of relief rippled through the party. "They will eventually discover they have been deceived, but we will be well away by then. We'll rest here for a few hours, so try to sleep if you can."

Linis walked over to Dina and motioned for her to follow him. Lee could see she was nervous; the last time she got too close to an elf, she nearly had her throat cut. She looked around and noticed Lee watching. He gave her a nod, hoping to offer some reassurance, and she returned the gesture before following Linis into the forest.

They returned an hour later. From his seat on a fallen tree, Lee could see that Dina looked both excited and terrified. Gewey, Millet, and Maybell had rolled out blankets and were sleeping under an oak, while Kaylia and the other elves stood nearby, speaking in whispers. Dina came over and sat next to him as Linis went to join the other elves.

"He told you?" Lee asked softly.

Dina nodded, her eyes staring into nothingness. "I don't know what to do," she said. Her voice trembled with emotion. "My mother may be alive. I never dared to dream such a thing was possible."

"What will you do?" he asked. "Will you seek her out?"

"No," she replied immediately. "At least, not yet. I have my duties, and I will not abandon them."

Lee reached over and put his arm around her, pulling her close. "When the time comes, I'll help you find her."

Dina put her head on Lee's shoulder, allowing him to comfort her. "Thank you," she whispered. Tears began to stream down her cheeks. "You're a good friend."

"Celandine," Linis called. "Come, meet your brethren."

Dina wiped her eyes and went over to the elves. They had all pulled back their hoods and were smiling warmly. Lee's heart lifted at the scene. Each elf took her hands and then embraced her. Kaylia motioned for Lee to join them.

"Lee," said Linis. "We have a favor to ask."

"I'll help if I can," he replied.

Linis took Dina's hand and looked into her eyes. "We ask that you watch over our sister and protect her," he said. "Kaylia has told us that you are strong and honorable and that your skill in battle is great. Celandine is the future of both our races, and she needs such a guardian."

Lee smiled broadly. "You need not ask," he said. "But I will swear to it."

"Your friends are of great worth," Linis told Dina. "Keep them close."

Dina nodded and embraced him tightly.

When the others awoke, Dina told them excitedly what had happened. Maybell hugged her repeatedly, while Gewey and Millet looked on happily. They promised her that they, too, would help to find her mother when the time came.

"It's like I have a family for the first time," Dina told Gewey as they walked on. "All my life, I've been afraid of being discovered. I still can't be out in the open, but I have part of my heritage back."

"I'm happy for you," Gewey said. His words were sincere, but he couldn't help but envy her newfound sense of belonging.

"We will take you as far as Gristol," Linis announced when they stopped for a midday meal. "We have brethren there who will help you."

"You won't be joining us the whole way?" asked Gewey.

"Unfortunately, we have other tasks we can't ignore," Linis replied. "But we will be leaving you in good hands."

"That will be perfect," Maybell announced, tearing off a piece of flatbread. "Though I am sad to leave your company."

"As am I," said Linis. "You would honor me with your company as we walk. I refuse to pass up the opportunity to speak to a human who has seen as much of your world as you have."

"Keep talking like that and you'll have me driving you mad with my stories," she said cheerfully.

"Nonsense," he replied. "Most of the humans we know are too young to have seen the changing world. To us, you contain a wealth of knowledge that we would prefer not to do without. It is two weeks to Gristol, and you will find that I will not tire of your stories."

"Don't say that I didn't warn you," laughed Maybell.

CHAPTER 20

For several days, they followed Linis and his Seekers along little-known trails and paths. The going was easy and everyone was in good spirits.

Dina spent most of her time among the elves, laughing and talking. Linis offered to assist Kaylia with Gewey's training. She gratefully accepted though it made Gewey feel uneasy. Linis remarked on how much Gewey had learned, and how quickly he mastered difficult techniques, but to Gewey's relief, the elf did not ask any awkward questions that would force him to lie.

True to her word, Maybell walked with Linis, regaling him with story after story about the life she had lived and the things she had seen. The elf listened attentively without ever seeming to tire of her tales, despite the woman's apparent ability to speak for hours without pausing.

Millet spent much of his time with Prustos, who turned out to be an expert in herbal cures and remedies. He showed Millet several common plants and mosses with healing properties that could be used to save a life if one were injured in the wilderness.

Lee continued to work with Gewey on drawing power from the earth, but Gewey was careful to take it slowly. After four days, he was able to control the flow of the power, even allowing it to enter into his body. The feeling was amazing. He felt invulnerable. Lee warned him not to take in too much too quickly, but Gewey couldn't stop himself from wanting more.

On the fifth day, Gewey completely opened himself to the strength and energy of the earth. At first, he felt invigorated, but eventually, the power overwhelmed him, knocking him to the ground. Lee helped him to his feet, reprimanding him sharply for such irresponsible behavior; secretly, however, he was pleased with Gewey's progress.

By the eighth day, Gewey was feeling as if he had no troubles at all. Linis was unbelievably adept at finding the easiest routes through the forest, making a full day's march seem like a leisurely stroll down a well-paved road. Laughter and storytelling were a matter of course, as they all sat next to the fire each evening.

It was just after noon on the tenth day—while Maybell was describing the Temple of the Far Sky to Linis—that things changed. Suddenly Linis stiffened and commanded everyone to halt and be silent. The other elves, including Kaylia, rushed to Linis's side, hands on their knives. Lee drew his sword and motioned for Millet, Gewey, Dina, and Maybell to move behind him.

"What is it?" Lee whispered.

"An elf approaches," Linis replied.

"Do you think the others caught up with us?" Gewey asked. He pulled out his own knife, holding it loosely as Linis had taught him.

"No," Linis replied warily. "I would have known if they were on our trail. Whoever this is, he wants us to be aware of his presence."

The tension grew as their eyes focused on the surrounding forest. A cloaked figure appeared from behind a young pine less than fifty feet away. His face was hidden beneath his hood, but Gewey could feel his gaze bearing down on them. He was shorter than Linis and leaner, and he wore a short knife that peeked out from beneath his cloak.

"Berathis," Linis said under his breath.

"Greetings, Linis," said the figure. His voice was deep and menacing.

"How long have you been following us?" Linis asked.

"Quite some time," Berathis answered.

"What do you want?" he asked.

"You know what I want. Give her to me, and I will spare the rest. I have no desire to see your blood flow."

"Then leave us in peace," said Linis.

Berathis pushed back his hood. His long white hair was pulled tight in a single braid that fell down his back. His face was smooth and ageless, but Gewey guessed he was much older than the other elves.

"You know I cannot," Berathis said. "You must yield."

Linis's face twisted into a pained grimace. "You taught me well," he said sadly. "I cannot yield my honor, even if it means I must face you."

Berathis's face showed both sorrow and pride as he looked at Linis. "You were always my best pupil. It saddens me to have to do this to you, Linis. It's not too late; you can still return to us."

"No," Linis answered with resolve. "It is too late for that. Things must change. I must follow the path my heart has shown me."

Berathis nodded and said, "I understand. I give you one hour. Then I shall return."

Linis and the other elves bowed and then watched silently as Berathis disappeared into the forest.

"Who was that?" Gewey asked. "And what happens in an hour?"

"Berathis is the greatest of all the Seekers," Linis explained. "He comes for Kaylia."

"He's only one elf," Gewey noted. "Surely we can stop him."

Linis shook his head slowly. "Berathis has spared us until now. He could kill us all at any time, and we could do nothing to stop him."

"What happens now?" asked Lee, sheathing his sword.

"He chooses to face us openly," Linis told them. "One of us must fight him."

"And what if he wins?" Millet asked.

Linis's face turned grave. "Then we must turn Kaylia over to him."

"No!" Gewey cried. "I don't care what happens. He's not taking Kaylia anywhere."

"I appreciate your loyalty," Kaylia said. "But if Berathis defeats our champion and I refuse to go with him, he will kill us all—one by one—until I comply."

"She speaks the truth," Linis agreed. "That he hasn't moved against us is only because he knows I will honor my word. If we lose, Kaylia must go."

Lee stepped forward. "I'll fight him," he volunteered.

Linis looked at Lee with admiration. "I cannot allow that. From what Kaylia has told me, you are an extremely skilled fighter. But Berathis is no human opponent; even among the elves, his skills are feared. I'm afraid it must be one of us."

Lee put his hand on Linis's shoulder. "If he's as dangerous as you say, then I'm the only one here who has a chance. I can't match you in the forest, but there's no elf alive that can defeat me in single combat. I'm what your people call a half-man, and I am the only hope we have to save Kaylia's life."

Linis stared at Lee in wonder. "Truly, the world is full of surprises," he remarked. "I never thought to meet a half-man.

While I understand your reasons for keeping it secret, I wish I could have availed myself to your experiences along our way."

"I thought it best to keep it to myself," Lee explained. "I ask that you do not spread this knowledge should I survive."

"You have my word," Linis promised.

When an hour had passed, Berathis returned. "Who shall meet the challenge?" he asked, removing his cloak. His eyes filled with surprise when Lee stepped forward. "I ask that you reconsider. You are brave, human, but surely Linis has told you who you face."

"He has told me," Lee replied, his sword in hand. "I wish that there be no deception. I meet your challenge in full knowledge and understanding, so I give you the same: I am Lee Starfinder, son of Saraf. I am a half-man, and well beyond your skills in combat. I ask that you remove yourself and leave us be."

"Half-man, eh?" Berathis said, intrigued. "Then today I rejoice. If death finds me, it will be at the hands of one who is great among men." He drew his long knife and smiled. "Let us dance, Lee Starfinder, and let the fates decide."

Lee crouched, leaning on his back leg and holding his sword low at his hip. The elf circled slowly to the right, his knife practically dangling from his hand. In a flash, Lee attacked high, forcing Berathis to duck and move away. Gewey had never seen anything move so fast. It was like watching two bolts of lightning do battle.

Over and over again, Lee forced Berathis back, making it impossible for the elf to counter. Seconds seemed like minutes, minutes like hours, and Berathis was clearly losing the advantage.

"You toy with me," Berathis accused. "Why don't you end this?"

"I only hoped you would see the futility of this fight," Lee pleaded. "You are by far the most skilled opponent I've ever faced. I have no desire to kill you."

"You honor me," the elf replied, "but you have no choice."

Faster than the eye could see, Berathis lunged with deadly intent, but Lee was prepared. He spun and brought his sword around, slashing across the back of the elf's hand, causing him to drop his knife to the ground. Berathis gripped his wound in pain, staring down at his fallen blade. Lee stepped forward, holding his sword in both hands, poised for the final blow.

Berathis laughed to himself and looked up at Lee. "The fight is yours," he said. "This is a good death."

"There is no need for you to die," Lee insisted. "Yield and withdraw. Your honor is secure."

"I wish you understood us better," Berathis lamented. "My death is required." He looked to Linis. "You know this."

Linis nodded his head with sadness and regret.

"That may be your way," Lee stated flatly, "but it is not mine. You fought with skill and courage, and I will not strike you down."

Suddenly, Berathis charged toward Lee. Instinctively, Lee lowered his sword to fend off the attack, impaling the elf on the blade. Berathis's arms flung around Lee's back, then slowly he slid to the ground. Lee stepped back, horrified.

Berathis gasped as blood trickled from the corner of his mouth. Tears streamed down Linis's face as he knelt down beside his former teacher and took hold of his hand.

"This is a good death," Berathis said weakly as blood spilled from his wound. "I go to see the Father with my honor intact."

"You shall be remembered," Linis wept softly. "Your spirit lives on, and I shall join you soon. You will always be the greatest among us."

Berathis reached up and touched Linis's cheek. "No, it is you who is great. You can see the future, while the rest of us live on in darkness. You are on the right path, brother. Walk it with honor." Slowly, his hand fell and his eyes closed.

Lee walked away and sat by himself against a young oak. Kaylia came over and sat beside him.

"It had to be this way," she assured him. "You honored him by allowing him to die by your hand."

Lee said nothing, but his eyes flamed with anger.

Kaylia touched his hand and raised herself up. "You may not understand us, and perhaps his death was senseless to your eyes. But that does not mean you did wrong. He wanted it so. If you had left him injured and defeated, he would have ended his own life in dishonor."

"Lee," Linis called over to him. "Will you join us as we lay our kin to rest?"

The elves were standing in a circle around Berathis's body. Lee got to his feet and approached them.

Gewey watched as the elves prepared a funeral pyre and torches. They placed Berathis's body atop the pyre and began the ritual. For hours, they sang songs in the ancient language, swaying back and forth around their fallen kinsman. Lee stood beside them with his head bowed low. Gewey and the others stood further back, watching quietly.

When the songs were over, Linis handed a torch to Lee and stepped aside. Lee lit the pyre and said a silent prayer. The elves backed away and got to their knees, watching as the fire blazed, consuming the remains of Berathis.

When the fire finally died and the body had turned to ashes, the elves solemnly rose to their feet and retrieved their packs.

"We must go," Linis declared. "I will not rest here."

The others followed without a word. They walked until dawn and then decided to rest through both day and night until the following morning.

"My heart is too heavy to continue," said Linis. "Come, Lee. Let me tell you stories of Berathis so that you may know him, and understand how happy he was that you provided the death he had always wished for."

Lee nodded and sat with the elf. He listened to stories of Berathis's deeds until it was close to dusk.

"Thank you," Lee said, once Linis had finished. "I still have much to learn of your kind. And though it still pains me to have ended the life of such a valiant person, I am grateful to have heard his tale."

"It is I who am grateful," Linis replied. "Because of you, I was spared the agony of fighting my teacher and mentor— though I doubt I would have prevailed."

"Why is it so important that Kaylia be killed?" Lee asked.

Linis sighed heavily. "There is a second split among the elves. I fear much blood will be spilled before it is over. Kaylia has a rich and noble heritage among our people; it would be a serious blow to the elders' cause if it were revealed that she has broken tradition and befriended humans. They cannot allow her to be heard and possibly sway the advantage away from them. As it stands, those who would see elf and human reconciled are greatly outnumbered, and we pose little threat to their power. But as our numbers grow, so does our influence. We've been able to avoid bloodshed so far, but the stronger our position gets, the more likely that is to change, and none of us want that."

"How do you hope to change the Elders' minds?" Lee asked. "I know elves are different from humans in many ways, but there is no doubt they share the same stubbornness."

"True," Linis agreed. "Our progress with humans has been slow, but it is progress. If we can only show our kin the possibilities and benefits of such a world, that might sway enough of my people to our cause and force the elders to relent."

"I fear that you will find resistance on all sides, my friend," Lee said with regret. "Humans don't tend to welcome change, and they hold tightly to their fears. But I wish you luck."

Linis laughed softly and put his hand on Lee's shoulder. "Two bullheaded races on a collision course with destiny. It is definitely luck that we will need."

Agreed on this, Lee and Linis moved their separate ways to rest for the next leg of the journey.

As they prepared to set off the next morning, Prustos ran ahead and disappeared into the forest.

"We arrive in Gristol in three days," Linis told the assembled group. "Prustos is scouting ahead to inform our friends of your arrival."

"I can't wait to meet these friends of yours," said Millet. "Are they elves or humans?"

"Both," he answered. "They are dependable and trustworthy. From there, they will see you the rest of the way. But for now, let us enjoy the time we have left together."

The rest of their journey was filled with merriment and song. It was almost enough to make Gewey forget the duel between Lee and Berathis, and the funeral that followed.

Each evening Linis continued Gewey's instruction in the arts of stealth and survival. He showed him ways to avoid leaving even the slightest trail, and how to read the forest in the dark when tracking prey.

Added to this, Lee allowed Gewey to push his limits a little further each day as he continued to practice drawing energy and strength from the earth. By the final day of their journey, Gewey was able to let the power flow fully into him. When he opened his eyes, it was as if he could see every detail of the world around him. His arms and legs felt stronger than they had ever felt before, and he could sense everything.

"Very good," Lee remarked. "Now you must learn to do this without meditation. Once you can do that, your physical strength will be unmatched."

Gewey could still feel the power coursing through his veins as he walked back to where the others waited.

"By the Creator!" Linis gasped as he saw Gewey approach. "You look as if all the power of heaven is inside you. What manner of creature are you?"

Linis's words set off a moment of panic in Gewey. All of the energy he had stored inside him was instantly released. The ground beneath the elf suddenly exploded, sending him flying through the air. He landed hard, and for a moment, he lay still. Lee rushed to the elf's side, but to his relief, Linis was uninjured. Linis began to laugh loudly as he struggled to his feet, while the others stepped away from Gewey, frightened.

"I'm sorry," Gewey stammered. "I didn't mean to..."

"I see now why your training is so important," Linis laughed, brushing the dirt from his cloak. "You are a mystery, young one. I hope one day to know just what kind."

Lee looked nervous. "I cannot answer questions regarding the boy," he said apprehensively. "I'm sorry, but you're better off not knowing."

"I'm just glad to know he's on our side," Linis replied. "But don't worry. I will keep my questions for another time. I do hope to one day have them answered."

Gewey was shaking at the thought of what he had just done. What if he had accidentally killed Linis—or any of the others, for that matter? Gewey swore to himself that he would learn to control his power. He would not cause the death of a friend through ignorance.

Linis could see how upset Gewey was. "Calm yourself," he soothed. "I am not hurt. But if you would allow me, I think I might be able to help."

Gewey looked at the elf in confusion. "Help? How?"

"Come with me," Linis instructed, leading Gewey away from the others. "There are those among my people who can feel the energy of the earth and forest. In ancient times, it is said some could even use that energy to change the earth according to their will. Seekers use a similar technique, though we can only harness very small amounts of it compared to what I saw in you. We can channel it to give us great stamina and strength."

"I can feel it," Gewey confided. "Even now. But I can't control it."

Linis smiled. "Do not try," he stated simply. "When you feel the flow enter you, do not try to channel it or direct it. Instead, picture it as a stream filling your soul. Once filled, let the rest pour over you and flow around you. Do not try to hold it in. Instead, simply replace it with more. Your body should become part of the energy flow, not a receptacle built to contain it. What happened earlier was caused by you holding on, when all you had to do was allow the power of the earth to continuously flow through you."

"How do I do that?" Gewey asked.

"By forgetting to try," he answered. "Do not think about it. When you hear the pulse of the earth, know that it was always there. Let your mind wander, and it will take its own course."

"I think I understand," said Gewey, nodding slowly in comprehension. "Thank you."

Linis slapped Gewey on the back. "What a Seeker you would make," he said. "One day, when our quests are done, I hope you will allow me to instruct you further."

"I would like nothing more," Gewey replied earnestly.

When they were about three miles from Gristol, Prustos returned. He spoke briefly to Linis and handed him a piece of parchment. Linis looked at it and smiled.

"Prustos has informed our people of your arrival," Linis announced. "They will meet you at the Bean and Broth tavern, and then escort you to a house where you will be safe."

"How will we know them?" Lee asked.

"Prustos has given them your descriptions," he answered. "They will speak my name so that you know them to be true. The road leading to the city is one mile north, and the gates are unguarded during the daylight hours. You should have no trouble."

"We can't thank you enough for all you've done for us," Lee said. "I am honored to have met you and your kin."

"The honor is ours," Linis replied.

Gewey and the others traded heartfelt goodbyes with the elves and then watched as they vanished into the forest.

Once the elves had gone, Millet turned to Kaylia. "What an extraordinary people you are," he remarked.

"Thank you," she replied. "I am pleased to have encountered them. I thought I would never speak to one of my kind in friendship again."

Lee started north toward the road, and the others followed close behind. Without their Elven friends, the march to the city gate felt dull and dreary. Gewey found himself missing their familiar laughter.

As Linis had said, the city gates were open and unguarded. The people of Gristol were far more accommodating than those they had encountered in other towns and villages, so they had no trouble getting directions to the Bean and Broth tavern. The tavern itself was nice, as taverns go. At first, Gewey worried that such a diverse group would stick out and raise suspicions, but none of the patrons seemed to take notice. They found a table and ordered ale and wine. They'd hardly had time to take a single sip when they were approached by a man wearing a long, worn, brown leather coat and tan shirt and pants. He had salt and pepper hair and fair skin. He smiled cheerfully as he scanned the group.

"Friends of Linis, I presume?" the man asked.

"We are," Lee responded, apprehensively.

"I'm Broín," he said, taking a seat. "You'll be my guests while you're here."

"We're pleased to meet you," Lee said, relaxing a bit.

Just then, the barmaid walked up to their table. "Good to see you, Lord Broín. The usual?"

"Yes indeed," he answered, before returning his attention to Lee and his friends. "I've looked far and wide, and have yet to find a plum brandy to equal that of the Bean and Broth. In fact..."

Struck with a sudden idea, he hopped up and whispered in the barmaid's ear.

"We're grateful for your assistance, Lord Broín," said Lee. "Our mutual friends speak highly of you."

"Thank you," he replied. "But you can drop the 'Lord' part; I'm not really a lord. About ten years ago, there was a massive fire here in the city, and I helped with the rebuilding. Since then, everyone started calling me Lord Broín. I'm actually just a merchant."

Lee gave a knowing smile to Millet. "Lordship is earned," Lee countered. "And clearly you have earned it if that's the title the people have given to you."

"I know," he said. "But I still find it a bit ... pretentious. I don't dress like a lord, and I certainly don't live like one."

"I don't know," Millet commented. "You look much like some lords I've encountered. Not all wear silk and satin."

"You sound like a man of experience," Broín complimented him, laughing heartily as the barmaid returned. She carried a tray full of small glasses filled with pungent plum brandy.

"Please enjoy," said Broín. "I would not have you visit our fine city without sampling what I consider to be its finest attribute." Everyone took their brandy and raised their glasses.

"To new friends," Broín toasted loudly, and they all took a sip. Gewey winced at the sweetness but found the aftertaste to be quite pleasant.

"When you're ready, we'll go to my home," Broín said, holding the glass under his nose. "I've had baths prepared. I know how time in the wilderness can take its toll."

"That would be marvelous!" Maybell beamed. "You must forgive my rude companions for not introducing themselves. I'm Sister Maybell."

"I'm pleased to know you, Sister," he replied, nodding his head. "While you're here, I'll have someone escort you to the Temple District if you wish."

"That would be perfect," she said graciously.

Embarrassed by Maybell's words, each introduced themselves in turn.

"What a unique band of friends," said Broín, his eyes fixed on Kaylia. "But enough of this. We should go, so you can wash off the dirt and grime of your long journey."

Lord Broín led them to his home. It was a modest two-story structure, but it appeared well-built with sturdy red brick and hard pine. It had a small white balcony overlooking the street, and a flower garden surrounded the entire house. Inside the foyer, a staircase led to the upstairs bedrooms; doors on either side of the stairs led to the dining room, study, and parlor.

"I must apologize in advance," Broín said. "I have only three spare rooms, but there are ample beds." A series of clanks and rattles could be heard coming from the back of the house. "From the sound of it, Angus is preparing dinner."

Broín led them to the bedrooms, where tubs of steaming water waited for them. Maybell took a room for herself, insistent that she be able to bathe in private. Kaylia and Dina shared the next room, while Lee, Gewey, and Millet split the third.

"When you've washed, please join me in the parlor," Broín said with a bow, leaving them to it.

"What do you think, my lord?" Millet asked once they were alone.

"I trust Linis," Lee answered. "But all the same, be alert."

CHAPTER 21

When all had washed and dressed, they went downstairs to join Lord Broín. The door to the parlor was open, and voices could be heard speaking softly from within. The parlor was sparsely decorated, with just a few paintings and some silver lanterns lining the walls. A cherry wood table holding a crystal decanter and a dozen brandy glasses stood in the corner. Three well-cushioned couches atop a thick woven rug formed a semi-circle in the center of the room, and at the far end, a small fire burned cheerfully in the fireplace.

Lord Broín was sitting on the middle couch, holding a spirited conversation with two unfamiliar figures. On his left-hand side sat a young-looking man wearing a red silk jacket and a black-buttoned shirt with black trousers. He had dark, curly hair. To Broín's right sat a blond elf dressed in common brown woodsman's attire.

"Ahh," Broín said as he saw them enter. "Please, join us." The man and the elf rose to their feet and bowed low.

"Let me introduce my friends," Broín said. "The young man here is Lord Ganflin from Althetas, and this is Malstisos."

Gewey and the rest introduced themselves in turn. Lord Ganflin turned to Kaylia, who was still wearing her hood.

"Please, my dear. You don't need to hide here," he said.

Kaylia nodded and removed her hood, although she didn't fully remove her cloak.

"Linis told us there would be both elves and humans," Lee remarked. "Still, it's odd to see." Broín laughed. "I know what you mean. I've been friends with Malstisos here for over a year, and it still shocks me when he removes his hood. A good lot, though—the elves, I mean. Once you convince them not to kill you."

"I only tried it that one time," Malstisos joked as he turned to the others. He smiled. "I'm sure Linis told you of our efforts to build relations with humans. As you surely know, it has not been well received by the elders. People like Lord Broín and Lord Ganflin provide a safe place where we can talk and plan. The elders may wish to stop us, but even they wouldn't dare assault us in a human city."

"In Althetas," Lord Ganflin added, "there are even elves walking openly in the streets."

Kaylia marveled at the idea. "I imagine that took a while to accomplish."

"Not as long as you might think," Ganflin replied. "You'd be surprised how quickly people can get used to something, though I admit there are still some who are opposed to the idea."

"Prustos left word that you would need passage further west," Broín interjected. "Where is it you need to go?"

"Actually," Dina answered, "we're headed for Althetas."

"Then you shall travel with me," Ganflin declared. "I will be here for two more days, and then I depart for home. I can delay if you need more time."

Lee looked at Maybell, who nodded in response.

"Two days should be plenty of time," said Lee. "We have some business here to attend to, but that should be completed by tomorrow."

"It's settled then," Broín said as he stood up and opened the decanter on the table. The air filled with the scent of plum brandy. "Until then, you shall stay here as my guests. My house is yours." He proceeded to pass around glasses of brandy to the entire table.

Dinner was pleasant. The dining room was large and could have easily accommodated twice their number, but the dark wood paneling and pastel drawings on the walls made it feel cozy. Angus, Lord Broín's servant, served the meal unaided with a speed and precision that impressed even Millet.

Conversation was light, focusing mainly on trade and merchant affairs. Malstisos spoke to Kaylia and Dina, telling them tales of Linis and his band. They had apparently traveled more than any other elves in history—or so it sounded the way Malstisos told it.

As they finished eating, Broín instructed Angus to see that there were enough chairs in the study to accommodate their guests. "I trust you've all had your fill?" he asked, wiping his hands with a napkin.

"Indeed," Lee replied. "I haven't eaten that well in quite a while."

"Then if you will join me in the study, we have matters to discuss," Broín said, pushing back his chair.

Broín led them from the dining room, across the foyer, and into the study. A large mahogany desk sat at the far end of the room next to a fireplace that glowed dimly as a small fire crackled and popped. Bookshelves lined the walls, and cushioned chairs had been placed in front of the desk. The lanterns in the corners had been dimmed, giving the room a very relaxed atmosphere. When they were all seated, Angus entered the room and gave them each a crystal glass filled with cider.

"My friends," Broín began. "As you all know, darkness is covering the land. In the north, Angrääl is gathering its strength and preparing to march. We've tried to warn the western nobles, but they refuse to listen. In fact, Angrääl already has representatives engaging in open negotiations with other northern kingdoms."

"Do you have word of Hazrah?" Lee asked anxiously.

"Not specifically, no," he answered. "But Hazrah is most certainly in danger. If you have friends or family there, you should get them out before it's too late."

Lee lowered his eyes in thought.

"I don't know what causes your flight west," Broín continued. "But I can guess you are not unaware of the things I speak of."

"We are aware," said Lee. "But I cannot tell you the reason for our flight. All I can say is that we have similar goals, and by helping us, you help protect your lands and homes."

"I thought as much," Broín said with a knowing smile. "You have the trust of Linis, so I won't press you to tell me things you think you shouldn't. But if you know anything about what we face, I hope you will share it."

Lee took a sip from his cup and looked at the tense face of Lord Broín.

"The power you face in Angrääl," Lee said, "is known as the Dark Knight, though some call him by other names. He is far more dangerous than you might have guessed. He has stolen a powerful weapon not meant to be wielded by mortal men. With it, he has locked the door to Heaven, and if he isn't stopped, he'll reshape the world into a living hell."

"You speak of the Sword of Truth," said Ganflin. "I've read about it, but I thought it was just a myth."

"I wish it were," Lee said solemnly. "The one who stole it is the power behind the trouble in the north. He seeks to destroy the gods, and with the sword, he might just find a way. He hasn't yet reached his full strength, but the longer he possesses the sword, the more powerful he becomes."

"How can he be stopped?" asked Broín. "I have heard of the Sword of Truth as well, and if the legends are true, then he now holds the power of a god."

"He may have their power, but he is not a god," Lee asserted. "He can be killed."

"Among the elves, hatred of the gods runs deep. There are many who would side with this Dark Knight," Malstisos noted. "If he is as powerful as you say, we will need to convince them to do otherwise."

"For that, we must count on you and your brethren," Lee said. "I'll aid you in any way that I can, but I doubt my interference in this particular matter would help."

"Hers might," Malstisos said, nodding toward Kaylia.

"They want me dead," Kaylia retorted. "They are even willing to ignore tradition to see it done. I doubt I can say anything to sway them."

"There is at least one elder who doesn't seek your death," he countered. "It may be that he is our only hope."

"He wants nothing to do with me," Kaylia replied coldly. "That my own kin has been sent to kill me tells me that."

"Who are you talking about?" asked Gewey.

"My uncle," Kaylia answered in a whisper. "He fought in the Great War alongside my father—his brother. After my father died, he raised me as his own. But that was long ago."

"Still, it might be worth the attempt," Malstisos argued. "He is not as stubborn as the other elders. He may listen to reason."

"He will not," Kaylia said firmly. Her tone was full of hate and anger. "My people could not have been sent to kill me without his consent. You would be better off if you told him you had murdered me yourself."

"I think you underestimate him," Malstisos said, his voice softening. "But as you wish, I will press you no more."

Kaylia got up and stood by the fireplace.

"In any case, we have further matters to discuss," Broín said. "There are rumors that the dead walk the earth. At first, I thought them nothing more than nonsense, but now I'm not so sure."

"They're not nonsense," said Lee. He told Broín what had happened with the baker's wife in Sharpstone, though he left out the name of the town.

"How is such a thing possible?" Broín asked, horrified.

"When the Dark Knight locked the door to Heaven, he trapped the souls of the living on Earth," Lee explained. "As his power has grown, there have been certain ... side effects. I believe it may be a result of his growing power. Whatever the case, it's effective in spreading fear, and that's his greatest weapon."

Broín took a deep breath and sighed. "Be straightforward with me," he said. Lee could hear the desperation in his voice. "Is there a way to fight him?"

"Yes," Lee answered with conviction. "He is not all-powerful—at least, not yet. Keep doing what you're already doing for now. Before it's over, we will need allies anywhere we can find them. It may not come to all-out war, but if it does, we'll need to be united and ready. My friends and I are journeying to a place that may reveal a way to end this without bloodshed, but there is no guarantee of success."

"Then we will aid you in any way you wish," Broín said with resolve. "Simply tell me what it is you need."

"There is only one thing I would ask," Lee replied. "It is a personal request, but one of great importance to me."

"Ask," Broín invited. "I will help if I can."

"There are people dear to me in Hazrah," he said. "I cannot abandon the things I must do, so I will send my friend and companion in my stead."

Millet's eyes went wide. "You don't mean to send me away!" he cried.

"Please," Lee begged. "You must see my wife and child safely away from Hazrah. I can trust no one else, and they will believe you when they see you."

Millet nodded his head and put his hand on Lee's shoulder. "I will do everything in my power to make sure nothing happens to them."

Lee turned to Broín. "I would not have him go alone, so I ask that you send someone to help him as he needs. I can pay all of the expenses, and whoever goes will be well rewarded."

"I will go," Malstisos volunteered. "But do not insult me with promise of reward. You are a friend to my kin, and that is enough." He smiled at Millet. "We leave when you are ready."

"Thank you," said Lee. "I hope one day to return the favor. Now, if you all don't mind, we've had a long journey, and I'm sure my companions are longing to spend some time in a warm bed."

"I agree," said Broín. "We can talk more tomorrow."

They all rose up from their chairs and bid one another goodnight.

Gewey went straight to bed, while Millet and Lee discussed the rescue of Lee's family. Kaylia stopped in to give Gewey his nightly dose of jawas tea, a routine he had come to look forward to.

"She certainly does take good care of you," Millet observed. "A thing not to be taken for granted."

Normally such teasing would have embarrassed Gewey, but tonight he just smiled and let the jawas take him away.

CHAPTER 22

Gewey was the first to rise the next day. He got dressed and wandered downstairs, following the smell of sausage. Angus was setting up the table when he spotted him at the door.

"Please sit," Angus urged him, pulling out a chair. "It's good to see an early riser around here."

Gewey thought about waiting for the others but dismissed the thought when Angus placed a plate filled with sausage, eggs, and fresh biscuits in front of him. To top it off, there was even fresh orange juice. In Sharpstone, orange juice was rare; the only times he'd had it before were when his father had taken him to visit Lee as a child.

The sun was shining through the windows and Gewey could hear the bustle of a new day beginning outside.

"It's been some time since the sun has broken through," Angus observed, pleased.

"Let's take it for a good omen," Broín said as he strode into the room.

Gewey felt embarrassed for not waiting to eat, but Broín didn't seem to mind. In fact, Angus brought him a plate and some juice and he immediately started in himself.

"You said very little last night, my young friend," Broín noted. "What are your thoughts on what goes on in the world?"

Gewey had to wash down a mouthful of sausage before answering. "Honestly, it's hard to make heads or tails of it. Compared with what I'm used to, things have been moving very fast."

Lord Broín nodded with understanding. "Yes, indeed. Things feel out of control, even for those of us who are more accustomed to dealing with the fast pace of the world. But I'm curious. How did you become involved in all of this, to begin with?"

Gewey was unsure how to answer. Broín could see his unease and waved his hand.

"Forget I asked," he said. "Let's talk about your companions instead. I've noticed you seem quite comfortable traveling with elves. Have you always been so accepting?"

"I think the elves are a wonderful people," Gewey replied earnestly. "After being around them, it's hard to imagine why they aren't welcome among us. They may be terrible and dangerous when they want to be, but they are also wise and full of joy. I've never seen anyone who loves his brother so selflessly or defends his honor so passionately. Of course, my experience is limited to the few I've met."

"You are wise beyond your years," Broín told him. "Now, if you would allow me, I would give you something."

"Please," Gewey protested. "Your hospitality is more than enough."

"But I insist," he said, leaving the table. A few minutes later, he returned carrying a long sword sheathed in a black leather scabbard. There were symbols running down the length of the scabbard in silver inlay, and to Gewey's eye, they appeared to be the same type of ancient writing that decorated Lee's box. Broín attached the scabbard to a studded leather belt and then handed it to Gewey. "This sword was given to me by the King of Gol'Giatha for saving the life of his son when I was a young man. I want you to have it."

Gewey stared at the weapon, stunned. "This is too much. I can't possibly accept this."

"You can, and you will," Broín said sternly. "Whatever quest your friends are on, I would have to be a blind fool not to realize that you are a big part of it. If I wanted to guess, I would say you're probably the most important part."

"Why would you say that?" Gewey asked nervously.

"You're not a servant," he replied. "You're not a warrior, either. And your friends take special care when anything to do with you comes up."

He leaned back in his chair, evaluating Gewey. "You're young—too young to be on such a dangerous journey by all accounts, and yet you carry yourself as a man ten years your senior. Whatever your reason for being here, I would have you as well protected as I can make possible. This sword will never break nor dull, and it has never been drawn from its scabbard; once drawn, only the person who has done this will be able to wield it, and no other. More than that, I do not know, but it is certainly a most special weapon. But for myself, I've always used the sword passed down to me by my father. I have no use for another."

"I can't thank you enough," said Gewey, looking the sword up and down.

"Now that's a kingly gift," Lee remarked as he and the others walked in. "May I see it?"

"Please do not unsheathe it," Broín requested. "As I told your young friend, once drawn, it will only serve one master—or so I was told."

Lee raised an eyebrow. "Interesting. Then, by all means, Gewey, draw your sword."

Gewey hesitated only for a moment before doing as instructed. The sword slid easily from its scabbard as if it had only just been oiled. The blade glimmered brightly, touched by the light coming in through the windows. Suddenly, he felt his hand grow warm, and the hilt began to throb. He wanted to throw the sword down, but he found himself unable to let it go. He gasped in shock, nearly knocking over the chair beside him. Then, as quickly as the sensation began, it was gone.

"What happened?" Gewey exclaimed. "Why did it do that?"

"Do what?" Lee asked, concerned. "What did you feel?" Gewey described what had happened.

"I know what you experienced," Dina announced, stepping forward. "Hand Lee the sword, but be careful not to lose your own grip on it."

Gewey held out the sword, holding the tip of the hilt in one hand and cradling the blade in the other. Lee touched the flat side of the blade and instantly drew back, wincing in pain.

"You've seen such a thing before," Dina said, referring to her medallion. "But I've never heard of a sword being forged like this."

"So what the King told me was true," Broín said, satisfied. "The Order of Amon Dähl would love to see this." Dina froze and stared at him.

"My dear," he chuckled. "I suspected at least one of you must be of the Order the moment I heard Lee's story last night. I guess now I know which one."

"Does anyone else suspect?" she whispered.

"Not likely," he replied. "Your lot is pretty secretive, and not too many people read as much as I do—no one I can think of, in fact. But every time I've ever run across stories about the Sword of Truth, the name Amon Dähl follows right behind. To tell you the truth, I wasn't certain until just now. Only someone of that order, or maybe an elf, would have seen a material like this being used. But don't fret; it's just another in a long line of secrets that will keep me company when I die."

He smiled pleasantly at Dina and then turned to Maybell. "But enough chit-chat. Angus will take you to the Temple District whenever you're ready, Sister."

"Thank you," she said, sitting down to eat.

"I'll be accompanying her as well," Lee added.

"Of course," he replied. "As for the rest of you, I assume you don't want to be spotted by unfriendly eyes, so please tell me if there is anything you need and I will see that you have it."

"A lifetime supply of orange juice," Gewey blurted before he could stop himself.

Broín chuckled loudly, nearly doubling over with his laughter. "A lifetime supply might be more than I can provide, but you will not want for it while you're here. It's a favorite of mine too, so I keep plenty."

Gewey turned red and thanked him.

Once everyone had finished breakfast, Angus showed Maybell and Lee to a waiting carriage and climbed up with the driver. Gewey and Kaylia sat in the parlor with Lord Ganflin as he showed them a popular card game from Althetas. An entire pitcher of orange juice sat on the table beside Gewey.

Millet busied himself with preparations for his journey. After a short but fierce debate with Lee the night before, Millet decided to venture out alone to purchase horses and provisions for the ride to Hazrah. Broín offered to accompany him, but Millet insisted he would rather be alone.

Dina, Malstisos, and Broín went to the study. Dina had planned to reveal her heritage to the elf, but apparently, Prustos had already done so. Malstisos offered to explain the Elven code of honor to her, and Broín insisted on joining them, not wanting to miss an opportunity to expand his knowledge.

After lunch, they all gathered together in the parlor to exchange tales and sing songs. Gewey noticed that many of the stories were just slightly different versions of those he had heard back home. The names and places were different, but the themes were the same. He had no voice for song, so he left the singing to Dina and Kaylia, who he thought had far more beautiful voices than his own.

Broín and Ganflin recited poems, but when it came to Gewey's turn, he could think of nothing to share.

"Come now," Broín encouraged him. "Surely you know a song from your home, or at least a story told to you as a child."

"Yes," Malstisos said, grinning merrily. "I weary of these lofty tales spun by men of learning. I would rather hear a simple tale told by simple folk." Everyone cheered him on until it was clear they would not be satisfied until Gewey took a turn.

Gewey took a deep breath and tried not to be too aware of all the eyes looking at him. "Long ago," he began, "there were two brothers named Bernard and Kyle, who were the sons of a farmer. The farmer owned two large pieces of land: one in the fertile lowlands, and one in the rocky hills. When he passed away, he left the brothers all his land and possessions. Bernard loved his brother very much, so when Kyle came to him and asked to be given the rich lowlands so that he would have the means to marry his love, Bernard agreed, even though this meant he couldn't afford to start a family of his own. Kyle swore that one day he would buy Bernard a farm next to his and share all that he had with his brother.

"Years passed, and Bernard waited as his brother took his wife and had three fine sons. He hoped that his brother would honor their agreement, but as the time wore on, he never did. Finally, Bernard became too old and weak to work his land, and because of his brother's betrayal, he had no sons to work in his stead. Kyle had become rich and bought up all of the lowland farms in the county, but because he was selfish, he never did anything to help his poor brother.

"One day, a great storm came, and the rivers overflowed. With nowhere else to go, Kyle went to the high hills with his family to take refuge. But because he was ashamed, he did not go to his brother for shelter. Instead, he sat with his family in the pouring rain atop a high hill and watched as all of their crops were swept away by the flood.

"The next day, the youngest of Kyle's sons became very ill, and in his desperation, he took the boy to his brother's house.

"Bernard greeted his brother with joy and helped him nurse his son back to health. 'Why do you help me?' Kyle asked. 'I have wronged you and broken my promise, and because of that you have no sons.'

"'Yes, you have wronged me, brother,' Bernard replied. 'You have left me alone here on this rocky hill. Your shame has kept you from me. But that does not change that I love you. And though I have no sons, what has been worse is having no brother.'

"Bernard's words held no hatred: instead, he wept with joy at the sight of the brother he had missed so much. Kyle vowed that when the water receded, Bernard could come live with him and his family.

"The farmer's heart swelled with joy, and when the land dried, they all headed down the rocky hill together. On their way down, they saw that the rains had uncovered gold that ran from Bernard's house, all the way to the basin. Kyle offered to have his sons collect the gold for Bernard, but Bernard insisted that they share it amongst themselves; as long as he was with his family, he had all that he wanted.

"The younger brother refused, and sent his sons to bury the gold, making them promise not to dig it back up until the two brothers were both dead. Together, they went back to the lowlands, where they happily spent the remainder of their days.

"When the brothers died, the sons went to find the gold, but it was all gone except for two interlacing veins. Try as they might, they could not remove this gold from the ground. It was then the sons knew that the spirits of their father and his brother rested there, so they left it buried for all time."

"Now there is a story for elf ears," Malstisos cheered. "Your father told you this?"

"Yes," Gewey answered. "When I was a small boy, he made sure to tell me a story every night. He even traded with the merchants for storybooks when he had told me all that he could remember."

"He sounds like he was a good father," Broín said.

"He was," Gewey agreed, suddenly missing him very much.

There was a loud knock at the front door. Broín went to answer it, and moments later he returned holding a letter. Concern showed on his face.

"What is it?" Lord Ganflin inquired.

"A letter has arrived for Gewey," Broín said, handing it to the boy.

"For me?" Gewey asked, startled. He opened the letter and read it. "You must find Lee right away." His voice sounded frightened.

"I will go to the Temple District and find him immediately," said Broín. "Do you know what temple he and Maybell would have gone to?"

"Ayliazarah," Gewey answered. Broín nodded and flew out of the door.

"What does it say?" Kaylia asked anxiously.

Gewey handed her the letter. His own name was written just above the broken seal.

To Gewey Stedding of Sharpstone

I wish to speak to you on behalf of my master. I mean you no harm and will be awaiting your presence at the Bean and Broth tavern. Bring who you wish, but I will be alone and unarmed. Do not flee. All of your movements are being watched, and it would be unfortunate if you did not hear what I have to say. I will wait for one hour.

It was signed:

Saylis Fernmen

"I will go with you," Kaylia said firmly.

At first, Gewey was going to tell her no—that he didn't want to put her in danger. But one look at her face told him there would be no argument.

"The rest of you must stay here," he said. Gales of protest came from the remainder of the group, but Gewey was determined. "We can't all be in the same place if this turns out to be a trap. The rest must stay here until I return."

"Do you plan to wait for Lee?" Dina asked.

"For as long as I can," he replied. "But if he is not back in time, then I must go without him."

Gewey went upstairs to retrieve the sword Broín had given him. While still in his bedroom, he drew it. The blade sang as it slid from its scabbard. He stared at it for a long moment and then sheathed it again.

"I hope you won't need it," Kaylia said from the doorway. "But all the same, it is good to be prepared."

She tapped her finger on the hilt of her long knife and smiled wickedly.

CHAPTER 23

It took the carriage thirty minutes to get to the Temple District. Lee had the box wrapped and stuffed inside a cloth sack. He hoped the Sister they were going to see would be able to help, but he wasn't optimistic. Maybell, on the other hand, was excited to see the woman and told Lee many times along the way about her unparalleled knowledge in lore.

"She is by far the most learned Sister in the order," she said. "If anyone can help us, it's her."

"No doubt," said Lee, smiling patiently. "And I'm sure she'll be happy to see you."

"We were novices together," she told him for the fifth time. "And best friends." Maybell had the excited look of a young girl seeing a temple for the first time. The carriage stopped in front of the Temple of Ayliazarah, and Angus hopped down to open the door for them.

"We may be quite a while," said Lee. "Feel free to leave. I'm sure you have other things that you'd rather be doing." He reached into his pocket and tossed Angus a silver coin.

Angus looked at the coin as if Lee had insulted him, and then passed it to the driver, who was more than happy to accept. "My instructions are to be at your disposal," he said. "I shall be here when you are ready to leave."

Lee could barely contain his laughter. He bowed to the man and walked Maybell up the stairs to the temple.

The interior looked much like the temple in Kaltinor, except that smaller statues of the other eight gods surrounded the large statue of Ayliazarah in the center of the entrance hall. In the corners of the hall, several plush chairs were set up in small circles, and a short brass table with a thick glass top stood in the middle. At least a dozen novices buzzed about their business, and nearly all of the chairs were filled with men and women reading and talking.

Maybell stopped a passing monk. "Is Sister Ruthisa here?" she asked him.

"She would most likely be in the archives," he answered courteously. "Do you need directions?"

Maybell smiled. "No, thank you, brother; I know the way."

Maybell led Lee up a flight of stairs and down a narrow hall to a marked door. Inside, tall shelves filled with hundreds upon hundreds of ancient-looking books lined the room.

"Ruthy," Maybell called out as she poked her head down each row of shelves.

"Here," an old woman responded, exiting one of the rows at the far end of the room.

Though Maybell had told Lee that she and the Sister were the same age, the woman he saw looked much older. She wore light blue and white robes, and her silver hair was wrapped in a thin silk scarf.

She was bent with age, and her stride was little more than a slow shuffle. In her arms, she held a thick leather book that was nearly half as big as herself. She looked up through a pair of thick spectacles and smiled widely.

"My word," said Ruthy, feigning irritation. "I thought you'd forgotten about me, you witch!"

"Don't just stand there," Maybell chided Lee. "Help her with that large and probably very boring book."

Lee suddenly felt like a guilty child, and he rushed to take the book from Ruthy's arms.

Ruthy looked at him firmly. "Don't let that old hag boss you around," she scolded. "The day I can't carry a bloody book on my own, I'll just go ahead and die."

The two women burst out laughing as Lee stood there, unsure of what to do. Ruthy handed him the book, then went over to embrace Maybell.

"By the gods, it's good to see you," Maybell said. Tears began streaming down her cheeks.

Ruthy stood back with her arms extended, still holding Maybell. "I'm so happy to see you, Bell. We heard about Kaltinor. I was afraid that demon-of-a-woman might have done you in."

"She wishes she had," Maybell replied. "But alas, I live to fight another day."

"Will you be staying?" Ruthy asked hopefully.

"Not quite yet," she answered. "I'm only here until tomorrow. I have something for you see, though."

Lee removed the box and handed it to Maybell. Ruthy's eyes grew wide as Maybell held it out.

"How did you get your hands on this?" she asked in a whisper. She trembled as she took the box and slowly ran her hands across the lid. "Do you know what this is?"

Maybell nodded. "The Book of Souls."

"Quite right," Ruthy replied as she traced the Elven letters with her finger. "I assume you have been unable to open it?"

"That's why we're here," Maybell explained.

"And I thought you had come to see me," she teased.

"Don't be cute," said Maybell.

Ruthy grinned mischievously. "This is better than a visit. Besides, you promised me you'd retire here, and it certainly doesn't look like you're ready for that just yet."

"Not quite," she replied. "Can you help us?"

"To open the Book of Souls? Not a chance. It can only be opened by one with the power of heaven, or so the legends say. The elves kept it for centuries, but that part you probably know. It was stolen in the Great War and was thought to be lost forever."

"What is it, exactly?" Lee asked.

"It's the very words written by the gods, is what it is," she replied as she turned the box over and over, examining every detail. "In their own hand. It is said that if a being with the power of heaven were to read from its pages, creation itself could be undone."

"No wonder the elves protected it," Lee said in awe. "Such a thing in the wrong hands could doom the world."

"Indeed," Ruthy agreed. "But I don't think there's much danger of that. Even if someone who possessed it intended to destroy the world, they wouldn't be able to get it open. The box itself is indestructible."

"I found that out the hard way," Lee admitted.

"The best thing you can do is return it to wherever you found it and leave it alone," Ruthy advised. "The mere thought of wielding such power is enough to drive men mad. Even if they couldn't get the box open, there's no telling what they'd do to possess it in the hope that they one day could."

Lee heard the door open behind them, followed by the sound of metal and leather. Suddenly, the hairs on the back of his neck stood up. He spun around and drew the short dagger he had brought with him, silently cursing himself for leaving his sword at Lord Broín's house. As he turned, he saw three men in studded leather standing just inside the door. Two carried crossbows, and the one in the middle held a short sword in one hand and a dagger in the other. Their faces were grim and weathered and bore the scars of battle.

"What fortune," said the man in the center. "I was only supposed to see that you remained here and out of the way, but now I find that you've brought a great treasure with you."

Lee glanced down at the box as he slid it in front of Ruthy. "Leave now and I'll allow you to live," he said threateningly.

"My dear Lord Nal'Thain," the man said with an evil smile. "Or do you prefer Lord Starfinder? I have no doubt you could kill every one of us. But if you don't do exactly as I say, I shall see that these two lovely ladies precede us to the afterlife."

Lee's muscles tensed as he tried to think of a way to kill the soldiers while saving Maybell and Ruthy, but the man was right. The soldiers on either side of him had their crossbows trained directly on the Sisters. There was no way to save them if he attacked.

"I'll give you nothing," Ruthy said defiantly, holding the box tightly to her chest. "Kill them. I've lived long enough."

"As have I," Maybell said, her head held high.

The man chuckled, still wearing a sinister grin. "Such courage," he said mockingly. "But I doubt Lord Starfinder wants the blood of two women on his hands. Isn't that right?"

Lee seethed with rage. He could not let the Book of Souls fall into the hands of the Dark Knight; with the Sword of Truth at his disposal, the Dark Knight might actually be able to open it. If that happened, all was lost.

"If I give you the book, you will leave my friends in peace and depart this city immediately," he demanded. "If you don't, I will make you pray for death."

"You are in no position to give commands," the man replied. "You'll give me the book, and I will keep you here as I was instructed to. After that, you'll find the reason for your quest no longer exists, so I suggest you return home and hope my master forgets all about you."

Lee felt a cold knot form in the pit of his stomach. It was clear they meant to keep him here until they had dealt with Gewey. He knew what had to be done. He readied himself to attack.

Just then, the soldier on the left yelped in pain as blood spewed from his mouth. The other two turned to look at their comrade, momentarily stunned. A moment was all Lee needed. In a flurry of motion, he sprang forward and slashed his dagger across the throat of the other bowman. Blood shot from the wound, spraying onto Lee's face. The remaining soldier tried to flee but was met by the sword of Lord Broín. He thrust his blade through the man's heart, watching as the soldier gasped and fell to the floor.

"Looks like I arrived just in time," Broín observed as he wiped his blade on the soldier's trousers.

Lee nodded to Broín, then turned to Maybell. "Wait here. I'll send word later."

Before she could argue, Lee was gone, with Broín following behind.

Lee raced through the streets of Gristol as fast as his legs could carry him, his dagger still in his hand. Broín could not keep up and soon fell far behind. The instant Lee reached the house, he flung the door wide open. Dina stood just inside, looking upset.

"Where's Gewey?" Lee demanded urgently. She recounted what had happened. "He left a little while ago for the Bean and Broth."

"Fool," he roared, running to his room to retrieve his sword.

"Where's Millet?" he asked Dina as he fastened the blade to his belt.

"He still has not returned," she replied nervously.

"When he does, tell him he leaves immediately," he ordered. "The rest of you get your things together. I'll return as soon as I have Gewey and Kaylia." With that, he took off toward the tavern.

Broín arrived a short while later, out of breath and holding his side. "By the Gods, that man is fast," he said, gasping for air. Dina told him what Lee had said and explained that Malstisos had been guarding the others.

"Tell him to keep vigilant. I'll be back soon." He caught his breath and shook his head. "Wonderful," he muttered to himself as he took off after Lee. "More running."

CHAPTER 24

Gewey and Kaylia paused as they approached the door to The Bean and Broth. He had waited as long as he could for Lee, but the time had come when he could wait no longer. Malstisos had offered to accompany them, but Gewey refused this. When Malstisos insisted, Ganflin helped a bit in convincing him to stay behind.

"I'm rubbish with a sword," he said to the elf. "Someone who can fight needs to be here."

Reluctantly, Malstisos had relented, allowing Gewey and Kaylia to leave for the tavern alone.

Gewey stared at the door and checked his sword for the hundredth time. "If anything happens, I want you to promise me you'll run," he said gravely.

Kaylia reached up, pulled his face to hers, and kissed him softly. Gewey stood stunned, momentarily forgetting the danger. "You will never get such a promise," she said firmly, but with a sweet smile. "I do not abandon my friends, and I certainly do not leave a suitor undefended." Gewey smiled back, and they entered the tavern.

It took a second for his eyes to adjust to the dim light of the room, and he could hear nothing but the sound of the barman cleaning mugs and glasses. He rubbed his eyes and looked around. The tavern was empty save for the barman and a lone figure sitting in a corner, facing away from them. The barman looked up at Gewey and motioned toward the figure. Gewey and Kaylia walked up to the table and stood behind the man. He had blond, shoulder-length hair that was tied in a short ponytail and wore a simple maroon tunic and pants.

"Unless you intend to stab me in the back, I suggest you sit down," he offered, sounding amused.

Gewey and Kaylia looked at one another for a moment and then took seats across from the man. To Gewey's surprise, he didn't look but maybe a few years older than himself.

"You're Saylis Fernmen, I presume?" Gewey asked. His hand had not left the hilt of his sword.

"And you are Gewey Stedding," he answered. "I see you have brought the lovely Kaylia with you—understandable, if unnecessary. I have come as I promised, alone and unarmed."

"Good," said Kaylia. Her tone was dangerous.

Saylis laughed confidently. "I didn't mean to imply that I am unprotected. But for the purpose of our conversation, I thought a show of force might be ... distracting."

"What do you want?" demanded Gewey.

"Me?" he replied. "Nothing. Nothing at all. But my master, on the other hand..." He motioned to the barman, who brought him a glass of wine. He looked over to Gewey and Kaylia. "Would you join me?"

Gewey glared in silence.

"That will be all," Saylis told the barman, tossing him a copper. "Now then, as I was saying, my master would very much like for you to come to Angrääl. There is no reason for you to run. He means you no harm and only wants your friendship."

Kaylia laughed. "You must think us fools," she sneered. "If that's all you have to say, then you've wasted your breath."

"Ah, the fury of an elf," he mocked. "Such passion. The fact is, he has no need of you, my dear. If young Gewey wishes it, you can accompany him, but my orders say nothing about you except that I should be careful regarding your temper." He leaned back and sipped his wine. "Oh yes, and if you should ask, I'm to inform you that your uncle has ordered your assassination."

Kaylia forced a smile. "You seem to know much," she allowed. "But if you think I'm not already aware of this, and your intent is to upset me and throw me off balance, you've misjudged me."

"Not at all," he replied. "I wish this encounter to be pleasant."

"If that is all you have to say, then I have an answer for you," said Gewey.

Saylis held up his hand. "Before you answer, you should hear the rest." He paused a moment before continuing. "You seek to destroy my master. He knows this but doesn't blame you. You have been deceived. He only wishes that you understand the truth and perhaps aid him in his cause. By now you have discovered what you are, but you have no idea how you got here, or even how to use your power. My master can help. All he asks in return is that you stop this foolish quest for his destruction."

"I've heard your master's lies before."

"Pure misunderstanding," Saylis said dismissively. "His reaction was ... unfortunate. Moreover, he wants me to convey his apologies. The truth is, he was shocked to discover of your existence, and he knows he acted unwisely. But now he is hopeful. That you have been abandoned on earth can be turned into a great boon for the whole world. If you join him, there is nothing that can't be achieved."

"It is your master's desire for power that caused me to be here in the first place," barked Gewey. "And I'm sick of listening to your lies."

"Careful," Saylis warned. His tone became dark and threatening. "Consider your words. If you refuse to listen to reason, you will not live to see the Temple of Valshara. But before you die, you will watch as your friends are tortured until they beg for death. Think about this. You can save yourself and your friends. All you have to do is come with me now. Bring the elf woman if it pleases you. I promise that the rest of your companions will be left in peace."

"For how long?" boomed a voice as the tavern door was flung open. It was Lee. His sword was in his hand and his face was spattered with blood and sweat.

"I see I should have picked better men," Saylis noted calmly. "I didn't expect you, but please, join us."

"No thank you," Lee snapped as he strode over to the table. "We're leaving."

"Don't you want to hear my proposal first?"

Lee reached down and grabbed Saylis by his hair, jerking his head back. "I'll give you a proposal," he hissed. "Tell your master that if he returns what he has stolen, he will receive a painless death. And as for you, if you are ever stupid enough to hinder me or my friends again, I will remove your eyes, cut off your hands, and set you loose in the wilderness." He slammed Saylis' head into the table, knocking him unconscious. "Let's go."

Gewey and Kaylia were stunned by Lee's outburst, but they stood and followed him to the door. Broín ran up just as they were leaving.

"If you think I'm running anymore, you're wrong," Broín told them, breathing heavily. Lee didn't say a word as he stalked away with Kaylia and Gewey trailing behind.

"Don't worry about me," Broín called after them. "I'm fine." He bent over and rested his hands on his knees. "I need a brandy," he muttered before setting off at a run again to catch up.

When they reached Broín's house, Millet was sitting on the stoop. "Good to see that you're unhurt, my lord," he said. "I see you've retrieved Gewey and Kaylia."

"Is everything ready?" asked Lee.

"I was only waiting for your return," he replied. "Malstisos is with the horses at the back. Everything is packed and ready. All that's missing is Sister Maybell."

"I'm not missing," said Maybell as she walked through the gate. She held the Book of Souls in her arms. "I'll be ready to leave presently."

"You'll not be coming," said Lee flatly.

"We've been over this before," replied Maybell. "I'll not be left behind, and that's that."

"I have no time to debate," growled Lee. "We ride hard and fast, and if you can't keep up you'll be left behind."

"my lord," interrupted Millet. "I only purchased two horses."

"I have enough horses for you stabled nearby," Broín offered. "I'll send for them now." He nodded to Angus, who immediately headed off.

Lee turned and looked at Gewey furiously as they entered the house. "Fool," he yelled. "Have you lost your mind? What were you thinking?"

"What did you expect me to do?" Gewey shot back.

"I expected you to wait for me," said Lee. "You could have been killed. Then where would we be?"

"I don't care what you say," said Gewey. "I did the right thing. Besides, I didn't go alone."

Lee took a deep breath and rubbed his temples. "You still should have waited," he said, calming himself. "I can't allow you to be killed. You don't understand how dangerous these people are. If it weren't for Lord Broín, Maybell and her friend would most likely be dead right now. If they have the chance, they'll kill us all. As it is, they set a trap that I walked right into."

"What happened?" asked Gewey as they walked up the steps to their room.

Lee recounted the events at the temple. "And that stubborn woman refuses to stay here," he complained, clenching his fists.

"Maybe she'll listen to you."

"I don't think she will," answered Gewey. "She believes all this is part of her destiny. Or at least, that's what she says. I must admit, she hasn't slowed us down yet."

"Yes," he agreed, "but she'll push herself to death before she'll admit she can't keep up."

Gewey thought for a minute. "Why not send her with Millet?" he suggested. "How could she refuse? There should be considerably less danger, and she might be a lot of help."

A huge smile slowly grew on Lee's face. "Now that's a great idea," he said and tore off down the stairs.

Kaylia came in a second later. "Are you all right?"

Gewey blushed, thinking about the kiss in front of the tavern.

"I'm fine," he replied shyly. "Lee just overreacted, but we settled it. He's going to ask Maybell to help Millet get his family out of Hazrah."

"I heard," she said, sitting on the bed. "That's not what I mean. I'm talking about the scum in the tavern. Are you all right?"

Gewey smiled. "Actually, I feel better than I did before. My enemy seems more human now. He may have been trying to sound powerful, but to me, he just sounded desperate. It gives me hope for victory."

"Good," she said and stood up. She placed her hand on his shoulder and squeezed almost imperceptibly. Gewey felt a pleasant chill run down his spine. Kaylia smiled back at him. "I think the Dark Knight should be very afraid," she said, and then left the room.

Gewey picked up his pack and headed downstairs, just in time to see Maybell storm past and slam her door shut. Lee was standing at the bottom of the stairs with a satisfied grin. Millet, on the other hand, wore a look of desperation.

"Please, my lord," begged Millet. "Don't do this."

"It's done," said Lee unyieldingly. Millet lowered his head and skulked away, muttering angrily.

Gewey couldn't help laughing at the scene. "I take it that all went as you expected?"

"They leave as soon as Maybell is ready," Lee replied.

Lord Ganflin came out from the study and handed a sealed letter to Lee. "When you get to Althetas, give this letter to Harlondo. He manages my affairs when I'm away. He will provide you with anything you need. You'll probably beat me there by several days, so you may also wish to visit the innkeeper at the Frog's Wishbone. That's where the humans and elves meet most of the time. Do not open the letter; Harlondo is not the trusting sort and may give you a problem if the seal has already been broken. But now you must excuse me. All this excitement has made me forget that I am overdue to meet the mayor for dinner. I detest the man, but I must maintain certain relationships. It was a great pleasure to meet you all."

"My thanks," said Lee. "I hope to see you again under better circumstances."

Lord Ganflin bowed low and departed into a waiting coach.

An hour later, Broín returned with three stable boys leading five magnificent horses. Lee stared at the animals in wonder.

"I see that you appreciate a good horse when you see one," Broín noted with pride. "These are the finest animals for a thousand miles. If those who pursue you want to catch you, they'll need to grow wings."

"Where on earth did you get such animals?" asked Lee.

"They're bred on the northwestern steppes by the nomadic tribes that dwell there. It wasn't easy to get them to part with these; I'm proud to say that I'm the only man to ever leave with so many."

"If our mission wasn't so urgent, I could never accept," Lee admitted. "You must at least allow me to pay you—though I don't know that I have enough money."

"You misunderstand," said Broín. "I have no intention of giving up my horses. I expect you to return them when all this is over and the Dark Knight has been defeated. But until then, they are yours to do with as you please."

Lee smiled, overcome with the thought of such a generous gesture. "I shall take care of them until then," he promised. "I hope one day I can talk you into taking another journey to the steppes with me ... if only to see if I can pick one out for myself."

"It would be a trip I would love to take."

Millet readied one of the horses for Maybell. When the three were mounted, Lee handed Millet a small bundle of letters and nodded as if asking a silent question.

Millet reached down and took Lee's hand. "All will be well," he said reassuringly. "I'll send word of our success."

Malstisos rode up beside Lee. "I will look after your family. They will have my protection until I deliver them to your care."

"Thank you," said Lee, trying to force back tears of worry. "I am deeply in your debt."

"You had better keep your word," said Maybell as she admired her mount. "I will see the Temple of Valshara once this is done."

"You don't need to worry," replied Lee. "You'll see it, even if I have to carry you there on my back."

Maybell tried to look angry, but seeing the worry on Lee's face, she said instead, "I swear that I will not step foot in Valshara until your family is safe."

Lee smiled and bowed. "Thank you, Sister. That means a lot to me." He realized what a good idea it was to send Maybell. She would lay down her life if necessary to protect his family, and her knowledge of the cities and temples could be invaluable.

Gewey and the rest bid them farewell and watched as they rode toward the east gate. Once they were out of sight, Lee called everyone into the parlor.

"Thanks to Lord Broín's generous loan," Lee began, "we should be able to make it to Althetas in less than seven days. We'll be moving fast. We have enough food and water for the whole journey, so we won't need to stop for supplies along the way. Once we arrive, Dina will make contact with her order, and from there on, we should be safe." His eyes focused on Gewey. "If anything happens and we're separated, we'll meet at the Frog's Wishbone in Althetas. Wait there until I, or someone from Dina's order, get there."

Dina stepped forward and pulled out her medallion so that Gewey could see it clearly. "If you are approached by anyone claiming to be in my order, make them show you this. Be sure to touch it. It should burn you. If it doesn't, then that person is an imposter."

"We need to be out of the city before sundown," Lee continued. "It's certain they'll see us leave, so we must move fast once we're beyond the gates."

"I'll send word ahead," said Broín. "I have a messenger flock on the roof. I'll instruct my friends in Althetas to aid you."

"Thank you," Lee replied. "That would be helpful."

"The horses have been saddled and packed," said Angus, sticking his head through the door.

Lee and the others went outside and double-checked their belongings. Once mounted, Lee looked at Lord Broín and nodded respectfully.

"Until we meet again," said Broín. "Angus is watching the gate and will tell me if you are followed." He stood just outside his door and watched as Lee and the others slowly made their way down the street.

The ride to the gate was tense, and no one spoke a word. As they approached the gate's heavy, metal doors, they saw Saylis Fernmen waiting for them. His head was bandaged, and his eyes were swollen and bruised.

Lee motioned for everyone to stop as he and Kaylia began scanning the alleys and rooftops for further trouble. Gewey put his hand on his sword, and Dina pulled out a small dagger.

"I thought I'd see you off," called Saylis. Despite his words, his face was grim. "I want you to know that I'll be there in the end, Starfinder. Mine will be the last face you ever see." He shot Lee an angry look, then ducked down a nearby alley.

"He won't try anything until we're outside the gates," Lee guessed, hoping he was right. "He may have set up an ambush. If that's the case, I'll handle it. The rest of you keep going and I'll catch up. That means you, boy." He looked straight at Gewey and didn't look away until the boy nodded in agreement. "Don't worry, I've had more capable men than this idiot think they could kill me. I'll burn before I'll let scum like him be the end of me."

They urged their horses on and passed through the west gate.

"Are you ready?" Lee asked the others. They nodded. "Then let's go."

Lee booted his mount, sending the horse into a gallop. Gewey and the others did the same, and they were off like bolts of lightning. Gewey had never ridden so fast. He could feel the sheer power of the animal beneath him, and it thrilled him. He smiled at the thought of anyone thinking they could catch them.

CHAPTER 25

Salmitaya tossed and turned in her bed. The dreams had gotten worse in the past few days. Since her return to Kaltinor, things had become troubled. The other temples had shunned her, even those that had once secretly aided her. She still had the governor and lords on her side, but their loyalty was bought. Should Angrääl get word of her failure, she would lose everything; it was their gold that kept her in power.

"Maudina!" she yelled. A young girl scurried into the room, rubbing her eyes and trying not to yawn. Salmitaya had hired her to replace Celandine the day after she got back. She didn't know what had happened to Celandine but swore to flay the girl if she ever returned.

"Yes, Your Holiness?" Maudina said meekly.

"I want some hot tea," she ordered, sitting up in bed.

"Right away," the girl replied, dashing off. Salmitaya got up and put on her slippers and a soft cotton robe. She hated the temple at night. The emptiness made her uneasy. The book she had been reading lay open on a small table next to a plush chair. Her thoughts kept returning to Gewey as she distractedly fingered through its pages.

Damn that boy, she thought. *If it's the last thing I do, I'll see him beg and scream.*

Several minutes passed and Maudina still had not brought the tea. "Blasted girl," she muttered. "What's taking so long?"

"You'll not be needing a servant, my love," came a deep voice from just outside the open door leading to the next room.

Salmitaya shot out of her chair. "Who are you?" she demanded. "Show yourself."

In stepped a tall, lean man dressed in a black shirt and pants with polished silver buttons. These were paired with an exquisite jacket with impossibly intricate white embroidery. A fearsome curved sword hung from a belt that sat loosely around his thin waist. His face looked young, and his brown curly hair fell to his shoulders. In his hands was a tray with two cups of hot tea. He placed the tray on her bedside table and handed her one of the steaming cups.

"Sit down, my love," he instructed as he pulled himself a chair from the corner. "We have much to discuss."

Salmitaya was terrified as she sat back down. "Who are you?"

"You may call me Yanti," he answered, smiling.

"Well, Yanti," she said, trying her best to sound unafraid. "You have trespassed in the Temple of Ayliazarah. Leave now, or I'll see you whipped and hanged."

Yanti looked amused as he blew on his tea. "That's not very hospitable of you, considering I'm here to save your life."

"What do you mean? Speak sense."

"You didn't think your failure would go unnoticed, did you?" he asked in a level tone.

"I—I..." she stammered with sudden realization. "I was going to report it. I swear."

"Of course you were. That's exactly what I told the master. I told him that you would never try to deceive him—especially knowing what would happen if you did."

"I'm sorry I failed," she said, desperately trying to hold in her sobs. "I was betrayed. Someone helped the boy escape. There's no way I could have known."

"Calm yourself, my love," Yanti soothed her, holding up his hand. "We already know what happened, and it's being dealt with. I'm here to offer you a chance to redeem yourself. You'd like that, wouldn't you?"

"I'll do anything," she vowed. Tears began to fall down her cheeks.

"I know you will, my love." He leaned back in his chair, stirring his tea with the tip of his finger. "The master does not doubt your loyalty, only your judgment. Normally that's enough to warrant ... discipline, especially considering the trust and responsibility that you've been given. But I've convinced him that you deserve a second chance."

Salmitaya slid from her chair and dropped to her knees. "Thank you!" she groveled. "Tell me what I must do. I swear I will not fail again."

Yanti sat his teacup on the arm of the chair and stood up. "There's no need for such a display," he said, helping Salmitaya to her feet. He lifted her chin and tenderly wiped the tears from her face with a handkerchief he'd produced from his jacket pocket. "I've left you instructions on the table in your study. You should open them right away, my love."

Salmitaya nodded her head slowly. Yanti smiled and turned to leave. "One more thing," he said, glancing back toward her. "It would be unfortunate if you failed again. I don't think I'd be able to intervene twice." Salmitaya watched silently as he left.

As soon as she heard the door to the main hall close, she ran to her study. Just as Yanti had told her, there was a sealed letter on the table. She opened it and read its contents. By the time she finished, she was weeping again. She looked around the room as if hoping someone might come to save her and then collapsed in a heap. Eventually, she gathered her wits and went to bed.

The dreams she had that night were the most terrifying yet.

CHAPTER 26

Lee marveled at how hard the horses could be pushed and promised himself to make good on the trip to the northwestern steppes with Lord Broín. They had been riding full speed for more than twenty minutes, and so far, he'd seen no sign of an ambush. If they didn't run into one by sundown, he thought it unlikely they would run into one at all. They'd entered the Great Faldon Plains that stretched all the way to the Abyss; though not impossible, concealing an ambush here would be difficult. The tall grass could easily cover a man's presence, but horses would have to be moved far enough away from the road so as not to be seen. The Plains were sparsely populated, dotted with ranches and farms. The few small towns were little more than trading posts frequented by drovers and travelers on their way west. A few shallow rivers and streams were the only real interruptions in the vast, flat landscape.

By the time they finally stopped to rest their mounts, they had already covered many miles. Lee looked behind them, pleased with their progress. A series of wells lined the road to Althetas, placed roughly every twenty-five miles to aid thirsty travelers. Lee knew some of them to be dry from his previous travels, but most made good spots to rest and water their horses.

"It doesn't look like anyone's waiting for us," Gewey observed as his horse drank from a small trough next to the well.

"So far," Lee acknowledged warily. "But I'd say we need to pass two more of these wells before we're far enough away to be sure. They may still be waiting for us. Hopefully, they're not clever enough to let us pass, then attack us by night."

"If they're foolish enough to attack an elf in the dark, then let them," Kaylia said, grinning. "It will be their last mistake."

"Actually, I think it more likely they'll ambush us with bows," Lee replied. "I doubt they'll want to risk getting too close unless they have to. It's what I would do."

The sun was going down, and Lee told them they would be riding through the night. It was fully dark by the time they approached the next well. Kaylia got off her horse, and she and Lee prepared to scout the area. Gewey wanted to join her, but Lee stopped him.

"Protect Dina if something happens," Lee instructed.

"I don't need protecting," Dina argued.

"We all need protecting," Lee replied. "But until we get to your people, you are our only means of making contact. So you will be protected."

Dina growled but held her tongue.

"Keep quiet," Kaylia scolded them. "I'll go alone. Lee can stay here and Dina... You can protect Lee," she said mockingly. She checked her knife and crept into the darkness.

When Kaylia returned, she motioned for everyone to get down and stay quiet. "There are men about," she whispered.

"Where and how many?" Lee asked, quickly drawing his sword.

"One hundred yards south of the well," she answered. "About a dozen."

"Could you tell who they are?"

"No, I didn't get close enough. We should move the horses back, then take a closer look."

"You two wait here," Lee told Gewey and Dina. "Kaylia and I are going to see what we can find out."

"I should go," Gewey asserted. "I've trained to hide in the shadows. They won't see me."

"He's right," Kaylia agreed. "You may be fierce in a fight, but you can't match him in stealth any longer."

Lee thought for a second, then looked at Gewey. "Observe only," he said firmly. "Nothing else."

Gewey nodded and removed his sword. "Take care of this for me," he said, handing it to Dina. She was careful to touch only the scabbard.

Gewey retrieved his knife and put it in his belt. He and Kaylia had only taken a few steps before they vanished from Lee and Dina's sight, as if by magic. Lee smiled with pride.

"He's learned much," Dina remarked.

"No doubt," Lee replied. "It's hard to see the boy who left the farm in the man who now travels with us."

Gewey followed closely behind Kaylia. There were no trees to hide behind, but still, he could see how the night changed and shifted ahead of him. The shadows were subtle, but they were there.

He allowed his eyes to penetrate and then eliminate the darkness, marveling at how much his training had changed his perceptions.

Gewey was able to see the men from about fifty yards away. They were kneeling down in the tall grass looking toward the well, though he was certain there was no way they could see it in the dark from where they were. He figured they were listening for the sound of approaching horses. He made out fourteen men, all carrying swords and wearing studded leather armor. Kaylia motioned for him to stay where he was, then circled around to look from the other side. Her graceful movements made it difficult not to watch her as she left. She returned a few minutes later, and together they headed back.

"Well?" Lee asked anxiously.

"They're not alone," Kaylia told him. "Another group of ten bowmen is waiting less than fifty yards west of the first group."

"Bait," Lee said. "They want us to engage close up; if we discover the first group waiting for us and attack them, the bowmen will rain down arrows killing everyone, including their own men. A clever plan, actually."

"Can't we just go around and avoid them altogether?" Dina asked.

"We could," Lee replied. "And if we were on foot, we would. But if they have any other men about that we haven't yet seen, they could alert the rest. And frankly, I don't want to face two-dozen men head-on. As it stands, they don't know we're here yet."

"So what's the plan?" Gewey asked.

Lee scratched his chin in thought. "They've set a trap, so we'll let them think it has worked. I'll sneak up and engage them from the north. The first group will be listening for horses to approach the well, so when I attack, they'll think we've spotted them and decided on a full frontal attack. Gewey, you and Kaylia will move in behind the bowmen. They'll hear the fight and think the trap is sprung. Once they've let loose their arrows on the first position, take them out. Don't give them a chance for a second shot. After the first volley, I'll move to your position and help you finish them off. Any survivors from the first group should be confused and scattered. If any are left, we'll take care of them last."

"And what about me?" Dina asked, not wanting to be left out.

"You stay with the horses," he answered. "If we're killed or captured, ride back to Gristol and tell Lord Broin what happened."

"I'll not stand by like a helpless child while the rest of you go headlong into danger," she said stubbornly.

"I have no time to argue with you, woman," Lee snapped. "You are capable, but you are not a warrior. You could get someone killed."

"How would you know what kind of warrior I am?" she challenged. "My order trains us in weapons. Some of us are among the best swordsmen that ever lived."

"Are you one of them?" Lee asked sarcastically. "If so, then by all means, ready your weapon. If not, we face two dozen men, and one weak link could get us all killed."

Dina glared at Lee for a moment, then threw Gewey his sword.

Satisfied, Lee turned to Gewey. "Listen carefully," he said. His tone was grave. "I know you've never killed before. But you cannot hesitate once the fighting begins. If you don't kill them, they will kill you."

Gewey nodded solemnly. "I understand." He had never really thought about what it would be like to kill a man, but now he was faced with that likelihood. He steeled his nerves and put on his sword. "But I have a question: when they fire their arrows, where will you be?"

"Hoping not to get hit," Lee replied. "Don't worry, I'll keep the soldiers between me and the bowmen. It's a risk, but one we have to take. If I am hit, don't stop fighting until they're all down. Understood?"

Gewey didn't like it, but he knew Lee was right. It was the only way to make it work.

"Let's go," Lee said. "I'll wait fifteen minutes for you to get into position. Remember; don't attack until they've fired."

Gewey and Kaylia moved silently around to where the bowmen waited. As soon as they were in position, they drew their weapons. Although more accustomed to fighting with a knife, for some reason, the sword now felt perfectly natural in his hand—probably because of the bonding that had occurred when he'd first drawn it, he imagined. He could sense the thumping heartbeat of the earth, and the sword was warm to his touch. Kaylia pointed to the left, motioning for Gewey to attack there first. She would go to the right.

A short time later, the night erupted into chaos. He could hear screams from the first group, and orders being barked out in the confusion as Lee wreaked havoc upon them. Gewey gritted his teeth, forcing himself to wait. Just as Lee had predicted, he heard the commander order the bowmen to make ready. His muscles tensed and his heart pounded in his ears.

Then it happened. The bowmen lined up in a single row and notched their arrows.

"Loose!" yelled the commander.

Kaylia burst from their hiding place just as Gewey heard the twang of the bows being fired. He flew out immediately after her, giving the soldiers no time to see them until it was too late. Kaylia slashed two across the throat and gutted a third. Gewey focused on a man standing on the far left of the row. He swung hard, and the sword passed clean through the man's leather armor. Gewey heard a scream as the man clutched his chest. A second soldier rushed at Gewey from his right, but Gewey stepped aside and brought his blade down across his attacker's bare neck, sending his head rolling across the ground. Suddenly, time slowed, and his sword struck home over and over again. The fever of battle overcame him as he continued to seek out new adversaries.

At last, the screams of the dying men became silent. He wasn't sure how much time had passed, or even how many men he had faced. His sword felt alive in his hand.

"Gewey," a voice called. It sounded distant and faint. "Stop."

He didn't want to stop.

"Gewey," it called again. This time, the voice was louder.

He felt the thump, thump of the earth coursing through his veins. He looked for someone else to fight, but there was no one.

"Gewey!" This time, the voice broke through. It was Kaylia.

He shook his head as the world crashed in. He expected to see the dead bowmen lying all around him, but he found he wasn't where he thought he would be. Instead, he was standing fifty yards away, among the first group of men. Lee and Kaylia were standing nearby, staring at him in awe.

"They're all dead," said Kaylia. She slowly walked over to him and put her hand on his sword arm.

"How did I get here?" Gewey asked, bewildered.

"You don't remember?" Lee countered.

"Not really," he replied, trying to make sense of what had just happened. "I mean ... I do, but it's like I saw it through someone else's eyes. What did I do?"

It was then he noticed the carnage around his feet. The dead were scattered everywhere, their limbs severed cleanly as if cut off by a razor instead of a sword. He heard the sickly squish of blood and earth as he shifted his feet.

"I watched you kill over a dozen men as if they were ants," Lee said. "Some of them you cut completely in half.

"I had just finished causing confusion in the first group when the arrows began to fall; only one or two of the men were struck, and none of them fatally. I was actually worried that this might not work when I saw you charging in. I didn't even have a chance to raise my sword again before you took out half of them. In all my days, I've never seen anything like it."

Gewey looked down at his sword. It dripped with blood. He couldn't believe what he had done, nor did he know how to feel about it. In a daze, he reached down, tore some cloth from one of the dead soldiers, and cleaned his sword.

"We should leave," Kaylia suggested. "I don't want to see what the dawn brings here."

"Agreed." Lee looked at Gewey with concern. "Are you all right?"

"I will be," he replied. "Eventually."

"I know how hard it is the first time you are forced to kill," Lee reassured him. "But you'll get through it. I'll help you."

"That's just it," Gewey replied. "It isn't the killing that bothers me, even though I know it should."

"What is it then?"

"It's the feeling," Gewey said coldly. "It was like something inside me took over ... and it felt ... good. I never understood what power is until that moment." He turned his back to Lee. "I don't think I can wield it. It's too much... too tempting."

Lee smiled and put his hand on Gewey's shoulder. "That's why you can," he said softly. "Understanding the danger of power is the only way to wield it wisely and with compassion. I'm sorry you had to learn it this way, but I am pleased that you understand the dangers. That gives me hope—for all of us."

Gewey looked over his shoulder and nodded. "Thank you. I'll be fine in a while. It's just that so much has happened so quickly. It's a bit overwhelming."

"I understand," said Lee. "I really do. But we need to leave now. We'll talk more when we stop again."

Dina was waiting with the horses when she saw them approach, covered in blood. The faraway stare on Gewey's face filled her with concern. She wanted to ask if he was all right, but he didn't even look up at her. He climbed in the saddle and sat there motionless.

"What happened?" Dina asked.

"They're all dead," Lee told her. "We should have no more trouble—at least until we get to Althetas."

They rode on until daybreak, giving Gewey time to think on what had happened. A flood of regret and anxiety filled his heart, and suddenly the faces of the men he had killed became clear. He could see the horror in their eyes as his sword cut through them. By the time he dismounted, he was weeping uncontrollably.

"I know, Gewey," Lee said comfortingly. "Most people who are forced to kill aren't put into a situation like that. I'd like to say it gets easier, but it doesn't."

"It doesn't seem to bother you or Kaylia," he sobbed. "I've seen you both kill. Sometimes you even look like you enjoy it."

"I never enjoy killing," Lee replied. "I feel it every time. It's just that I've come to terms with it. And I was much older the first time I took a life."

"It is right that you weep," Kaylia interjected. "As the elves say, you have become a bringer of death."

"That's enough," Lee snapped.

"No," Gewey said, "Let her speak. I want to hear it."

"You are not a human," Kaylia continued. "But nor are you an elf. You are a power in this world, and death will follow you wherever you go. But you must learn that without it, there can be no victory. Those men you killed tonight stood against all that you love and honor. Suppose you found a way to let them live. Do you think they would thank you, return to their homes, and raise crops? No! You would find yourself facing them again and again.

"You should weep because you have left a part of yourself behind that is innocent. Mourn the loss, but rejoice that you have gained the strength to protect those that you love from the evils of this world. We elves do not take a life lightly, but once done, it cannot be undone. We gain strength in the knowledge that each person we kill is set free and cleansed of all evil. To meet the creator, purified, is the greatest gift one can bestow."

"Are you saying you believe that a person can only be for-given if they are killed in battle?" Gewey asked.

"Not at all," she replied. "We believe that all spirits are pure. Only in life is someone evil. We do not believe that the sins of this life continue to the afterlife. How could we? Atonement would be impossible, and we would be doomed for all eternity."

"I just wish the pain would go away," said Gewey. "At first, it was different... I felt almost numb. But then it all came rushing in. I know I must cope with this, but I think it will take time to learn how."

"There are no easy answers," Lee acknowledged. "But the fact that you're asking questions tells me that you're on the right path. In time, you'll find a way to deal with the pain. But I don't think you'll ever forget it; I know I haven't."

Gewey lowered his head in thought. "I wish I understood what happened. It was as if the sword came alive in my hand. I could feel the power of the earth like never before. It was intoxicating."

"I think I might know what happened," Dina chimed in, approaching the trio. "I think it had something to do with the bond between you and your sword."

"My sword?"

"It's made from the same material as my medallion. It's more than just a way we identify one another. We also use it to focus our energy when we meditate. The more talented among us can use it to project their spirit and see other places without physically being there. I think your sword may have amplified your abilities in some way. I'm not sure how, but perhaps someone at the temple could tell you when we get there."

"If that's the case, you should be careful until we under-stand it better," Lee advised.

Gewey nodded. It made sense. He thought about the heat of the sword and the pulse of the earth coursing through his body; it was as if he and the energy were one. He would definitely have to take care. They ate a quick meal of dried figs and water, then continued on. The remainder of their trip was less than comfortable; Lee refused to allow a fire, and the nights were cold. Kaylia huddled next to him on several occasions. At first, he felt uneasy, but by the third night, he looked forward to it. Their speed had them just outside of Althetas in only six days.

The few towns along the way were easy enough to avoid. Gewey marveled at the endurance of their mounts; even after a hard ride, they acted as though they were ready to run some more. It was little wonder the people of the steppes guarded their animals so jealously—just one would be worth a dozen of any other horse he had ever seen. He promised himself to return to Sharpstone with one of his own. The whole village would be envious of him. He smiled at the thought.

When they were ten miles from the city, Lee told them to make camp. He and Kaylia would scout ahead, just in case there were any more surprises waiting for them. Gewey told him that he wanted to join them, but Lee stubbornly refused.

"I'll not have you captured or killed just before we reach our destination," said Lee. "Besides, I need you to guard the horses." He was careful not to say that he also needed Gewey to protect Dina. He wasn't in the mood for that argument again.

To Gewey and Dina's delight, Lee decided it would be all right to risk a small fire.

"At least we won't be sitting here in the dark while they're off having fun," Dina said after Lee and Kaylia had departed.

"I was getting a bit tired of sitting in the dark too," he admitted.

Dina got some dried meat and flatbread from her pack and split it with Gewey.

"I have a surprise," she said impishly, then pulled a small flask from inside her saddlebag. When she opened it, the smell of plum brandy filled the air. "Broín gave it to me just before we left." She took a sip, then passed it to Gewey.

Gewey hadn't really been a big fan of plum brandy, but he took it anyway. The far-too-sweet taste made it hard to swallow. "Thanks," he said, forcing a smile.

Dina laughed. "I see how much you enjoy plum brandy," she teased. "Still, I refuse to drink alone." She grabbed the flask and took a sizable mouthful. "I've noticed that you and Kaylia have become rather … close?"

"What do you mean?" Gewey asked, suddenly embarrassed. "We're friends."

"Is that how you feel about her?" she replied with a slight grin.

Gewey became painfully aware of Dina's eyes on him and noticed that she had moved closer. "Of … of course," he stuttered. "What else would I feel?"

"That's not for me to say," she said, handing him the flask again. "But I see how she looks at you."

"How's that?" Gewey asked, not really wanting to hear the answer.

"Like one who is in love." Her eyes twinkled in the firelight and her voice was playful. "Don't pretend you don't know what I'm talking about. I've seen the way you look at her, too."

"I … I didn't mean to… I wasn't…" He couldn't find the right words. His heart was beating so fast, he felt as if it would burst from his chest.

Dina draped her arm around his shoulders and met his eyes. "It seems like you are in quite a dilemma, wouldn't you say?" Suddenly, she jumped up, spun on her toes, and danced around the fire. "Don't worry. These things have a way of sorting themselves out."

Gewey wasn't sure if the whole thing was just a cruel joke or not. For the next few hours, he tried to avoid conversation, but Dina kept at him until he finally stormed off and pretended to check his horse.

When Lee returned with Kaylia, Gewey could barely look up at her. He was afraid she would see him blushing, and he'd had quite enough embarrassment for one night.

"Everything looks fine all the way to the city gate," Lee told them as he retrieved his blanket from his saddlebag. He sniffed the air. "Is that plum brandy I smell?"

"It is indeed," Dina answered cheerfully, throwing him the flask. "I saved you some." Lee nodded gratefully and took a sip.

Kaylia noticed Gewey was out of sorts. "What's wrong?"

"Nothing," Gewey lied. "I'm fine. I'm just tired."

"We should try to get a good night's sleep," Lee said. "Tomorrow should be a telling day."

They all rolled out their blankets and settled down. Gewey tried to place himself as far from Dina and Kaylia as he could, but he somehow ended up between them in spite of his efforts.

Sleep did not come easily, even after a larger-than-normal swallow of jawas tea.

CHAPTER 27

Gewey couldn't help but be excited as they approached the gates of Althetas. From more than a mile away, he could see the buildings rising above the city wall. Some looked to be over five stories tall.

"Is the whole city like that?" Gewey asked.

Lee laughed lightheartedly. "A good portion of it. Althetas is the largest city on the Western Abyss. All the cities and towns for hundreds of miles come here for trade."

"How far are we from the Abyss?"

"Not far," Lee replied. "Less than thirty miles, I should say."

"Why not build it on the shore? Wouldn't it be easier for shipping?"

"Long ago, Althetas was on the shore," Lee explained. "But a great storm nearly destroyed it, so they moved it here. Most towns along the shore now are small ports and fishing villages. The storms of the Western Abyss are enormous. They don't hit often, but when they do, everything is destroyed."

Gewey nodded, wondering what it would be like to see such a storm up close.

The walls of the city were twenty feet high and ten feet thick, made from gigantic blocks of black granite. As they approached, the guards waved them to a halt.

"State your business," called the guard, seemingly bored.

"Trade," Lee replied.

"How long will you be staying?"

"Three days."

The guard gave their party a quick once-over. "If your stay lasts longer than one week, you'll have to register at the clerk's office. Welcome to Althetas." He waved them on without enthusiasm and then went back to his post, where a chair and a jug of ale awaited him.

As they passed the gates, Gewey stared at the sights of the city, unable to believe his eyes. The streets were jammed shoulder to shoulder with people—some selling wares, others trading, and even some who were standing on boxes shouting quotes from various scriptures at the crowds. Most of the taller buildings had balconies on each floor where people were eating and drinking far above the hustle and bustle. Gewey stared, wishing he could see the city from their vantage point.

Lee noticed Gewey staring at the balconies. "Impressive, isn't it? Millet loves Althetas. He and I once stayed here for six months. There used to be a great sword master that lived here, and his home was in one of the taller buildings. While we're here, I'll see if I can arrange for us to visit one. At the north end of the city, there used to be some taverns on the top floors; I'm sure some of them are still there."

Gewey beamed with excitement. "Do you think Lord Ganflin's house is anything like this?"

Lee laughed. "Certainly not. From the directions he gave me, his manor is in the southern garden district, where they prefer traditional, two-floor houses. The aristocrats consider the rest of the city to be somewhat tacky."

Gewey looked at Lee in amazement. He couldn't imagine anyone thinking such wondrous buildings to be tacky. "The lords here must be a bunch of idiots."

"I'll tell Ganflin you said so," Lee teased. "I'm sure he'll agree."

"Maybe that's not such a good idea," Gewey said with a smile. "Considering we're staying at his house."

Just then, Gewey noticed something he didn't expect: an elf. He was standing in front of the door to an inn, talking to a short human. Kaylia noticed too.

"I know they told us that elves walk freely in this city," said Kaylia, "but to actually see it..."

"You should remove your hood," Gewey suggested.

Kaylia paused for a moment and then did just that. Her auburn hair flowed freely, and she closed her eyes, letting the sunshine on her face. With her bronze skin glowing in the sunlight, Gewey thought she looked beautiful. He scanned the crowd to see if anyone had noticed. A few people cast a quick glance in their direction, but for the most part, they were ignored.

"How does it feel?" he asked.

"Strange," she replied. "But good. I hate hiding."

"You shouldn't have to hide," Dina said. "None of us should."

Kaylia nodded in agreement. "Maybe one day we won't have to."

Lee led them through the crowded streets to the southern garden district. Just as Lee had said, the houses in this area were single and two-story dwellings, their brick walls covered in ivy and protected by wrought iron gates. The streets were clean and far less crowded than the rest of the city. Fine coaches, driven by haughty men in red and gold jackets and pulled by horses nearly as well adorned as the drivers, navigated the wide avenues. Lords and ladies in elegant attire strolled down the broad sidewalks.

Lee stopped in front of an immense manor and dismounted. The double-gated wall was at least ten feet high. A man in a gold silk suit and waistcoat stood at the gateway.

"Is Harlondo in?" Lee asked politely.

"He is," the gatekeeper responded. "Might I tell him who calls?"

Lee pulled the letter Lord Ganflin had given him from his pocket. "I have a message from Lord Ganflin."

"I see. Please wait here." The man passed through the gate and disappeared inside the manor.

Gewey was amazed by the size of the estate; it was bigger than most temples. The entire structure was made from polished white granite and sat upon at least three acres of land. The vestibule was lined with stone columns supporting a veranda that spanned the entire front of the house. The driveway was almost as wide as the avenue, and the well-manicured lawn and gardens held plants and flowers of so many varieties that it would take someone an entire spring just to name them all. He recognized flowers such as roses and tulips from back home, but others looked as though they belonged in a fairytale. Low-lying lavender blooms sprinkled with deep yellow swirls followed a stone path leading to a white, ivy-wrapped gazebo.

At the center of the yard was a marble fountain created in the likeness of Althetas Mol, the Goddess of Wisdom and Compassion, the patron goddess and namesake of the city. Beautiful carved wooden benches faced the fountain at six-foot intervals, and a small table had been placed beside each of them.

When the gatekeeper returned, he was accompanied by a short man in a gray-buttoned shirt and trousers, together with a thin black jacket. His hair was jet black and slicked back with oils. He wore silver reading glasses and was carrying a leather binder under his arm.

"You have a message from Lord Ganflin," Harlondo said by way of greeting. His voice was high and almost feminine.

Lee handed him the letter and waited as he broke the seal and read.

"I see," said Harlondo, putting the letter into his pocket. "Greetings, my lords and ladies. Welcome to the house of Lord Ganflin. I have instructions to treat you as I would Lord Ganflin himself. Clearly, he holds you in high regard." He gave a loud whistle, and four young boys ran from the house. "Your horses will be well-tended and your belongings brought to your rooms. Will you be sleeping separately, or shall I have couple's suites prepared?"

"Individually will be fine," Lee answered.

Harlondo raised an eyebrow. "Excellent. Please, come with me."

"You didn't want a couple's suite, did you?" Lee whispered to Gewey, trying to hide a smile. Gewey clenched his jaw and shot him a dirty look.

The inside of the manor was even more impressive than the outside. On either side of the large foyer sat marble basins full of perfumed water that gave the air a pleasing scent of lavender. Beyond the foyer, an alabaster staircase rose majestically before splitting into two spirals that led to opposite sides of the house. The polished marble walls were covered with elaborate tapestries and fine oil paintings depicting members of the Ganflin family in various heroic acts. To the far left were large double doors that led to the formal dining room, and in the corner was a smaller wooden door that provided access to the rear chambers. On the right-hand side were three separate doors leading to the studies and offices. Directly behind the stairs, a huge archway opened up to a ballroom, where an exquisite crystal chandelier hung from the vaulted ceiling. Though the room was currently unused, it was well-lit, and the lights beamed and reflected from around the steps to sparkle against the pink marble floor.

"We have hot showers in each room," Harlondo informed them. "However, a bath can be prepared if you prefer."

"A shower?" Gewey asked. "What...?"

"Showers will be fine," Lee said, cutting him off.

"Martin will show you to your rooms," Harlondo continued, motioning to a tall, silver-haired man in a straight-cut, blood red suit and jacket. "I have business to attend to, but I'll be joining you for dinner this evening. I can see you've traveled light, so a change of clothing will be brought up directly."

"Thank you, Harlondo," Lee said graciously. "That would be much appreciated."

Harlondo bowed and took his leave. Gewey smiled, thinking that Lee was right at home in this environment.

Martin led them upstairs and to the left. At the end of the hall, they turned right and were shown to their rooms in turn. Gewey couldn't believe his eyes when he entered his own suite; it was as big as the common room of most inns. An oak feather bed—large enough for three grown men—sat flush against the back wall, and to its left was a glass dressing table and mirror. To the right was a small, round breakfast table with two chairs, and beyond that stood a tall, carved mahogany wardrobe with polished brass handles.

In the near left corner was by far the most interesting feature: a round curtain hung from the ceiling above a section of black tiles. Gewey pulled back the curtain and saw three copper pipes protruding from the ceiling. The first of the pipes hung about a foot below the eight-foot ceiling. At the end of this pipe was a cone-shaped attachment with tiny holes drilled into the solid facing. The other two pipes ran down to his chest level, each one fitted with a small brass handle. Attached to each handle was a tray; one held a small bar of soap, and the other a square piece of pink coral. He knew what the soap was for, but had no idea what purpose the coral might serve. Curious, Gewey grabbed one of the handles and turned. Water sprayed down from the pipe above and poured over his head. It was hot—scalding hot. He screamed in shock and leaped away. He watched the water spill onto the tiles and swirl down a recessed drain in the center.

Gewey heard Lee laughing behind him. "I was just coming to show you how to use that. I guess I'm a bit late."

"This must be a shower," he said as water dripped down his face. He wasn't looking at Lee at all. "What a marvel!"

"I thought you'd like it," Lee said. "Dina's showing Kaylia how to use hers right now."

Lee showed Gewey how to adjust the water temperature by manipulating the handles and explained that the coral was used to scrub off dead skin.

"Be careful with it, though," Lee warned. "Scrub too hard and you'll peel your skin right off."

Gewey relished his first shower. He had never felt anything like it, and he swore that when he finally returned home, he would build one for himself.

Martin came in during his shower and announced that he had placed Gewey's belongings next to the wardrobe and laid out fresh clothing on the bed.

"Your friends will join you in the parlor," Martin told him. "This is to the left from your room, at the end of the hall."

When Gewey stepped out of the shower, he felt refreshed—even more so than after a good night's sleep. The clothing Martin had supplied was every bit as fine as the suit Lee had bought him for his coming-of-age party, which he'd sadly had to leave behind in Gristol. His fresh attire was a cream silk shirt with gold buttons and gold stitching, along with a pair of shiny black trousers. A short black jacket, soft leather shoes, and a belt with a gold buckle completed the ensemble. Gewey quickly dressed, but as he was about to head to the parlor, there was a knock on his door. Gewey gaped as a young woman wearing a baby blue housedress stood smiling in the doorway, a small basket propped against her hip.

"Lord Starfinder said that you were in need of grooming," she said, scrutinizing Gewey. "I can see he was correct. Please sit down." She motioned toward the chair in front of the dressing table.

Gewey wasn't sure what to do, so he complied. "How long will this take?" he asked. "My friends are waiting in the parlor for me."

"Your friends are being tended to as well," she assured him. "To think of beautiful young women in such a state. Your elf friend—what was her name?"

"Kaylia."

"Yes, Kaylia," she continued, brushing the knots from his curls. "Such a lovely girl. Elsa couldn't wait to get her hands on that one. Elves have such natural beauty. But when Elsa's finished with her, she'll be a goddess. The other one too. Celandine. That one is less accustomed to dirt and grime ... if you ask me. Such a gorgeous complexion on her. Well-tended skin and hair. It's nice to see a woman who knows how to take care of herself. Don't get me wrong, elves take care of themselves too, but it's just different." For the next hour, the woman talked and talked as she worked.

Gewey chuckled at the thought of Kaylia being fussed over and made up.

After a while, he found the process wasn't so bad. The girl shaved him, then rubbed a sweet-smelling cream on his face, letting it dry as she trimmed his hair. When she wiped the cream off with a warm towel, his skin felt alive, as if it had never felt the air before. *So this is how a lord lives*, he thought. *No wonder they always look so healthy and clean.*

He had never spent much effort before in grooming, and by the time she was done, he almost didn't recognize himself. He cut his own hair most of the time. Occasionally, one of the women of the village would do it instead, but none had ever made him look so ... lord-like. Refreshed and filled with a new confidence, he thanked the woman and headed down the hall to the parlor. Lee was already there, sitting in a large cushioned chair and sipping a glass of brandy. He was wearing a navy blue suit and jacket, and an ash walking stick with a silver knob was leaning on the side of his chair.

Lee smiled as Gewey entered. "Now you look presentable. I almost didn't recognize you."

"Thank you," said Gewey. "It feels different."

"We still have plenty of daylight," Lee observed. "I thought we should see if Dina can make contact with her people. I also think we should make contact with Lord Ganflin's friends at the Frog's Wishbone."

"Don't you two look handsome," Dina remarked as she walked in. Kaylia followed close behind.

Gewey's jaw dropped when he saw them. Dina was wearing a dark blue satin dress that hugged her figure lightly. Her hair was lifted away from her face and tied with a silver band, allowing it to fall loosely down her back. Kaylia wore a smooth silver dress with a small diamond cut in the midriff. Her hair had been left down, but Elsa had added shining gold strands that caught the light when she moved.

"By the gods..." Gewey gasped.

"I'll take that as a compliment," Dina teased. She did a little twirl, causing the skirt of her dress to swish and spin around her.

Kaylia, on the other hand, looked very displeased. "I refuse to go out in public wearing this," she growled. "How am I expected to fight in such clothes if something happens?"

"Don't worry," Lee assured her. "You'll be back in your old clothes before you know it. I admit it's a bit early for such attire, but they probably assumed we intended to stay in until the evening."

"Actually, I think we should do just that," Dina suggested. "My people are hard to find in the daytime, but I know where to find them after dark. We should wait until then."

"Excellent," Lee said. "I asked Martin about the Frog's Wishbone, and he said it's a very nice establishment. It turns out that Lord Ganflin bought it a few years back and completely remodeled the place."

"He should have changed the name ... if you ask me," Dina said. "It sounds like a low-class tavern."

"Maybe, but from what I've been told, it's anything but," Lee replied. "The good news is that we can keep wearing these fine clothes a while longer."

"Wonderful," Kaylia grumbled.

Just then, Martin walked in, followed by three men carrying a lute, a harp, and a flute. He served everyone a glass of honeyed wine as the musicians began playing softly. Gewey took a seat and allowed the music to take him. The songs were sweet and intricate—much different from the music he had heard at the taverns, or even at the festival of Gerath. When the first song was over, he actually sighed.

"There's so much left for you to experience," Lee said to Gewey, noticing the boy's expression. "When all this is over, I promise to show you as much as you want to see."

"That would be great. But right now, I wonder if I'll ever see home again, much less the rest of the world."

"You'll see your village again," Kaylia vowed. She had been listening to the music as well, but now a fire lit her eyes. "That I promise you." Gewey smiled, but he was saddened by thoughts of home.

They talked until dusk, keeping the conversation lighthearted. When Lee noticed the fading daylight, he called for Martin.

"Will you be dining here tonight?" Martin asked.

"No," Lee answered. "Please inform Harlondo we will be at the Frog's Wishbone."

"I shall send for the coach, my lord," he said, backing out of the room.

"We'll stop by the tavern first and make certain all is well," Lee told them. "Then Dina and I will make contact with her people."

"Shouldn't we all go?" Kaylia asked.

"I didn't really want to take Lee," Dina admitted. "The order is very secretive and distrustful of outsiders. For me to bring one person may be a problem; if they see me with three others, things could get ... complicated."

"You two will wait for us to return to the tavern, assuming all is well there," Lee instructed. "Then we'll come back here to regroup." They all agreed, though Kaylia still wanted to change her clothes.

Martin returned shortly after to inform them that the coach awaited them downstairs. They thanked him and left.

Lee told Gewey to make certain that he wore his sword. "It's fashionable here," Lee said as he dropped by his room to get his own. "As for the ladies..."

"I'm armed," Kaylia assured him. "As is Dina." Gewey tried not to think about where they had hidden their knives.

"We're off then," said Lee, and they all walked down to the waiting coach.

CHAPTER 28

When they arrived at the Frog's Wishbone, Gewey was surprised to see that there were a dozen fine coaches parked out front. The building had clearly been renovated, though Lord Ganflin had allowed the old, faded sign depicting a frog with a wishbone in its mouth to remain. Before they had a chance to exit the coach, the door flung wide to reveal Harlondo smiling in at them.

"I was just about to head back to the manor to join you for dinner," he said. "But I see that you've decided to join me instead."

"Lord Ganflin recommended this place to us," Lee replied as they stepped from the coach. "And since Martin informed us that he owns it, we thought we should see it while we're here."

"His Lordship finds it to be prudent to have a place where old prejudices aren't allowed," Harlondo told them, glancing at Kaylia. "You'll find that everyone is welcome here."

Harlondo walked them inside and instructed the barmaid to find them a good table. The tavern was by far the most elegant Gewey had ever seen, though, of course, he was no expert. Still, the floors were laid with solid stone tiles, and the sturdy wooden tables would have made anyone in Sharpstone proud. Fine lanterns hung from the ceiling, and the walls were decorated with beautiful oil paintings.

A marble fireplace had been built at the far end of the hall, and leather couches had been placed on either side of this. A lutist strummed lightly from the near corner, enthralling the small crowd gathered by him. Looking around the room, they found they were by no means over-dressed; lords and ladies in fine dress were everywhere, and scattered among them were at least a half-dozen elves. The barmaid showed them to their seats, and Harlondo ordered a bottle of wine for the table. Lee spotted a man he assumed to be the inn-keeper talking to a group of three elves near the fireplace.

"The food here is excellent," Harlondo declared after the wine arrived. "Lord Ganflin is very particular when it comes to cuisine." He looked at Kaylia and smiled. "They even serve Elven dishes, if you'd like."

Kaylia looked surprised. "Really? I haven't had mint roast lamb in a while. I wonder if they have it."

"They do indeed," he answered cheerfully. "It's a favorite here. In fact, if your friends have never tried it, I must insist they join you."

"Unfortunately, Dina and I must leave shortly," Lee replied. "But I would appreciate it if you would have some sent to the manor for us."

Harlondo looked a bit disappointed. "I am sorry you won't be able to join us. But I will see to it that you both have a dish awaiting you. Might I ask why you must leave? The nights are quite entertaining here, especially when the elves start singing—such magnificent voices they have."

"Nothing of consequence," Lee answered dismissively. "But I must attend to it before morning—a nuisance, really."

"I understand."

Lee excused himself and spoke briefly to the innkeeper before returning to the table. "We must go," he said. "We'll be back soon."

"Take your time," Gewey told him. "I think I'll have a fine time right here."

"If you're delayed, I'll see them back to the manor," Harlondo promised. "I have a carriage outside."

Lee nodded in thanks, and he and Dina took their leave.

Harlondo took the liberty of ordering for the group, and they listened to the lutist as they waited for their meal.

"Greetings, sister," said a tall elf who had seen them from the fireplace. He was dressed in a green ruffled shirt and pants with black buttons and had a long knife at his side. "I'm Drantolis. I hope I'm not disturbing you."

"Not at all," Kaylia replied. "I'm Kaylia. This is Gewey and Harlondo."

"Harlondo I know," he said. "But you say you're Kaylia? It is truly an honor to meet you." He bowed low. "We have anticipated your arrival. Lord Broín says that Linis speaks very highly of you."

"Is Linis here?" Gewey asked.

"No, I'm afraid not. He wanders the land, as Seekers do. We rarely see him. But Lord Broín sent word that you and the lovely Kaylia would likely come here. But where are your other companions?"

"Attending to some business," Kaylia replied. She sounded uneasy.

Drantolis gave her a knowing look. "It's strange the first time, speaking openly among humans. I still find it hard not to cloak myself. And the clothes are a bit difficult to get used to."

Kaylia was suddenly aware of her all-too-human attire and blushed. "It is strange," she agreed. "Especially the clothing."

The elf scrutinized Kaylia for a moment. "They certainly know how to bring out the beauty in a woman though," he said with admiration. "Please, join us once you've eaten. The rest of my kin will be excited to meet you."

Kaylia nodded, and the elf politely excused himself. Gewey felt a familiar twinge of jealousy that Kaylia immediately picked up on.

"At least something good has come from this evening so far," she observed.

"And what's that?" Gewey asked, trying not to sound upset.

"You get to feel as I have during our trip," she replied, looking satisfied.

Gewey looked confused. "I don't know what you mean."

"Don't try to understand the fair sex, my lord," laughed Harlondo. "It will only cause you grief. Just accept that they know more than you, and try to keep up as best you can."

"Wise words," Kaylia agreed with a smile.

The meal was very good. The mint lamb had a uniquely wholesome flavor that made Gewey think of spring.

More and more elves filed in as they ate, and he could tell by the wandering eyes that they had become a topic of discussion among both humans and elves alike.

When they had finished, Gewey was stuffed. He leaned back in his chair and sighed heavily.

"So what did you think of it?" Harlondo asked.

"As good as I've ever tasted," Kaylia said, wiping the sides of her mouth with a napkin. "Thank you."

Gewey only nodded and smiled with satisfaction.

"Wonderful," Harlondo replied. "But if you will excuse me, I must attend to some business while I'm here. Looking after Lord Ganflin's affairs takes constant vigilance. Might I suggest you join Master Drantolis and his friends near the fireplace?" He rose to his feet. "I shall return shortly."

Kaylia and Gewey went over by the fireplace where Drantolis and two other elf men were sat on the couches talking.

"Good of you to join us," said Drantolis as they all rose. "This is Pilianos and Salmitoris." The elves nodded in turn. They were dressed much like Drantolis, and each wore a long knife at his hip. "It's good of you to join us."

"It's our pleasure," Gewey said. Suddenly, he felt two small hands on his lower back.

"You didn't think you could keep the new arrivals all to yourself, did you?" came a woman's voice.

"Allow me to introduce Lady Fritzina," Drantolis said, gesturing toward the woman.

"Charmed," she laughed as she slipped around Gewey and took his hand. "I hear you're friends of Linis and his band. How exciting! He's like some hero right out of a legend, wouldn't you say?"

Lady Fritzina wore a fire-red gown that twirled easily around her feminine figure as she moved. Her red hair and silk gloves made Gewey think of the sirens his father had told him about as a boy. The stories of sailors being lured to their deaths by the sirens' song always frightened him.

"Kaylia and Gewey are highly regarded by Linis," Drantolis told her. "No doubt they are heroes in their own right if they traveled with such a worthy Seeker."

Lady Fritzina looked intrigued. "Is that so?" she said, eyeing Gewey with interest. "By all means, do tell us of your exploits. On the rare occasions Linis comes here, I have to ply him with drink all night before I can get a peep out of him. Perhaps you'll be more forthcoming?"

Gewey gave her an embarrassed smile. "There's really nothing to tell, Lady Fritzina. Most of my life has been spent on a farm."

"Oh, do call me Zina," she insisted. "Everyone does. You're a commoner, you say? How delightful. Please sit next to me and tell me of life on the farm." She sat on the couch and patted the spot next to her. "I'm always cooped up here in the city. I think it would be lovely to breathe fresh air for a change."

Gewey timidly sat next to her. Kaylia looked none too happy as they all took a seat.

"Tell me, Lady Fritzina," Kaylia began, purposefully using her full name. "How do you feel about the elves in your city?"

"I think it's the best thing to ever happen to Althetas," she replied. "Hopefully we can be an example to other cities." She slid closer to Gewey. "Tell me, Gewey, how have you enjoyed our city so far?"

"It's big," Gewey blurted, nervously. "I mean, it's very nice."

"A man of action, not words," Zina teased, wearing a mischievous smile. "I like that."

"Leave the boy alone," the innkeeper scolded as he brought their wine. "He's a guest of Lord Ganflin. I don't think he would appreciate you embarrassing the boy."

Zina laughed. "I was only trying to make him feel welcome. But being that you're an honored guest of Lord Ganflin, I think I need to try harder."

Kaylia seethed and leaned forward. "What do you know of Elven courtship, Lady Fritzina?" she asked, forcing a smile.

"Nothing, I'm afraid. But I'm eager to learn. Please tell me."

"It can be perilous at best," Kaylia said darkly. "When a man declares himself as a suitor, the woman takes the responsibility to guard him from potential rivals—sometimes with deadly consequence."

"Has someone made such a declaration to you, my dear?" Zina asked as she slowly edged closer to Gewey.

"Perhaps. But I believe that would be a bit too personal to speak of around strangers."

"Nonsense, we're all friends here," Zina replied. "Now, take young Gewey, for example." She seemed unconcerned in the face of Kaylia's growing anger. "For the sake of argument, suppose he had made this 'declaration' to you. How would you protect him from a rival?"

"If I felt it was warranted, I would challenge that rival to single combat," she answered, feigning an innocent grin. "To the death."

"I see," Zina said, smirking. "It's a good thing we don't do that here in Althetas. There would be duels in the street on a daily basis."

"Such a declaration made by anyone other than an elf would be a first," Drantolis noted, very interested. "If that were to happen, it should be kept secret—even from the more enlightened of us."

"Relax, Drantolis," Zina laughed. "We're just speaking hypothetically. Isn't that right, dear?"

Kaylia nodded and smiled sweetly. "Of course," she replied, staring into the woman's eyes. "But you're right, Drantolis—such a thing would need to be kept secret."

"What would be the repercussions if such a union were discovered?" Gewey asked.

"There was only ever one union between human and elf that we know of," Drantolis told him. "It was not well received by our people. Linis recently sent word that he'd discovered of a child that came from this union."

"Really?" Zina exclaimed. "I wonder what the child looks like? And more to the point: I wonder how the other elves will react?"

Gewey and Kaylia shot a glance at one another.

"Those that have been with us from the beginning will not think it anything but a natural result of our interaction with humans," Drantolis explained. "But there are those among us that still struggle with certain ideas. Elves such as Linis, who is revered among our people, must help them to understand."

The other two elves nodded in agreement as Drantolis continued. "Linis's word holds great weight with us and our kin. Of course, there are also many elves who would kill the offspring of such a union on sight."

"Then let us hope this child meets you first," Zina said, holding up her glass.

"Yes," Drantolis agreed, tipping his glass against Zina's in a toast. "Linis believes she represents hope for the future, and I, for one, agree."

Zina turned toward Kaylia. "My dear, I would speak to you alone, away from these fine gentlemen."

"Regarding what?" Kaylia asked suspiciously.

"Certainly not to fight to the death," she teased. Kaylia was not amused. "Please, let me make up for my earlier behavior. I know something you may want to hear." She got up and held out her slender, gloved hand. "We won't be but a moment."

Kaylia took Zina's hand and allowed herself to be led through the crowded tavern.

Once they had left, Drantolis leaned closely toward Gewey. "You play a dangerous game, young one," he whispered. "If you court an elf without full knowledge of our ways, you put both her and yourself in danger—especially if what I suspect is true. Did you say the words?"

Gewey was afraid to speak as the three elves stared at him intently.

"You have nothing to fear," the elf assured him. "We have been here from the beginning and are not offended by your courtship. But please, do not insult us with lies. The ancient words of declaration have definitely been spoken to Kaylia; we can see it in her eyes, and in her behavior. And, unless I've missed the mark, I think it was you who spoke to them. If you did, you need to hear what I have to say."

Gewey took a deep breath. "I spoke the words."

The elves looked at one another gravely. "Then you have done a thing that even elves have not done since the time of the Great War. You have made the bond of courtship. It's a prelude to the joining."

"I don't understand," Gewey said. "When I spoke to them, I didn't even know what I was saying. I know the traditions of your people can't be ignored, and I accept that, but I doubt she really intends to marry me."

Drantolis burst into laughter. "Tradition? Tradition has nothing to do with it. Has she told you nothing? My young friend, the words are meaningless unless spoken from the heart. That you spoke them without knowledge of their meaning tells me that the bond between you is unbreakable and possibly dangerous. Have you not noticed how things have changed between you? You can feel what the other feels—joy, fear, pain: all are shared until the time of the joining."

"Then what happens?" Gewey asked.

"Then your spirits become one in the same until you both leave this life."

"She told me she has one year to accept," said Gewey. "And that if she rejects me, we're to never see one another again."

"What she told you is only part of it," Drantolis replied. "When you spoke the declaration, her spirit attached itself to yours, bonding you together."

"You mean I forced this on her?" Gewey cried.

"Absolutely not. She wanted it, even if she didn't know it at the time." He chuckled and shook his head. "If not, the bonding would have failed. As young as she is, I'm sure it came as a great shock."

Gewey remembered the terrified expression on Kaylia's face when he had spoken the words.

"After a year, the bond will break if the joining is not made," Drantolis continued. "But it is disastrous when the bond is broken—even more so when the bond is as strong as yours seems to be. If the joining is not made, you will lose a part of your spirit. She wouldn't be able to look upon you because it would tear her apart. But should you complete the joining, you would be bound together forever—even in death."

"What!" Gewey exclaimed. "You mean...?"

"I mean, if one should die, the other would soon follow," Drantolis told him somberly. "This is why the bonding is no longer done; the Great War caused many deaths, and their mates died along with them, leaving thousands of orphans. What troubles me is that when the bond is too strong and the joining not completed, it can tear the spirit to shreds, leaving one empty and desolate. For an elf, such a fate is worse than death."

Gewey put his head in his hands, his mind spinning. Drantolis reached over and squeezed his shoulder. "Take heart," he said. "She is a fine elf, beautiful and fierce. Anyone, elf or human, would be fortunate to have such a mate."

Just then, Harlondo rejoined them by the fire. "Are you all right?" he asked Gewey.

"I'm fine," he replied weakly.

"Come then," Harlondo beckoned. "I have something you must see."

"If you will excuse me," Gewey said, rising from the couch.

"Return soon, young human," said Drantolis. "I have enjoyed your company."

"I will," Gewey promised, then followed Harlondo through the crowd to the corner of the room.

"A man gave me this a moment ago, with instruction to give it to you," Harlondo said, handing Gewey an envelope. "Who knows you're here?"

Gewey felt a chill. "No one," he said as he opened it and removed a small note from within.

*I have your elf woman. Meet me one
mile south of the city wall.*

*There is a path. Follow it until you
see a clearing. I will be waiting.*

*Come alone, or the last thing she will
feel is my knife sliding across her throat.*

"Kaylia!" Gewey gasped.

"I saw her leave with Lady Fritzina a little while ago," Harlondo said. "She seemed well at the time, though not very happy."

"Did you see what direction they went?" Gewey cried, grabbing him roughly by the shoulders.

"I'm sorry. I only saw that they walked out together."

Gewey ran to the door, sending unwary patrons flying as he passed. The street was busy as Gewey searched the crowd, hoping to see Kaylia.

"What has happened?" It was Drantolis' voice, coming from behind. He stood with his two companions, long knives drawn. "Where's Kaylia?"

Gewey knew he had to think fast. The note had said to come alone, and he wouldn't risk the elves insisting on coming with him. "She left with Lady Zina," he said, trying to sound calm. "I think I upset her earlier." Drantolis looked hard at Gewey and then sheathed his blade.

"Find her then. There is nothing worse than an angry Elven woman." The others laughed heartily and turned back to the tavern.

Gewey sighed with relief. He checked his sword and bolted toward the city gate.

CHAPTER 29

L ee and Dina's coach had just entered City Square when
Dina called for the driver to stop.

"Wait here," she told Lee. "One of my people is near."

"How can you tell?"

"When we bond to the medallion, it gives us the ability to
sense others of the Order when they're close by—so long as
they're also wearing their medallion," she answered. "Give
me a few minutes."

Lee waited, watching the people of Althetas through the
coach window.

It pleased him to see that the darkness had not spread
so far as to kill the spirit of such a great city. He thought
of his childhood, and of when his father had brought him
here for the first time. His home village was only a five-day
ride to the south. Once a year, his father made the journey
to Althetas to attend the annual meeting of the Fisherman's
Guild. It was the month before he died when he took Lee
along. His mother had said she wasn't up to the trip, and at
first, he'd been afraid he wouldn't be allowed to go without
her. But his father had looked at him and said, "A promise

is a promise. Just you be sure to do as you're told." Lee could remember how excited he'd been—just him and his dad for the first time.

His father had taken him on a walking tour of the city, even talking their way into one of the tall buildings so that they could look out on the city from the balcony. He'd asked his father if they could come live in the city. His father had simply smiled and mussed his hair. It was the best time Lee could remember.

Lee's musings were interrupted as the door to the coach opened and Dina got in. She was followed by a gray-haired man in a plain tan shirt and trousers.

"This is Ertik," Dina said in introduction. "One of my Order. He needs to speak with you."

Lee held out his hand, but Ertik simply scowled and sniffed.

"We know who you are, Starfinder," he said briskly. "And your presence is unwanted."

"That may be," Lee replied, withdrawing his hand. "But it's necessary. The Dark One moves, and I have with me the only hope for victory."

"You think that being the child of Saraf will save us?" he scoffed.

Lee was taken aback.

"Yes," Ertik laughed. "We know all about you. We've followed your progress for years."

"Then why haven't you contacted me?" Lee asked with irritation. "Angräal is on the move. I would think you would gather allies where you can."

"I suppose you think that being a half-god would be a boon to us, but you put us in danger simply by being here; the Dark Knight can sense your kind. If I bring you to the temple it would endanger the lives of more than a hundred men and women, not to mention risk the destruction of the one safe haven we still have."

"Safe haven?" Lee retorted. "There are no safe havens anymore. The evil is spreading as his power grows. He already has agents openly dwelling in the northern kingdoms, and it won't be long before they come under his rule. The dead rise from the earth, their souls forced into decaying bodies. His agents and soldiers assaulted us less than seven days east of here. All this, and you dare speak of safe havens? How long do you think it will be before he finds your precious Valshara?"

"We know all of this," Ertik replied calmly. "If you think we have been idle, you're wrong. We haven't the power to face him openly. If you expose us too soon, then the last hope of regaining the sword will die with our destruction."

"You are not the last hope," Lee countered. "I have brought the last hope. And he is the only reason I have sought you out."

"Not another half-god," Ertik sneered. "Even a thousand of your kind would not be able to defeat the Dark Knight; you truly don't understand the power he wields."

"No, not another half-god," Lee replied sarcastically. He glanced at Dina, who nodded slowly. "I have brought the only child born from the union of two gods."

Ertik laughed at first, then stopped. "You're not serious. There is no such creature. We would have known."

"We did know," Dina said. "Or at least, we knew there was something the Dark Knight was after—something he would do anything to get his hands on. Why else would the High Lady have sent word to be on the lookout for them?"

"She has her reasons, I'm sure," Ertik maintained. "But if you expect me to believe that you travel with a god..."

He hesitated. "You have proof of this?"

"I have all the proof I need," Lee answered. "My kind can recognize each other by touch. I know what he is."

"Do you think the Dark Knight would go to all this trouble just to kill a half-god and his companions?" Dina asked flatly. "The Dark One is aware this god exists, and if he succeeds in killing him, then all hope is truly lost."

"If he is a god..." Ertik began. "And I'm not saying he is ... but if he is, then death cannot touch him."

"He was bound to earth when he was a baby," Lee revealed. "How and why is still unknown, but it makes him very human in many ways. He is only now discovering his power. If The Dark Knight finds him before he's ready, then he'll kill him—or worse, capture him and break his mind."

Ertik looked hard at Lee, then got out of the coach.

"Is that how you expected it to go?" Lee asked.

"I was hoping for a bit better," Dina admitted, forcing a smile.

A moment later, Ertik returned. "Take me to him," he demanded.

Lee told the driver to take them back to the Frog's Wishbone.

"How did you discover all this?" Ertik inquired. Lee recounted the events leading up to the night when the Oracle's messenger entrusted him with Gewey as an infant. He also told Ertik about his subsequent move to Sharpstone and Gewey's upbringing in the Stedding household.

"I assume you've been training the lad?"

"I have," Lee replied. "Along with Kaylia."

"Kaylia?"

"An elf woman we are traveling with," Dina explained.

Ertik rolled his eyes. "Just how many of you are there?"

"Four now," she answered. "There were six when we began, but two are off on an important errand. They will be joining us as soon as they are able."

"You assume that anyone but the boy will be coming," Ertik said.

Lee leaned forward. "You will find that the boy's companions will not abandon him. If your intention is to separate us, then you may as well get out now."

"Then you would sacrifice the fate of the world for your own selfish desires."

"Think what you will," Lee retorted. "But so far, you've given me no reason to leave the only hope this world has in your hands. All I've seen is arrogance and an unwarranted, self-important attitude that makes me think coming to you may have been a big mistake."

Ertik glared at Lee. The tension was palpable.

"Ertik," Dina soothed, trying to calm things down. "Lee has watched over Gewey for seventeen years, sacrificing everything in the process. You can't think he would just leave him and move on. Besides, I doubt Gewey will go anywhere without his friends; he can be very stubborn."

Ertik pursed his lips and grunted. "I suppose the elf will want to come as well. That should be interesting."

"I would watch what you say when you meet Kaylia," Lee warned. "She has something of a temper."

"I'm not surprised," Ertik replied under his breath.

When they arrived at the Frog's Wishbone, Lee told Ertik and Dina to wait in the carriage while he went inside to look for Gewey. The tavern was still crowded as Lee pushed his way through the throngs. He could see no trace of either Gewey or Kaylia. Finally, he tracked down the barmaid who had served them during dinner and asked her if she'd seen Gewey.

"Oh yes," she told him. "He and the elf woman were talking to Drantolis, last I saw." She pointed over to where Drantolis and his two friends were still sitting near to the fireplace. Lee thanked her for her help and made his way over to the elf.

"Yes," Drantolis replied when Lee asked him about Gewey. "Kaylia left with Lady Fritzina. The boy seemed to think she was upset with him and went after her. I haven't seen them since."

"Do you know Harlondo?" Lee asked him.

"Yes. He left about the same time as the boy."

Probably went back to the manor, Lee thought as he returned to the carriage.

Once back at Lord Ganflin's manor, Lee and Dina scoured the house, but Gewey was nowhere to be found. Martin informed them that no one had returned since they had all left together.

"Where do you think they are?" Dina asked Lee.

"Harlondo probably offered to show them a bit of the city," he guessed. "We'll give them some time before we start to worry."

"I can see how well protected he is," Ertik sneered.

"Watch it," Lee warned. "I'm not beyond throwing you into the street. He may be young, but the boy is very capable."

Dina frowned, placing her hands on her hips. "I refuse to listen to the two of you squabble," she said. "Unless you intend to start scouring the city, we have no choice other than to wait. But if you refuse to be civil, you can both wait in separate rooms—at least that way I won't have to listen to your childish bickering."

Lee and Ertik looked like two scolded children.

"Of course you're right Sister," Ertik offered, holding out his hand to Lee. "I apologize."

"As do I," Lee said, taking the man's hand. "Now let's put this behind us and wait in the parlor. I'll have Martin bring us some wine."

Dina showed Ertik upstairs to the parlor. Lee joined them a few minutes later, followed by Martin, who carried a tray of glasses and a bottle of good wine.

"Tell me about Gewey," Ertik requested. "How old is he?"

"Seventeen," Lee replied. "But you'd never know that by looking at him."

"Seventeen," Ertik repeated softly. "So young."

"Yes, but he has shown great maturity," Dina pointed out. "It's easy to forget how young he really is."

"He has shown discipline during his training as well," Lee added. "That comes from his father, I suspect. The man who raised him was an exceptional person. That's why I chose him."

"Do you know who his real father is?" Ertik asked.

"I have my suspicions," Lee said. "He draws massive strength from the earth, so I think his father must be Gareth, but I can't be certain. As for his mother, I don't have a clue. Maybe someone at your temple will have a way to find out for sure."

Ertik scratched his chin. "Possibly. It would certainly be helpful if we knew. It's still hard to imagine ... a god, here on Earth."

"I know," Lee agreed. "But once you get to know him, you'll see that he's, in fact, very human."

Ertik opened his mouth to reply, but suddenly, the whole house began to shake violently, as if struck by an earthquake. Pictures fell from the wall, and the sound of breaking glass echoed through the halls. Lee grabbed Dina, protecting her body with his. After a few seconds, the shaking stopped.

"What was that?" Ertik cried.

Lee ran downstairs and out of the front door. Dina and Ertik followed closely behind. People on the streets were screaming and crying in fear. The front gate had come loose from its hinges, and the gatekeeper was still crouched down on the walkway.

"It's Gewey," Lee said, his voice filled with fear. "I know it. He's the only one who could cause this."

"We must find him before he brings down the whole city," Ertik said in a panic.

"Can you tell where it came from?" Dina asked.

"No," Lee replied. "But if it's inside the walls, he will be easy to find. Wait here until I return."

Lee ran off as fast as his legs could carry him. As anxious as he was to find Gewey, he was also very afraid of what he might find when he did.

If Gewey had let loose that kind of power inside the city, the devastation would be unimaginable.

CHAPTER 30

Gewey found the trail just south of the city wall. The trees were sparse and thin, but the light of the full moon offered ample shadows in which to hide. He unsheathed his sword and made his way south, keeping a few yards off the trail. He tried to stretch out his senses, but the roar of the nearby city drowned everything out. The trail itself provided little help; it was too frequently traveled for him to make out any distinct tracks. As he approached the clearing, he could see the light of several torches burning brightly.

No way to approach unseen, he thought. *Whoever this is, they either know I've been trained, or they got lucky.*

The clearing was about one hundred feet in diameter, and torches had been placed around its edge in six-foot intervals. In the center, he saw Kaylia, gagged and on her knees, bound at the wrists and ankles. Lady Fritzina stood next to her with a vicious-looking dagger in her hand.

"What's the meaning of this?" Gewey yelled, stepping into the clearing. Kaylia looked unhurt, though anger burned in her eyes.

"So fierce," Fritzina laughed. "No wonder the master wants you ... taken care of."

"Release her and I will let you live," he offered, taking a step forward with his sword still drawn.

"Stop there, my handsome peasant," she warned, holding her dagger close to Kaylia's throat. "Or I might just have to bleed this ... elf." She looked down at Kaylia with contempt. "She loves you, you know."

"What is it you want?" Gewey asked through his teeth.

"Don't you want to tell her you love her too?" Fritzina replied, ignoring Gewey's question. "Just once, before you watch her die?"

"If you hurt her, I swear you'll beg me to kill you," he roared. "You don't think you can run from me, do you?"

"Run?" she repeated, amused. "It is you who should have run." She pressed the blade against Kaylia's throat. Gewey saw a trickle of blood fall down her neck.

"Wait," Gewey cried. "Just tell me what you want."

"Lady Fritzina," came a voice from just beyond the clearing. "Enough."

Gewey turned toward the voice. "You?" he said, his voice a mixture of confusion and rage.

Harlondo stepped from the shadows. His voice was now deep and menacing, rather than high and feminine. He held a curved saber in his hand.

"Take the elf just outside the clearing," he commanded Lady Fritzina. "Do nothing until this is over. Then," he said, waving his hand carelessly, "you may do whatever you like with her."

Lady Fritzina grinned fiendishly. She grabbed Kaylia by her hair and pulled her across the clearing to its edge. Gewey jumped forward in response, but the dagger in the woman's hand held him at bay. He couldn't risk it—at least, not yet.

"I see you're every bit as stupid as I'd hoped," Harlondo said. "It's a marvel you've made it this far, even with that idiot Starfinder helping you."

"Why are you doing this?" Gewey asked. Gripping his sword tightly, he could feel it starting to come alive in his hand, drawing in the power of the earth around him.

"Why?" he replied scornfully. "Because you weren't wise enough to join the master when you had the chance—not that I ever thought it was a good idea to let you join us in the first place."

"Let Kaylia go, and I'll come with you."

Harlondo laughed. "It's far too late for that. Besides, I'd rather you were dead; the last thing I want is more competition. We don't need your help to win. The master is nearly at his full strength, and with you gone, there will be no one else nearly powerful enough to challenge us."

"If you hurt her, I swear you'll pay for it with your life," Gewey warned, his tone dark. "You have no idea what you're getting yourself into."

"She will not be harmed until after I've killed you," Harlondo promised. "Actually, you have Lady Fritzina to thank for that. She wants her to watch you die."

Gewey grinned wickedly as the power of the earth flowing through him increased. "I look forward to gutting you. Then her. Then Lord Ganflin, just for good measure."

"Ganflin?" Harlondo chuckled. "That fool knows nothing about this. We have agents in key positions everywhere, even in your beloved Sharpstone. Ganflin provides access for me, nothing more. He's too damned thick to serve the master. In fact, I think I may make him my slave as a reward for killing you."

He stepped forward menacingly. "Speaking of which."

Harlondo's left hand shot out. Gewey barely had time to react as a small knife whizzed past his head.

"Not bad," Harlondo said with approval. "I was afraid this would be too easy to be proud of."

By now, the power of the earth flowing through Gewey was like a raging river. Time began to slow, just as it had done when he'd fought the soldiers. He leaped forward, slashing down at Harlondo's head, but the man moved easily away. Gewey stared at him in shock for a moment, then attacked again. Over and over, his sword found empty air as Harlondo countered with virtually no effort. Gewey had seen only one man move like that.

"You're a..."

"Yes," Harlondo interrupted, smiling. "You didn't think Lee Starfinder was the only one, did you? But it's worse than that, boy. The master has empowered me with energy from the Sword of Truth itself."

Gewey felt his confidence drain.

"Don't feel too bad. You're not the first to underestimate me. Once I'm finished with you, I'll find the rest of your friends and make sure you're not the last."

Gewey filled with rage at the thought of his friends falling to this demon. He ran headlong at Harlondo, thrusting his sword at his opponent's belly. But Harlondo merely twisted and stepped away before bringing his own sword down. Gewey felt searing pain as the blade cut deep across the back of his shoulder. He spun around, sword extended. Harlondo ducked, and again his blade found Gewey's flesh, this time slashing open his upper thigh. Gewey backed away as Harlondo pressed the attack. He tried to block the onslaught, but Harlondo was too fast. Again and again, Harlondo's sword cut deep, opening new wounds. Blood soaked Gewey's clothes, and the wounds on his arms and shoulder made his sword feel heavy and awkward. His legs throbbed and shook with pain. He felt weak with blood loss and could hardly hold on to his sword as Harlondo came in for another attack. This time, Gewey was barely able to duck quickly enough to keep his head on his shoulders. The blade sliced the top of his scalp, sending him tumbling to the ground. He rolled back, then stumbled to his feet.

"Why prolong the inevitable?" Harlondo asked. "You have fought well. Let me end your pain."

Gewey glared at Harlondo and squared his shoulders. He looked to the edge of the clearing and saw Kaylia, tears streaming down her face. *I'm sorry,* he thought. Kaylia's eyes filled with sadness, as though she had heard him.

"Still some fight in you, eh?" Harlondo laughed. "Good."

In a flash, he was on Gewey again. This time, Gewey was able to fend off the blade, but Harlondo closed in and smashed the hilt into the side of Gewey's head. Gewey fell to the ground, dazed and with blood pouring into his eyes and mouth. His surroundings began to feel dull and distant. He wondered if this could really be the end. He attempted to stand up, but Harlondo merely laughed and kicked him back to the ground.

Harlondo stood over him with a satisfied smile. "And so ends the only child of heaven," he mocked. "I'll send your regards to your friends, starting with that one over there."

"Don't give up." Gewey could suddenly hear Kaylia's voice. It was as clear as day in his mind. "Please don't make me watch you die." Pain and desperation filled Gewey's heart as Harlondo raised his sword for the final stroke.

But the final stroke never came. Suddenly, the earth rumbled, and the ground began to shake violently. A moment later, Harlondo's eyes shot wide as the forest floor beneath his feet literally exploded. Both men were sent flying. The last thing Gewey saw before darkness took him was the ravaged body of his enemy lying next to him. Gewey smiled with relief. *This is a good death,* he thought, as the world around him faded to black.

Lady Fritzina struggled to her feet. In front of her was a crater ten feet wide and three feet deep. The mangled body of Harlondo lay only a short distance away from her, alongside a pale and lifeless Gewey. She stared at the scene in horror. Kaylia lay on the ground next to her, struggling against her bonds. She picked up her dagger and pulled Kaylia to her knees.

"I could kill you," Fritzina warned. Her voice trembled with fear and shock. "But if you promise that your friends will leave me alone, I will let you live." She pulled off Kaylia's gag. "Swear to it!"

"I swear none of my companions will touch you," she said, her voice dripping with malice.

Lady Fritzina slowly backed away, then took off into the night.

Kaylia struggled to her feet and hopped over to where Gewey's sword lay. By working the rope that held her against its razor-sharp blade, her bonds were quickly cut. She then ran to Gewey. She put her hands on his face and closed her eyes. His life force was faint and fading. Replacing his sword in its sheath, she attached it to her belt, ignoring the searing pain as it touched her skin. Tears fell down her cheeks as she pulled his body upright. Using all of her strength, she threw him over her shoulder. The mile-long walk back to the city gate seemed to take a lifetime; she could feel Gewey getting weaker by the minute. By the time she arrived, he was barely breathing.

The city was in turmoil. The guard post was empty, and the gate had been left open. Kaylia found an abandoned wagon and put Gewey in the back. Panic in the streets made it difficult to maneuver, but eventually, she arrived at Lord Ganflin's manor. The gatekeeper was trying to fix the broken gate when Kaylia jumped from the wagon.

"Help me!" she commanded.

The gatekeeper looked in the wagon and gasped. "Was he hurt in the earthquake?"

"Are you deaf?" she screamed. "I said help me." The gate-keeper flinched but obeyed.

They hadn't gone more than a few feet when Dina and Ertik came running from the house. They gingerly lifted Gewey from the wagon and rushed him inside. As soon as Martin saw what they were doing, he directed them to a nearby study where they laid Gewey down on a couch. Kaylia knelt down beside him, holding his hand.

"Get me something to make bandages," she cried. "I must stop the bleeding."

Martin went to a closet and retrieved a linen sheet. Kaylia tore it into strips and began binding Gewey's wounds.

"I'll fetch a healer right away," Martin said, bolting from the room.

"What happened?" Dina asked. "Who did this?"

"It was Harlondo," Kaylia told her. "He is an agent of the Dark Knight."

"Where is he now?"

"Dead," Kaylia answered.

"Are you sure?" Ertik asked.

Kaylia shot to her feet, suddenly noticing the new face among them. "Who are you?" she demanded.

"It's all right," Dina assured her. "He's a member of my order. He's here to help."

Kaylia looked at him for a moment. "Do you have skills as a healer?"

"No. But if we can get him to Valshara, there are those that can help him. We have the best healers that have ever lived."

"How far is it?" Kaylia asked as she knelt back down beside Gewey.

"We can be there in two days," Ertik replied.

"We leave as soon as the local healer arrives. Go get the carriage ready."

"We should wait until he's been treated," Ertik advised. "That will take time."

"No need," Kaylia replied. "Whoever Martin brings will be coming with us." She brushed back Gewey's hair. "She can treat him on the way."

"Kaylia," Dina said. "We should…"

"I said get the carriage ready," Kaylia yelled, cutting her off. "Now."

Dina nodded and left the room. Ertik followed.

A few minutes later, Lee came running in. He saw Kaylia kneeling down at Gewey's side, her eyes closed. "How is he?" he asked softly.

"He lives," Kaylia answered. "But not for long if he doesn't get help."

"Dina said a healer is coming. She also told me you plan to take him to Valshara tonight."

Kaylia nodded.

Lee stood there for a long moment, considering. "You need to tell me exactly what happened. I'm sorry, but I need to know before we leave."

Kaylia recounted what happened. She was unable to hold back her tears when she told him of the fight between Gewey and Harlondo.

"Then I should make ready," Lee said, once she had finished. "Harlondo may be dead, but there's no guarantee he's alone. I'll gather your things as well. Don't worry, he's strong. He'll make it."

"Thank you," Kaylia said, wiping her tears.

When the healer arrived, she told everyone to get out. Kaylia resisted, but Lee assured her it was for the best.

"I need to treat his wounds before he is moved," the healer explained. "Otherwise, the wounds may open on the road and he'll bleed to death. How he's alive now, I have no idea, but don't worry—I won't leave him until he is stable."

"Then you will accompany us," Kaylia said flatly. "We leave in two hours."

"You're joking, of course," she said, not amused.

Lee reached into his belt and pulled out a pouch. "This should compensate you adequately," he said, handing her four gold coins.

The woman stared at Lee and then at the gold. "Well then. My name is Ezmerial, from the temple of Helenasia, goddess of Healing and Knowledge, and I am at your service." She bowed. "Now get out."

Lee, Dina, and Kaylia waited just outside while Ezmerial went to work. Ertik left for his home to gather his belongings.

"It must have taken great strength to carry him to the city gates," Lee remarked. "Let me find you a chair. You must be exhausted."

"I don't need to sit," Kaylia said, as she anxiously paced back and forth.

"Please," Dina said, grabbing Kaylia's hands. Kaylia winced in pain. Dina saw the burns made by Gewey's sword.

"It's nothing," Kaylia said sharply, shaking herself free of Dina's grip. "I'll be fine."

"It's not nothing," Dina replied, then turned toward Martin. "Please, bring us some water so that we can get her cleaned up."

Lee brought a chair from the next room, and Dina sat Kaylia down to clean the dirt and grime from her burns.

"How will you be traveling, my lord?" Martin inquired. "Should I ready your horses?"

Lee thought for a moment, then nodded. "Yes. Gewey, Sister Ezmerial, and I will ride in the carriage. Ertik can take my horse for now. The one remaining will stay here until it can be sent back to Lord Broín."

Martin nodded quickly and left.

"How were you captured?" Lee asked Kaylia.

Kaylia scowled. "She must have had something on her gloves; she took my hand just before she led me outside. By the time I got to the door, I could barely stand. The next thing I remember is lying on the ground, bound and gagged in that clearing."

Lee nodded and put his hand on her shoulder. "It's not your fault. It could have easily been Dina or me. You couldn't have seen this coming."

"I should have," she spat, shrugging off his hand. "The bond between Gewey and myself has blinded me."

"That bond is what gave you the strength to save him," Lee said. "While I don't understand elf ways, I do know that with injuries like those, Gewey should be dead right now. And if it wasn't for you, he wouldn't have made it."

"If it wasn't for me, he would never have been there in the first place," Kaylia shot back. "They used me to get to him."

"Don't be foolish," Lee scolded. "They would have found another way. We are lucky that you were there to help him. If he had been alone, he would still be out there—probably dead by now."

Kaylia looked up. "It won't happen again," she said with determination. "He will never have to fight alone, ever again."

"I understand," Lee said. "But still, you must not blame yourself for what happened. What's done is done. All we can do now is hope he'll recover."

Dina finished cleaning Kaylia's wounds. "Please, don't get up. We need you strong if we're leaving tonight."

"No doubt," Lee agreed. "If Harlondo wasn't alone, we may have another fight ahead of us."

Hours ticked by as Ezmerial tended to Gewey. Kaylia checked on her progress several times, but the woman kept telling her to leave her alone to work.

Finally, the door opened. The healer stood in the doorway and sighed heavily.

"How he still lives, I can't imagine," she said. "I've never seen a man as injured as that who didn't bleed to death."

"Will he live?" asked Lee.

"I don't think so," she replied somberly. "He's beyond my skills to heal. I would say that I've managed to stop the bleeding, but I don't see how he has any blood left. I'm sorry."

"We're moving him to the carriage," Kaylia instructed. "Now! You will ride with him, healer."

"My dear," Ezmerial said gently. "There is no hope. It's just a matter of time now."

Kaylia stepped menacingly toward the woman. "I said now."

"As you wish," the healer replied. "I will try my best to help him."

"Is Ertik back?" Lee asked.

"I am," Ertik replied as he walked in. "I was just getting the horses ready. All of our things are packed."

Lee gave Martin a letter. "Give this to Lord Ganflin," he said. "It will explain everything. I will send his carriage back as soon as possible."

Martin nodded and put the letter in his pocket. "May the gods keep you—especially your young friend." They carefully lifted Gewey and brought him to the waiting carriage. His skin was pale, and he looked as though life had already left him. Lee climbed into the driver's seat and took the reins.

"If anything happens, stay close," Lee advised the group. "We will not stop until morning. Ertik will take the lead once we're outside the gates."

Without another word, Lee snapped the reins, and the horses bolted forward.

The gate was still open when they approached. They ignored the guards, who were motioning them to halt, nearly running them down as they passed. Screams of alarm faded as Ertik led them west toward the Abyss.

"By the gods!" screamed Ezmerial. "You'll get us killed."

Lee ignored her and pushed the horses to move faster. Time was running out. Somehow, he could feel it. If they didn't get to Valshara soon, all would be lost.

CHAPTER 31

T he landscape flew by in a blur as they raced into the night. Ertik led them west for ten miles, then south along a less traveled road. They kept going until an hour before dawn when Lee called for a halt.

"Why are we stopping?" Kaylia demanded.

"The horse you ride could keep running for much longer, but if the ones pulling the carriage give out, we're in trouble," Lee answered. "We need to rest them for a while."

"And I need to check the boy's wounds," added Ezmerial. "I can't do that when he's being jostled about."

Kaylia grumbled angrily. "One hour. Then we move on."

"You heard her," Lee told the group. "One hour. So rest while you can."

"Kaylia, my dear," said Ezmerial. "I need your assistance."

Kaylia jumped into the carriage without hesitation. The healer told her to hand her dressings and a sweet-smelling salve. "This should help keep the wounds closed," she explained. "If you would, I could use your help whenever we stop. I don't know what's keeping him alive, but I believe that the power of love and prayer heals. It's obvious you care deeply for him; I see it in the way you look at him. Your love for him is giving him strength somehow."

Kaylia stared down at Gewey's ghostly face. He looked peaceful as if merely resting. Ezmerial touched Kaylia's hand.

"I'm sorry for not giving you more hope back at the manor, but I spoke truth. Now, I'm starting to believe you won't allow him to die. Take comfort and stay strong ... for him."

"You are kind," Kaylia said. "But you were right not to give false hope. I am bonded to Gewey in a way I am too inexperienced to fully understand, and I feel him fading."

"Bonded how?" she asked in a whisper. "Tell me, my dear. I will keep it to myself."

"He spoke the ancient words of my ancestors to me, and my spirit reached out and joined with his. He is a part of me in a way you couldn't understand; even I don't fully comprehend it."

"Then perhaps your bond is helping him to hold on," said Ezmerial. "I have no other way to explain it, but you should be grateful for it."

Kaylia squeezed the woman's hand. "I pray you're right. Thank you."

By the time they had finished tending Gewey's wounds it was time to move on again.

"We are heading north until we reach the Stone of the Tower," Ertik told them as he mounted his horse. "Once we get there, stay close. The road that leads to the temple is hidden and winds through a labyrinth of jagged rocks."

They hurried on, only stopping when they needed to rest the horses. Kaylia rode close to the carriage and assisted Ezmerial at every stop.

"You should try and sleep, Sister," Lee told the healer. "There's room in the carriage for you to lie down."

"Not until we reach this temple of yours," Ezmerial replied stubbornly. "Is it really the Temple of Valshara?"

"It is," Lee assured her.

"It's said that within the Order of Amon Dähl there is knowledge of healing unknown to anyone else. To think, I may get the chance to watch them and learn."

"You keep him alive, and I'll see to it that you will," Ertik promised. "Perhaps I can even arrange for you to stay on for a while."

Her eyes brightened. "That would be a dream come true," she replied. "The things I could learn there, the knowledge I could pass on to my order..."

Ezmerial worked with renewed vigor. "Don't worry; if it means I have to stay awake for a week, he'll be alive when we get there."

It was dusk when they saw the silhouette of the Stone of the Tower in the distance. It was flat at the top and stood fifty feet tall. The sides were smooth and round, as if they had been carved by a stone worker of unimaginable skill.

"What a strange sight to see on the plains," Ezmerial remarked as they came near.

"Legend says it was carved by Hephisolis, the God of Fire, as a present for his wife, Islisema," said Lee. "It was once covered in gold and jewels, but Dantenos, God of the Dead, coveted Islisema and told his followers to strip it bare. Only the stone remains."

Ertik smiled. "Your knowledge of lore is impressive, Starfinder."

"My library is extensive," Lee replied. "And life in a small village gives me a lot of time to read."

When they reached the Stone, Ertik called for a halt and began searching for the trail. "It's been some time since I was here, and this way is rarely used."

He returned after about ten minutes and led them around the far side of the tower toward what appeared to be nothing more than a pile of loose rocks. As they approached, they could see that the rocks staggered and turned, revealing a well-disguised trail.

"We'll need to lead our horses for a while," Ertik instructed. "About two miles from here the path gets easier. We should be at the temple by dawn."

When they finally arrived at Valshara, they came upon a natural stone archway that served as the entrance to the temple. Two men in black robes stood at the threshold, each wearing a sword. Ertik halted and got off his horse.

"Stay here until I call you over," he told them. "We are unaccustomed to visitors."

He walked over to the men and talked to them for several minutes. Finally, he motioned for the rest to approach.

"You must leave your weapons," said one of the robed men. Lee and Kaylia removed their weapons and handed them over.

Dina retrieved Gewey's sword and kept it with her. "I must show this to the High Lady," she explained.

"Then Ertik must carry it, Novice," the man growled. "And you must surrender your arms as well."

Dina nodded and handed the sword to Ertik, then removed her dagger. The man motioned for them to continue.

Once past the entrance, a broad stone path led up an incline to a large wooden door. The walls of the temple were plain gray stone and twenty feet tall, extending for several hundred yards in either direction. Ertik pulled a rope that hung from the top of the door, and a bell echoed loudly in response. Moments later, the doors slowly swung open, revealing a massive courtyard.

Multicolored slate formed a walkway around the outer edge of the yard, enclosing an inner yard of well-manicured grass. In the center stood an eight-foot tall golden sword, its point buried deep into a marble slab. On either side of the courtyard were covered walkways that led deeper into the temple grounds, and at the rear was another double door, nearly as large the first.

There were at least a dozen men and women walking about the yard. None of them wore ceremonial dress or anything else that might indicate they were part of a temple, and all of them stopped and stared at the newcomers suspiciously. From the far left corner, a young woman began walking rapidly toward them. She went directly to the coach without saying a word to anyone else and looked carefully at Gewey.

"You're a healer?" she asked Ezmerial.

"I am," Ezmerial replied.

"You two," the woman said, pointing to Ertik and Lee. "When the stretcher arrives, bring him to the healing chamber. You do remember the way, don't you, Ertik?"

Ertik nodded, trying to hide his embarrassment. "I haven't been away that long,"

The woman harrumphed, unimpressed.

A few moments later, a young boy came running across the yard with a stretcher on his back. Lee and Ertik carefully placed Gewey on the stretcher and followed as the woman strode off. It only took a few seconds for them to lose sight of her, but Ertik did, in fact, know the way.

"How did she know about the boy?" asked Ezmerial. "She walked straight to him."

"Many of our healers can feel when someone is sick or injured," Ertik replied. "Wileminia is extremely sensitive. I'm sure she has had them preparing from the moment we got to the archway."

"Amazing," she whispered.

Ertik led them through a series of stone hallways to an open door. Inside was a bed, several tables with various bottles and plants, and a stone basin in the center.

Three women were busy at the tables preparing medicine, while Wileminia waited by the bed.

"Lay him down," she directed. "Then Ertik will show you to your quarters. The Sister that has been tending the boy will stay and help."

Lee and Ertik put Gewey on the bed and began to leave, but Kaylia refused to go.

"I will not leave him," she said defiantly.

"My dear, you must," Wileminia said in a much softer tone. "The High Lady of Valshara herself will be here in a moment to personally tend to him. She has commanded that you all be removed until it's over. He could not be in better care anywhere in the world, I promise."

Kaylia stood silent for a moment, looking at Gewey's nearly lifeless body, and then lowered her head. "Please tell me the moment you know something," she pleaded.

"You shall be the first," Wileminia promised, placing her hand over her heart.

Lee stepped forward. "Before you attempt to heal him, there's something you must know. Gewey isn't an ordinary human. In fact, he's not really human at all. He's a god."

Wileminia looked at him, her eyes skeptical and slightly amused. "If you mean he's like you, then you needn't worry; treating a half-god is no different than treating a typical human."

"That's not what I'm saying," Lee insisted. "He isn't half anything."

The realization of what Lee was saying struck her. "I see. Are you certain?"

"I am," Lee replied. "There is no doubt."

Wileminia looked thoughtful for a moment, then said, "I will inform the High Lady. Now if you would please go, we have work to do."

Ertik led them to a large but empty den with several couches and chairs angled around a lit fireplace. "Please, sit and rest while I attend to your quarters." They sat in silence until a young woman in a blue housedress entered, giving them each a cup of honeyed water.

"No one wears robes here?" Lee asked once the girl had left.

"Only during certain ceremonies," Dina replied. "Our order is very informal when it comes to things like that. Only the guards wear robes at all times."

"The High Priestess," Kaylia said pensively. "She is a skilled healer?"

"She is most skilled among us," Dina replied. "However, you should refer to her as High Lady. We have no priests or priestesses. The order does not center on rank as much as others do. After you advance past novice, you become either a cleric or a knight, but there's nothing above that, save for the High Lady."

She took a sip of honeyed water before continuing. "A knight trains as a guardian of the order; they are among the finest warriors in the world. If you achieve the rank of cleric, you choose a focus of study that you spend the rest of your days trying to perfect. For example, I intend to become a temple historian."

"What does a historian do here?" Lee inquired.

"They travel to different cities, towns or temples to observe and record events as they unfold,"

"Sounds like an enjoyable life," Lee said with approval.

"Yes," she agreed, a touch of sadness entering her voice. "But with the way things have turned out, I doubt it will ever be."

"Why would you say that?" Kaylia asked, trying to keep her mind off Gewey. "You are a part of one of the greatest stories in known history. Who better to record and tell about it?"

"When Gewey and I met Felsafell and stayed in his house, he woke me in the middle of the night and told me a different story," Dina said. "He said that as a child of two worlds, I would have to sacrifice myself to make the world whole again. Of course, he said it in his odd little way—but there was no mistaking the intent."

"Mind his words," Kaylia advised. "They do not always mean what they seem to. As I told Gewey..." She paused, wincing slightly upon saying his name. "As I told him, Felsafell is dangerous, and you risk great peril if you take his words at face value. You may yet have the life you want."

Dina smiled. "Thank you, Kaylia. I hope we all get the life that we want."

When Ertik returned, he escorted them down the hall and showed them each to their rooms. The rooms were plainly furnished with a bed, a small table, and a chair. A washbasin with hot water sat in one corner of the room, and their belongings had been placed in another.

"Once you've rested and washed, you may wander freely—with the exception of the healing chamber," Ertik told them. "If you need me, I'll be in the den awaiting word of Gewey."

"I think we'll all be joining you there shortly," Lee informed him. Dina and Kaylia nodded in agreement.

Lee was the first to return to the den. Ertik was sitting in a chair by the fire, thumbing through a leather-bound book, humming to himself. When he saw Lee, he sat the book on the arm of the chair and gestured for Lee to sit across from him.

"You look ... cleaner," Ertik noted. "Though I'd wager, you must be exhausted."

"My kind doesn't tire very easily," Lee replied.

"Yes, I forgot," Ertik said thoughtfully. "It must be quite a burden."

"Why would you think that?"

"Such strength and power breeds jealousy. Hiding who one is all the time can't be easy."

"It can be tiresome," Lee admitted. "But I have Millet. He's been with me a long time, and he shares my secret. It makes it easier to have someone like him with me."

"He sounds like a good friend. Where is he now?"

"On his way to Hazrah to take my wife and child out of the city," Lee answered. "With the Dark Knight on the move, I couldn't risk leaving them so close to his borders."

"Hazrah?" Ertik repeated, suddenly looking troubled. "How long ago did he leave?"

"More than a week now. He should be there in about two more weeks. Why? Do you know something?"

"I got word that Angrääl now has dominion in Hazrah. Whether the city was sacked or they simply surrendered, I don't know—but your friend is walking straight into the heart of the Dark Knight's power."

Lee closed his eyes tight, trying to still his mind. "Can you send word to Hazrah?" asked Lee. His voice was unsteady. "Do you have a messenger flock that travels there?"

"I'm sorry," Ertik replied regretfully, "your friend will arrive well ahead of any message I could send. Still, I will try."

"Thank you. I need to have Lady Nal'Thain and her son evacuated from Hazrah and taken to the city of Dantory. It's a small oasis in the eastern desert. Tell them to mention Millet if she questions the truth of the message. I will pay anything it costs, ten times over, if they are brought safely there."

"Payment is not necessary," Ertik assured him. "I will send the message now. There are no messenger flocks between here and Hazrah, so the message will have to be carried much of the way by members of the order. Still, I shall see to it at once." Ertik got up and hurried away.

Lee sat there, holding his head in his hands, as Kaylia and Dina entered.

"What's wrong?" Kaylia asked as she took a seat next to Lee. Dina followed close behind.

Lee told them what Ertik had said.

"Millet will get them out," Dina said, confident. "I know he will."

"I hope you're right," he replied.

"Millet is wise and capable," Kaylia added. "Much more than any other human I've met thus far. Even if there is an army guarding their door, he will find a way to get past them."

"You're right, of course," he agreed. "It's just the feeling of helplessness I can't stand."

"Believe me, I understand," said Kaylia. Lee looked at her and nodded knowingly.

After an hour, Ertik returned. "I sent your message. I also sent word to Dantory to be on the lookout for them."

"I'm in your debt," Lee said graciously.

"Not at all," Ertik replied. "You have done us quite a service."

"There's something else you should know," Lee said. "I believe I have the Book of Souls in my possession."

Ertik froze. "Where is it?"

"In my room. I was hoping someone here would know what to do with it."

"Are you sure that's what it is?" he asked.

"Not completely," Lee answered. "But from what we've learned, we're as certain as we can be."

Ertik clapped his hands. "That is news. We must tell the High Lady when she is finished with your friend. She will be overjoyed."

"If she can heal Gewey, she can have it," said Lee.

"It will be some time before we know if he will heal," said a voice from the doorway. It was Wileminia. They all stood up.

"What's happening?" Kaylia asked anxiously. "Will he live?"

Wileminia sighed heavily. "He has been struck by the power of the Sword of Truth. If it had been the Sword itself, it would have destroyed him. Thankfully though, it was not. We have removed the energy that prevented his body from healing, but it has left him near death. He may not recover."

"He's a god," Kaylia cried. "He will not die."

Wileminia stared at Kaylia for a moment. "God or no, he is in mortal form. But he is strong—stronger than any I've seen. Now that the bite of the Sword's power has been removed, his body may heal on its own. But I'm more concerned with his spirit."

"What do you mean?" Lee asked.

"His spirit wanders," she answered. "And it has not found its way back."

"Can't you help him?" Kaylia asked desperately.

"We are trying," Wileminia assured her. "But if he's a god as you say, it explains our inability to reach him. His spirit would be different from our own, and we have no way to call out to him. Even if we did, we wouldn't know how to guide him back. The places he goes, we have never been."

"I can find him," Kaylia said firmly.

"I know you think that," she said softly. "And I know as an elf you have tremendous strength of spirit; it's a wonderful trait of your kind. But he is not an elf. It seems his spirit travels in realms where mortals cannot go."

"My spirit is bound to his," she contended. "Even now I feel him. If he needs a guide, then I am the only one."

"She speaks the truth," Lee affirmed. "They were bound together by words in the ancient language. I have no doubt she is his only hope."

Wileminia thought for a moment. "Come with me then. I will take you to him. You may sit next to him and reach out as you can."

Kaylia nodded and followed her to the healing chamber.

Ertik stretched his arms and yawned. "I need rest," he said reluctantly. "I hate sleeping before nightfall, but I think tonight I'll manage to sleep until dawn." He slowly rose, grunting with each movement, and walked out.

As Ertik made his exit, a young girl entered. "Lord Starfinder?" she asked. "The High Lady would like to speak with you before you retire."

Lee looked to Dina.

"I'll be fine," Dina told him. "I think I'll walk around for a bit and maybe get something to eat."

Lee nodded and followed the young girl out of the room and down the hallway. He was amazed by the sheer size of the place. He remembered Ertik saying there were about a hundred people here, but from the look of it, five times that number could live comfortably. They passed at least three dining halls and several libraries as they walked, as well as a variety of recreation and training areas. Most of the walls were bare, aside from a few elaborate tapestries and etchings near the libraries.

At the end of a long hall, the girl stopped in front of a plain wooden door. "Please go right in. She's waiting."

Lee thanked the girl and opened the door. Inside he saw a small study with a nicely carved wooden desk that had papers scattered about it. There were a few shelves and cabinets along the wall, and brass lanterns hung in the corners; all in all, there was almost nothing to indicate that this office belonged to a leader of one of the most ancient orders in existence.

The chair at the desk was facing away from the door, but Lee could tell someone was sitting there.

"High Lady," Lee said. "You asked to speak to me." There was a long pause.

"I've often wondered what I would say to you when the time came," said the High Lady, still facing the wall. Her voice sounded strangely familiar. "Now that you're here ... I just don't know."

Lee was both puzzled and troubled by the High Lady's words. Trying not to let this confusion show in his voice, he said: "I would like to thank you for what you are doing for Gewey, and for the rest of us. I am deeply grateful."

"Are you?" she asked. "If I were you I would not be so quick to give me your gratitude."

The High Lady then stood and faced Lee. He staggered back in shock. She was older and grayed, but there was no mistaking her.

"You..." he whispered. "How are you here? I spent years looking for you, and you were here the whole time?"

"Not the whole time, son," she said, smiling sadly. "But most of it, yes."

"But why?" Lee asked, trying to slow his racing mind. "Why now? Surely you could have let me know where you were before now."

"Please sit," she said. "I swear I'll tell you everything. I will hold nothing back."

Still dazed by her appearance, Lee pulled up a chair and sat down, unable to take his eyes off his mother's face.

CHAPTER 32

"I know you must have a million questions," Selena began. "But please wait until I tell you my story. Otherwise, I don't know if I can get through this."

Lee slowly nodded but said nothing.

"When I was a young girl before I met your father, my parents sent me to Althetas to study at the Temple of Saraf. My father was a blacksmith and did well enough to be able to support my studies at the temple. They hoped I would become a priestess some day, and I probably would have if not for your father."

"I'm warning you now," Lee interrupted. "I'll not hear you speak ill of my father."

"Why would I speak ill of him?" she asked. "I loved him... I still love him."

Her voice trailed off for a moment, then she regained her composure. "I met him in Althetas during my studies at the temple. I was in the market square the first time I saw him; he had come to the city to meet with the Fisherman's Guild. Your grandfather had died a few months before, and your father had taken ownership of his boat. He was supporting both himself and your grandmother.

"I had just bought some spices and herbs when a young rogue snatched my purse right off my belt. It was all the money I had. My father was not rich, so the money he sent me each month had to last. Without it, I had no way to feed myself and would have had to return home. I chased after the thief, but he was too fast. Then, out of nowhere, your father tackled him and took back my money. He looked so handsome and dashing, I think I must have fallen in love with him right then and there."

Lee grumbled with disbelief.

"I know you think I might have felt differently," she said. "But you only see things from a child's perspective. I know you are a man now, but your memories are that of a child. I did love him. I was only fourteen at the time, but still, I knew what I felt. He gave me my purse and offered to buy me a sweet apple." She started laughing.

"I was so angry at that. A sweet apple? I wanted a candlelit dinner or a moonlight walk, and here he was buying me a bloody sweet apple as if I were a child. However, he was twenty at the time, and to him, I was a child. He walked me back to the temple holding my hand. I was so excited; this handsome hero was holding my hand. We talked the whole way there, and I made him promise to write me, which he did of course. I didn't see him again for a year.

"But just as he'd promised, he wrote to me once a month. As soon as the letters arrived, I'd eagerly run back to my room at the temple to read them. He wrote mostly of his day-to-day life and the goings on in the fishing village, but to me, each letter might just as well have been a love sonnet. I wrote back to him, careful not to be too forward and scare him away. Even then, I knew he was the man I would marry.

"The next year he came to Althetas again to meet with the Fisherman's Guild. You could have told me the gods themselves were coming and I would not have been more thrilled; I must have spent three hours getting ready, determined to look perfect for the man I loved. We met in the same square where my purse had been snatched. This time, I was determined not to get a sweet apple.

"He was as kind and thoughtful as I'd dreamed he'd be. He took me to lunch, and we walked all over the city. At the time, it was the best day of my life. I nearly cried when it was over. I made your father promise to show me his village when I was old enough to travel on my own. He confessed to me later that it made him nervous to think of me realizing how poor he really was.

"I wept for three days when he left.

"A few months later I was chosen to be one of the attendants accompanying our High Priestess on her journey to Manisalia to see the Oracle. I had never traveled so far, and the thought of it frightened me. The trip was long and hard, but as it turned out, I had a grand time. The High Priestess was young, cheerful, and played games with us at night. She even told us old tales of the world before the Great War. I felt lucky to have been chosen.

"When we got to Manisalia I waited outside the pavilion with the rest of the attendants while the High Priestess went inside. She was only inside for a few minutes when she came out and told me that the Oracle wanted to see me. I was terrified.

"When I went inside, she was sitting on a pillow, tossing nuts in the air and catching them in her mouth—not really what I expected, to say the least."

Lee chuckled, in spite of himself. "No puppy?" he asked. "She played tug-o-war with a puppy when I went to see her."

His mother smiled. "No puppy. Still, as you know, she is not what one expects when you think of the Great Oracle of Manisalia. She asked me to sit and offered me some water.

"She told me she'd been expecting me, and that she regretted having to give such ominous news to a child. I hated being called a child, but I was too nervous to say anything in return. She reached over and took my hands. She told me she could see I was in love, and I turned so red I probably glowed. But then, she told me that I mustn't marry—that if I did, it would end in tragedy.

"I jerked my hands away and stood up. Her words scared me, and my fear became anger. I told her that your father didn't want to marry me, and if he did, I would wed him in an instant, no matter what she said.

"She looked at me with a sympathetic smile. She told me that your father loved me even then, and was waiting for me to come of age. But she warned again that I mustn't marry him; if I did, he would die, and I would hate myself for the rest of my life.

"I sat back down, but I did not hold her hands. Hesitantly, I asked her how he would die.

"She admitted that she didn't know, but told me I was part of an important destiny, that my child—a child not fathered by the man I loved—would help to save the world.

"I laughed so hard that I almost fell over. I'd bear a child with the man I loved and no other, and I told her as much.

"She insisted that I would have a child and that one day I would have to let him go. She told me that he would one day be called to serve a northern lord and that I should not interfere with this." Selena paused, her eyes guilty and troubled. "And once he was gone, she said I was not to contact him again. She said my son would find me one day when there was a great upheaval in the world, but I could not allow him to find me before then or he would surely die.

"The Oracle could tell that I didn't believe her. 'It seems you will marry your handsome fisherman anyway,' she said. 'But upon his death, remember my words.' I left angrier than I had ever been in my life."

"I take it you ignored her," Lee said.

"To my everlasting regret," Selena replied. "Your father and I kept writing to one another, and each year he made sure to attend the annual fisherman's meeting in Althetas. When I came of age and was old enough to leave the temple, we married. My family was furious. They wanted me to continue my education and become a novice, but I refused. As a result, my family ostracized me. I never saw any of them again.

"Your father always regretted that I had to sacrifice so much for him, but as long as we were together I didn't care. For a time, we were very happy. I had all but forgotten what the Oracle had told me. Fishing was good in those days, and though we didn't have much, we had enough to get by.

"Then, in a flash, it all changed. I was walking along the shore, collecting shells for a basket I was making as a present for one of our neighbors. I heard a clap of thunder over the water, and I looked to see the ocean boiling. Steam rose and became a hot mist. It was then that I saw him, walking across the waves toward me and smiling. It was Saraf, the God of the Sea. Somehow, I knew who he was instantly, and he was the most beautiful thing I had ever beheld. I nearly fainted at the sight of him."

"What did he look like?" Lee asked.

"It's impossible to describe," she answered. "Not like a man, but not unlike one either. Even now, all I can remember is the sheer beauty of his presence. He took me in his arms and loved me. I could not help myself. It was as if a spell was cast over me. Once in Saraf's embrace, I didn't care about anything else—not even your father.

"He left me on the shore, and I watched as he faded into the ocean. It wasn't until he had gone that the realization of what had happened set in. I was wracked with guilt and self-hatred. I had betrayed the man I loved, and I could not live with it. I knew I had to tell him, but I was afraid he wouldn't believe me. I sat on the beach and cried for hours.

"The sun had already gone down when your father found me. I told him what had happened and begged for his forgiveness. He said that a water spirit had warned him that Saraf would come to me that very day. He said the spirit was a vile thing, and that it told him he should kill me for such a betrayal.

"I told him that the spirit was right, and he should do just as it said. But instead, your father looked at me tenderly and held me close. He said he didn't blame me, that the fault was with Saraf.

"I wanted him to blame me, though. I wanted to be punished for what I had done, and after a time I grew resentful of your father's forgiveness. I hated myself and wanted him to hate me too.

"Then, I found out I was with child.

"I remember the look on his face when I told him. Both of us knew who the father was, but he told me it didn't matter, that he would love you all the same. I should have been grateful, but I wasn't. I was angry—angry at him, angry at myself, and angry at Saraf.

"I know you must have thought I didn't love you or your father, but that isn't true. Once you were born, all I could think about was what the Oracle had told me. It was coming true, and I knew what would happen next.

"The day your father died, Saraf returned to me. I was outside gathering wood when I heard a voice call my name. I looked up, and there he was. This time he appeared as a shimmering light, but his voice was sad and full of remorse. He knew my husband was dead, and he told me he was sorry. I stared at him in disbelief. I screamed at him, calling him a liar.

"He moved closer and told me it was the spirits of the water that caused my husband's boat to sink. They were jealous that Saraf had loved me. When they failed to convince my husband to kill me, Saraf had hoped they would let go of their envy and move on. Instead, they waited. They waited until they thought Saraf had forgotten, and then they struck. They knew that an attempt on my life would be more than he could forgive, so instead, they took my husband. They knew it would hurt Saraf to see me in pain.

"I couldn't believe it. I wept, unable to understand why the spirits would do such a thing.

"Saraf told me that the spirits could not bear to share their love with another; they wanted it all to themselves. He told me again that he was sorry. He tried to stop them, but he was too late. By the time he realized what they had planned, it was over.

"I ran at him then, intent on killing him, but I passed right through him as if he wasn't there. I told him he knew nothing of love, cursing him as I fell to the ground, weeping. Saraf vanished, and I never saw him again.

"It was then I knew what I would have to do. I returned to the temple and made sure we were sent north. When Lord Dauvis took you in, I fled and eventually found this place. At the time it was a place of retirement for the Order of Amon Dähl. I told them my story and they allowed me to join the order and remain. When the Dark Knight destroyed the original Valshara, we reformed the Order from here. I sent people to Hazrah to keep an eye on you, but I was afraid to make contact because of the Oracle's words. I would not see you die because of my own foolishness. I'm sorry I was not there for you, Lee. I'm sorry that I caused you pain. I never wanted this, I swear."

Selena's tears welled as gazed into her son's eyes. Lee stood and walked around the desk. "For years I was angry with you," he said, his voice trembling with emotion. "But I see now why you did what you did."

"Can you forgive me?" she asked, rising to her feet.

"Mother," Lee said tenderly. "I am alive because of your sacrifice. There is nothing to forgive." He reached out and embraced her tightly, and they both wept joyful tears.

CHAPTER 33

Lee and Selena talked for hours, catching up on years of lost time. They stopped only when Lee noticed the fatigue in his mother's eyes.

"We can speak more tomorrow," he said. "You need to rest."

"I know there are important things we need to discuss," she said, embracing him again. "But I've wanted to just sit and talk with you for so long. I'm afraid I'll wake up and this will all have been a dream."

"I'll be here when you wake up," he promised. "And there's time enough to discuss everything. For now, I just want you to sleep and regain your strength."

He left his mother and made his way back to the healing chamber where he found Kaylia sitting in a chair next to Gewey's bed. She was holding his hand. Her eyes were shut, and she swayed back and forth slowly. Gewey's face was still pale and covered in bruises. Bandages had been wrapped over nearly his entire body. Lee marveled at the fact that he was alive at all. He had seen many wounded men, but never anyone who had taken this much punishment and still drew breath. He placed his hands on Kaylia's shoulders.

"How is he?" he asked quietly.

Kaylia gradually opened her eyes. "He is lost. The healer was right; he is in a place no mortal has been. I can hear him, but it's like trying to hear a voice in a storm."

"Do you think he knows you're there?"

"I don't know," she replied somberly. "But I do know that I am the only one who has a chance of bringing him back. I sense his struggle, but I can't see what he struggles against."

"Perhaps you should rest," Lee suggested. "You can try again later."

"I swore to never let him fight alone again," Kaylia said, her resolve absolute. "Whatever danger he now faces, I will face it as well. I will not leave his side."

Lee heaved a sigh. "At least let me get you some food."

Kaylia nodded reluctantly.

"I'll return shortly," he said as he set off to look for the kitchen. While still searching, he ran across Ezmerial, who was on her way back from one of the dining halls.

"This place is wonderful," she said. "They've offered to let me stay for a while and study their healing techniques. I'm so grateful that I came with you—not that Kaylia gave me very much choice in the matter. But still, I must remember to thank her."

She reached into her pocket and pulled out the four gold coins Lee had given to her.

"I wouldn't feel right keeping this. I had planned to give it to the temple, but as I won't be returning for some time…"

Lee shook his head. "Keep it. When you do return, use it to buy what you need to teach others what you have learned here."

Ezmerial bowed, then kissed him lightly on the cheek. "You're a good man, Lee Starfinder. May the gods keep you safe." Lee watched as she walked away, humming happily.

When Lee found the kitchen, he had the cook prepare a plate of roast beef and corn for Kaylia. The cook took one look at Lee and insisted that he take a plate for himself as well. Lee hadn't realized how hungry he was until that moment.

"One of these wouldn't be for that lovely elf woman, would it?" asked the cook.

Lee nodded.

"Then you eat this in the dining hall, while I cook up something special for your friend," she said, handing him the plate. "The moment I heard there was an elf here, I got out my old recipe book and found an authentic elf dish. I've been waiting ages for an excuse to use it. Please, the hall is just through that door. It won't take me but a few minutes."

"I'm sure she'd appreciate it," Lee said before passing through the door shown to him.

The hall was almost empty of diners. The afternoon meal had already been served, and several young men and women were busy cleaning.

He sat down, and his mouth began to water as he drew in the smell of hot beef and corn. One of the men cleaning asked him if he wanted any wine.

"That would be excellent," he said, forking a large bite of beef into his mouth.

He was only halfway through his meal when he heard his name being shouted from outside the dining hall. He jumped up and ran out to see who was calling. A young girl saw him as he exited. She hurried over, out of breath.

"Lord Starfinder," said the girl. "It's the elf. Something's wrong. You need to come quickly."

Lee bolted down the hall and back to the healing chamber. Two women were holding Kaylia in their laps. His mother had her eyes closed and her hand on Kaylia's head.

"What happened?" he cried.

His mother opened her eyes and rose to her feet. "I don't know—at least, not for sure. I came to check on the boy before going to bed and found her lying on the floor unconscious."

"Can you help her?"

"I think she has managed to reach Gewey," Selena said. "If that's so, then there is nothing we can do but hope they both find their way back together."

Lee walked over to Kaylia and knelt down beside her. She was drenched in sweat, and her body twitched every few seconds. He brushed back her hair and kissed her forehead.

"She is with him," Lee said somberly. "She fights alongside his spirit, just as she said she would."

Selena immediately ordered a bed be brought in for Kaylia. The bed was set directly next to Gewey's, and they gently placed Kaylia's limp body on the mattress. Lee sat next to them, staring into nothingness, barely noticing when Dina pulled up a chair next to his.

"Lee," Dina called gently.

Lee looked up with a blank expression. Without a word, he wrapped his arm around her. Dina put her head on his shoulder. They sat like this for hours, saying nothing.

Despite her obvious fatigue, Lee's mother checked in on them from time to time. She had water brought for them to drink, but neither he nor Dina touched it. Night turned into dawn, and still, neither Gewey nor Kaylia had moved. Selena came in and sat on the edge of the bed to examine their two fallen friends.

"Ertik told me you have brought the Book of Souls," she said as she checked Gewey's bandages. "Is that true?"

"We think so," answered Lee. "The box is unbreakable, so there's no way to know for sure."

"You must give it to me," she said. "If I can find a way to open it, there may be something within the pages that can help your friends."

Lee nodded and got to his feet. "I'll bring it here now," he said, quickly leaving to retrieve the book from his room.

"Do you really think you can open it?" Dina asked.

"I don't know," Selena replied. "But it's either that or simply wait and do nothing."

Lee returned with the box and handed it to his mother. She looked at the lid intently, then turned it over.

"This is the Book of Souls," she said finally and sat it gently on the bed.

"Can you open it?" Lee asked, hopeful.

"I don't know. I will try, but it will take time. I need to contact Althetas; there's an elven sage named Theopolou who might be able to help. I'll need to send word to him. Of course, when he finds out we have the Book of Souls, he might very well try to kill us and take it for himself. The elves have been looking for it since the Great War. How did you come by it?"

"Dauvis Nal'Thain had it," Lee explained. "It was among his possessions when I claimed my inheritance."

"You took his name then?" she asked.

"I did," Lee admitted. "He was good to me. When he died, he left me his title and position."

For a second, her eyes misted over. "Lee Nal'Thain," she whispered to herself.

The moment of reflection quickly vanished. She cleared her throat and wiped her eyes. "Well then, I need to get word to my contacts in Althetas right away. They will know how to find Theopolou. It will probably take him many days—if not weeks—to get here, so please make yourselves at home. Explore the temple if you wish. Dina, am I correct in remembering that you wish to become a historian in the order?"

"Yes, High Lady," Dina replied earnestly. "Very much so."

"Then you shall be. As of now, you are a cleric of Amon Dähl, but the formal ceremony will have to wait."

Dina's eyes shot wide. "I ... I don't know what to say."

Selena smiled warmly. "Say that you will be truthful in all your accounts. You live in historic—though terrifying—times, and an honest account will be important. You travel with my son and he trusts you; that is enough for me to know your worth. I hereby welcome you, young cleric."

"Your son?" Dina exclaimed in shock.

Selena smiled. "I'm sure Lee will tell you all about it. For now, I think both of you should get some rest."

"We will, Mother," Lee said. "But I think I'd like to sit here for just a while longer."

"I'll stay with you," Dina offered.

"You can tell a person's value by their friends," Selena remarked. "You, my son, have great value from what I can see."

Lee smiled, and Dina bowed low.

"I'll see you tomorrow, son," she said as she left.

"Your mother?" Dina said incredulously. "Why didn't you say so earlier?"

"I only just found out," he replied.

Dina looked at him in wonder. "You are full of surprises," she said. "I must say, meeting you has been an experience of a lifetime."

Suddenly, Kaylia shook violently. Lee reached out to grab her, but she stopped shaking just as he touched her arm.

"I hope this Theopolou can help," Dina said as Lee wiped the sweat from Kaylia's brow.

"So do I," he replied gravely. "So do I."

End Book One

BOOK CLUB QUESTIONS

1. Who is your favorite character? Why? What about them make them enjoyable to read about?

2. How well does the author follow the formula of the hero's journey while making the story unique in its own right? Has the journey held true from book to book?

3. How well developed do you feel the character arcs are? And how do you think they develop throughout the book and series?

4. Do you feel Gewey will be the savior he is prophesied to be or will he succumb to the temptations of power?

SPECIAL THANKS

Brian and Jonathan would like to thank: George Panagos, Gerald and Donna Anderson, Jacob Bunton, Jennie Bunton, The DiBattista family (especially Kyle who was one of the first to read it), The Ramos family, the Gnyp family, Sean and Jess, Bob Brandt, Hammza (Jon's best friend), Tara Ramirez, Vincentine Williams, Hunter and Sarah Anderson, Vicki McManus, Bryan Lee, Jen Couch, Clarisse Castro, Ariis Lopez, Czupacabra Czeslovski, Calib Rains, Leigh Riddle, Antonios Seif, Tyler Jensen, Adaria Welborn, Tracy Baggett, Kira Melamed, Greg Peacock, Natasha and Rob Cousens, Veronica Dread, Mike Bailey, Shannon Bilbrey, Karen Cooper, Onna Layton, Mitchel Lee, John Cooper, Angie Barlow, Jeff Bradey, Missy Mcanally, Chris Hergenroder, Raymond and Nadia Awika, Daniel Jones, Andrea Adams, Giulia Iuppa (the world traveler), Sharone Purer, Russell Lehmann, Raven Moore, Moe Yabdayoui (the ladies' man), Tracy Duarte, Shelbie Jones, Jared Larkin, Amanda Shiver, Lee Conleen, Keith Parker, Jeff Knapp, Amamda Phillips, Rachel Heeter, Denise Cruz, Andrea Klumpp, Gilberto Quinonez, Stephanie Iturrino,

John Bange, Caby Nedvarda, Anne Yeates, Doris Watson, Faith Nyou, Tyson Lee, Regina Beaty, Jeanie Nash, Ismael Robles, Robyn Underwood, Edsan Caliso, Athena Papadatos (world's greatest second grade teacher), Christina Tettonis (a true educational innovator), The New York Public School System. Authors Brian D. Anderson and Jonathan Anderson

ABOUT THE AUTHORS

Brian D. Anderson was born in 1971 and grew up in the small town of Spanish Fort, AL. He attended Fairhope High, then later Springhill College, where his love for fantasy grew into a lifelong obsession. His hobbies include chess, history, and spending time with his son.

Jonathan Anderson was born in March 2003. His creative spirit became evident by the age of three when he told his first original story. In 2010, he came up with the concept for The Godling Chronicles. It grew into an exciting collaboration between father and son. Jonathan enjoys sports, chess, music, games, and, of course, telling stories.

Discover more at
4HorsemenPublications.com

10% off using HORSEMEN10